Sparrow

L.J.SHEN

Cover Designer:
Sofie Hartley at Luminos Graphics House

Interior Designer:
Cassy Roop at Pink Ink Design

Editor:
Karen Dale Harris

Proofreader:
Cat Elliott

"Though she be but little, she be fierce."

William Shakespeare

Sparrow

PROLOGUE

TROY

Trinity Chapel
South Boston, Massachusetts

SILENCE. THE MOST LOADED sound in human history.

The only sound audible was the *click, click* of my Derby shoes against the mosaic floor. I closed my eyes, playing the game I relished as a kid one last time. I knew the way to the confession booth by heart. Been a parishioner in this church since the day I was born. I was christened here. Attended Sunday mass here every week. Had my first sloppy kiss in the bathroom, right fucking here. I would probably have my impending funeral here, though with the legacy of men in my family, it wouldn't be an open-casket event.

Three, four, five steps past the holy water font, I took a sharp right turn, counting.

Six, seven, eight, nine. My eyes fluttered open. *Still got it.*

It was there, the wooden box where all of my secrets were once buried. The confession booth.

I opened the squeaking door and blinked, the smell of mold and the sour sweat of sinners crawling into my nose. I hadn't set foot in reconciliation in two years. Not since my father died. But I guess confessions were like riding a bike—once you learned, you never forgot.

Though this time, things would go down differently.

It was an old-fashioned booth, in an old-fashioned church, no living-room bullshit design and fancy, modern crap. Classic dark wood covered every corner, a wire grille divided the priest and the confessors, with a crucifix hung above it.

I settled in my seat on the wooden bench, my ass hitting the scarred pew with a bang. At 6'4" I looked like a giant trying to fit into a Barbie Dream House. Memories of sitting here as a boy, my legs dangling mid-air as I told Father McGregor about my small, meaningless sins raced through my mind, tangling into a messy ball of nostalgia. The thought of how big my sins were turning out to be would make McGregor sick to his stomach. But my rage toward him was stronger than my morals.

I folded my suit coat on the bench beside me. *Sorry, old man. Today you'll meet the maker you've been preaching about all these years.*

I heard him sliding his side of the screen open with a screech, clearing his throat. I did the sign of the cross, reciting, "In the name of the Father, and the Son, and the Holy Spirit."

His chair creaked, his body stiffening at the sound of my voice. He recognized me. *Good.* I relished the thought of his death, and to some people I guessed that would make me a psychopath.

But it was true.

I was fucking thrilled. I was a monster, out for blood. I was vengeance and hate, fury and wrath.

"Son…" His voice trembled, but he stuck to the usual script. "How long has it been since your last confession?"

"Cut the bullshit. You know." I smiled, staring at nothing in particular. Everything in the place was so goddamn wooden. Not that I expected an interior designer's touch, but this shit was ridiculous. It looked like the inside of a coffin. Certainly felt like one.

"Can we move on?" I cracked my neck and rolled up my sleeves. "Time is money."

"It's also a healer."

I clenched my jaw, balling and releasing my fists.

"Nice try." I paused, checking my Rolex. His time was running out. Mine, too.

Tick tock, tick tock.

"Bless me, Father, for I have sinned. Two years ago, I killed a man. His name was Billy Crupti. He shot a bullet straight into my father's forehead and blew out his brains, causing my family pain and devastation. I killed him with my bare hands."

I let the weight of my confession sink in and continued. "I cut his arms and legs, just enough so he wouldn't bleed to death, tied him up and had him watching as a pack of fighting dogs fought over his parts." My voice was eerily calm. "When everything was done and dealt with, I tied a weight to his waist and threw him from a commercial pier on the bay, still twitching, to die a slow, painful suffocating death. Now tell me, Father, how many Hail Marys for a murder?"

I knew he wasn't the type to bring a cell phone into the booth. McGregor was too old and cocky for modern technology. Even though he went rogue on my father, he never imagined he'd be caught. Least of all by me. Least of all like *this*. I waited patiently for two years for the perfect moment. For him to be exposed, off-guard and alone at church.

Now, as I confessed my sin, he knew I was going to wait at the other end of the booth and claim his life, too. He had no way out.

He was mostly silent, calculating his next move. I heard him swallow hard, his fingernail scraping at the wooden chair he sat on.

I crossed one leg over the other and cupped one of my knees, amused. "Now your turn. How 'bout we hear about them sins, Father?"

He released a breath he'd been holding in a sharp sigh. "That's not how confessions work."

"Don't I fucking know it," I snorted. "This one's a little different, though.

So..." I brushed the screen dividing us with my glove and watched as he flinched on the other side. "I'm all ears."

I heard the clatter of his rosary beads as they dropped from his hand and the creak of his chair when he kneeled down to pick them up.

"I'm a man of God," he tried to reason with me.

I seethed with resentment. He was also a man who spilled secrets from the confessional.

"Not a soul on earth knew about the whereabouts of my father every Tuesday at ten p.m. Not a soul other than him and his mistress. And *you*," I drawled. "Billy 'Baby Face' Crupti tracked down my father, unprotected and unarmed, because of *you*."

He opened his mouth, intending to argue, but clapped it shut, thinking the better of it at the last minute. Somewhere in the distance a dog was barking and a woman was yelling at her husband in their backyard. Classic Southie reminders of the people I used to know before I moved to a skyscraper and reinvented myself.

McGregor gulped, stalling. "Troy, my son..."

I stood up, pushing my sleeves farther up my arms. "Enough. Out you go."

He didn't move for a few seconds, which prompted me to take out my knife and slice the grid open with a ripping sound. I shoved my hand into his booth, grabbing him by his white collar and pulling his head through the hole so I could take a good look at him. His gray hair stood out in all directions, damp with sweat. The horror in his eyes lightened my mood. His narrow, thin mouth hung open like a hooked fish.

"Please, please. Troy. Please. I beg you, son. Do not repeat the sins of your father," he chanted, crying out in pain as I jerked him closer to my face.

"Open. The fucking. Booth." I extended every word like it was a sentence of its own.

I heard a sleek *click* as he fumbled for the door. I released his hair out of my fist, and we both stepped out.

McGregor stood before me, several inches shorter. A chubby, sweaty, corrupted man pretending to be God's messenger. A tasteless joke.

"You're really going to kill your priest," he pointed out sadly.

I shrugged. I wasn't a hitman. I drew a thick red line somewhere near homicide, but this was personal. It was about my father. The man who raised me while my mom was too drunk on Bloomingdales sales and Sunday-brunch cocktails. She was so absent from my childhood, not to mention adulthood, that I was practically half orphaned. If nothing else, my father deserved closure.

"You're just like them. I thought you were different. Better," McGregor accused.

I pressed my lips into a thin line. My job had nothing to do with Irish mobsters. I didn't need the Feds crawling up my ass every time someone farted in my direction and certainly had no interest in the framework of gang leaders and soldiers. I was a lone wolf, who hired a few people to help him out when help was needed. I had no buffer between me and my clients, colleagues and enemies. And most importantly, I sailed smoothly under the radar. Didn't need to hide behind a dozen soldiers. When I needed someone gone, I handled them myself.

And Father McGregor had to pay for his sins. He was already supposed to be dead—collateral damage. But he hadn't shown up where he was supposed to when I took out the guy he'd ratted my dad out to. Billy Crupti. The asshole.

So now I had to do this in a fucking church.

"Be quick," he requested.

I nodded grimly.

"You were always his child. Had the Irish mob gene, the ruthlessness in your blood. You had no fear. Still don't." He sighed, extending his hand to me.

I stared at it like it was a ticking bomb, finally shaking it. His palm felt clammy and cold, his handshake weak. I pulled him into my body for an embrace, and clasped the back of his neck with one hand.

"And I'm so sorry," he continued, sniffing into my shoulder, his whole body quivering as he struggled to hold back the tears. "Lapse of judgment on my end. I knew that he'd kill them, both of them. But at the time, I thought I'd be doing everyone a favor."

"It was money, wasn't it?" I whispered into his ear as we clasped each other, me pulling a knife from a sheath at my waist. "Billy paid you?"

He nodded, still sobbing, unaware of the knife. Someone had to pay him off, and pay him good to spill the beans about my dad. Someone who wasn't Crupti, who couldn't even afford the fucking special of the day at his local diner.

"Not just for the money, Troy. I wanted Cillian out of this neighborhood, out of Boston. This place had suffered enough under the realm of your father. Our people deserve some peace."

"*Our* people are not your fucking subjects." I dragged the knife along his neck until I found his throbbing carotid artery and slashed deep, immediately shoving his body backward into the booth so that the spray of blood wouldn't touch my newly tailored suit. "You should have minded your own business."

He gagged and jerked on the confession floor like a fish out of water, losing buckets of blood. The scent—sour, tinny and thrilling—fogged the air and I knew it would linger in my nose for days to come.

When his spasms died down, I got down on one knee, staring back at his brown irises, still open, still filled with horror and regret. I pulled out his tongue and cut it from his mouth.

This was gang-member code for a snitch. Let the police try and figure out what the fuck Father McGregor did to deserve it and which of the hundred Boston gangs killed him. There were too many of them to count and hell knew they were intertwined with one another more often than not. Gangs had taken over the streets, filling the void left when my father was dethroned from his seat as the Boss of Boston when I was still a kid.

Ironically, in trying to give them peace, Father McGregor had sentenced his parishioners to lives of panic and fear.

The streets were still chaotic—some would say more than ever—with the crime rate picking up at an alarming speed. Keeping an eye on the Irish

Mob, I assumed, was far simpler than trying to tame dozens of gangs running the streets.

I knew the police would never get anywhere near me with this murder case.

And I'd also known where I'd bury father McGregor's tongue. In his own backyard.

I casually wiped my knife clean on his pants leg and pulled off the leather gloves I was wearing, shoving them in my pocket. I took out a toothpick and put it in my mouth. Then I rolled down my sleeves and retrieved my suit coat. When I got out the door, I glanced around for potential witnesses, just in case.

The neighborhood was deader than the man I had just dealt with. Going for a stroll wasn't really our thing in South Boston, especially not around noon. You either worked hard, took care of the little ones at home or nursed a fucking hangover. The only witness to my visit to the church was a bird, sitting on an ugly power line up above, eyeing me suspiciously from the corner of its eye. It was a bland looking sparrow.

I crossed the road and got into my car, slamming the door behind me. Taking out a Sharpie from the glove compartment, I crossed another name off my list.

1 – Billy Crupti

2 – Father McGregor

3 – The asshole who hired Billy?

I sighed as I looked at number three, shoving the crumpled yellow paper back into my pocket.

I'll find out who you are, motherfucker.

I looked out the window. The sparrow didn't move, not even when a gust of wind sent the power line dancing and the bird lost its balance. The irony wasn't lost on me. Fucking sparrow, of all birds.

I fought the urge to throw something at it, revved up the engine and spat the toothpick in my mouth into the ashtray after it was thoroughly chewed.

I thought I saw the stupid bird still following my car with its tiny eyes as I stopped at a red light and looked out my side mirror. Averting my gaze down, I checked for blood traces. There weren't any.

McGregor was dead, but the void in my stomach didn't shrink an inch.

It was alarming, because in order to keep my promise to my dad, I had another name to handle that wasn't even on my list.

But this wasn't a person I was supposed to kill. This was a person I was supposed to resurrect.

I, of all people, needed to be her savior.

Other people—normal people, I guess—would have never agreed to sacrifice this part of their lives for their father. But other people didn't live under Cillian Brennan's shadow, didn't feel the urge to constantly step up their game to be equal to their late legendary sire. No, I'd follow his wishes. And I'd even make it work.

All I knew when I drove away from my childhood church were two things:

My father had sinned.

But I was to be punished.

The sparrow is associated with freedom. At one time, sailors got a tattoo of a sparrow for every five thousand nautical miles they traveled. Sparrows were believed to bring good luck. Sometimes the sailor got his sparrow tattoo even before leaving the docks, hoping it would act as a talisman and help bring him safely home again.

ONE

SPARROW

Three years later

"I**S IT POSSIBLE TO FEEL YOUR HEART** breaking, even if you've never fallen in love?" I stared back at the woman in the mirror, chewing on my lower lip until the tender flesh cracked. I looked like a stranger.

Sorrow slammed into me like thunder. Sorrow for the man I would never meet, for the first love I would never experience, for the romance I would never have. For the butterflies that would never take flight in the pit of my stomach. For hope, happiness and anticipation, things I would never feel again.

"I didn't spend three hours doing your makeup so you can munch on your lipstick like it's a bag of chips, sweetheart." Sherry, the makeup artist, fussed around me.

Just then, the hair stylist, a gay man in his late twenties, marched into the room, carrying a bottle of hairspray, and sprayed my hairline again without warning, spritzing the cold liquid all over my eyes. I blinked, fighting the burning sensation both on my face and from the inside.

"You done harassing me yet?" I hissed, stepping away from the mirror and walking to the other side of the luxurious presidential suite.

My first stay in a five-star hotel. And it made me feel like a glorified hooker.

I retrieved a champagne glass I was pretty certain wasn't even mine and downed the whole thing in one gulp, slamming the glass against the fancy silver tray, fighting the urge to wipe my mouth with the back of my hand so that Sherry wouldn't kill me. The glass broke into two pieces, and I grimaced, looking back at the crew Troy Brennan has appointed to make me look like the perfect little bride.

"I'm sure Mr. Brennan will have no problem footing the bill for this... too." Sherry waved her hand, her overdone platinum hair stiff as a rock on her head.

She had a cleavage so deep you could almost see her belly button. She looked like a showgirl from one of the joints Pops used to work at, not exactly the kind of person I'd take fashion and makeup tips from. Then again, I had no say in anything about this wedding.

"As long as you didn't hurt yourself," said Joe, the stylist, wiggling his index finger at me. He pried the broken stem from between my fingers with his free hand. "Don't want you bleeding all over the dress. It's a vintage Valentino, mind you."

I didn't even pretend to look like I knew what a vintage Valentino was. Why would a girl from my tough South Boston neighborhood know anything about couture? Ask me about coupons and how to sneak into the subway for free, and I'd tell you all about it. High fashion, though? Yeah, not for me.

I rolled my eyes and walked into the bathroom to wash my hands. If I had nicked my finger, I wouldn't want to infuriate Brennan by staining the costly rental dress. The counter was littered with hair products and makeup, as well as creams, spa essentials and my cell phone. I jumped when the phone bleeped with a text.

Eying the group in the other room, I eased the door mostly shut.

Lucy: *Still not gonna make it to class today? Boris is teaching us how to make stock. x*

Me: *Sorry. Caught a bug or something. Been throwing up all night. Text me the recipe when class is over.*

Lucy: *You got it, babe. Hope you feel better.*

Me: *Have a feeling the worst is yet to come. x*

I put the phone down and prayed, for the millionth time that day that Lucy would be too busy to read the society page tomorrow. Troy Brennan was the kind of guy to show up in the local news for all the wrong reasons. He was trouble—hot trouble, flash-fire-on-the-stove hot trouble—and I knew that his wedding would likely be spread all over the local news like salmonella from a dubious food truck the minute he said, *I do.*

And me? I'd never attracted too much attention. My social life was as active as a dead turtle. I didn't have many friends. Those I had I'd kept oblivious to my shotgun wedding. I was pretty frightened of the groom, embarrassed with myself for agreeing to do this in the first place and too confused to deal with their potential (and understandable) questions.

Sadness pierced my heart when I turned on the faucet. My fingers brushed my engagement ring under the stream of running water. It had a diamond the size of my fist at the center, and two, smaller ones on each side. The band itself was plain, a thin platinum shackle, but the weight of the bling—literally, figuratively, freaking mentally—screamed *nouveau riche* to the sky and back. It also yelled money, power, and look-at-me pretense.

But there was one thing it didn't even whisper—*my name.*

Me, Sparrow Raynes. Twenty-two. The child of Abe and Robyn Raynes. An avid runner. A tomboy. A lover of blueberry pancakes, hot chocolate, sweet summer air and unapologetic boyfriend jeans. *That kid.* The girl who sat in the first row of every class and fiddled with her lunch box during school breaks because no one wanted to hang out with her. The woman who never cared about fashion. The poor chick who thought money was overrated, glitzy cars equaled small dicks, and that happiness was Irish stew and *Kitchen Cutthroat* reruns under the covers.

This ring belonged to someone else. A Real Housewife of Whatever-suburb. A trophy bride of certain tastes and status. A girl who knew who Valentino was and why his dresses were so goddamned expensive. *Not. Me.*

I turned off the faucet and took a deep breath, running my fingers over my incredibly stiff hair.

"Just deal with it," I prompted myself quietly. Marrying a wealthy man who was known as one of the most sought-after bachelors in Boston was hardly considered a punishment. "Not your choice, but roll with the plan."

I closed my eyes and shook my head. First-World problem or not, the last thing I needed was for *him* to take care of me. A soft knock on the bathroom door made me swivel my head in its direction. Sherry's face, plastered with makeup and a fake smile, peeked through the cracked door.

"Mr. Brennan's here to see you," she announced in her syrupy-sweet, insincere voice.

"It's bad luck to see the bride before the wedding," I gritted out, clenching my fists together and allowing the monstrous ring to dig into my flesh. The pain was a welcome distraction.

"Trust me, it's even worse luck to piss off your future husband." I heard his iron-cold tenor cutting through the air outside the door.

I took a step back, hugging myself protectively. The door swung open, and he stepped inside, looking so much bigger than life and any of the pep talks I kept drilling into my head.

He wore a formal black three-piece suit and leather wingtips. He owned the small bathroom, sucking all air and my presence out of it. Suddenly, I felt even smaller than my already tiny frame. His icy glare peeled my walls of defense, exposing me for what I really was—a sweltering ball of nerves.

"Unfold your arms so I can see you," Brennan ordered sharply.

I did as I was told, not out of respect, but out of fear. My arms hung at my sides as I gulped hard. He'd never looked twice at me before. Not in the eighteen years we lived in the same neighborhood or in the last ten days. This was the first time he'd acknowledged my existence this personally. *The day of our wedding.*

"You look beautiful." His tone was detached.

I knew the dress was spectacular. Phrases like "mermaid silhouette" and "Queen Anne neckline" flew in my direction when I first tried it on at the bridal shop. Not that I chose it myself. Joe, the stylist, got his orders directly from my dear future husband. So did Sherry and the hair stylist whose name I couldn't remember and even the woman who chose my jewelry for the event. I had no say about anything when it came to this wedding. Just as well, as I wasn't exactly Bridezilla. I wanted this wedding like a bad case of gonorrhea.

"Thank you," I finally managed to reply and despite my simmering rage, felt oddly compelled to reciprocate with, "You look nice, too."

"How can you tell? You haven't looked at me once since I stepped into the room." Brennan's voice was frosty and unapproachable, but it didn't sound like he cared.

I gingerly lifted my chin and dragged my gaze to meet his eyes, every muscle in my face tightening as I watched him. "Very nice," I repeated, not a trace of sincerity in my voice.

I heard Sherry fussing over God knows what in the other room and Joe talking on the phone, or at least pretending to. Meanwhile, the hair stylist and Connor, the bodyguard who followed me everywhere, were silent, which was coincidentally louder than any of Sherry and Joe's futile attempts to sound busy. The buzz of a disaster rang between my ears.

He has a troubled past.

A disastrous future.

And I'm about to become a part of his present, whether I like it or not.

"Connor, Sherry, everyone—get the fuck out," my groom ordered as he continued staring me down through narrowed eyes.

I twisted my fingers together and felt my mouth drying up. This wasn't me. The insecure, little Mary-Sue wasn't the Sparrow I had built over the years. But he was dangerous, and I was giving him trouble.

I was giving him trouble because ten days ago, completely out of the blue, he dragged me out of my house (a guy who was no more than a distant childhood memory in an expensive suit and a shady reputation) and threw me into his luxurious penthouse and announced (two days after he left me there with nothing and no one but a bodyguard and a number for a takeout joint) that we were going to get married.

Yes, Troy Brennan was one hell of a sociopath, and he didn't bother disguising his nature and putting on a mask when he faced the world.

He stood in the presidential suite's bathroom, looking at me like I was a bitter pill he had to swallow. It didn't seem like he was mildly interested in me. He'd barely spoken to me, and when he had, a mixture of disappointment, boredom and apathy leaked from his gaze.

I was beyond confused by his behavior. I had heard of powerful, rich men forcing themselves on women before, but usually they desired the women they pursued. This wasn't the case with Troy Brennan. The way he acted, it almost seemed like he was doing this because he'd lost a bet.

I stared back at my future husband, waiting for him to do something. Hit me, yell at me or break the whole thing off.

I wasn't sure why the hell he wanted me in the first place. We grew up in the same Boston area, a blue-collar sketchy neighborhood. Our childhood scenery consisted of barred windows, ripped posters, old buildings in desperate need of repair and empty cans rolling down the street. But that's where our similarities ended.

While I was the poor, working-class daughter of a drunken bum and a runaway mother, Troy Brennan was Boston royalty, and grew up in the nicest house in our zip code. His father, Cillian, once ran the infamous Irish mob. By the time I was a toddler, Cillian had moved on to more legitimate businesses, and by "legitimate" I meant strip clubs, massage parlors and other sleazy South Boston entertainments for guys barely making the rent. My dad, one of his last loyal soldiers, had worked as a bouncer in more than a few of Cillian's joints.

Troy was an only child, with people saying Cillian's wife couldn't have more kids. He was therefore the apple of his father's eye.

And while Troy might not have carried on with all of his dad's old businesses, he was no choirboy either. Rumors about him spread like wildfire on the streets of our neighborhood, and at this point he was so talked about he was almost a legend. Word was that politicians, businessmen and rich people from all over the state reached out to him when they needed someone to do their dirty work.

And dirty work he did, and got paid plenty for it.

People called Troy "The Fixer." He fixed stuff. Not in the handyman sense, mind you. He made people disappear faster than characters in Dennis Lehane's books. He could cut your prison sentence in half and fix you up with a passport and a fake Social Security card in hours. In days, he could even convince the people who were after you that you didn't exist. Troy Brennan was Boston's master manipulator, pulling strings like we were all his puppets. He decided who lived and who died, who disappeared and who made a comeback.

And for some unknown reason, Mr. Fixer chose to marry me. I had no way to fight, escape or even defy his irrational decision. All I could do was beg for a feasible explanation. So I decided to use our first encounter together alone—without Connor, Sherry or any of Troy's staff—to do just that.

"Why me, Troy? You never spoke a word to me all those years we lived on the same street." I gripped the creamy vanity top behind me, my knuckles whitening. Maybe calling him by his first name would inspire him to be nicer to me.

He cocked an eyebrow, an expression that looked like *Well, shit. She can talk, too.* He buttoned his suit jacket with one hand and checked his cell phone with the other.

I was wind, I was a ghost. *I was nothing.*

"Troy?" I asked again. This time he lifted his eyes to meet mine. My voice dropped to a whisper, but I kept my stare trained on him. "Why me?"

His brows furrowed, his lips thinning into a hard line.

He didn't like the question, and I wasn't satisfied with the answer.

"We don't even know each other." My nostrils flared.

"Yeah, well..." He kept punching his cell phone, his eyes dropping back to the screen. "Familiarity is overrated. The less I know someone, the better I usually like them."

This still doesn't explain why you thrust yourself into my life with the finesse of an army tank.

I glared at him under my newly fake eyelashes, trying to figure out whether he was even good-looking or not. Troy Brennan was never on my radar, but he was on everybody else's. He was like the IKEA canvas pictures of London and New York in bachelor apartments, like fast food, like Starbucks, like a freaking Macbook Air for a preppy student—mainstream and well liked. At least among women. Buying into his bad boy, influential, rich mobster's appeal was the polar opposite of who I was.

And still, even under the unforgiving bathroom light, I could see he might be a monster inside, but on the outside, he was anything but.

His thick black mane—so dark it had an almost bluish hue—was trimmed into an expensive haircut with smooth and soft edges. He had the palest, frostiest blue eyes, and a slight tan that made them pop even more. From afar, he was old-fashionedly good-looking. Tall as a skyscraper, wide as a Rugby player and with prominent cheekbones you could cut diamonds with. As he neared you, though, the dead expression behind those baby-blues made you want to run the other way. His eyes were always lazily hooded, vacant of any trace of emotion. Almost like if you looked deep enough, you'd see all the horrific things he'd done to his enemies running in slow motion.

Then there was also the sneer. The challenging smirk plastered on his face 24/7, reminding us all just how unworthy we were in comparison.

I feared and loathed Troy Brennan. He was practically untouchable in Boston. Loved among the cops and respected by the local gangs, he was able to get away with murder.

Literally.

Three years ago, Troy had been the prime suspect in the murder of Billy "Baby Face" Crupti. There wasn't enough evidence to make the charge stick, but word on the street was the murder was payback. Supposedly Crupti was the one who'd killed Cillian Brennan. No one knew who had sent the simpleton gangster to off Troy's father or why. The timing was odd. Cillian's illegal activities were pretty irrelevant to gangland Boston by then. Then there was also the Father McGregor tale, about how Troy killed him too, for ratting about his father's whereabouts to Crupti.

Yeah, Troy Brennan wasn't one to take any prisoners.

I still remembered how, growing up, I used to wait for my turn to ride Daisy's bike (she was the only girl in the neighborhood to have one, and with training wheels, too), and watch in awe when he ran into the cops. I swear the police patted down the boy down the street more than a newborn puppy. They were waiting impatiently for teenage Brennan to follow in his father's footsteps. He got slammed into the hood of every patrol car that rolled by, and every cop on our beat knew the curve of his ass by heart.

Now cops were too scared to even look at him.

As I stood in the hotel suite's bathroom, staring at his expressionless face, I realized that I had no cards to play. And even if I had cards, he owned the freaking table.

I was completely trapped, a caged bird with clipped wings.

"Can I still work?" I asked through a strangled voice. Mob wives were not allowed to, but Troy was not a mobster. *Technically*. He took a step closer, his breath falling on my face.

"You can do whatever the fuck you want. You have a long leash."

I felt his lips traveling inches from the crook of my neck, and I stilled. Thankfully, he didn't touch me.

"But let's get one thing straight—when it comes to men, I'm the only fucking one for you. Do not test me on this subject, because the consequences will be grave for you...and for him."

He was being deliberately obnoxious, but his words still stung. I tried to focus on the small victory I was granted. I could still work. Still get out of the house and avoid him. Now it was just a matter of finding a job to keep me busy.

"If my leash is so long, why is Connor following me around?" I lifted my chin, challenging him.

"Because I always protect what's mine."

"I'm not your property, Brennan." I seethed, narrowing my eyes. Yes, I was scared, but more than anything, I was royally pissed off.

"The fact that you're in a wedding dress and have my ring on your finger begs to fucking differ," he said, his voice flat and calm. "But even if you weren't, with the amount of enemies I've collected in this city, anyone affiliated with me needs protection. Now if you'll excuse me." He turned on his heel and headed out the door.

It was only after he left my personal space that I released the breath that was trapped in my lungs for what felt like a decade. Why was he so hell-bent on reminding me how dangerous he was?

"You're not going to get away with doing this to me, you know," I called out after him, watching his broad back.

"That's where you're wrong, Red. I get away with everything. Always." He didn't even bother to turn around to face me.

Did he just call me Red?

"Oh, so now I have a nickname? This marriage isn't real, Brennan. No matter what will happen in church this afternoon."

That finally made him react. He turned his head in my direction. Our eyes locked. His frosty blues pierced through my greens, burning an imaginary hole all the way to the back of my skull.

Stupid girl. I felt my pulse—wild and manic—behind my eyes, at my throat, in my toes, pumping, pounding, my heart trying to break free out of my skin and run for its life. *Why provoke the guy if you can't even handle a stare-down?*

There was a brief beat, and then Brennan offered me one of his unpleasant I-Will-Destroy-You smiles.

"Dear future wife…" He smirked in a way that made me want to beg for mercy. "If you think you're going to give me trouble, think again. I invented trouble. I stir it, I mix it, I fucking fix it. Don't try my patience, because you'll discover I have absolutely none."

My father was giving me away at the Sacred Heart Catholic Church, conveniently located in the center of the city. The guest list was full of people I didn't know or care about. A mish-mash of high-profile businessmen, a handful of politicians, one senator and endless socialites.

A trail of black stretch limos lined up in front of the old church. Sophisticatedly clothed matrons poured out of the cars, assisted by their husbands, sons and daughters. The attire was formal and oozed power, as the men puffed on cigars, laughing with each other and patting shoulders good-naturedly, certainly enjoying the event more than I was.

By the number of security guards marching through the entrance, you'd think I was marrying the Pope.

As my gaze roamed the entrance of the church from the limo I sat in, it occurred to me that the flower arrangements flanking the doors had probably cost more than a year's rent at the apartment Pops and I shared for the past twenty-two years. The mere thought of marrying someone so obscenely reckless with his money sent a cold shudder down my spine.

I was trying to control the hysterical emotions swirling in me when Pops took my quivering hand in his warm, rough one and squeezed it tight for reassurance.

"You're doing the right thing, you know that, right?" Hope gleamed in his eyes.

As if I was given a choice.

But I knew what my father didn't have to tell me. Even if he hadn't accepted Brennan's request to take me as his wife (and Troy Brennan was undoubtedly one of those hypocritical, old-fashioned assholes who asked your dad for your hand), Brennan would have made it happen one way or the other. *No* was simply not in his vocabulary. What he wanted, he took.

And right now, he wanted little old me.

It made no sense at all. I wasn't particularly beautiful, or at least not in the way to attract the attention of men of his caliber. My lips, probably my best feature, were pink, narrow and heart-shaped, but otherwise I was ordinary at best. I had a short, scrawny frame; long, fire-engine red hair; almost sickly pale skin and freckles peppering every inch of my round face. I was not Troy Brennan's type.

I knew this with certainty, having flipped through the gossip pages of the local newspapers here and there. He was always seen with glamorous women. They were tall, curvy and gorgeous. Not mousy, ruby haired and a little on the odd side. So as I sat in the limo, about to walk into a church I'd never been inside, full of people I didn't know, to marry a stranger I feared, a chant rang between my ears, its echo bouncing on the walls of my skull.

Why me? Why me? Why me?

"We're up next," I heard the limo driver announce, as the vehicle dragged leisurely forward.

My heart picked up speed, banging wildly against my sternum. A thin layer of sweat formed over my skin.

I wasn't ready.

I didn't have a choice.

Dear God.

The irony wasn't lost on me. I was praying for God to step in and prevent the ceremony from happening, even though I was at his holy home.

A small, quiet but persistent, voice in me taunted that this was my punishment for being a bad Catholic. For not giving the Almighty the respect he deserved. I'd stopped going to church long ago, and even as a kid, I wasn't particularly interested in faith.

All those years drifting off as a child at Sunday mass.

All those years attending youth group solely for the cookies and to ogle the young, handsome man who lectured us about God's marvelous ways. Tobey, I think his name was.

All those years and now it was payback time. And Karma? She was well known as a hormonal, raging bitch. God was going to punish me. I was going to marry a monster.

"Here we are," the driver said, tilting his hat forward.

I caught him eyeing me curiously from the rearview mirror, but at this point I no longer cared. Better get used to it, because once I was Brennan's wife, people would ogle me like I was a unicorn at a magic zoo.

"Everyone's taking their seats inside. Shouldn't be more than a couple more minutes, ma'am."

I looked back to my father as he handed me the purple bouquet. He leaned forward, kissing my forehead gently. He reeked of alcohol. Not the cheap kind either. Brennan must've spoiled him with the good stuff now that we were all about to become one big, unhappy, screwed-up family.

"I wish your mom was here to see this." He sighed, his wrinkled forehead collapsing into a frown, his eyes two pools of grief.

"Don't," I cut him off flatly, relieved to hear there was not a trace of emotion in my voice anymore. "We haven't laid eyes on that woman since I was three years old. Wherever she ran off to, she doesn't deserve to take part in this, or anything else in my life. Besides, you did a good job taking care of me on your own." I patted his thigh awkwardly.

It was true. Robyn Raynes wasn't my mother, she was a woman who gave birth to me and left shortly after. I supposed most people would feel more strongly about it on the day of their wedding, but (a) this wasn't my wedding, not my real one anyway, and (b) when your parent deserted you, you had two choices: you either let it define and rule you, or you moved on, making a point to show the world that you didn't give a rat's ass where your mother had gone.

I tried falling into the second category, and I rarely slipped.

Pops loved what he was hearing. His eyes shone with pride and surprise. Of course, I'd sugarcoated the hell out of our history. But somehow, I recognized today was just as difficult for my dad as it was for me. A raging alcoholic or not, he'd always put a distance between me and his job with the Brennans, and I knew he wanted nothing more than to shield me from these people.

As for his parenting abilities, truth be told, he had taken care of me on his own ever since I was a toddler. He was never abusive or impatient, even if he was a little on the clueless and insensitive side. There were even women he'd dated who'd played house and were my temporary "mommies" until they realized my father's love for the hard stuff would always run much deeper than his love for them. Mostly, though, it was just me and him.

Well, me, him and the alcohol.

Even though I loved him, I knew my father wasn't a good man. When I was growing up and he worked for Cillian Brennan, too often he came home bruised from fights. I dealt with surprise visits from the cops, and I brought him fresh clothes and cigarettes plenty of times when he was arrested. He was now employed by Troy, probably doing something just as illegal.

Pops was an alcoholic and a terrible Casanova with the ladies, but he was also the only person who loved me, who cared, who burnt himself on the stove trying to make chicken noodle soup for me—not the canned type, the real deal—when I caught pneumonia.

He deserved a little happiness, even if it was on my account.

"I love you, Birdie." He let a single, fat tear roll down his wrinkle-mapped cheek as he pressed both his paws to my face.

I nodded, leaning my face into one of his palms. I stroked his forehead with the pads of my fingers. "Love you too, Pops."

"Alrighty-o. Ready? Here we go." The cheery driver pushed his door open and walked around the limo, opening the door for me.

I slid out carefully, noting that the front yard of the church was mostly empty, other than few elderly men scattered around, still caught up in business talk. Pops followed behind, but broke to the left where he spotted the small group of washed-up men.

"I need to catch a word with Benny. I'll be back in a minute. Let the groom wait a little while. Be right back, little darlin.'" He winked and marched toward the herd of suited men at the corner of the cobblestone church.

I frowned, adjusting my dress. It was an uncharacteristically cold June day, but I knew better than to think goose bumps broke on my skin because of the chill. I eyed the opening in the high stone wall beside me and spotted a tiny garden with a bench. I wished I could hide there.

Then I heard him.

A man speaking softly to his son on the other side of the wall. His voice was gentle, but still throaty and gruff at the same time. I'm not sure why, but the sound of him seeped into my body like warm liquor on a stormy night.

"Of course, Abraham wasn't a bad man, but he did what he thought he had to do, and that was to sacrifice his child to God."

A trail of cold sweat dripped down my spine, and I leaned forward on one heeled foot toward the voices, straining my ears.

"But Daddy, dads love their children, right?"

"They do. More than anything else in the world, Sam."

"And God loves his children?"

The man paused briefly. "Very much."

"So how come God did what they did to Isaac?"

"Well, God wanted to test Abraham's faith. Isaac was okay at the end of the day, remember, but God received proof that Abraham would put his adored son at the altar for him."

"Do you think," the little boy pondered, and by his voice, he couldn't have been much older than five, "that God is just testing our Abraham? Maybe his daughter and Mr. Troy won't get married today."

The man chuckled to himself humorlessly, and I felt my heart sinking.

"No. That's not a test, little champ. People want to marry each other. It's not punishment."

"Did you want to marry Mommy?" Sam asked.

Another silence filled the air before the man answered.

"Yes, I wanted to marry Mommy. Which reminds me, where is *our* mommy?"

Just then, the man's strode through the opening in the wall and his hard body bumped into mine. I squeaked, almost falling flat on my ass, but managed to grab the wall with my hand that wasn't clutching the bouquet.

"Shit, sorry," he said.

I straightened, raising my head, and my eyes bugged out and my mouth dried up instantly. He was handsome. No, scratch handsome. He was a masterpiece in a sharp black suit, stealing my breath and momentarily shaking me free of my mental breakdown.

He was about six two, a little shorter than Brennan, and just like my husband-to-be, the way he filled his custom-made outfit told me he made it a point to work out at least four times a week. His chestnut-brown hair, wavy and thick, tousled and soft, stuck out in a few directions, despite his best effort to slick it back. His gray eyes studied me, narrow and intelligent, as he rubbed his strong jawline.

"You said a bad word!" His son practically bounced with happiness, waving a little blue truck in his hand. "You need to put a dollar in the jar when we get back home."

But Sam's dad seemed to have been sent to a parallel universe, judging by the way his gaze held mine. He looked surprised to see me, and I wondered how much he knew. I froze, trying to shake off the weird effect he had on me.

"I wasn't eavesdropping," I hurried to explain, smoothing my dress. His eyes dropped to where my hand stroked the fabric of my vintage Valen-something, and I immediately jerked it away, feeling self-conscious.

"I wasn't accusing," he answered serenely. That voice. That authority. He was one of Troy's crew, I immediately knew.

"Of course you weren't." I blushed, turning away toward the church door. "It's my wedding in there. So, you know, I better…" My dumb mouth kept spitting out stupidity. *Yes, Sparrow. It is your wedding. Otherwise, you just showed up in the most inappropriate dress on the planet.*

"It is. And I'm sorry," he said gravely, his meaning clear.

More emotions stormed inside me, and my stomach flipped at his minor act of kindness.

He was married, with a son, I reminded myself. Oh, and also, I was about to get married in approximately five minutes to one of the most dangerous men in Boston. This made him firmly off limits. And me, a raging idiot.

I rubbed one hand over my face, grateful that Sherry wasn't there to yell at me for messing up all the layers of makeup she'd caked on my skin.

"Me too." I shrugged. "I hope you and your family enjoy the ceremony."

He opened his mouth to say something, but I couldn't deal with more of his kindness. I didn't trust men these days, especially not those who were hypocritical enough to offer solace.

Turning away, I put two fingers to my lips and whistled to my dad. "Hey, Pops…" I waved him over with one hand as all the men in the churchyard stared at me, dumbfounded. I bet they thought Brennan would marry a lady and not some weirdo tomboy redhead. "Let's get this over with."

Pops jogged the short distance between us. Panting, he acknowledged the beautiful man with a nod. "Brock."

"Abe," Brock returned with his own nod. "Congratulations on the wedding. I trust you know I'm here should any of you need anything at all." Brock turned his gaze back to me, and my heart squeezed just a little more with self-pity.

Brock and Sam turned around, walking into the church, hand in hand.

Pops took a step closer and grasped me by the shoulders. "It's show time. Let's get my little Birdie married."

Objectively speaking, my wedding to Troy Brennan was a beautiful event. Obscenely lavish and obnoxiously wasteful. Brennan spared no expense when it came to what was his. Be it his penthouse, his cars, his women or his wedding.

The candles, floral arrangements, aisle runner, soloist, organist, floral archways and extravagantly decorated pews were all impeccable and plush. In fact, I was surprised the altar wasn't built exclusively from blood diamonds and rolled one-hundred-dollar bills.

Nonetheless, to me, it was as pointless as Henry Cavill with a shirt on. So much detail and beauty shouldn't be wasted on fraud. And that's what

Brennan and I were—a lie. A charade. Doomed people trapped in a marriage built on the ruins of extortion and lies.

We exchanged vows in front of four hundred guests, all teary-eyed and joyful. Father O'Leary performed the ceremony with grace, or so I assumed, seeing as my vision was blurry and my head spun. I tried not to sweat away the equivalent of my body weight in anxiety and mimicked what the priest was saying whenever appropriate.

Brennan wasn't exactly basking in the attention, but he didn't seem too bothered by it either. Overall, he looked tough, unfazed and a little irritated with the time he had to waste on the mundane event.

"Since it is your intention to enter into marriage, join your right hands, and declare your consent before God and His Church," O'Leary instructed, and my emotions got the better of me.

I gasped when the groom took my small hand in his big one, clasping it firmly. While the people in the pews chuckled, thinking it was the sweet, authentic reaction of a nervous bride, black dots clouded my vision and I thought I was going to faint. He stared daggers at me, his jaw stiff as stone, and I forced myself to smile weakly, continuing with the charade.

"I, Troy James Brennan, take you, Sparrow Elizabeth Raynes, to be my wife. I promise to be true to you in good times and in bad, in sickness and in health. I will love you and honor you, all the days of my life."

Women were wiping the edge of their heavily mascaraed eyes with handkerchiefs, sniffing their noses as they nodded their approval. Men exchanged contented grunts, sticking their chins out like this freak show was genuine. My face drained of color, blood and life.

My turn.

The priest turned to me and asked me to repeat his words, which I did, albeit with a shaky voice. "I, Sparrow Elizabeth Raynes, take you, Troy James Brennan, to be my husband. I promise to be true to you in good times and in bad, in sickness and in health. I will love you and honor you, all the days of my life."

The priest continued rambling, but I tuned him out at this point, concentrating solely on the fact that I was almost married to this man. A criminal. *A murderer*. My promise to Troy Brennan left a bitter taste in my mouth.

A part of me wanted to yell at everyone sitting in front of us and smiling like idiots, to lash out angrily. I was twenty-two. He was thirty-two. We hadn't even gone out on one date.

Never been out together.

Barely spoken to each another.

This was a lie. How could they let this happen?

My shaky relationship with humanity took another nosedive when Brennan's best man, a plump man with ratty, mean eyes handed him my ring.

"Take this ring as a sign of my love and fidelity. In the name of the Father, and the Son, and the Holy Spirit." Brennan slid the ring down my finger.

When it was my turn, I spewed the words on autopilot. Plucking my husband's ring from a pillow held by a young girl—she and my three bridesmaids, all complete strangers to me and probably hired—I slid the band onto his finger with a quivering hand.

"You may kiss the bride," the priest announced with a satisfied grin when the deed was done.

Brennan didn't wait for me to move or get hold of my emotions. Showing off his wolfish grin, he stepped into my personal space and tilted my head back, holding my neck like he'd done it hundreds of time before.

And I bet he had, just with so many women who weren't me.

His taste exploded in my mouth as his lips crushed mine. Surprisingly warm and unapologetically masculine, he conquered my mouth. A mix of bitter stout beer (Guinness probably), the sweetness of a cigar, and freshness of mint gum swirled on my tongue. I stiffened, pinching my lips instinctively, not allowing more of him to invade me.

But my new husband would have none of it. He engulfed me with his arms, his broad shoulders shielding our faces from the crowd that stood up and cheered, clapping, whistling and laughing, a firework of happiness. The church boomed with ecstasy, while I worked hard on trying not to throw up in his mouth. His lips left mine, traveling up to my cheek, leaving traces of hot, charged breaths on my skin, before settling on the shell of my ear.

"Pretend to be happy, or I will provide you with a real reason to be sad."

His hissed whisper sent a jolt of panic straight to my stomach. His eyes were still heavy lidded with the kiss when he leaned back, looking down at me. I squinted at him, but didn't kick his balls with my impossible stilettos like I so desperately wanted to.

"Am I clear?" He dipped his chin, lips thinning into a hard line.

I swallowed. "Crystal clear."

"Good girl. Now let's shake some hands, kiss some babies and get back to the limo. I have a surprise for you."

FOR THE NEXT HOUR, I played the role I was cast in. I shook hands, smiled big, hugged people I didn't know and whenever things got too real, reached for a glass of champagne and numbed the bitter bite of reality. Brennan wanted to get the guests happy-drunk before we all left for the reception venue—and so bizarrely, there was an open bar on the sidewalk in front of the church.

While we mingled outside, occasionally, a photographer would gingerly interrupt whatever we were doing and ask to take a picture of us. Both my new husband and I complied. He looked at ease, clutching my waist assertively and placing a rough hand on my shoulder whenever was appropriate. Me? I stared back at the camera like I was begging the person behind the lens to call the police and save me. I knew I looked awkward, like my body was a rental I had yet to learn how to operate.

My father steered clear of me and my groom, opting to stay at his spot near the deadbeat wannabes of our neighborhood, all of them men who somehow found themselves being bossed around by the younger generation of criminals. Some because they lacked the intellectual ability to lead, like

Sloppy Connelly, who according to the rumor, was just a few brain cells better than a potato, and some because they lacked discipline, like my drunk father.

Depression washed over me every time I glanced his way and saw him clinking a glass with his friends. The bitterness of my situation, paired with the lingering taste of Brennan's kiss and the fact that I, too, drowned my sorrows with alcohol today, made me feel hopeless.

I saw Brock, Sam and his mother minutes before we walked back to the limo. The small family approached to give us their blessing and good wishes, just like all the other guests who treated Brennan like subjects kneeling in front of their king.

Brock was stunning, so I shouldn't have been surprised to find out that his wife was as equally breathtaking. She looked Hispanic, with smooth golden skin, endless legs and curves that went on forever. I figured standing next to her made me look like a poor excuse for a teenager. She had short, coffee-hued hair cut in a stylish bob, while mine was long, straight and sunset red. Her eyes were the color of whiskey, a little slanted and inviting, while mine were light green and wide. She oozed sex appeal—I barely looked legal.

Still, it occurred to me that Troy Brennan could have taken her for his wife had he wanted to. It wasn't that Troy had more charm than Brock. Quite the opposite, if you asked me. It was just that Troy had made a name for himself as a human bulldozer.

Brock's wife bowed deep, her cleavage almost popping from her hot, tight red dress as she greeted Troy. "You make one hell of a handsome groom." She gave him a lingering kiss on his cheek, leaving a lipstick stain on the edge of his jaw. "And what a lovely bride. I'm Catalina Greystone."

We shook hands, Catalina applying enough force to break a bone or two in my fingers as she scanned me like I was a contagious disease.

"Pleasure," I lied, a toothy smile frozen on my face. "I'm Sparrow."

"Well, that's a peculiar name." She pouted, narrowing her eyes.

"Well, that's a predictable comment," I retorted.

She dropped my hand like it was made of shards of glass.

Brennan lifted one brow, amusement dancing in his cold blue eyes. So he liked my bitchy comebacks. Good, because he'd need to get used to 'em.

Brock and Troy shook hands and exchanged pleasantries. Despite being similar in height and bone structure, Brock was more of a pretty boy and Troy was rougher, rugged in features and a lot scarier. Brock looked like a poem; Troy, like a heavy metal song.

"My good man," Brock said to Troy as he clapped his shoulder. "Lovely ceremony, gorgeous bride. Take care of her."

Troy brushed his thumb over his lips, scanning my body like it was dessert. "I intend to."

"Nice to meet you, Mrs. Brennan." Brock nodded to me, not giving away for a second the fact that we had already met.

I blushed for some unknown reason.

Looking for a distraction, I squatted down and offered Sam my hand. "I'm Sparrow," I said, ignoring the grown-ups. It's not like I felt like I was a part of them anyway.

"I know," he answered matter-of-factly, and everyone, including me, broke into a relieved laughter. "It's a cool name. Is it your real name?" he continued, his face serious but open. "Not a nickname?"

"I'm afraid it is." I wrinkled my forehead, my smile growing wider. "I guess my parents felt original." Not that original, my mother's name was Robyn, but this was my standard line.

"Mine didn't." Sam shrugged, returning his attention to the blue toy truck he was holding in his small fist. "My real name is Samuel. It's just a boring old name."

"I think it's pretty. And I bet you aren't a boring boy. In fact, I'm sure you're really bright. Don't you think so, Troy?"

For the first time in my life, I voluntarily acknowledged my new husband's presence. He seemed as taken aback by the gesture as I was, but recovered quickly, taking a slow slip from the whiskey he cradled in his palm and looking down at the glass, avoiding the little boy.

"Too soon to tell." His dark smirk told me he was enjoying offending everyone around us, me included.

Catalina's forehead wrinkled into a frown, but she kept her eyes trained on my husband, not her son. Brock jerked Sam to his side, stroking his head as he fought an angry twist in his lips. Sam was too focused on his little truck to care what the grownups were discussing.

I realized I was gaping at them when Troy nonchalantly used his pointer finger to press on my chin and close my lips with a snap.

"Careful," he mocked, taking a step closer and whispering into the crook of my neck, "don't want a fly to wander into that pretty mouth of yours."

When we got into the limo taking us to the historic manor where nearly four hundred strangers would celebrate our fake wedding, rain knocked on the tinted windows. I swallowed a sarcastic remark. I might be a June Bride, but of course it was going to rain on our wedding day. Some people claimed rain meant good luck, but I knew better.

A handful of guests went through the usual motions, gathering on the sidewalk and throwing birdseed at our vehicle. *Birdseed.* At least my new husband wasn't as predictable as to try and make a joke about my name. Instead, as we merged into the busy Boston traffic, he handed me a wide, deep white box tied with a pink satin bow.

"From me, to you," he said, his expression emotionless.

I took the box carefully from his hand and untied the bow with shaky fingers. Pausing, I glanced up at him, suspicious. Dammit, would I ever stop acting like a sheep led to slaughter around this man?

"Sorry I didn't get you anything," I said, ignoring his predator eyes. "As you're aware, this wedding was pretty rushed and unexpected."

"I'll live," he said tonelessly.

Yup, unfortunately. I bit my lip to suppress the nasty comeback.

He waved his hand impatiently. "For fuck's sake, Red. Unwrap the damn thing."

I ignored the fact he called me Red again. Yes, I was a redhead, but he was an asshole, and you didn't see me walking around calling him that without making sure he liked his new pet name first.

I poked aside the tissue paper in the mysterious white box. When the contents registered, bile shot up my throat and my blood froze. Almost screeching, I threw the box in his lap like it was a nest of snakes.

My gift was very revealing and degrading lingerie items. I'm talking leather, fishnets and all that crap.

Tears stung my eyes. I fought them, not wanting to give him the satisfaction of seeing me cry. A traitorous tear managed to sneak out, rolling down my right cheek. I swiped it away and clenched my jaw to stop my chin from quivering. If this asshole was hungry for my pain, I planned to keep him starving.

Brennan's stony face broke into a taunting smirk. "What's that, Red? Not even a thank you?" His low voice crawled deep under my skin.

I shook my head no. I assumed sex was going to be a part of the package, but in the ten days he'd caged me in his penthouse, alone and afraid, he hadn't visited more than once, let alone tried to touch me.

This was a reminder that just because he hadn't yet, didn't mean that he wouldn't.

"So you need a leatherette bra and a vinyl teddy to be turned on? I didn't peg you for a cliché, Brennan."

His eyes lit with something devilish. "And I didn't peg you for someone who answers back. Don't worry, little birdie. We'll have plenty of time to explore one another."

I stared straight ahead, focusing on the back of our driver's head and biting my tongue. I hated that he called me *Birdie*. Only people I loved called me that.

"Chill out, Red. I have no interest in tapping your ass unless you're willing and begging."

"That's interesting, because you sure seem to have a healthy interest in lingerie shopping. Too much spare time?" I deadpanned.

His smirk widened. "I didn't pick those items." He tilted his chin to the gift nestled in layers of tissue paper.

"No?" I blinked slowly.

"No…" He leaned forward, bringing his mouth closer to mine. "My mistress chose your gift."

Sirens wailed in the distance, a truck beeped as it reversed and the angry hum of my blood buzzed in my ears. Still, somehow, time completely stopped despite the busy streets of Boston flashing by outside. Our driver kept swallowing hard and looking straight ahead robotically, but I knew he was listening. Saying I wasn't comfortable having this conversation in front of a complete stranger was the understatement of the century.

I pressed my lips between my teeth, trying not to launch at my husband like a cornered animal. This man promised me his faithfulness in front of a priest less than an hour ago. I wasn't naïve enough to believe he'd ever take this marriage seriously, but he didn't have to rub his affairs in my face.

"She really doesn't like you if she goes around buying lingerie for your wife." My voice barely trembled.

"She just knows what's best for her. Maybe you could learn a thing or two from her."

I tucked my hands under my thighs to keep from trying to strangle him. "Tell her to send me the syllabus. I'm especially interested in How to Tame the ManWhore 101." I offered him a sweet smile, folding my arms over my laced-covered chest.

Just then, the limo came to a halt and the driver rushed to help us out of the back and onto the steps of the eighteenth-century landmark where the wedding reception was taking place. Troy got out first, offering me his hand. I didn't move, ignoring his gesture.

"Remember, play nice." He kept his palm open, yet uninviting.

"Whatever. Fine," I muttered slapping my hand into his. We walked and waved, smiling to our guests through plastic grins.

"But I like your fight," he said softly through our make-believe joy as we made our way, arms linked, like the two happy lovers that we weren't. "Can't wait for you to show me some of it in my bed."

TWO

SPARROW

I should have known he was a man of his word.

But he should have known that on top of hating his guts, I was also a virgin.

A virgin, despite my best efforts.

Contrary to what anyone might think, I wasn't especially keen on saving my virginity for that special someone. I'd grown up in a rough neighborhood, among people who didn't buy into fairytales. Prince Charming was about as feasible as Santa Claus to me, if not less. There was not one romantic bone in my scrawny body.

No, my cliché virginity was due to the fact that I just hadn't met anyone who wanted to share more than a few kisses and the occasional grope with me. I was notorious for my bad luck with the opposite sex. True, I wasn't particularly striking or sexy, but I wasn't a hag either. Yet somehow, guys always kept their distance from me.

At school.

At work.

And especially in and around South Boston.

So I'd quietly carried the burden of my virginity, hoping I'd find a man who'd be sweet enough to guide me through the dos and don'ts of lovemaking.

I had a feeling Troy Brennan, with his physical size, strength and brutal way of living, was not the best tour guide for a beginner like me. If there was one ray of light in my grim situation, it would have been my hope that Troy was too busy messing around with half of Boston to notice I had a pair of boobs and an ass, too.

But he did. He noticed.

Right after we got back from our wedding celebration, to be exact.

We arrived back at his glitzy penthouse in Back Bay, thoroughly drunk and understandably flushed.

Brennan walked into his lavish bedroom and started taking off his clothes silently, folding them in a neat pile on a sleek black bureau near the huge king-size bed. He stripped down to his briefs, giving me a full view of his muscled body. All male, not an Abercrombie & Fitch-ad type of guy, but a real, hairy, big, demanding one.

Furious and frightened, I walked swiftly into the master bathroom, shutting the door behind me with a loud bang and locking it for good measure.

"Don't be long," he instructed from the bedroom.

I ignored him, took a seat on the edge of his giant Jacuzzi and, regulating my breathing, plucked out the hairpins that dug into my skull one by one. I threw them into the sink with a blissful *plink*. Then I tackled the impossible dress, struggling to reach the laces in the back and shimmying until I finally managed to crawl out of the corset more fitting for a Barbie doll.

I opened drawers and cabinets. *Stalling, stalling, stalling.* After all, he was drunk. Maybe he'd fall asleep, pass out...or throw up and choke on his puke. Maybe I had nothing to worry about.

After forty minutes, I tiptoed back to the bedroom wearing a pair of socks and my old PJ's—gray sleep shorts and a white cotton tee—and crawled onto the far edge of the immense bed. I wanted to curl into myself and disappear between his sheets as far away from Brennan as I could manage.

Not breathing, barely moving, I peeked sideways to check to see if he was safely asleep.

His eyelashes fluttered up and down against the red and blue city lights spilling into the darkness. He was staring at the ceiling, lost in thought, the covers thrown back on his side.

"Scared of sex, huh?" His menacing voice cut through blackness with an amused bite. "Well, no surprises there."

I didn't fail to notice that he was shirtless, wearing nothing but a pair of Calvin Kleins. They were white, tight and emphasized his erection.

His body was muscled steel. Tantalizing and smooth, with the exception of three, old scars running from his stomach to his chest, his shoulder to his bicep, and a smaller one near his throat. A shamrock was tattooed on his chest across his heart, timeworn and faded.

A flashback of my friend Daisy and I eavesdropping on the teenage girls whispering in our apartment building's stairwell made my heart stutter. I was just a kid, six years younger than the high school girls, when one of them excitedly told her friends that she'd finally managed to bed Troy Brennan. That he was a certain kind of guy: his body was built for fighting and fucking, and he did both with a passion, rage and brutality most girls wouldn't forget.

But even if I wanted to get nasty with my husband, *I* couldn't forget who he was—the guy who murdered Billy "Baby Face" Crupti, a murder so brutal the media reported that Crupti's body had been chewed on by animals prior to being dumped in the water. And there was a priest who'd been found dead in our parish church, his tongue cut out.

Everyone in South Boston knew that Troy had killed them both.

No one said a word.

That should have told me a thing or a dozen about my husband.

His cruelty was infinite. His hands had touched blood, weapons, knives, dead bodies. Thinking about him caressing my body with those hands should've made me nauseous. Yet somehow, it didn't...

"Not scared at all. You don't know anything about me." I turned in bed, offering him my back and hugging my knees to my chest. I buried my face in the soft pillow.

His side of the mattress lifted unexpectedly. I heard him pad across the floor to the bathroom, but he didn't bother to close the door. I listened closely. He took a leak and washed his hands, whistling. When he returned, he stood there at the end of the bed in his underwear, his cock saluting in my direction.

"First time you've seen a boner?" he mocked.

I didn't want to tell him the truth. *Yes.* So I gulped and looked up, concentrating on a piece of modern art, a painting of a naked woman behind him. I shrugged. "Yours is nothing special."

"That's where I can prove you wrong." His smile almost passed for human.

"Thanks for the offer, but beside the fact I'd rather chew on used needles, I just got my period." I pulled the duvet all the way up to my nose.

"Bull-fucking-shit." His mouth twisted into a vicious smirk. "Let's see it."

"What?"

"Let's. See. Your period," he said slowly. "Take off your briefs."

I scooted away from him, looking around me, trying to marshal my thoughts. "You're not serious?"

"I don't do humor, Sparrow. Besides, you've shown some spine so far, don't wanna ruin it by chickening out on me, do you...*wifey?*"

"But..."

"The butt is a good option," he said evenly, not a trace of amusement in his voice, "but I'm more interested in seeing your blood right now."

I glanced around me, looking for...what? Sharp objects to throw at him as I ran? He could probably kill me just by breathing in my direction. Instead of taunting him like a three-year-old, I should've told him the truth.

"I'm not chickening out."

He moved closer toward me. "Actions speak louder than words."

Screw it. He wanted to play, and I was starting to understand his twisted game.

I stood up in front of him and peeled my PJ shorts down an inch at a time. My fingers scraped my pubic bones and despite my hatred of him, I found myself self-conscious about my scrawniness. I bet he was used to sleeping with women who were all curves. And I looked like a boy, with my pale skin, fragile frame and bonfire hair.

But he'd challenged me, and I had my stupid pride to keep intact.

"Underwear, too." Brennan sat, falling onto my side of the bed with a soft thud as I stood in front of him, removing my clothing inch by inch.

My body vibrated as I held back my hatred. His gaze zeroed on my pelvic area, tucking one hand into his underwear and stroking himself leisurely. I took off my underwear, feeling a mixture of disgust and thrill with the situation. *What the hell is wrong with you, Sparrow?* Appalled, I wet my lips, watching him. *Are you freaking high?*

"Show me your blood," he rasped.

I winced again, sucking my lower lip and releasing it slowly. My body hummed with embarrassment as I slid one of my index fingers between my folds, scraped the surface of my inside shallowly, and displayed my finger, showing him a scarlet smear of fresh blood.

I'd put the blood there while I was in the bathroom, purposely cutting my foot open with his razor and letting myself bleed so I could insert it between my legs. I'd closed the cut with the styptic pencil I'd found next to his razor and then rolled on a pair of socks to hide what I'd done, just to be safe. I knew it was sick, but desperate times called for desperate measures.

And I was desperate not to give Brennan what was mine, in case he decided to have me on our wedding night.

Troy inspected the blood on my finger, raised his eyes to meet mine and licked his lips, top to bottom. He looked like he was going to pounce and rip me open at any moment. Whether it was with lust or hate, I wasn't completely sure. Either way, he was raw, untamed. *Trouble.*

"Do you really think a man like me will be put off by blood, *Red?*" he asked.

"Quite the opposite," I said, using every ounce of confidence I still had in me. "But rape is beneath you. I know that."

I hoped that.

Troy stopped stroking himself and leaned forward. I barely managed to control my quavering thighs when he parted his lips and took my bloody finger in his mouth while his eyes zeroed in on mine. He sucked my finger clean for a whole minute before releasing it with a pop and snaking his hands behind me, cupping my ass cheeks and jerking me toward him. I collapsed on the bed, straddling him. He smiled that mischievous smirk that seemed to highlight his startlingly handsome features, his eyes wild with abandon. My thighs clenched on either side of his waist.

Damn thighs.

Hell, this was bad. I needed to stop, this much I knew. My body, however, had very different plans.

"I won't do anything that you don't want me to do," Brennan said finally. "But so far you haven't stopped me. Now why is that?"

I shut my eyes, taking a deep breath.

"I haven't stopped you because I don't want you to hurt me." I put my hands on his bare chest to balance myself. His muscles were flexed, hard. Something about what he said annoyed me. He made it sound like I enjoyed his attention, the way he sucked on my blood. I didn't. True, I didn't feel violated—for some screwed up reason I wasn't eager to explore—but I certainly didn't ask for it.

A moment of silence passed between us as we looked at each other, my eyes imploring and his, contemplating. The only noise was the sound of faraway cars honking in the downtown Boston night and the lash of rain washing against his floor-to-ceiling windows.

"I don't find you attractive." My voice was hoarse.

A lie.

"Say that to your pussy." He wasn't offended one bit. "My briefs are soaked, Mrs. Brennan."

A truth.

I blushed furiously, scrambling off his lap and almost kneeing his junk in the process. I darted to the end of the bed, desperate to avoid him. Resting on his elbows, he turned his head, his eyes narrowed on mine, challenging again.

"You're wasting your time." I covered my lower body with my hands, feeling my ears pinking before I even whispered the words. "I'm a virgin."

"I had a feeling you would be." Amusement danced in his eyes as he rolled closer and reached out to draw circles on my pubic bone. "That can be rectified."

"I don't want it to be," I fired back, feeling all kinds of ashamed, annoyed and…Hell, who was I kidding? Troy Brennan really wasn't that bad to look at. If you were willing to ignore the monstrousness lurking behind those ice-blue eyes, he might not be the worst candidate as a lover.

Of course, that was the last thing I was going to admit to him or anyone else in this lifetime.

"This period of yours…" He licked his lips, keeping his voice businesslike and ignoring my last comment altogether. "When is it going to end?"

"Four, five…*years*," I answered, my lips twitching, but I thought about how it'd feel to have him, even five years from now. "What can I say, Mother Nature can be a bitch."

"And she's not the only one." He flattened his hand on my stomach, and I let his heat seep through the fabric of my cotton shirt.

His master bedroom was magnificent, with marble flooring, a huge black-leather headboard, gray and white satin throws, rich beige rugs and custom lighting. It looked like something out of a catalogue. Breathtakingly impersonal and too sterile to feel at home in.

Just like its owner. But just like its owner, it was unbelievably striking.

It was different.

It was insane.

It was…something I didn't hate, even though I desperately wanted to.

"Something tells me that if Mother Nature was in charge right now, you'd be riding me like a jockey." He sat up and hauled me back toward his body, his breath caressing my skin.

I let out a soft moan and fought the urge to lean into him.

His lips traveled oh-so-briefly over my wrist, his words sharp as a razor but his voice surprisingly sweet. "Why don't you show me this spine of yours, Sparrow? Why don't you take a look at what you did?" he urged, looking down at his underwear.

My pulse hitched, my eyes slowly traveling down to his groin. A faint trail of pink blood stained his white boxers, watered down by my wetness against his bulge.

I hated him for showing this to me. I hated myself for doing this to him.

"I'm nowhere near ready to have sex with you, Brennan. Not now. Probably not ever." But even as I said the words, I knew they were a lie. Hell, he probably knew that, too.

At the same time, I hated him so much it burned through my skin, made my bones ache with rage.

"Sparrow Brennan…" He tasted the name on his tongue, clucking it in approval. "One day I'm going to fuck your brains out, until you won't be able to walk the next day."

One day, my brain processed. *But not tonight, asshole.*

"You know that. And I know that," he continued, "so if you want to lie to yourself, by all means, be my fucking guest. But we both know you're already mine. Mind…" He reached up and stroked my temple softly.

A shiver ran down my spine.

"Body…" His hand traveled down to my chest, groping my right breast suddenly and circling my erect nipple with his thumb.

I dropped my head back, letting him touch me.

"Soul…" He continued down to my stomach, underneath my shirt, his fingers brushing every inch of my flesh.

Oh, hell.

"*Heart*…" His hand glided back up to my left breast where he paused for a second, snorting a sarcastic laugh. "Well, the heart you can keep yourself."

Then, without a warning, he flipped us both in one fast movement. He was now on top, with me writhing underneath him, stomach to stomach. His weight pressed on my pelvis, and before I could muster the courage and brain cells to give him another mouthful, he ground his bulge against me, nothing separating us other than the stupid fabric of his underwear.

Heat swelled inside me. I sucked in a breath, biting my lip furiously to suppress a moan.

"Should I stop?" he asked, his arms boxing me in as he continued grinding.

"Y-yes," my weak voice stuttered. I did want him to stop...*didn't I?*

He paused, but his smile grew bigger and more shark-like. He dipped his head, his mouth finding mine as he rolled off of me. He spoke into my mouth, his lips hovering over mine, but not kissing me. "Someday, I'm going to get us kicked out of this place, when you scream my name so loud in this bedroom that everyone can hear."

I frowned at him. "I doubt anyone would kick you out of the building, considering your reputation."

Troy threw his head back and laughed a wholehearted, joyful laugh. He loved my last statement. *Loved being feared.*

"That much is true." His hand moved to my throat, his finger tracing an invisible line. "You know, Sparrow? Maybe we could play together after all. There's some fun hiding underneath your layers of goodness."

I had a feeling there was nothing fun hiding underneath his layers of darkness, but I didn't say a thing.

THREE

SPARROW

Five Days Later

ONE DAY SWALLOWED THE NEXT one, time sticking together like pages in a new, unopened book. And me? I was running out of options to entertain myself between the thick, suffocating walls of Troy Brennan's penthouse.

When he'd imprisoned me for ten days before our wedding, he only visited his tastefully furnished, clinical-looking apartment once, and that was to tell me I was going to be his wife. Back then, I'd wondered if he wanted to scare me or give me time to come to terms with the new arrangement. Now, I knew for certain that his absence had nothing to do with me and everything to do with his job.

These days, he came home every night long after I pretended to be asleep, reeking of stout beer, other women's perfume and the sour-sweet scent of a man's sweat. He left for work early, so when I woke up, his side of the mattress was always cold and empty.

He didn't try to touch me again. Hell, he didn't even try to strike up a conversation the few times I saw his face. And for the most part, I was content with this arrangement.

I left the penthouse for my morning runs and for my evening culinary classes. I visited Pops twice, cooking and cleaning for him out of habit, with Connor shadowing my every move, following my every step like an eager Pit Bull puppy. I wouldn't let him inside my father's apartment, so he sat outside the door, in the kitchen chair I dragged into the hallway, patiently waiting, chewing tobacco tucked in his jaw and, undoubtedly hating every second of me being out of his sight.

Any attempt by me to leave the penthouse late at night (and there were attempts to do so, especially the first couple of days) was blocked by my sturdy, bulky bodyguard, who looked like the human equivalent of an industrial fridge. Connor would wordlessly fold his arms over his gorilla-like torso, marching in my direction as I stumbled back into the apartment, my head hanging low.

For the first time since I was fifteen, I had a curfew. I hated Brennan for imposing restrictions on me, interfering with my life even without taking part in it.

But at least I had other company.

Troy had a housekeeper named Maria, a small, cranky, sixty-something woman with white hair and brown skin, who came in every other day, working for both Troy and for his mother, Andrea, as the family help since Brennan was a kid.

Maria didn't speak good English, so we communicated in the most universal way humanly possible—with food.

I spent hours practicing and cooking for no one in particular. I prepared delicious dishes only to admire them silently, tuck them into disposable Tupperware and hand them to the closest homeless shelter. But first, Maria would help herself to a serving or two and offer great input about the spices, tastes and flavors (mostly in Spanish.) Her suggestions and compliments made me happy, her presence a drop of solace in the sea of desperation I was drowning in.

Almost a week into our fake marriage, I got back to Brennan's penthouse after my morning run and walked straight to the first floor bathroom. His apartment was a modern two-story affair, with the master suite and study upstairs. I always used the bathroom near the guest room on the first floor, because it felt less his. It wasn't personalized with his products, towels, razor and singularly manly scent. With *him*.

Ever since our wedding night, I'd tried to keep my exposure to Brennan to an absolute minimum and treated him with a suspicion usually saved for convicted terrorists.

I kept a small knife under my pillow, the one I used in cooking class for removing meat from the bone. I added 911 to the speed-dial on my phone. Like a good Girl Scout, I was always prepared.

Today, I kneeled down in the bathroom and ran myself a bath, throwing salts and other luxuries I wasn't even aware were on the market in the tub. I toed off my running shoes and threw my yoga pants and soaked shirt into a sweaty pile in the corner next to the sink.

Then I heard the front door slam, and my heart gave a leap. Maria was already in the apartment.

Connor was peacefully (albeit unprofessionally) napping on a sofa in Brennan's study upstairs after trying to keep up with me on my run.

Troy never came home this early, and he wasn't the kind of man that you dropped in on for a friendly visit.

This meant alarm bells. Aware this might be someone not so friendly, I jumped into a bathrobe and searched the bathroom cabinets and drawers. Nail scissors weren't much of a weapon, but they were small and sharp, and capable of taking out an eye. Truthfully, arming myself with scissors in a mobster's apartment was about as practical as learning how to swim in the kitchen sink, but I wanted to be on the safe side.

Heart hammering in my chest, I cautiously stepped into the gigantic foyer. The whole first floor—kitchen, dining and living rooms— functioned together as an open space, and I took comfort in the fact there were no hidden corners or dark curves a potential attacker could hide behind. Once I heard a soft laugh coming from the direction of the kitchen, my shoulders eased.

The voice was male and vaguely familiar, but it was different than Troy's. It wasn't so cold.

"Were you going to attack me with a pair of scissors?" he inquired in a smooth voice.

I stopped in front of him and narrowed my eyes. *Brock.* He was sitting on an elegant white leather barstool at the stainless kitchen island, sipping a cup of coffee Maria must have just poured for him. Our maid gazed at him with adoring eyes, beaming like he had just found the cure for cancer and stupidity all at once.

I released my grip on the scissors, placing them on the counter and breathing deeply to try and ease the unexpected increase in my heartbeat.

"Well," Brock said, saluting me with the mug he was holding, "you came prepared."

"I'm sure you're more prepared than I am." I shot him an accusing glare. If he was anything like his law-bending friend, Brock would come armed with enough ammunition to conquer a medium-sized dictatorship.

He stood up, lifting his arms in mock-surrender, and pivoted slowly to show me that he didn't have a gun. His beauty lit up the room, and I hated myself for noticing this. He was clean-shaven, his brown hair a disheveled mess. He wore slim dark denim, a gray crewneck that complimented his eyes, and a white cotton shirt underneath. He looked like the dreams they try to sell you in *Cosmo* and *Marie Claire*, like a gift wrapped in sophisticated clothing.

And he's married, I reminded myself. So was I.

"What are you doing here?" I demanded, short of breath.

"I came here to give Maria a few things she needed." He plopped back down on the stool and took a sip of his coffee. "Then she offered me the good stuff. Can't say no to caffeine. It's like middle-class crack. *Gracias*, Maria." He tipped his mug at her, winking playfully at the older woman.

"*De nada.* I go back to work now, *mijo*." She planted a peck on his cheek. I almost stumbled back in shock. Maria was about as motherly as a scouring pad. Kissing and fussing were not in her nature. She might have taken a shine to me because of my cooking, but she scowled at the very mention of Troy and Connor. Both men had a shady job and at least some history with pissing off the law. I didn't know what Brock did for a living, but if he was granted access to this penthouse, I was guessing he wasn't a respectable police officer or justice-seeking prosecutor. No, he had to be another bad guy.

But in his case, Maria didn't mind. I watched her climb up the curved staircase to the second floor, disappearing into the master bedroom, probably to change the sheets, like she did on every visit so far. Not that Troy and I were leaving anything on the sheets that made washing them necessary.

"Did you drug her or something?" I jerked my thumb in Maria's general direction.

"I only drug people when I really have to." Brock laughed over the rim of his coffee mug. "Normally, I'm more of a live and let live type of guy."

I couldn't help but admire his smile. He didn't look scary and didn't act like a silent, unpredictable sociopath. *Like my husband.* It made hating Brock a challenging task.

I snorted, desperate to gain some control of the situation. Even if it meant being bitchy to him for no reason. "Thanks for sharing, Buddha."

"Actually..." He looked around him to make sure no one was listening and leaned forward as he dropped his voice. "I wanted to check on you. You seemed upset at the wedding."

I looked away. *He doesn't care.*

He eyed me intently, ignoring my grouchiness. "Talk to me. I'm not one of the bad guys."

"Pretty sure you're not one of the good ones either."

He paused, actually considering my statement. "I'm not here because Troy sent me to sniff around, if that's what you think. I'm just...worried. Talk to me, Sparrow. How's married life treating you?"

"Badly," I deadpanned, "and since I heard the secret to a happy marriage is to want to be married to the person you're with, guess I'm screwed."

I was so brutally honest it almost felt reckless. *Almost.* I wasn't afraid of him telling my new husband how I'd badmouthed our marriage. Brock knew I was forced into this bond. I'd read that between the lines when he spoke to his son at church the other day. But even if he did decide to rat me out to Brennan, it's not like what I shared with him would be news to my husband.

"It gets better," Brock said softly, rubbing the back of his neck and looking adorable.

The air thickened.

So did my voice. "Does it?" I cleared my throat.

"That's the rumor, anyway." He downed the rest of his coffee like a shot and banged his mug down on the kitchen island. Getting to his feet, he grabbed his jacket, draped on the back on the chair, and shot me a charming smile, flashing those pearly-white teeth and making my knees weak.

"You'd better check on your bath before it overflows." He nodded in the direction of the distant sound of streaming water.

I nodded wordlessly and turned, walking back toward the bathroom. I was glad to put some distance between us. Being attracted to him was not something I was proud of, and I knew it'd only bring more complications to my already messy love life.

"Sparrow…" His voice halted me mid-step. "What do you do all day?"

I didn't turn around. Was afraid he'd read the confusion on my face.

"Sit around here," I answered, my voice brittle with the burden of the truth. "Mostly just trying to remember who I am, figuring out what to do next."

"Your husband is a very capable man, you know."

I gripped the belt of my robe, my teeth digging hard into my lower lip. "So people keep telling me."

I turned around now, and our eyes locked. There was some space between us, but not much. Not enough for me to ignore the heat pouring from his body.

"What I mean is…" He licked his lips before taking another step in my direction. "Troy owns a restaurant just off Tremont Street. Rouge Bis. I manage it for him. Maybe you'd like to help out there."

I almost clapped a hand over my mouth in disbelief. Rouge Bis was widely considered the most romantic place in Boston, so it was comical to find out that it was owned by the least romantic man in New England.

"Wait, how do you know that I'm a cook?" I frowned.

"Maria mentioned you keep making a mess in her kitchen. Plus, I noticed the fridge's full of stuff that's not just condiments. That's a first in the Brennan household. Also, there's the newspaper." He nodded toward the island where he'd sipped coffee. "You highlighted a job as a cafeteria cook in the local schools. So, yeah, you're not really keeping a low profile about it. Look, I'm sure you can give us a hand at the restaurant. You should probably ask Troy about it."

"I doubt he'd be too happy to have me around."

"He's not there all that much." Brock's tone held a hint satisfaction, almost like he, too, couldn't stand the presence of my husband. "If he's game, I promise I'll make it work. Instead of wandering, find yourself again, Sparrow. I'll help if I can."

I looked down, biting back my smile and fighting the butterflies that took flight in my stomach in full force.

Is he playing me?

Is he genuine?

Am I an idiot for feeling grateful?

"Okay," I finally said, looking up to meet his eyes. "I'll ask him. Thank you."

"Sure thing. Thanks for the coffee."

"Have a good day, Brock," I said as he headed for the door.

"You too, sweetheart."

THAT NIGHT, I CRAWLED TO BED with a headache as oppressive as the thunderstorm outside pelting the windows with rain. Summertime my ass. It was like the lack of sunshine mimicked my feelings.

Brock's words looped in my head all day, and I tried to think of ways to convince Troy to let me work at his restaurant. It was the first time in the last two weeks I was feeling a little hopeful.

Ever since he'd taken me from Pops, I felt like I was handcuffed and locked inside a brakeless car, rolling downhill at the speed of light.

Working in a kitchen was something I'd dreamed about ever since I was in middle school and watched *Ratatouille*. Pops gave me the DVD for Christmas and I played it so many times over, I remembered every single sentence. I'd worked my butt off, taking every class and course I could afford, to make it happen.

Now I was close. So close. The only thing standing between me and fulfillment was him.

Food. I loved making it. Loved watching people enjoy the fruits of my labor as I served my dad and his buddies with a hearty meal. They'd sit there with their shirts open, undershirts beneath, their white-haired chests and bellies poking out against the small wooden table in our kitchen and shovel in my food. Be it Irish stew, homemade pasta with fresh sauce, or just my famous blueberry pancakes. Cooking and baking made me feel like someone, and someone was better than being the no one I was growing up to be.

Everyone was known as something. The pretty one, the athlete, the nerd, the bitch, the accountant or the mobster. I was known as the one with no mom, and I wanted to reinvent myself as the girl who could make mean blueberry pancakes. *The chef.*

I waited for Brennan in bed for what felt like a decade. The clock ticked, painfully and almost deliberately slow, as my thoughts swirled in circles.

Will he be his usual, asshole self?

Will he surprise me and agree?

Is this even a good idea, to work for my fake-husband?

I heard the door open and slam shut at around two a.m. downstairs. Brennan's place barely had any furniture, and so the echo carried all the way to the second floor. At first, I waited patiently in bed, but when fifteen minutes turned into thirty I hopped to my feet. My long hair flowed over my shoulders, tickling the small of my back as I climbed down the stairs. By the time I was in the dimly lit foyer, I started tiptoeing. I always treaded lightly around this man.

Brennan had his back to me, scanning the view overlooking the city skyline from his high-rise penthouse, and downing a tumbler of whiskey in big gulps. The scent of the alcohol was like my past slapping me in the face, and memories of my dad passed out on our couch punched me in the stomach.

Only difference was Troy's alcohol didn't smell of hardship, of Bushmills and sour sweat.

I stood there silently, trying to think of what to say or do. His dark suit, pressed and new looking, masked the obvious realities of his line of work. There was a dangerous buzz around him. He sometimes radiated it. Tonight, I suspected, was a bad night to ask for a favor. Something in the air around him felt wrong. Stormy, like the weather outside. The apartment was stark and chilly, but his body poured angry heat in waves. My stomach tightened as I contemplated whether I should just turn around and go back to bed. I could always ask him for a favor when he was in a better mood.

"You're up late." He crushed some ice between his teeth, making me shudder. His voice was gruff and thorny.

Like all sociopaths, I suspected my husband was emotionally impotent. From the week we've lived together, I knew that he rarely showed any feelings, and when he did, they were usually on the detached and disinterested spectrum.

"I waited for you," I answered, a little surprised that he'd heard me.

He turned around, inspecting me with his piercing eyes like he was trying to see beneath my words. His jaw stiffened. So did his fist around the whiskey glass.

"You look…upset," I whispered.

"Am I usually the jolly kind?" he mocked.

"You're usually not miserable. Just scary as hell," I shot back, eying the bruise on his forehead.

His shoulders rolled back, making him look a little less guarded. I noticed that he enjoyed my unapologetic comebacks, especially when they were at his expense. I wondered if it was refreshing, having someone answer back for a change. And I was stupid enough to be that person.

The change in his expression increased my confidence. I erased the space between us, flattening my palm against his chest. The gesture felt unnatural but necessary. I was used to putting up with bad behavior from years of living with my dad, but mostly I just wanted him to hate me a little less. I needed him for this job, after all.

"Bad day at the office?" I tried.

"Your pretense insults me," he said evenly. "No need to act like you care. You already have my credit card."

"Not all women are interested in only money, Troy. Especially if the money is dirty," I clarified.

I realized I'd called him by his first name and pressed my palm deeper into his hard chest. I wasn't sure if I was trying to soothe him or me, but his name and the human touch were consoling. Like we weren't complete strangers.

"What do you do for a living?" I asked, more proof of how little I knew my husband.

"Money," he answered. "I make it."

"What do you do for this money?" I pressed.

"I have a grocery store, a restaurant and a few private poker joints. Your dad is a bouncer in one of them. You know this shit."

"The grocery store in Dorchester was losing money even before it opened. The poker joints are small and people always owe you money. That's not how you pay for a Maserati and a penthouse the size of a football field."

He arched an eyebrow, giving me a slow once-over with those frosty baby-blues. "She's sharp, too."

"There's a lot you don't know about me," I croaked.

"There's one thing I do know, and it keeps me from spilling my shit in your ears—you hate my guts, Red."

"I don't hate your guts." It took all the effort in the world to say it. Because I did. I hated Troy Brennan for marrying me, caging me, owning me and chaining me to his grim life and destiny for no reason other than because he could.

"Anyone ever told you that you're a terrible liar?" His nostrils flared, but he kept his cool. He jerked me closer, wrapping his hand around the nape of my neck, his breath falling on my face with a whisper. "You wear the truth on your sleeve."

I tiptoed my hand up to his face, my heart picking up speed as I stroked his bruise. Ballsy move, but I was afraid of him. Afraid that his frustration with me would swell and that he'd send me off back to the bedroom.

Fear is a prison, and in prison you played by different rules to survive.

Troy's eyes narrowed on mine skeptically. The epitome of ruthless, his lips turned into a challenging smirk. "Prove you don't hate me."

And I did. I leaned up and pressed my lips against his softly.

I kissed him.

I kissed the husband I hated so much. Against reason, against logic, against everything my heart was telling me.

I kissed him because I wanted something from him. A job. A chance at happiness. Some *freedom*.

He fisted the hem of my nightshirt and in two big steps shoved me to the nearest wall, slamming me against it. My back felt the impact, and I arched to soothe the pain trickling down my spine. It felt different than the usual ache of flesh hitting concrete. Made my body buzz with something unfamiliar. Desire bit at my insides, and just like that, I got lost in his touch again.

His lips searched for mine angrily as he took one of my thighs and wrapped it around his waist, lifting me off the floor, only him and the wall supporting my weight. His erection pulsated beneath the fabric of his suit pants, and I resisted the instinct to grind against him. I lifted my arms to touch his smooth hair, running my hands down his slick mane.

He was a cheater.

A criminal.

A murderer.

And I was…fascinated.

If I was trapped in his golden cage, might as well enjoy the perks that came with it.

I traced his muscular chest with my fingers, roaming, exploring, longing. When my hands traveled down his abs, he stopped me, clasping my narrow wrist with his huge palm. I shrieked when I realized why.

"Careful now, Red," he groaned into my mouth, removing my hand from his holster and catching my lower lip between his straight teeth.

Holy shit. I tried not to freak out and yell. *I just touched a gun.* I'd never touched one before, and even though I knew Pops owned one, I'd never seen it up-close.

"Oh." I collected my wits, still flushed. "That was your gun? I thought you were just happy to see me."

He laughed a hearty laugh and carried me with my legs wrapped tightly around him to the leather sofa. The persistent, cold summer rain knocked on the windows, but the living room felt hot and charged with what was happening between us.

What the hell was wrong with us? We couldn't hold a five-minute conversation, and our only communication so far involved heavily making out and taunting each other like high school kids. Nevertheless, I felt like a bundle of quick-firing nerves in his arms.

"Troy…" I moaned his name into his mouth, giving in to the moment of sudden lust, tasting the Johnnie Walker Black Label on his breath and trying hard to suppress the memories that particular smell—a brand my father would never be able to afford—brought with it. The stranger who ruined me, whose name I never told anyone.

"Are you still on that period of yours?" He bit my neck, wrapping my hair around one of his fists and dragging his tongue down my cleavage. His other hand roamed my body—my chest, ass, legs—familiarizing himself with every angle and sliver of flesh.

I froze. Even though my body reacted to him like he was crack cocaine, my mind knew better than to jump into bed with a man who'd forced me to marry him. I didn't know what the hell had come over me when I kissed him. Maybe I wanted to give this unwanted life a fair chance. Maybe it was the job. Hell, maybe it was just me being human. But it had to stop.

"Yes." I stilled, our lips disconnecting. "Still on my period."

"God-fucking-dammit," he breathed into my mouth.

He peeled his suit coat off angrily, leaning backward to give me space at the same time. Disappointment crashed into me at the loss of his touch. His body was sculpted, strong, freaking perfect. And a part of me, an adventurous part, wanted to know what the girl down my hallway talked about when she said he fucked like an animal all those years ago.

Sleeping with him could be a dream or a nightmare. Either way, I refused to fall asleep.

"This was a mistake," I said, my chest rising and falling to the rhythm of my heart.

"Fuck you." He got up on his feet from the sofa, running his fingers through his raven black hair.

"Hey," I argued softly, following his movement through my lashes, "I'm new to this."

To *you*.

"Sparrow…" he sneered, shaking his head slowly, like I was a stupid kid. He never called me Sparrow, only Red, and my name sounded like a curse leaving his lips. "This is not junior high. I don't need your wet, hesitant kisses."

I darted up after him, knowing I was about to pick another fight. How dare he speak to me like that! "I'm not the one who insisted we get married. So save the attitude, Mr. I-Deserve-Anything-I-Want."

"It's not what you did, it's what they did *to us*, Miss Annoying-As-Fuck." He untied his tie, throwing it on the sofa. "We're done here. You can go back to pretending you're asleep."

Was he kidding me?

"Who are *they*?" I roared. "What did *they* do to us? Did someone force you to do something against your will? You can't just drop a bomb and pretend it's nothing." I followed him around the room, trying to get him to look me in the eye.

The idea that Troy was caged in this situation just as much as I was never occurred to me before. But it made sense.

It made a lot of sense.

He looked at me like I was a cockroach, his expression turning from furious back to his usual default of cold and vacant. "Don't make me laugh." He turned his back on me, pouring himself another drink. "I would never do anything —or anyone—who isn't worth my time. Of course it was my choice to marry you."

"Bullshit." I smiled bitterly, knowing that I'd hit a nerve. He was as chained as me. Something drew us together, and it wasn't love. Wasn't lust either. "You're just as miserable about this as I am."

A brief silence filled the room while he took a sip of his drink, brushing his fingers over the neat row of expensive whiskey bottles in his bar.

"You probably don't remember, Red, but when you were a kid, you sat two rows in front of me in Trinity Chapel every Sunday at mass. Your dad used to fall asleep on your little shoulder because he was drunk, but you would stroke his gray hair, like the loving daughter that you were, and help him walk all the way back home afterwards. You were always giving hugs to all the kids your age and younger. You even used to make fucking lopsided cupcakes when someone had a birthday. You were all fucking heart despite your shitty upbringing—the no-mother part and the drunk-father reality. And you didn't drop out of school, didn't do drugs, didn't become a slutty biker chick. You finished high school, worked your ass off in a shitty diner and took night classes to become a chef.

"You..." He pivoted, shoving an accusing finger to my chest with the hand that still held the whiskey glass. "You're so good, too fucking good. And whenever I looked at you—from afar, of course, because my family didn't mix with your nobody father—I thought to myself one day, my children will have a mother this noble. A mother whose goodness would rub off on them, because their dad is bad. Really. Fucking. Bad."

I was shocked, confused, and underneath it all, maybe even touched. I fiddled with my hair. "You know stuff about me? I didn't realize…"

"That I noticed you? Yeah, I'm not exactly the flowers and chocolate type of guy." He loosened his collar, and my gaze dropped to catch the sliver of skin he exposed. "You better get used to it, or you're in for a miserable-ass life. Now what the fuck is it that you want, Sparrow? Why did you wait up for me? It wasn't to ask how my day was or what I do for a living."

I caught my bottom lip between my teeth, rubbing the back of my neck. Somehow, it seemed difficult to ask him for a favor when he'd shown me a glimpse of honesty. Of romance. Even if this favor was only a request to let me out of his house to work at his restaurant, the first part of which he'd already agreed to on our wedding day.

I forced a patient smile, despite the impatient need whirring in me to break free. "It can wait. Can we talk about it tomorrow? You obviously had a shitty day, and it's three a.m. and…I don't know, maybe in the light of day, we'll be able to communicate like two grown-ups and not like dogs in heat."

He brushed my shoulder as he walked past me, not sparing me even a second glance. "Go buy yourself something half-decent tomorrow. I'll take you out to dinner and we can discuss whatever it is you have in mind. And Sparrow, I'm *not* a nice guy." He emphasized every word. "So if you're looking for favors, you better start reciprocating. Start acting like a goddamned wife and not like a prisoner. Oh, and a few more days of that magical period of yours and I'm sending you for a checkup in the ER. Don't want you to bleed out, huh?"

With that, he disappeared up the stairs, leaving me high and dry.

Jesus Christ. This man.

FOUR

TROY

THE INVITATION TO DINNER WAS an impulse I might regret. Taking her out on a date? What the fuck was that all about? This wasn't *Pretty Woman*, and Red sure as hell wasn't Julia Roberts.

I'd made up the story about church. I hadn't watched her. In fact, I'd tried my best to pretend she didn't exist, suppressing the idea that one day this kid would be my wife. Even when her preteen friends inched close to me after mass, giggling, and she stood beside them, shyly eyeing me like I was fucking ET. Even back then, I knew that Sparrow Raynes was not for me. Her quiet behavior screamed something I didn't want to hear. I knew her mother deserted her and her father was an alcoholic, that life had fed her shit from all directions. But she never got under my skin. Not many people did, and only one woman ever had.

So, truly, the feelings I had for Sparrow Raynes were the same as I had for every women other than the bitch who broke my heart—a big, fat, hollow nothing.

I took a leak and shower, letting the water wash off the last of my crappy day and not caring if she'd followed me to bed.

The only reason I'd given her false hope that we shared some kind of history together, at least from my end, was because I wanted to shut her up. She was getting all let's-talk-about-it on my ass, and it reminded me of the stupid, misguided women who'd tried to get through to me over the years.

I admit I was a little intrigued when she came out of the bathroom the night of our wedding and produced blood from her pussy. I saw the socks on her feet, her slight limp when she entered the room like a mouse with a thorn in its foot instead of the lion. She'd purposely hurt herself to buy time. She chose pain over humiliation. The daughter of the drunk, the spawn of the runaway mother, had pride and wits.

I shouldn't have been surprised by it, but I was.

As it turned out that night, Sparrow was the only girl from our neighborhood who didn't lose her shit and drool over any affluent, suited man who walked down the dark path.

Even before she marched out of the bathroom dripping blood, I knew she wasn't one of those girls who'd just spread her legs for me. She probably thought I'd rape her. That she'd just lie there and take it like a dead body. That we would both hate the situation—and one another—but with a bit of luck, I'd manage to knock her up and hope that would shut her up for the next nine months.

But that didn't happen. See, Sparrow Raynes had a little fight in her, and I was intrigued. So much so, that I tried to test her boundaries, scare her. Play with her a little.

The sexy gift wasn't my idea. I wasn't the one who picked it out, and my mistress would pay for distressing Red too soon and too fast.

But the blood? That was all on me. When I tasted her blood, knowing it was from her foot, I searched her face for a reaction. She looked appalled and shocked, but held back the tears. And underneath the distress…she fucking loved it. She had a dark little soul, just like mine.

Yes, Red was brave—so much braver than some of the men I had to deal with every day that I felt compelled to spare her virginity. I had very little interest in it anyway, even though she was hot and ready for me. I knew *want*, recognized it from miles, and Sparrow's body reacted to me so fast, so hungrily that I had to make a point.

She was mine to take if I wanted her, and that was good to know.

Since that first night, work had taken over. I was too busy to try and fuck her. Frankly, she didn't look like she was worth the time. Inexperienced, innocent, and pretty but in a pasty, wallflower way.

Red was cute, but was also categorically not my type. Her dress sense made me want to lock her in a designer store with a herd of stylists and come back for her next year. She wore Keds, black hoodies and casual mom jeans. Sure, she had a banging runner's body and an ass to fill those pants like nobody's business, but a little effort wouldn't hurt.

I supposed it might not be that hard to get used to that sort of look. A part of me hoped she'd take offense to my remark about her going to buy something nice for herself. Somewhere in the back of my mind, I'd almost come to terms with her feistiness.

Of course, when she'd stood in front of me in the living room, trying to strike up a conversation, all I could think about was how screwed up my day had been.

I'd begun the day by crushing the kneecaps of two ambitious little gang nobodies. A job for one of my clients, an up-and-coming rich politico who happened to like it rough and was a sub for a transgender girl who tried milking him for half a million dollars after she secretly videotaped them. Normally, I'd settle the score directly with the girl, only in this case, things got messy.

The gang members broke into the girl's apartment, stole her shit and unfortunately her camera too. Instead of erasing everything on it and selling it, they found the video footage of the politician and his dom doing ungodly things. Things respectable, proper community leaders like him weren't supposed to be doing. Somehow, don't ask me how because gang members are usually as stupid as turds, these two realized the full potential of what landed in their laps and decided to blackmail the preppy bastard, too. Only they wanted a million. I had to step in and do some damage control.

Getting myself into trouble by solving other people's shit was part of my job description. This wasn't a first, but it had still sucked ass. By the time I got to the office at Rouge Bis, I'd looked like shit.

I walked in with a lump the size of a baseball on my forehead, courtesy of one of the blackmailing lowlifes.

And *he* sat there behind his desk, typing on his laptop.

Brock took care of my legitimate businesses. I mostly hired out for the illegal stuff to people like Connor, but Brock managed the fronts I used to launder the money I was paid by people like the fucking politician. Along with Rouge Bis, Brock handled the grocery store and the gambling joints. (Strictly speaking, those joints weren't legal, but the police overlooked this little fact for the right price.) Brock also had one other skill. The sonovabitch knew how to perform as a field doctor and could detox junkies as expertly as I broke faces.

"Shit hit the fan?" he asked, not looking up from his Excel spreadsheets.

I took off my blazer and blood-stained black shirt (I knew better than to wear white on workdays) and tossed them into the trash. I opened one of the drawers in the filing cabinet and pulled out a plastic bag of instant-ice and one of the clean shirts I kept stashed there.

"Smashed their kneecaps with my Callaway golf club," I grunted, squeezing the bag and pressing the now ice-cold rectangle against the knot on my head

Brock kept typing. "And you're bummed because they'll never be able to walk again?" He sounded skeptical.

"I'm bummed because I fucked up my Callaway's shaft. It was my favorite." I buttoned up my clean, crisp black shirt

His expression hardened, but not with nearly as much disgust as six years ago, when he first started working for me. "Does your new wife know how sick you are?" Disapproval dripped from his voice. He still didn't look up.

"Probably, if she's got half a brain." I mentally added, *but your wife knows exactly how sick I am.*

His fingers stilled on the keyboard, and this time he did look up. "Don't feel obligated to act like an asshole to her." He was talking about Sparrow. "She didn't do anything, and it's bad enough what you did to her mother."

My fist tightened around the ice pack. I slowly raised my chin, a patronizing smile on my face. "Mind your own fucking business, Greystone."

And before he could retrieve some of his pride, before he could answer back, I turned around and walked out the door.

I'd leave him a note to replace that golf club later. Treat him like he was the secretary. Like a waitress at Hooters. Then I'd take him out for a beer. After all, we were friends, weren't we?

Keep your friends close and your enemies closer, they said. Brock's leash was shorter than my temper, and I made sure that I was always three steps ahead of him.

And that I always had the upper hand.

I FINISHED OFF THE disastrous day by paying a visit to Catalina, thinking I'd let off some steam and give her a piece of my mind about Sparrow's inappropriate wedding gift.

Catalina was my Friday piece and only long-term mistress. Tonight was an unscheduled visit.

It was a risky thing, like anything else worth doing. Brock worked late at the restaurant on Fridays. I always made sure he was extra busy those days so I could play with his wife, even though a part of me really did want him to find out.

Tonight, I wasn't in the mood for fucking. Maybe it was the Callaway, and maybe it was the fact I knew I'd be going back to a penthouse full of Sparrow, a chick I didn't know or like. Hell, maybe it was just me growing bored with my mistress's crazy antics.

Catalina was a virus encased in a sexy dress. Easily spread, but you know that shit is bad for you. There was a time—it was long ago—that she made me believe she was an innocent little lamb, in need of rescuing. Today, I knew she was the person people needed to be protected from.

Either way, I was feeling extra devilish. "Kneel," I ordered coldly when she walked into her dark bedroom.

She jumped, surprised and startled by my presence, but then quickly dropped to her knees, her breath already growing heavy. I pushed myself off the window sill I was leaning against, closed the short distance between us and slammed the door shut so her son wouldn't hear. Her cleavage rose and fell with the rhythm of her breaths. She wanted this so fucking bad, it was almost a turn-off.

Looking down at her, I unzipped my pants. "Now suck."

She didn't budge. The bitch wanted to play, but I wasn't game. I repeated my request.

"No. Do me first." Her voice was shaky.

My jaw twitched. I didn't have time for this. Fisting her dark hair from the base of her skull and yanking her closer to my junk, I murmured, "If you won't, Sparrow will. I've been meaning to test-drive her."

Her lips pinched, and she drew a long breath before moving her face to my cock. A quivering hand wrapped around my shaft.

My threat had worked. Cat had a problem, and her problem was me. I was her ambition, her love, her hate and every other feeling occupying her cold little heart. It was sad, but true.

After I came, I zipped up before she even had the chance to wipe her mouth with the back of her hand. Slumping onto the floor, she dragged her gaze up to see if I'd return the favor.

I was not a good lover. Always took care of myself first, never thought twice about the women I was with. Women overlooked my moody behavior and shortcomings because I never gave them a chance to object. And Cat? She fucking lived for my cruelty. Loved it, lusted after it. The more monstrous I was, the hotter she was for me.

So I was the nastiest to her.

That particular night, I was in no mood to do her, let alone go down on her. I hadn't gone down on a woman in years.

When I started for the door, she peeled her eyes away from my face, crawling on the floor, clasping my leg. "Don't go to her," she whined in decibels more fitted for a slasher film.

My cum was still dripping down her full lower lip and onto Brock's carpeted floor, but she didn't seem to give a damn that her son was downstairs and could probably hear her. I shouldered into my jacket as I watched her squirming at my feet. Recently she'd started crying. A lot. Cried when we fucked, cried when we didn't, and especially every time I left. Surprisingly, I didn't enjoy seeing her like this. I seldom enjoyed the misery of the weak—it was the resilient that I wanted to bring to their knees.

I spat out my toothpick, watched it roll under their bed and shook my head at her. "You're a mess."

She sniffed, bending her head down. "It kills me that you're with her now."

"Don't butt into my shit, Cat. You have a kid to take care of and a life outside this cushy arrangement. We can stop if this is getting to be too much for you. I'm not the only person in the world with a dick. Your husband's got one, too."

"No, no." She got up to her knees, looking like Alice Cooper, the mascara running down her cheeks in chunky strikes. Her palms were pressed together and she matched my pace, crawling on her knees.

Make no mistake, she loved this mess. Would never quit this affair, this drama, or *me*.

"I'm good. I'm just…you know, with you getting married and…" Her eyes fluttered shut as she heaved a sigh. "You're right." She shrugged, forcing a cunning smile as she got to her feet. "It's just something I need to get used to."

I would give her a piece of my mind about that slutty gift. But not tonight.

When I walked out of her house, Sam was in the living room, watching a cartoon in the dark, clutching a teddy bear under his armpit. "Bye, Mr.

Troy," he muttered almost to himself, eyes still glued to Bugs Bunny and Road Runner.

I grunted in response.

I was the scum of the earth.

The biggest scum on the planet.

And still, I couldn't help myself.

So, WHEN I GOT BACK home, poured myself a drink and heard Sparrow's little feet climbing down the stairway, I decided I'd done enough damage for one day and spared her the truth about our marriage.

She was trying to be nice, and I was trying not to resent her.

The truth about our marriage was that I wanted nothing more than to be out of it. But as it happened, my father had made me promise I'd marry Abraham Raynes's daughter.

Until his murder, I couldn't, for the fucking life of me, understand why.

Raynes was a loser, a drunk, a man with no prospects, who never even made it to becoming a real mobster back in the day when every illiterate piece of shit was a legitimate part of the mob. He used to get the shittiest jobs the organization had to offer. My father let him work with the rookies. Abe extorted like a teenager, threatening people who owed us money, and he had some gigs as a bouncer and filled in for our errand boy when the latter was sick.

My father always spoke fondly of Sparrow Raynes, Abe's daughter. Which didn't explain why, when I turned eighteen, he invited me to his office (something he very rarely did, despite us being close) and made me promise that one day I would marry her and bring her into the family.

Marry. Sparrow. Raynes. The kid who was so off my radar, I wasn't even sure I'd understood him right.

But I loved my father fiercely, adored him and would have died for him, so I rolled with the plan. I was eighteen, and she was eight. It was twisted and barbaric, and it was my very first taste of the unfairness of life, but it would be years before I'd have to worry about it. I put that plan on the backburner.

Needless to say, as we both got older the very idea of marrying the Plain Jane down the road sounded about as appealing as fucking a hedgehog. I warned everyone around Sparrow to stay the fuck away—guys were not to look, take interest or touch her. Always made sure the bad crowd kept away from her, not that she was drawn to it in the first place.

And always, always pressing my father to tell me why the hell I had to marry the little redhead. He never did.

The day he died, I found out why.

See, I always knew da had a side piece, but finding out it was Robyn Raynes – the runaway mother next door – made sense.

By then, I was older, wiser and colder, after having my heart broken into a gazillion pieces. I knew that the road to success was paved with sacrifices.

Sparrow Raynes was my sacrifice. I promised I'd marry her, and I had.

Truthfully, I would have happily waited a few more years, but my father's lawyer made it pretty fucking clear that I wouldn't see a dime or an acre he had left me until she had a ring on her finger.

And Cillian Brennan wasn't taking the "all the days of my life" part of the wedding vows lightly. Clause 103b of his will stated that if Sparrow and I divorced, she would get the majority of my inheritance.

The majority. Un-fucking-believable.

At thirty-two, I was ready to collect what was mine. What had always been mine—my father's hard-earned wealth.

The money was especially needed, now that my mother had decided to leave Boston in favor of a place in Nice, France. Most folks retired to Florida or Arizona. Andrea Brennan, though? Fucked off with her younger boyfriend to one of the most expensive places on earth. The French Riviera. And she didn't even have a job to retire *from*.

Someone had to pay for her fancy shit, for the fact Maria was still needed at her house three fucking times a week because my mother let her lazy friends stay there every now and again. And despite her lavish lifestyle, my mom was a little strapped for cash. Most of the family money was invested in stocks and properties for tax reasons.

I couldn't help but think that Andrea and Catalina had a lot of things in common.

Anyway, if Red learned the truth—why my father made me marry her in the first place and how I kept her virginal and untouched just for me all those years, scared all those potential suitors away—not only would she try and kill me, she could also go to the police, and have me locked up. For life.

So I was trying to be civil with my new wife.

Only now I had no fucking idea what to do with her. Court her? Ignore her? Fuck her against her will? The first and third options weren't my style. Ignoring her had worked for a week, but left me annoyed. I was sick of hearing she was aimlessly wandering my apartment most of the day and pretending to be asleep whenever I returned home.

And then the shit in the living room happened downstairs, and she was so miserable and vulnerable, I'd spat some bullshit story about seeing her at church and even offered to take her to dinner.

A dinner date. First one since *her*. I tried to remind myself dates were like sex. You never forget how to do it.

BY THE TIME I FINISHED my shower, Sparrow was already asleep, and not faking it this time. I slid into bed beside her and watched the rise and fall of her chest, but she was far from peaceful. I knew she was keeping a knife under the pillow. It amused and impressed me all at once. Not that she could do anything with that knife if she ever confronted me, but I liked her assertiveness.

She was nothing like her father. *Nothing.*

My initial expectation after the wedding—that she'd lock herself in a room listening to man-hating Taylor Swift songs on repeat as she cried her eyes out—was proving premature. She might be innocent, but she wasn't stupid. Hardened by her circumstances and toughened by our neighborhood—Red was no pushover.

I turned my back to her and turned on my bedside lamp, taking my iPad from my nightstand drawer. I went through everything I had to do the next day—a meeting with an asshat who was running for governor and needed to find his bitter stepdaughter and convince her not to talk shit about him; an appointment with a local property tycoon who got into trouble with some Armenian gang members because he didn't want to pay them protection money.

Fucking Armenians ran the underworld of Boston nowadays, and they were a grim reminder of what could have been mine had my father been more careful with the family business.

The Brennans were infamous in Boston not only as the royal crime family of the city, but also because we'd been smart enough to donate to schools, churches and local charities. We dropped enough cash to have hospital wings, bars and babies named after us. People liked us because once upon a time we'd been generous with our earnings, and we'd kept the city mostly clean of the bad stuff (prostitution and drugs).

Sure, we were criminals, but we kept the innocents' innocence intact and never hurt a soul who didn't deserve to feel the wrath of our fists. Loan sharking, extortion, illegal gambling and money laundering. We did it all, and we did it well.

Now, the Armenians and local unorganized gangs were ruling the Boston underworld, and it was a mess. No moral codes, respect or honor. Just a bunch of fucking bullies who got their hands on unregistered guns.

After going over an email from another client and cursing the Armenians again, I put my iPad back in the drawer. Taking one last glance at Red, I noticed her cell on her nightstand was glowing with a new text message. It was four a.m. Who the fuck would text her this late?

My eyes shifted to her face, and back to her cell.

Don't do this.

Do this.

Don't do this.

Fuck it.

I'd only seen this woman on a few occasions, when she was just a girl, playing kick the can with the other dirty kids when I was busy scoring chicks, smoking cigarettes and leaning against muscle cars that weren't even mine. For all I knew, Red could be a snitch. Work with the police. Could be a serial killer.

Ha.

I reached over, my arm stretching above her nose, and picked up her phone.

Then I started digging. Deep.

Sparrow Raynes didn't have many friends. She'd always been an odd bird, no pun intended, and I guess her social life reflected it.

Based on her incoming messages, a girl named Lucy appeared to be her closest friend. (But not close enough for Sparrow to invite her to the wedding, God forbid.) There was a guy named Boris, her culinary teacher, who'd already been warned off. There was also a girl named Daisy who I remembered from our neighborhood.

What struck me as peculiar was the timing of the most recent conversation with Lucy. The timestamp was after our little encounter earlier, downstairs in the living room. While I was in the shower, Sparrow had been on her phone. In fact, the flashing of her cell phone was Lucy answering Sparrow's last text.

Lucy: *Drinks tomorrow? Usual spot. Just got paid. My treat.*

Sparrow: *Wish I could. Got a job interview.*

Lucy: *What? When? Where? Why am I out of the loop all of a sudden? Spill!*

Sparrow: *It's for Rouge Bis. That super-expensive French restaurant we always promise we'll go to and dine and dash.*

Lucy: *No way. Isn't the owner Troy Brennan? The only Brennan who isn't dead or locked up. Haha.*

Sparrow: *Yeah, they didn't get to him yet. Hopefully they'll wait until after my interview. I'll keep you posted. Wish me luck.*

Lucy: *Don't make friends with him. They call him The Fixer for a reason.*

Sparrow: *I know he's a fishy guy. He's my dad's boss, remember?*

Lucy: *I remember, I'm just making sure that you do too.*

Sparrow: *Love you.*

Lucy: *Love you more. Xx*

Then there was the final unanswered message.

Lucy: *P.S. Don't feel bad if you don't get it. Rumor has it he's a world-class asshole.*

Guess this was the reminder I needed. She hated me, wanted to use me, and thought I was scum, just like my dad.

And just like that, any resolve to make her life a little less hellish disappeared.

FIVE

SPARROW

I SCURRIED MY WAY TO the kitchen at dawn. Confused about my last encounter with Troy, I wanted nothing more than to be on his good side.

Fine, I would just admit it—I wanted that job.

And let's face it, it moved something inside me to know that he'd noticed me at church. That he'd noticed me at all. So I decided that I was going to give Troy Brennan an honest chance not to be a world-class jerk.

I fixed him breakfast, fluffy blueberry pancakes with maple syrup and a cup of hot chocolate—my personal favorite—and greeted him with a big smile when he walked down the stairs, squinting away the morning sun. He was still wearing his briefs and sporting some serious morning wood. And when I said "wood," I meant more like a forest.

My curiosity got the better of me and I peeked down, trying to calculate the size of him as I pretended to straighten the silverware and napkins I'd set out on the island.

I was no expert, but his junk looked like something that could comfortably fit into the exhaust pipe of a truck and not, so help me God, into my vagina. I might have taken a moment or three to stare, interest and fear flickering in my eyes.

"Don't worry, Red. It doesn't bite." He yawned into his forearm, nudging me out of the way to reach for the coffee pot on the counter behind me.

"But it can spit," I offered over my shoulder, smiling coyly.

He sent me a crooked, condescending smirk. "Not at you, with the way you've been treating it so far."

He was being an ass again, but I kept trying, not letting my ego get the better of me. I pointed at the large dish on the island. "Pancakes. Right here, hot and fluffy. And hot chocolate, too. Do you want some whipped cream?"

I wanted him to remember the girl he wanted to marry. I wanted myself to forget that he was the man my father worked for. I wanted us to try and be something, even if it was stupid and naive.

"I don't eat sugary crap," he answered unapologetically, his voice bone-dry. "And I definitely don't drink hot fucking chocolate. But next time I'm hosting a tea party, I'll borrow a tutu and you can help me fix some cupcakes."

My ears pinked as I withdrew the plate of hot pancakes from the placemat, swallowing back the bitter lump in my throat. I marched to the sink and dumped the food with a loud clank. I broke his stupid, precious, probably expensive plate. *Good.*

Silent, Troy plucked a banana from the wire bowl on the countertop. He opened the fridge, pulling out some OJ and plain yogurt, and banged the fridge shut with his foot.

Still mostly naked. Still hard as stone.

"I'll be in my office upstairs. Don't forget dinner tonight," he said, walking away. "I left another credit card on your nightstand. Try to look your part. No Keds bullshit or emo-kid hoodies. Got it?"

"Jesus Christ." I scowled. "Chauvinist much?"

"Not much, just enough to want my wife to look like a woman and not a twelve-year-old boy who raided Hot Topic."

I wanted to tell him he was being a dick, but knew it wouldn't help my chances of scoring the job. Instead, I balled up my fists, ground my teeth and stormed out of the apartment, banging the door shut behind me.

I was practically able to feel the hair on my head graying when I jabbed at the elevator button aggressively, gave up after a few seconds—too pumped on my own boiling anger to stand still—and took the stairs down to the lobby of his building, two at a time. I climbed down all freaking fourteen floors and started my morning run without my gear or running shoes. Just Keds. *The ass.* All I had was tons of energy to burn.

And that was enough.

When my feet hit the cold, damp sidewalk, my breath evened. Finally, a minor bliss.

As I plugged in my earbuds and played "Last Resort" by Papa Roach to accompany my run—I needed something angry just like me—I already felt Connor on my heels, trying to catch up with my pace.

I was going to waste the day away, and fantasize about the million opportunities I'd have to shove a fork into my husband's chest at dinner. The last thing I'd do was follow his instructions and become a sweet, pretty wife in a dress.

And every time he pushed—I'd pulled harder.

I DIDN'T BUY ANYTHING SEDUCTIVE or alluring for our dinner out, like Troy had ordered. In fact, I refused to leave the kitchen, drowning my frustrations in making food. Tons and tons of food. I used all the ingredients in the cupboards and fridge, and spent the day fussing over food for the shelter.

Hours of solitary cooking made me finally come to terms with the gravity of my situation. Until last night, I hadn't exactly been sure what was happening. I hadn't fully digested the fact that I had married this man.

But now it was real.

And it was scaring the hell out of me.

Connor was pacing back and forth in the living room, talking on the phone. I was almost tempted to use the opportunity to try and run away. Then again, where the hell would I go? My dad would hand me right back to Brennan, fearing the consequences of thwarting his boss. I couldn't burden Lucy with my presence, and no loan shark was going to hand me enough to flee town, seeing as they all knew my husband or one of his family members, and at the very least, didn't want to mess with him.

At four p.m., Maria stormed into the kitchen with a face like thundercloud, informing me that it was time to clean up all the mess I'd made and that I had to evacuate her kitchen before she grabbed me by the hair and did it herself (not in so many words, but her shouting in Spanish and hand waving certainly implied it). She was extra pissed off today, with a dash of furious, because she had a double shift both at Andrea's and at Troy's. Apparently he spilled some OJ in his study earlier in the morning, and of course, his hands were too precious to clean up the mess himself. Now she had to clean my mess, too.

She announced that Mr. Brennan would pick me up at eight p.m. from the lobby of our building and that I should be ready in an evening gown. I snorted into my chest, deeply focused on packing a double batch of mac and cheese. The amount of food I'd prepared could probably feed a whole army, and not a small one either. But cooking was therapeutic, and I needed a way to distract myself from my reality. From *him*.

"I don't have an evening gown," I grumbled, pivoting to the oven and taking out the coconut pies. I only had one little black dress in my closet. I wore it to weddings, funerals and I was planning to wear it to my first-ever date tonight. Anything in-between didn't require fancy attire. In my opinion anyway.

"Too late to go buy," she barked at me, disappointed with my inability to follow simple instructions from my husband. "What do you do? Mr. Brennan will be mad!"

"He's always mad."

Maria let out an exasperated sigh and turned around, fishing her cell phone out of her apron. She pressed the phone to her ear and shot me an annoyed glare. When the person on the other line answered, she started talking to them animatedly in Spanish. I wiped my hands on my pants, mildly interested in this turn of events.

Finally, after a few minutes, she hung up on the person and wiggled her finger at me. "My daughter will give you nice dress. She your size. But you no dirty it and you give back after dry clean. *Comprende?*"

I nodded, a little shocked and a lot relieved. I couldn't, for the life of me, understand why she'd want to help me. Either way, I was glad Brennan would see me in something presentable and perhaps give me this job.

"Thanks, I guess." I followed her movements as she began cleaning up after me.

"You," she said furiously, scrubbing pans and shielding me away from helping her with her shoulder, "are little girl. He," she continued, pointing upstairs with her chin to where the bedroom was, "a big, powerful man. You no annoying him, or he dump your ass."

I couldn't help but break into a laugh. "Dump your ass" was just about the funniest thing Maria had ever said to me.

I shook my head and walked to her, pouting my apology. "You're right. And please don't clean after me. I can do this myself." I carefully tried to pry a dirty pan from her hand.

She rolled her eyes and elbowed me away. "Let me clean, silly girl."

I packed up all the food that I'd made and dispatched it to the homeless shelter, via a taxi and a big tip from Connor, who refused to let me deliver it myself.

I didn't get to meet Maria's daughter. She left the cocktail dress for Connor to pick up in the lobby along with a pair of high heels while I was in the shower. Those, too, were exactly my size. When I walked into the bedroom, the gown was already laid out on Troy's big bed. It was a peach-colored and sleeveless, with a sweetheart neckline and a thin gold belt.

At 7:45, I zipped it on me, added some makeup (not too much, just a little mascara and lip gloss to cover up my freckles and hours of self-pity) and rode the elevator down to the lobby.

Not to my surprise, Troy was late. I texted Lucy and Daisy while sitting in one of the creamy leather chairs, waiting for him. A sudden urge to wrap myself up in familiarity, in their friendship, gripped me. Plus, it was evident they were more than a little suspicious about my sudden disappearance from our neighborhood.

Me: *Hey, girls, want to have drinks next week?*

Lucy: *You tell us.*

Me: *?*

Daisy: *Stopped by your house. Your dad said something about you moving out. What're you hiding, Birdie?*

Shit. Shit, shit, shit. Guess the reassuring messages I'd sent my friends hadn't really make the impact I was hoping for.

Me: *You must have misunderstood. I'm not hiding anything. Just busy. My interview is in a few minutes, btw.*

Lucy: *You worked at a diner and take cooking classes. Now all of a sudden, you have a job interview at Rouge Bis? One to ten, how stupid do you think we are?*

Me: *Mmm...5?*

Me again: *Kidding. Look, I can explain.*

No, I couldn't. And that was the worst part. I knew they'd find out eventually, but I didn't want to deal.

Daisy: *You better. We'll be waiting for you @ our usual spot. Good luck with the interview.*

I was about to fire Lucy and Daisy another message when I heard footfalls and my eyes shot up from my cell. I recognized his walk. It was elegant, self-assured and claimed the space he'd just entered. He wore a pale gray suit that somehow made him look even taller and broader. I stood up, smoothing my dress with my hands and looking at him like a guilty kid.

"How were the pancakes?" Brennan placed a dry, impersonal kiss on my cheek.

Like he had to. Like I was an annoying aunt. He also seemed to have forgotten (or not noticed) I'd thrown the stack of pancakes in the sink. Wow, what an attentive husband. Lucky me.

"Worth all the sugary *crap* in them." I tipped my chin up defiantly, then rethought the attitude. I *wanted* that job. "Like my dress?"

Brennan frowned, but his expression looked more puzzled than angry. "You picked this dress yourself?" He took a step back, examining me. His frown made him no less easy on the eyes.

In fact, any expression other than his cold shark-gaze made my pulse increase. He wasn't unattractive, and it bothered me. *A lot.*

"Shopping wasn't first priority," I admitted, making sure there was enough distance between us. Brennan was hot. Not just figuratively, he actually radiated warmth. "Maria was kind enough to call her daughter and ask if I could borrow a dress from her."

"Her daughter?" He studied my face as we made our way out of the lobby, like he didn't believe me.

"Yeah, her daughter. Why? Is it too peachy for your taste? Or maybe you were expecting a leather thong like my wedding gift?" I cocked an eyebrow, shivering as we exited into another cold, drizzling night.

He simply pressed his palm possessively into the small of my back and led me out to the awning-covered sidewalk. I tried to ignore the bolt of lust shooting down my belly at his touch. I wanted to move into his heat. Probably just the fact I had little to no experience with the opposite sex, I tried convincing myself. After all, I hated this man. My body, as it turned out, didn't share the sentiment.

"You look nice," he offered, though everything about his compliment felt like it had a hidden meaning, as per usual.

"Thank you."

The street was buzzing with traffic and pedestrians. I recognized his car from his visit to my neighborhood. The white Maserati—a stark contrast to a mob-style black Mercedes, I didn't fail to note—was double-parked in the middle of the one-way street in front of the building. He'd created an unapologetic traffic jam, blocking the way of a dozen vehicles behind him. People were honking and swearing, waving their fists out of their car windows despite the rain.

But when they saw it was Troy Brennan who approached the shiny GranTurismo, they swiftly tucked their heads back into their cars and rolled their windows up. I actually heard the *clicks* of the closest doors locking in unison.

Embarrassed beyond words and horrified by my other half's arrogance, I shook off his touch and picked up my pace to his car. He carried an unopened umbrella, but didn't increase his speed or spare me a second glance as I rushed to avoid getting wet. I still couldn't believe it was so rainy and cold in June. It was like the whole world had conspired against Sparrow Raynes. It was bad enough to deal with this guy without nature deciding to taunt me with constant clouds.

"Did you *have* to block all those people?" I asked as I fastened my seatbelt.

"No." He met my gaze, unblinking, as he climbed behind the wheel. "Just didn't care enough not to."

I stared out the window with pursed lips and thunder in my eyes as the car rolled into Boston's unforgiving Friday-night traffic, trying to let the chilly leather seat cool my temper. The radio station played "Heavy Is The Head" by the Zac Brown Band and Chris Cornell. Pretty ironic, I thought bitterly.

"You can wipe that satisfied grin off your face," I said after a steadying breath. I could see his amusement from my peripheral vision. "Rudeness doesn't impress me. I've never seen the appeal of the whole angry-asshole façade, and I'd definitely never fall for someone like you."

"Troy Brennan. Nice to meet you. There's always a first time for everything."

"Maybe this…" I waved my finger between us. "Will be the first time you realize that not all women are the gold-digging, cookie-cutter, cardboard stereotype you've been dating so far."

"If I were you, I wouldn't burn all your bridges to my good graces." His smirk somehow broke into an even wider smile. "You have something you want from me tonight, Red."

"How can you be so sure?"

He flashed me a quick glance before training his amused gaze back on the road. "Because you agreed to have dinner with me."

I blew some air out of my lungs, rubbing my bare arms. He noticed and turned on the heater. Sadly, it was the nicest thing he'd ever done for me.

"Okay, you're right. I have a suggestion I need to run by you." My voice was thick.

"Later," Brennan said, and I decided not to push for now.

As the silence stretched. I adjusted my dress, pried at the high heels that felt too tight.

"How's your foot tonight?" he suddenly asked.

"Better," I answered automatically, then bit my inner cheek once I realized what I'd done. *Shit.*

I was collecting *shit*-moments by the second this evening.

His lips pressed together in a thin line. "I'm a lot of bad things, but an idiot is not one of them. I figured you cut yourself on our wedding night to avoid consummating our marriage. You wearing my socks, and the blood I found on my razor was a big fucking clue. I'm not a rapist, Sparrow."

Feeling my cheeks heat, I rubbed my forehead. "With all due respect, Brennan, with your track record, I decided it was better to be safe than sorry."

"My track record?" He hissed out a breath. "Please educate me on what the fuck you're talking about? And quit calling me Brennan. I'm your husband, not your boss."

I needed to backpedal my last remark. What was I supposed to answer? *Everyone knows you killed Billy Crupti? People say you break bones for a living? You make my knees weak with fear?*

"My point is," I said, "intimidating a woman with sex is disgusting. I didn't want you to touch me." I folded my arms over my chest, trying to catch my breath again.

That was my constant physical state around this man. I could run for hours on end and sing simultaneously without missing a note, but I couldn't, for the life of me, talk to him for a few seconds without feeling like I needed an inhaler.

"Whatever helps you sleep at night, Red. But if I recall, on our wedding night you creamed my boxers like they were a fucking birthday cake."

This man was so disgusting sometimes the need to hurt him overwhelmed me.

"Thanks for the poetic analogy. And still, I don't want to have sex with you."

"Yes, you do." His lips curved seductively, his eyes still narrowed on the car in front of us. "Your eyes wander to my morning wood. You grind yourself against me when given the opportunity. Your nipples were so hard when I sucked on your blood, they almost cut through your shirt." His right hand traveled from the gearbox, hovering over my thigh, but never touching. "And you kissed me last night and moaned my name. *You.*"

Damn, it was hot. I could feel the warmth of his skin, even through the dress's fabric.

"You're ripe, Red. And you want to have sex. It's just a shame you want to have it with a man you hate."

I shook my head. "Unbelievable."

He shrugged, holding the steering wheel in one hand and drumming on the gearbox with the other, moving away from my thigh. "Love and hate are similar in a lot of ways."

"Is there a way to love you away from me?" I snapped.

"No, but you could hate-fuck me all you want."

I flushed lobster red, a jolt of warmth finding its way to my groin. Troy Brennan was perfectly content with talking dirty, whereas I was embarrassed at simply thinking about sex. Yet again, he had the upper hand.

I stretched, straightening my spine, wishing we weren't in the middle of the traffic jam from hell. I had a feeling we weren't going to make it to the restaurant even if he made reservations for nine o'clock.

I changed the subject. "We're going to miss our reservation with this traffic. Maybe we should just forget dinner." The less time together, the better.

"I don't need reservations. I own the place. They'll serve us at four in the morning if that's what I feel like."

Just like that, a gap opened up in the traffic. He sped through a light, and my heart picked up speed, along with the car. We were going to visit Rouge Bis, the restaurant I so desperately wanted to work at. This brought new possibilities and hence new hopefulness to my mood. I perked up in my seat, trying to keep my smile to myself.

Back to plan A.

Back to playing nice.

Back to building bridges.

I decided calling him by his first name would be a good start.

"Can you tell me a little more about why you chose to marry me, Troy?" I stared straight ahead to avoid the sting if he decided to award me with another snarky comment.

He was navigating the streets like a fire-spitting monster was on our heels, violating every driving law known to man, and inspiring some new laws in the process.

"When you were nine and I was nineteen…" He paused, letting the gravity of our age difference sink in. "There was a wedding. Paddy and Shona Rowan, remember them? She was his third wife, I think."

I swallowed hard, nodding. One of the only mobster weddings Pops was ever invited to, and, boy, was he proud. The groom was a man who dabbled in real estate and drug smuggling after the FBI threw his friends in jail. He didn't mind socializing with peasants like my dad.

And on his wedding day, I found out why.

Paddy Rowan was high on my shit list, one of the first two people up there, along with the man who sat right next to me. The only difference was that I hated Troy and wanted him out of my life, but Paddy? I wanted Paddy dead.

"I remember," I said, pain already tickling the pit of my stomach. "'Saving All My Love For You.'"

"Excuse me?" he said, sounding amused.

"The name of the song we...you know." My face was on fire. I was embarrassed to admit that I remembered. "We danced to it. "Saving All My Love For You" by Whitney Houston."

"Yeah, sure." He shrugged a shoulder. "Anyway, my family shared a table with yours, much to everyone's surprise."

Just in case I'd forgotten just how low-class I was.

"But," he continued, "Paddy was always a clueless prick. Anyway, you sat across from me. I didn't pay much attention to you, because you were nine, and that was too fucked up even by my standards." He shook his head, almost cringing. "I remember you were the cutest, politest little thing. You asked my mother tons of questions. At one point you asked her if her teeth were real. Then you tried to convince me to dance with you."

"You agreed." Memories slammed into me. I dug my fingernails into my palms, pressing my fists on my thighs, hoping he wouldn't notice. I tried to focus on the part of the day he was talking about, the sweet memory of my dance with the much older boy, a memory I'd somehow completely erased until now.

"Yeah." He raised one eyebrow. "You were hell-bent on dancing a slow dance." He suppressed a chuckle. "Even then, Red, I was your first."

My fists tightened and I continued to stare out the window. It wasn't embarrassment that he was my first slow dance that shook me to the core. It was what happened after that dance that made it one of the worst days in my life. So bad, in fact, that it made my mother leaving me seem like child's play.

I cleared my throat, suddenly realizing how exposed I felt. "The line to the valet is two-blocks long. Pull over and I'll let someone know we're here."

"I own the place." Brennan—no, make that Troy—laughed, delighted by my unintended joke. "Watch."

He slammed the Maserati into park in the middle of the busy street, slid out and threw his keys to a uniformed valet who was leaning against a wall in the alley and smoking a cigarette. The valet, who was about my age, caught the keys in his palm and nodded furiously at Troy, dropping the cigarette like it was a ticking bomb and jogging to the Maserati's driver-side door.

As another traffic jam formed behind my husband's vehicle, I began to suspect he was the sole reason for bad traffic in Boston. It was entirely possible that if it weren't for him, we wouldn't need the T.

"Smoke again during your shift and you're fired. Scratch my car and you're dead, get it?" Troy barked at the guy with his keys.

He sauntered over to my side of the car and opened the door. I stepped out, accepting his hand and allowing him to guide me by the waist as he ushered me into the glitzy restaurant. Two other restaurant staff already held the door open for us. Faint elevator music wafted through the doors, along with the smell of mouth-watering food and pale, sandy light.

"You're not nine anymore," he said gruffly as we waltzed in.

"And thank God for that," I muttered, my thoughts traveling back to Paddy Rowan.

Block it, I ordered myself, just like I always did. Just like I blocked everything else.

SIX

TROY

CATALINA SENT HER DRESS AND heels so Red could wear them tonight to fuck with my head. It worked. Because when Red wore Cat's dress, unlike my mistress, she didn't look like a wrapped candy waiting to be unfolded. She looked like a sweet fucking princess who is about to lose her innocence at the hands of the big bad wolf.

I fed my personal little Red Riding Hood more sweet memories to keep her happy, my words like music to her unsuspecting ears.

Guilt was a thief. It would steal your mind, mess with your priorities and would eventually steer you from your original plan. I couldn't allow it any room in the life, so I pushed it aside, convincing myself that on some level, these moments we shared weren't lies. Just half-truths.

We did slow dance at the wedding.

But I never thought she was endearing in any way.

In fact, at nineteen, I already knew that she was destined to be my wife. When I danced with nine-year-old Sparrow, all I'd felt was anger. Mostly for me, a little bit for her.

All that mattered now was that Sparrow bought it, and she was beginning to crack. Rays of light streamed through her walls of defense. Even though I liked their warmth, I was careful not to give her too much hope. We weren't a real couple, and this wasn't a love story.

A waiter showed us to the best table in the restaurant. My wife took in the room wide-eyed, and I knew why. Before me, she could hardly afford a Happy Meal. Now, she was gaping at the waterwall dividing the brass bar from the bronze concrete tables. Hell, the lighting here alone cost more than her father's annual salary.

People swiveled their heads in our directions, gossiping in hushed tones over their overpriced meals, probably wondering how I, of all people, had settled down—and with an average Catholic girl, no less. They were swallowing her whole with their gazes, following her wobbly steps, like there was a secret hiding behind those innocent green eyes and that crimson hair.

I straightened to my full height, towering almost a foot over my wife, my hand guiding her narrow waist as I led her to our seats.

"Everybody's watching us. People are talking about us," she said, her voice small.

"Do you care?"

She hesitated, looking down at the high heels she swayed in, before lifting her face up, her expression resolute. "No."

"Good, because opinions are like assholes. Everybody's got one, and they usually stink."

"Well, that's just *your* opinion." She chewed on a smile, and the cleverness of her comment didn't escape me.

I bit back a grin, feeling a tad less annoyed with being seen with her. She wasn't supermodel material, but fuck it, her mouth was good for more than licking and sucking, and that was refreshing, I supposed.

Red spilled the beans about what she wanted from me while we were sipping Kir Royale. I had a feeling if she knew a single cocktail was $125, she wouldn't have polished off three in a row just to get the liquid courage to ask me if she could work at Rouge Bis.

A part of me liked that about her. She wasn't particularly interested or impressed by my money, even though she had none. That showed character. Or endless stupidity. I was leaning toward the former, though.

I clenched my drink and pretended ignorance, like I hadn't already done the math the night before, when I went through her texts. I inspected the room while she rambled on, trying to sell herself as a valuable employee.

She sat across from me, tapping her foot beneath the table and watching me for a reaction. She was so caught up in trying to see what I was thinking she paid little attention to the way people were still staring at us. Sparrow was an observant little thing most of the time, but as opposed to my so-called "string of cookie-cutters," she seemed to rarely give a damn about what people thought.

It was a liberating quality in a woman.

"So you want to work here?" I folded my arms behind my neck and leaned back when she finally stopped talking to take a quick breath. I didn't hate the idea. Maybe if she worked here, she wouldn't be grating on my fucking nerves whenever we were both under the same roof. Getting her out of my hair was an idea I was warming up to.

She nodded. "I'll do anything. I don't mind starting from the bottom." She cleared her throat nervously, but I spared her the sexual innuendo. "I worked at a diner as a cook. It may not sound like much, but I can also wash dishes or work as a waitress or…"

She was rambling again. Lifting one hand, I cut off the stream of words. "Time to be blunt. What the fuck makes you think you're good enough for the best place in Boston?"

Her face fell. For a second, I almost felt sorry for her for marrying a bastard like me, but then I remembered she was a fucking headache I inherited from my old man, and I stiffened my back in my chair.

She squared her shoulders back, taking a deep breath. "I'm a great cook, Troy. Try me," she challenged, calling me by my first name. She only did it when she tried to be nice, which wasn't very often. Her eyes were almost pleading, but her tone let me know she wasn't going to beg.

I let my mouth curve into a slow smile. That hint of fight gleamed behind her eyes again, dancing like flames. I stood up, offering her my hand.

"What are you doing?" She looked a little confused, but took my hand and followed suit, her chair screeching behind her.

"I'm going to see if you're as good as your word, Mrs. Brennan."

I led her to the back of the restaurant, barging through the swinging double-doors in a confident stride. The minute I stepped into the hectic kitchen, the hustle and bustle stopped. Everyone paused shouting over the dishes. Staff who ran from one station to the other halted, staring at me. Mouths fell open, dishes crashed against the floor and eyes widened. Hell, you'd think I walked in there with a loaded Uzi and not a frightened chick.

Guess my staff was surprised to see me. After all, I was notorious for being a short-tempered, snippy asshole. And the fact that I'd never bothered to meet any of my employees didn't exactly push me up the list as Boss of The Year. They were waiting to see what I'd do. I was a case study. I was the psychopath. That's the legend I fed, and that's the legend I had to live up to, even if it wasn't the whole truth.

The place was as hot as a furnace, and I grunted my disapproval, wiping off my forehead. Sparrow was standing behind me, clutching my hand in a death grip. She was scared shitless, and I kind of liked it.

"Who's the head chef around here?" I asked, and watched as people flinched. No one spoke. No one breathed. No one fucking moved. Their terror echoed and bounced on the walls.

After a few seconds, a large man with a dark porno moustache and stained, white chef's coat stepped forward, wiping his hands with a kitchen towel before tossing it on a chopping board and offering me his sausage-thick fingers for a handshake.

"That'd be me, sir. Name's Pierre."

I didn't even look at his hand, let alone shake it. "Don't really care. Now, this girl right here…" I turned around, pointing at Sparrow, whose eyes grew wider by the second. "She wants a job working in this kitchen."

"We don't need any new employees, but she can leave her contact number and—"

"I don't remember assigning you as my HR manager," I snapped. "Test. Her. Now."

Hushed gasps filled the room. Some girl shrieked in the far corner of the kitchen. All eyes were on Sparrow, desperately trying to figure out why I wanted to help Plain Jane get a job at one of Boston's finest. Guess they didn't get the memo about the wedding of the month. The sound of something sizzling on a frying pan was the only thing audible in the crowded kitchen. Something other than my short fuse was burning.

"For the love of God, drag your asses back to work before you set my place on fire," I roared.

Everybody jumped back to their stations, other than the head chef. He eyeballed Sparrow like she had just kidnapped his family at gunpoint and thrown them in a cellar full of venomous snakes. I turned around to glance at my wife. Despite her obvious embarrassment, she returned a challenging glare to the chef. She wasn't going to be intimidated by his stink eye.

Atta girl.

I curled my finger behind my back, signaling her to step deeper into the kitchen. She did. I kept my eyes trained on what's-his-name, who bit his hairy upper lip in barely contained frustration.

"Go on," I murmured, my scowl lingering on his face. "Test her."

He blinked a few times, trying to digest the situation. Then he sighed, looking around him for support. No one even dared to look at us now.

"Come with me," he instructed her.

I followed them. Pierre—he introduced himself again when I referred to him as "the cook"—plucked one of the menus from beside the stove and shoved it into her hands. He didn't have a clue that she was my wife, and I wanted to keep it that way. To find out whether she really knew what she was doing.

I wanted her out of the house, but not at the expense of giving my customers food poisoning.

Pierre stabbed at the menu with his oily finger, leaving a stain on the parchment as he pointed at one of the dishes. I couldn't help but notice it was the most expensive, long-titled entrée on the menu. A fucking trap if I ever saw one. My eyes narrowed in annoyance, but I didn't move. Just took out a toothpick from my breast pocket and placed it between my lips, rolling it from side to side with my tongue.

"Roasted venison loin, grains, parsnip puree and sauce *poivrade.*" His smile was triumphant.

Sparrow turned her gaze to him, not a muscle in her round, freckled face flinching. "It takes about three and a half hours to make this dish," she stated matter-of-factly.

"I have time," the chef hissed, nostrils flaring.

A sudden, unexpected urge to cut the son of a bitch to tiny pieces washed over me, but I leaned against one of the steel counters instead, looking both bored and content. "So do I."

She looked between us like this was a conspiracy, but threw her red mane behind her shoulder and shrugged off our attitude. "Better get started, then."

Sparrow got down to business straightaway. She almost flipped Pierre the finger when he sarcastically offered her an apron. I watched as she filled up the empty station he assigned her with the ingredients she needed. Her movements were swift and confident as she got comfortable and found everything she needed. I knew the chef set her up with an unfair task. He just gave her the name of the dish and hoped she'd fuck up. But by the look on his face every time she ran from side to side, holding carrots, beef stock and bay leaves, I had a feeling this girl knew her way around the kitchen, much to his dismay.

While I watched her cook, I suddenly realized it was her art. The pan was her canvas, the ingredients her paint. She cooked with fire in her eyes, with passion in her soul, with love in her heart.

Occasionally she'd wipe her forehead with her milky-white, freckled arm and smile apologetically, probably thinking she looked like a mess.

But she was wrong. This was a much-needed reminder that Red was kind of hot, in her own quirky way, anyway.

Like the way she curled the tip of her tongue on her upper lip when she concentrated. Something about it made me so hard I almost shoved her against the stove and proved to her just how much we could enjoy each other's company. Or the way my wallflower suddenly became the center of the room, working the hardest without calling attention to herself or rambling about it. She glowed. Corny as it sounds, she fucking *glowed*.

"Hey, can you fetch the red wine from over there?" she asked at some point, running between one point of the kitchen to the other. I was so taken aback by her request, I felt almost offended.

"No, I cannot," I answered evenly. "Can you not overstep your fucking bounds? You're here auditioning for a job."

"Someone's on that special time of the month," she grinned, grabbing the wine bottle by its neck.

"Just do your thing, Red."

"O-*kaaaay*," she drawled, still wiggling her ass to an inaudible tune in her head. "So just look over the pan and make sure the olive oil's not overheating while I get the bottle opener."

She finished making the dish a little after the restaurant closed for the night. Her red hair was everywhere—face, neck, sticking to her forehead—and Cat's dress looked like she had just lost a food fight. But she looked happy, and that's a look I'd never seen on her face before.

I ordered Pierre to follow me to one of the black leather banquettes, where he poured us both red wine while she served the food.

"Gentlemen." She couldn't contain her wide beam as she presented us with the plates, repeating the name of the dish and finishing off with a little bow. "Enjoy your meal."

We both picked up our silverware and stabbed into the food. The minute I shoved the fork into my mouth, I was done for.

Yeah, she was that good.

I knew Pierre thought so, too, by the way his mouth hung open halfway through his bite, looking up at her with hate-filled eyes.

"Too salty," he gritted through his teeth.

"Bullshit," I sneered. "It's excellent."

Her gaze bolted to me, her face opening up with something sincere I probably didn't deserve. She was just as surprised as I was by my compliment. "You think?"

"Yeah." I threw my cloth napkin on the table and stood up. "Tell your culinary class friends your evenings are no longer free. You can start a week from Monday. I'll let Brock know so he can do the paperwork." I turned to Pierre. "Don't give her more than five shifts a week. Make sure she's always stationed doing something meaningful. I don't want her cutting vegetables or working an intern position. You report back to Brock about the new employee, should any difficulties occur. And you..." I nodded toward her. "Ruined that dress. No surprises there. Let's go home."

Pierre jumped to his feet, looking like a heart attack waiting to happen. Judging by his puzzled look, a dozen questions were swimming in his head, but the only thing he seemed to have managed to stutter was, "H-home?"

Her hair smelled of onions and garlic as I dropped my arm around her shoulder, just to see the blood draining from the fat chef's face. But I was surprised when Sparrow's reaction was to wrap her hand around my waist like we were an actual couple. We walked out of the restaurant, and she looked up at me, her eyes bright.

"Stop smiling at me," I said.

She started laughing.

"Cut it," I groaned. Positive attention is the kiss of death to natural born killers. We just don't know how to deal with reassuring feedback.

"I can't!" she giggled. "I can't. I'm sorry. My friend Lucy is going to piss in her pants when she finds out."

For the first time since we got married, I didn't feel the bitterness that accompanied looking at her face. The burden I had to endure when having her around.

We walked into the chilly summer night and I disconnected from her touch. The valet who'd parked my car immediately broke into a run, cutting into the alley where he'd left the Maserati. I gave him a fat tip for the extra hours and for waiting, and ushered Sparrow into the car. She was still laughing like a drunk.

Secretly, I had to admit, her laugh was not that horrible to listen to.

That should have been my first warning that Sparrow wasn't the only one cracking up. Her laugh was not that horrible to listen to. At all.

SEVEN

SPARROW

DRUNK WITH HAPPINESS AND high on bliss, I could barely contain myself during the drive home. The thought of working in the kitchen of a high-end restaurant made me want to break into a silly dance in the middle of the street. I was going to get five shifts a week, which meant my culinary school days were over. But my real career was only just beginning.

Sparrow Raynes. Runner. Summer-air lover. Boyfriend-jeans enthusiast. *Chef.* Hear that, Mom? *Your daughter, the girl you so easily tossed away like an empty soda can, is someone.*

Will be someone.

My imagination went wild. I could gain some experience and then go and do my own thing. Truth be told, I wasn't the fancy-food type of girl. I'd buy a food truck and serve blueberry pancakes to all the suits working in downtown Boston. Be the height of their gray working day. I'd hire Lucy to work alongside me, and maybe Daisy, too. She couldn't bake or cook to save her life, but she was always good with people.

I practically jumped up and down in my seat next to Troy. He shook his head and ignored me for the most part, but occasionally, I'd glance sideways and catch him grinning to himself.

Something in him had cracked. I could feel it, and despite my best intentions to stay away, to protect myself, it stirred something in me. Did he feel it, too? Did he care?

In the elevator, I studied his face, drinking in his reaction. Searching, guessing…

"You care."

"Don't be ridiculous," he scoffed.

Yeah, he definitely cared.

Even though I wasn't tired, I danced my way upstairs and into the bedroom. Troy was left behind to get himself another whiskey and to lock the front door. He had a habit of checking all the rooms in the apartment, looking for God knows what before he went to bed every night. I'd heard him when I was pretending to be asleep.

I guess I, too, should have been worried about my safety, but everything about his security measurements pissed me off.

And especially Connor, my very own guard dog.

I felt Troy enter the bedroom, my back to him, a few minutes later. I was pulling my PJ's out of my drawer, just about to go into the bathroom and change.

The thing about Troy was that he always walked into a room bringing the atmosphere he wanted to convey. Like a human thermostat, he not only controlled every situation, but also the mood you were in. Sometimes he brought anger and rage, sometimes gloom, sometimes terror and very rarely something positive and hopeful.

Tonight, he brought lust.

He took a step toward me, and then another one.

More heat gripped my body. I blamed adrenalin and the damn alcohol— I'd downed three more drinks while Troy and Pierre were tasting my food. The drinks and the rush from my new job were a lethal combination.

Something buzzed in the air, something that made the space between my thighs quiver in response, a pool of heat washing over my lower belly.

I knew if I opened up to him, it would end in tears. The writing was on the wall, the text smeared in blood, no less. *Stay away, Sparrow. Don't let your curiosity get the better of you.*

The floor-to-ceiling windows were fogged with condensation, and my breathing grew heavy. My back still faced him, and I knew that if I turned around, I'd cave. I was holding the top of a six-drawer dresser, the expensive kind, my feet still clad in those goddamned high heels. He closed the space between us and stood behind me, his body pulsing heat at mine, wave after wave.

But he didn't touch me, and somehow, it made me want him even more.

My body froze, legs clenched together in fear and...No. He was corrupted. A monster. *No.*

My mind raced and I struggled to read my own feelings. He said I needed to reciprocate. But also that he wasn't a rapist. That with him, I'd want it. So right. So wrong. I closed my eyes and took a deep breath.

"Bend over," he ordered, his lips pressed behind my ear. I wanted to respond, but felt his fingers already moving down my back, unzipping my dress slowly, deliberately brushing my spine in the process. I leaned forward to take off my heels, and he yanked me closer to his body by my waist, my ass hitting his groin. "Leave them on."

My dress fell on the floor, exposing my simple cotton underwear and matching white strapless bra. I stepped out of the pool of fabric beneath me. He kicked the dress into a pile and, still behind me, trailed one of his long fingers along my collarbone. A shiver tickled my skin, raising goose bumps in its wake.

"Spread your legs."

I did.

He moved away from me for a second. My heart drummed fiercely with anticipation as I placed my palms on the dresser, my body bent and my ass up in the air. I heard something click and watched as his hand snaked from behind my back, reaching over my shoulder. He put his gun on the dresser top in front of me. His holster dropped to the floor with a thud. Still completely and impeccably clothed, he trailed his lips over my neck, just barely touching me.

My skin was on fire and I lowered my head, staring at our feet. I was so needy I thought I'd collapse.

"Hold the dresser real tight unless you want a busted lip. I don't want you hitting something." His hand covered my throat as he pulled me into his face.

I had no sexual experience to speak of. I didn't know what was about to happen. But truthfully, I didn't *not* want it to happen either. If there ever was a good night to do something with Troy, this would be it. Hell, I wanted to experience what other girls were having.

I gripped the edge of the dresser, sucking on my lower lip.

"How's your magical period tonight?" he taunted into my ear.

I moaned, arching my back to meet more of his body. He shoved his huge, warm hand into one of my bra cups, massaging and tugging at my nipple. I groaned, not uttering one word.

"Tell me you don't want this." His tongue flicked over my earlobe as his hand moved down to my stomach, his rough fingers caressing my skin. His mouth traveled down my jawline, stopping inches from my lips. "Tell me that you're not ready yet, that you want me to stop." He nipped the tip of my chin seductively, and my head dropped backward, to his chest.

Suddenly, it felt so hot in the room I was barely able to breathe.

I cleared my throat. "Would it even matter?"

He nodded yes into my shoulder, his firm body pressing into mine. I didn't want him to stop, thought I'd die if his hands left my wanting body, but I hated to admit that he was right. I loathed him but loved his touch.

"Don't stop," I barely whispered, my self-control evaporating.

Troy dropped to his knees behind me, ignoring my silent plea for him to keep teasing my nipples. His head disappeared between my thighs, and then he tipped back his head, pressing his lips upward to my underwear. He kissed my opening through the cotton. A shudder ripped through me, head to toe. I gripped the bureau tighter.

"You've never had oral sex." His voice was silk, traveling the short distance between my thighs to my pussy.

It wasn't a question, so I didn't answer. There was something intoxicating about seeing him below me like this, this powerful man, on his knees for me. His coal black hair contrasting with my white skin, his mouth so hot, so close...

"So this..." His long finger trailed between my folds, over my panties. "Has been waiting for me all this time. Did someone ever touch you there?"

I thought back to that awful day when someone did, despite my pleas, and all the days he did it over and over again after. I shook my head no, fighting my gag reflex. Brennan wouldn't care, and it was too intimate to share with him anyway.

"You're lying," he said, hooking his index fingers into my underwear from each side, his voice suddenly harsh behind me.

Another statement.

His mouth was there again, between my thighs. I squeezed my eyes shut, feeling my legs shaking. Desperate... wanting...falling in lust with this twisted man. One step from grinding my crotch against his face.

"I know how to smell bullshit from miles. So tell me now, who was it?" His warm breath felt good on my skin, especially as I could barely make out his face from that angle and didn't know when it was coming. "Who was stupid enough to mess around with you?"

It sounded peculiar, even insulting—why would a guy be stupid to be with me? But at that moment, logic and thinking weren't the thing on my mind. With my head hanging low, I felt the familiar burn behind my eyes and the lump in my throat.

"Paddy." My voice thickened. "At his wedding. When I went to the girls' room. Paddy Rowan touched me there. And many times after. It became a hobby of his at some point." I swallowed a bitter lump. "I was only nine."

I didn't break down in tears. Instead, I delivered the information like

I was talking about someone else's problems, someone else's sexual abuse. Maybe because I'd hidden it for so long, a part of me almost doubted it had really happened.

After all, no one knew. Not a soul. It went on for nearly a year, and yet, nobody knew. I couldn't tell my father. He was working for Paddy and Cillian back then, and I knew how much he feared them and needed the paycheck. I had to choose between the truth and food on our table. So I kept it to myself.

Until now.

Admitting this to Troy made me feel more naked than I physically was— it was like giving up an imaginary bulletproof vest. A part of me wanted to see if it would push him away. After all, now I was damaged goods. Tainted by his father's right-hand man. Troy's shiny new toy was broken and cracked. Would it put him off? Would he back down? I wanted to know if taking off my armor would inspire him to shoot me where it hurt.

I peeked down to search his face, but he was still behind me.

"What did he do exactly?" He pressed his face to my panties, inhaling gently. He sounded composed and attentive, but clipped. Even though his voice barely gave him away, the sudden twitch of his hand caressing my lower stomach did the job. He was disturbed by what I'd said, but not disgusted by me.

I let out a relieved breath when I realized he wasn't going to be snide or cold about my confession.

Human, after all.

"He..." I didn't want to elaborate, but not seeing his face when I spoke about it was liberating. So was getting this secret off my chest. "He didn't rape me. But he was violent. He shoved his fingers into me. He was drunk, and I was small. Paddy was one of my father's bosses. I didn't want to make a scene."

More silence. Not the judging kind, though.

I released my breath, shaking my head. "I'm a little drunk. My normal self would never share something like this with you," I admitted. "Let's just drop it, okay? I just want to mess around tonight."

Troy spun me around by my waist to face him. Still on his knees, he kissed each of my pubic bones, his firm hands keeping me in place. I think I might have loved him in that particular moment. Just for a second. For listening. For being there. For not being terrible for once, even though it was in his DNA. In his nature.

"Is that why you've never slept with anyone?" he asked.

I shook my head. "I don't think so. I just...never got around to it." I knew this wasn't exactly dirty talk between the sheets. Thankfully, I didn't spend too much time worrying about trying to impress my new husband.

His eyes pinned me to the dresser, trying to estimate how upset I was. There was no need for that. Paddy happened a long time ago, and I was ready now. Ready for more of those kisses all over my sensitive area.

"I won't make you do anything you don't want to do, Red." His voice was grave. "But I feel like it is my duty as a husband and a human being to tell you, sex can be great. Giving up on it just because one asshole..." He grunted his last sentence, pressing his face to my stomach and shutting his eyes, "Or even because we don't see eye to eye—it's a big mistake. You can hate me and still love how I make you feel."

His eyes dropped back to my white panties, and he tugged them down to my knees, kissing the spot just above my slit gently. He then parted me carefully with both thumbs, leaning forward and inhaling me with his eyes shut. It was slightly embarrassing...but incredibly arousing.

My eyes met his as my hand brushed through his hair, so implausibly soft in comparison to the tough man it belonged to. I stepped out of the panties. "I know," I exhaled. "I don't want you to stop what you're doing."

He pressed his mouth to my center. Darting his tongue out, he explored me, every bit of me, building anticipation. I felt wetness pool inside me and leaned onto the dresser behind me, trying to stay upright. It was only then that his mouth sought—and found—my bundle of sensitive nerves and sucked on it, long and hard, building and releasing pressure like he was pumping a delicious drug into me.

I moaned and fisted his hair, tugging, urging him to continue. Everything tingled. My toes curled inside the high heels. I rolled my hips forward, wiggling out of his strong arms around my waist and wanting, searching, aching for more.

Troy sucked on my clit and pulled it between his teeth, applying more pressure. "Stand still," he commanded, his hands roaming my body.

Stomach, hips, inner thighs…

"God, I missed eating pussy," he sighed into me. "And you're so delicious and tight."

I blushed, smiling to myself. At least he didn't do this to everyone. That made me feel stupidly special.

Troy ate me alive, making happy noises throughout. Little grunts and moans that told me he was enjoying this no less than I was. It was probably the first time I ever saw him happy, licking the length of me, sucking on my sensitive part and pumping his tongue in and out of me. He draped one of my thighs over his shoulder, digging his head deeper between my legs, and I threw my head back and cried out his name.

He stopped sucking and slid his tongue into me, in and out, in and out. My vision clouded, my body shook all over. Even though the sensation was insane, it also felt like he was playing with my body and refusing to take it over the edge. He was teasing me, but every time I got closer to tipping over, an orgasm threatening to tear me from the inside out, he slowed down. On purpose.

"Please," I panted, not really sure what I was asking.

"Please, what?" he urged.

That was a good question. I could see the gates of heaven open up, but Troy wouldn't let me walk through.

Unable to form a coherent sentence, I kept on pulling his hair almost violently. When he picked up the pace pumping his tongue into me, and I literally saw stars. My knees finally gave in and I buckled, collapsing down on him. He hit the beige carpet with a thud.

"That's better." Troy put his hands on my waist to root me into place. "Ride my face, Red. Now…you were saying?"

"Make me come." I panted harder, shamelessly grinding myself against his mouth. God, I would never be able to look at him again after knowing his tongue was buried so deep inside me.

He smiled into me—I actually felt it, shuddering violently against his lips—and went slower, licking more thoroughly and gently, while shoving one hand back into my bra, pinching my nipple hard. The bastard.

"I hate you." I let out a grunt, meaning to rise and stand up from this delicious torture, but he jerked me back into his face, laughing into my core. His laugh vibrated inside my body. He was getting off on my frustration.

"Let me go," I hissed.

"Say the magic word," he answered, amused.

"Asshole." I threw my head back, both turned on and exasperated. I was still riding his face, and had a feeling I would be, for hours, if I didn't put a stop to it.

Holy Jesus. Riding his face? My mind was filthy around this man, and I had absolutely zero filters when it came down to what I wanted him to do to me.

"That's not the magic word. Beg me..." He dragged his tongue along my slit from top to bottom. "And I'll let you come."

"Keep dreaming," I moaned.

His sucking became more intense, and he bit on my throbbing clit. My fingers dug into his skin.

"Beg," he repeated. "Say what you want to say."

It was tempting, but I couldn't let go of my ego, of my sliver of self-control around him. We were not on the same team. Just because he indulged me tonight, didn't mean he'd acknowledge my existence tomorrow morning.

"No," I answered again.

He laughed long and hard, drunk on my resistance, loving that I hated his game. He spread my legs so I was wide open in front of him, took my clit in his mouth again and rubbed my entrance with his thumb in delicious up and down movements.

This time I knew I was really on the edge. All I needed were a few more strokes. I didn't know what was going to happen with Troy, but I knew it would be worth more than the begging. It was magic. It was giving your body to someone else, feeling every single one of your muscles tighten deliciously, feeling a swell of pleasure about to overtake you like a tsunami…

"Beg," he demanded one more time, and I knew it'd be the last.

"No."

His wet lips left my skin as he dragged his body up so he could kiss my lips, inserting his tongue into my mouth and swirling it teasingly, forcing me to taste myself.

"This was fun." His throaty voice tickled me, and I felt shattered. I wanted to come so badly. "Now let's see how long you can manage without begging me to be balls deep in you. I like a challenge."

"Good, 'cause you're in for an impossible one." My teeth chattered from the impact of his touch, but at least I managed a comeback.

He gave me another deep, intoxicating kiss, darting his tongue and twirling it over my lower lip. I felt his smile.

"Your spine…" He ran his index finger along my back. "Is beautiful. And here, I thought I could snap you like a twig."

He propped himself up, leaving me to lie there on the floor, naked other than my bra and heels, as he walked out of the room unaffected, like nothing happened.

A chill gripped my body when I felt his footfalls in the hallway, echoing on the bedroom floor. He opened a door down the hall, probably his study, and banged it shut after him.

The pit of my stomach turned, worry and anxiety swirling inside. I buried my face in the crook of my elbow.

He could still snap me like a twig. He'd just decided not to…*this time*.

EIGHT

TROY

THERE WAS NOTHING MORE dangerous than a person with nothing to lose. That's why I'd hired Sparrow to work at Rouge Bis, even though I knew she'd be close to *him*.

I wasn't the controlling kind when it came to women. With my business, hell yes. But with a woman? If my wife wanted to work and was good at what she was doing, she can bust her ass for all I cared.

And Sparrow? She'd turned out to be a breath of fresh air. I was so used to the women around me not working or even entertaining the radical idea of doing something with their lives that I was genuinely surprised with how much Red wanted to work at the restaurant.

Love and compassion had nothing to do with my decision to give Sparrow a job. Having her out of the apartment occasionally might be nice. Her wicked smart mouth and endless questions grated on my nerves. Plus, putting a smile on her face wasn't the worst idea I'd ever had.

I had to admit, the taste of her pussy in my mouth was fucking amazing.

Not sure if it was the thrill of tasting what's mine, only mine, pure and untouched before (other than that asshole, Paddy) or if it'd been so long since I went down on a woman that I forgot it was literally sweet. Either way, I'd enjoyed watching her as she crashed down, so close but not there. I wanted to snap that little spine of hers. Have her begging. Leave her wanting and lusting. Wanted to prove to her that she wanted me no less than I wanted her.

Well, her body, anyway.

But now I had to take matters into my own hands, so to speak. Bring my body down to a sensible temperature.

I hadn't jerked off in maybe fifteen years, but when I leaned with one hand against the glossy black tiles, under the stream of scorching water, masturbating like a fucking teenager, I admitted it was oddly exciting. I laughed to myself like a madman as my hand relearned how to pump hard and fast to the beat of my new fantasies. *Sparrow*. Sweet, fucking Sparrow. Tight, lean, intelligent, annoying Red…

I'd forgotten how good it felt to want something and not get it in a matter of hours.

I pumped harder, faster, imagining her legs wrapped around me. I came in my hand, squeezing the warm cum between my fingers, thinking about how good it'd feel to shoot my load inside her.

Yearning.

I hadn't felt it in forever, and now it was growing on me.

And so was the thought of her warming my bed.

I BURNED THE REST OF the weekend doing fun stuff, like drinking in my study, plotting to destroy Rowan and thinking about eating my wife.

Brock's weekend, meanwhile, seemed to have left him drained and irritated. A bonus, as far as I was concerned.

On Monday, he walked into his office at Rouge Bis—no, fuck that, *my* office. I was the one who footed the bill for the place. Not that he saw it that way. He stood in the doorway, his arms crossed over his chest, eying the glass desk as if I'd invaded his space.

"You look like shit." I spat out my toothpick and wheeled the office chair backward so I could take a better look at him. "Rough night with the missus?" I cocked an eyebrow.

"Fuck you."

I smirked. He and Catalina weren't fucking nowadays.

I nodded at the chair in front of the desk, inviting him to sit down. He tugged at his breast pocket, fishing out a pack of smokes, his ass hitting the seat. He lit a cigarette, inhaling deeply and exhaling through his nose. The way he held the cigarette, between his index finger and thumb, like he was Clint Eastwood in a Western, made me want to laugh out loud. Instead, I glowered quietly.

"Smoking inside this building is prohibited." I pointed to a sign saying just that behind me, barely containing my glee.

"So is every single thing you do, Troy. Don't give me shit. I've had a rough morning. You needed me?" he asked.

"Trouble in paradise?" I tilted my chin toward the cigarette that hung in the corner of his mouth. Fuck, I bathed in his misery like it was pure water in the Sahara desert.

Brock sucked hard on the cig. This time his mouth hung open after he exhaled, a swirl of smoke traveling upwards. "Cat treats Sam like dirt." He ran a hand over his hair. "This morning, he went to school wearing filthy clothes because she's decided he's not worth doing the laundry for. I almost flipped when he tugged at his shirt, seconds before I dropped him off, sniffing it to make sure he didn't smell too bad. He said that he didn't want kids to make fun of him. Man, this is the kind of shit that breaks your heart."

He rubbed his eyes, continuing before he realized it was me he was confiding in. He must've been desperate. "Anyway, I did a U-turn. We ended up buying fresh clothes at Target, and he changed in the bathroom before I dropped him off. Spent the next thirty minutes sitting in my car in front of his school, practicing this stupid-ass breathing exercise from that tape you bought me for Christmas."

I almost snorted. This was too much. The only reason I'd given him the tape was to piss Catalina off. She was whining like a bitch about Brock being too good and proper. It was a joke aimed at him. And he'd walked right into it.

Brock looked up at me, searching for my response.

I eased back into his soft leather chair and knitted my fingers together. "Some piece of work, your wife is. If you ask me, I always preferred the single life."

"You're married now," he reminded me.

"I guess sometimes it's easy to forget," I said through my smirk.

He lolled his head sideways, stubbing the cigarette into an empty mug with a picture of him and Cat. Something she gave him to remind me of her every time I walked into his office.

It was cute how she thought I cared.

"I'm guessing you're not here to discuss my marital problems." Brock leaned forward, elbows propped on his knees, and tapped his fingertips. "Why are you here, Troy?"

"Patrick Rowan." I cut straight to the chase, looking out the window, people-watching as I spoke. "I wanna know what ties he has left in Boston."

Brock raised his brows, throwing himself back and sighing loudly. He didn't like this turn of events, and I had no idea why. Rowan, my father's right hand before everything flushed down the shitter, was just an old washed-up mobster. He'd kept the gambling piece of my father's empire alive for him for a while even after my dad was dethroned, but eventually Paddy had branched out on his own. He'd high-tailed it out of the state to Miami when the Armenians decided they wanted his head on a plate. I discovered why a few months after my father was killed.

Yeah, Rowan had left enemies everywhere, but on Friday night, he'd made one too many of them in the form of me.

"Rowan?" He frowned. "Why?"

My jaw tightened when I thought about the answer to this question. Did I still hold a grudge against Rowan for stealing money from my father years ago? Sure. Did the fact that he touched my wife act as an incentive to finally seek retaliation? Hell yes. Was I in the mood to watch bad people paying for their sins? You fucking bet.

I'd hit a dead-end with my *Kill Bill* list, still not sure who sent Crupti to kill my father, and I wanted to play. Dealing with Rowan might take off the edge.

"Find out how to contact his second wife." I ignored Brock's question.

"What crawled up your ass? Got a new beef with Rowan all of a sudden? He's rotting of cancer, you know. Leave him alone. You're beating a dead horse."

"Not dead enough for me," I countered, picking up my own cell and punching the touch screen furiously. "I'm going to pay him a visit in Miami."

"Are you sure? I'm not feeling comfortable about you harassing a guy who is dying of cancer."

"I'm not paying you to feel comfortable, Brock. I'm paying you to follow orders."

He stood up with thunder in his eyes, about to storm out of the room, when he stopped in his tracks. "Is he the guy who sent Crupti?" His voice cracked as he half turned.

Brock knew I was after the anonymous motherfucker, even had helped me seek him out.

"Just do as I asked. By the way…" I cleared my throat, avoiding the stream of *hellos* coming from my phone and watching Brock intently. "I hired my wife to work at Rouge Bis. Get whatever paperwork you need together for her. She's starting next week. Make sure she and the chef don't stab each other's eyes out with a spatula."

He turned back to face me. There was something unsettling underneath those gray eyes, and I wanted to rip them out of their sockets just to find out what.

"She's going to work? Right here?" He glanced sideways, like there were hidden cameras watching him.

I nodded slowly. He knew that we had an arranged marriage, or marriage of inconvenience, or whatever the fuck Sparrow and I were.

He also knew why Sparrow was so important to my father.

I shrugged into my Armani suit jacket, looking bored with the topic. "She was nagging. Who the fuck cares anyway. If she wants to bust her ass instead of living a life of luxury, it's her grave."

"Mmm." Brock scanned me, searching my face. "So, the tension is high between you two?"

"Not that it's any of your business, but no. We're fine."

"And Pierre? He gave her trouble?"

"Who?" I didn't even bother to pretend to recall the name, then remembered I still had my travel agent on the line. I swiveled the chair so my back was to Brock and waved him off, dismissing him like he was an average-looking day-shift stripper ogling me for tips. "Yes, I'd like to purchase two first class tickets to Miami..."

NINE

SPARROW

THE SUN WAS SHINING ON MONDAY morning when I arrived at Quincy Market, but the improved weather tense did little to improve my mood. I had no idea what made me do what I did with Brennan on Friday night.

Lapse of judgment on my part, but who could blame me? He was basically the only guy who'd tried to touch me in God knows how long, and let's face it, he was so hot the temperature in the penthouse soared every time he entered the room. True, he was also cruel—a savage in a tailored suit— but at the same time, he'd never hurt me.

Not physically, anyway.

My fear radar, sharpened by a tough neighborhood, had impeccable instincts when it came to danger. With Troy, I felt safe.

Nonetheless, the pressure between my legs was a constant reminder that my husband was an asshole. Who did a thing like that? Was it even allowed? Shouldn't it be illegal in a modern Western society to stop someone from climaxing after getting her to a point where everything was tingling with pain, pleasure and lust?

The weird sensation lingered throughout the weekend. My unfinished business left me craving more, and the nagging feeling I had down there made a small part of me want to beg Troy like he had asked. Luckily, the bigger, saner part of me remembered he still had a lot of questions to answer before we'd be on good terms.

There was one thing he was right about, though. Regardless of what I thought about him as a person, I craved him like a crackhead.

Troy Brennan was the devil, but sometimes, even good girls wanted a healthy dose of evil in their lives.

He'd spent Saturday and Sunday mostly holed up in his office, but this morning I'd hoped to try and make him breakfast again. Stupid, I knew, but feigning emotional attachment made what we did together seem less dirty. More real. But by the time I woke up after another night of tossing and turning, he'd already left for work.

Whatever *work* meant in his world.

I was almost glad I'd rescheduled my plans to meet Lucy and Daisy, my childhood (and essentially only) friends, and agreed to join them for late morning coffee. Anything was better than another day in the empty apartment. Well, empty except for Connor, that is.

Lucy and Daisy waited for me on our usual bench, sharing a box of donuts and coffee. Lucy, a plump, pretty chick with curly blonde hair and freckles like mine, cradled the donut box as protectively as a newborn baby. Daisy was holding our foam cups. Daisy used to work in a strip club not too long ago. Men dug her raven black hair, shapely legs and impressive bust. She reminded me a little of Catalina. A less bitchy version of her, anyway.

Lucy and Daisy got along like the Starks and the Lannisters, meaning they were at each other's throats every time I wasn't looking, but they kept things civilized for my sake. Each of us had her own reason for being lonesome and together. We were all outcasts, but at least we had each other.

The minute my friends spotted me, they got up from the bench and threw their arms over my shoulders. Daisy placed a cup of hot chocolate in my hand. I was always the only one not to drink coffee.

Lucy tucked the donut box under her arm and brushed a few strands of red hair off of my forehead, inspecting my face. "Are you okay?"

My cheeks heated, and I hid the lower part of my face behind the foam cup. I'd taken off my engagement ring and wedding band minutes before I got out of Connor's car, but somehow still felt them on my finger. Guilt gnawed at my gut, but I tried not to squirm.

When I didn't answer, Lucy and Daisy exchanged meaningful looks and frowned in unison.

"Where do you live nowadays?" Lucy shoved the donut box into my chest, daring me to lie.

Well, that was fast. Not even a *Hello, how have you been?*

"Home," I said, trying to muster some conviction. "At Pops's."

I had no idea where I was going with this. There was no plan, other than vehement denial or breaking down in tears and admitting to everything, or maybe stalling by hyperventilating.

"You never seem to be there." Daisy narrowed her eyes, her glossy lips pouting in disapproval.

I started walking deeper among the tourists and locals, passing stands and people. I wasn't planning on buying anything but time that day. Time was all I needed to figure out how to break the news to my girlfriends.

"Gee, thanks for the vote of trust." My mouth twisted. "You think I'm hiding something?"

"I *know* you're hiding something." Lucy cocked her head to one side before pointing her thumb in the other direction. "And I was hoping you could start by shedding some light on why that six foot giant is following you. And don't tell me that you haven't noticed him, because you kept glancing his way before you saw us sitting on the bench."

I silently cursed Connor. He was following me 24/7 and being about as discreet about it as Paul Revere announcing the British are coming. But I couldn't explain Connor, because I couldn't explain my marriage to Troy, because I didn't understand it myself. My friends knew my dad was not exactly Father-of-the-Year material, but even I found it difficult to tell them I suspected he'd sold me to the son of a dead mobster.

"I don't wanna talk about it," I said.

"No shit." Daisy threw her hands in the air.

A bunch of kids in matching shirts on a fieldtrip ran between our feet, and I used my friends' distraction to look behind me. Connor was there, still following me like I was a moving target.

Lucy, the voice of reason among the three of us, spun on her heel and sent him a threatening glare. "Take another step forward, buddy, and I'm calling the cops."

But Connor continued flowing with the crowd, doggedly moving in the same direction as us, his eyes dead. With every step he took, my lies suffocated me a little more, the walls inching closer in on me. The box Troy put me in was becoming ridiculously small, even for a petite girl like me.

"Is he a bodyguard? Are you in trouble?" Daisy panted as Lucy quickened her pace and we followed suit. "And more importantly…is he single?"

I shook my head, snorting a tired sigh. I wasn't in the mood for jokes.

Lucy was power-walking away from Connor as fast as she could. "Please tell me your dad didn't get you into trouble."

I stopped walking and stared down at my Keds. There was no more point in hiding what they'd pretty much already figured out. I was stupid to try and hide it from them in the first place.

"Don't freak out," I warned.

"The bastard." Lucy strangled the donut box she carried and swung toward my bodyguard. I hoped she wouldn't do something stupid like try and hurl a chocolate glazed at him. She would, too. If I was fire, she was an active volcano.

"It's not Pops's fault."

"Fine," Lucy backtracked. "No judging. Just tell us already."

"I married Troy Brennan last week. He…he asked my father for my hand and Pops agreed. Probably because he didn't have much choice. You know they say Troy is some kind of a hitman. A wealthy one, at that. And Pops works for him, so…" I trailed off.

Lucy and Daisy stared at me, bugged-eyed. The three of us stood in the middle of the crowds, with people pushing and shoving us from all directions.

"Sorry I didn't tell you sooner. It's not really a piece of info you want to share with the world. And the last thing I wanted was to drag you into this mess."

I thought Lucy was going to faint, but Daisy gathered her senses quickly. "But we grew up with Troy Brennan. He never looked at you that way. Never even tried to slip his tip in."

I frowned, annoyed as usual at the way my childhood friend spoke about the opposite sex. Well, about sex in general. "You can like someone without sleeping with them, you know. It's not like he screwed everyone in South Boston."

Daisy fanned herself. "Bitch, please. With the amount of pussy your husband's dick has trekked through, I'm surprised it doesn't have its own National Geographic show. He is so…mature and old and stuff. Your husband, that is, not his dick." She licked her lips, thinking. "Wait. Birdie, this makes you rich!"

Rubbing my face, I checked to make sure Connor wasn't close enough to have heard her. Daisy was too much of a free spirit to offer comfort. She took everything in stride, even when the circumstances demanded some serious running. I turned from her to my best friend. "Lucy, please say something."

Lucy looked away from me, gripping the edge of a stand and nearly toppling a display of sand art. Her eyes glinted with sadness, the tightly bunched muscles in her neck telling me the lump in her throat was as big as mine.

I threw my hot chocolate in the trash and grabbed her hand, desperate for her touch. It was silly, but I was feeling all sorts of guilty for not inviting them to my fake wedding, now that I had told them about it.

"Birdie, honey, he is…you know that people say he killed a man?" she mumbled.

I nodded. "Yeah, I know, but rumors run marathons in small

neighborhoods."

"It may not be what you want to hear, but you should be scared," Lucy said. "Terrified, to be exact."

"You would think so." I managed to muster a faint smile. "But he won't hurt me. I've gotten to know him a little. He's not like that."

"Okay, so he's not going to hurt you," Daisy said, "but the rest doesn't make any sense. How does he go from unattainable lady killer to someone who forces a girl he doesn't even know to marry him?"

I had the same nagging question in my mind.

"No offence, Birdie," Daisy continued, "but Troy Brennan has one of the hottest asses in Boston. They say he's a beast in bed, and he's done well for himself financially. Why would he pick you? He could have anyone he wants."

"Thanks." Leave it to a friend to tell you the truth.

"I still say you should be scared," Lucy argued.

My head felt like it was ten times heavier than it was when I first arrived. It was bad enough to deal with what Troy stirred in my head, what he kindled in my body. And now the Paddy stuff was out in the open. I had so many fires to put out, it felt like my whole life had burst into disastrous flames.

"Look, he is not that bad." I exhaled, walking again to put some distance between us and Connor. I didn't want him to listen to this conversation. "And he's the owner of Rouge Bis. I'm going to start working there next Monday. I'm sure it will all be okay."

It was anything but.

"Does he not trust you? Is that why you have a bodyguard?" Lucy squinted over her shoulder at Connor.

I shook my head. "I'm allowed to do whatever I want. I think the guard is to keep me safe from all the *nice* friends he's collected over the years." I offered a sad smile.

"Protecting you? That's actually kind of hot," Daisy mused. "How's he in the sack, by the way?"

I sometimes wondered if she knew life wasn't some big, ongoing sexual joke.

"Daisy!" Lucy swatted her shoulder. "Birdie isn't going to sleep with him just because her poor excuse of a father sold her to him."

I felt my skin heat again as I buried my lower face inside my jacket. I enjoyed the night of our date more than I was willing to admit.

Lucy turned to me, her face twisting with dismay. "Jesus Christ. Don't tell me—"

"Of course I didn't sleep with him," I said, cutting her off.

"Not that it would be the worst thing in the world," Daisy interjected. "A few of my friends rolled between his sheets. Rumor is The Fixer can fix you up with multiple orgasms and is into some pretty kinky shit." She stopped, picking up a bottle of perfume and examining it with interest, popping her pink gum loudly.

She was completely oblivious to the fact Lucy and I wanted to get rid of Connor. Lucy took the bottle from her and grabbed her arm, tugging her along.

"Geez, what's the rush?" Daisy flipped back her glossy hair.

"So, did he make you sign a prenup, or what?" Lucy asked, always the practical one.

I moved my jaw back and forth. I hadn't considered it before. "No," I said, as surprised as Lucy was to hear my answer.

"Really?" Daisy looked intrigued.

Lucy glanced behind us and dropped her voice down when she saw Connor was just a few feet away. "I'm pretty sure the guy's loaded. Heard he's living in Back Bay."

"He is," I confirmed, "and he drives a Maserati."

Daisy nodded. "I'll bet his dad left him a couple of trust funds and a ton of real estate before he was murdered and dumped in the woods. I dunno, Birdie. If he didn't make you sign a prenup, looks like he's planning to keep ya."

I opened my mouth, just about to answer, when I felt a strong hand grip my elbow and pull me out of the throng.

Lucy's spine straightened, and she spun in my direction, knocking into a woman pushing a stroller. A diaper bag spilled at her feet.

I turned to face the person the hand belonged to. *Connor.*

He'd never touched me before. His face was expressionless, and a cell phone was suddenly glued to his ear. He was nodding and kept repeating my name. *Shit.* I'd talked about Troy and now I was going to pay for it. I knew my mouth was going to get me into trouble the minute he told me he'd marry me.

Stupid you, Sparrow. Why couldn't you just accept your fate?

"What's your problem?" I asked him, realizing it was one of the rare times we'd spoken.

I was scared and angry, and the last thing I wanted was to involve Daisy and Lucy after my claims about Troy not being so bad. Connor worked for Troy, and he'd grabbed me like I was a teen caught sneaking out of her room at night.

"Should I call nine one one?" Lucy asked. Daisy's mouth rounded in an O.

"No, it's fine. I just need to go. I'll text you later."

I let Connor lead me away, giving them a wave and forcing a smile, but as soon as I was sure we were out of sight, I jerked hard on my arm.

Connor grunted and held tight, hustling me, with a little force and a lot of determination, through the shoppers and sightseers. People were looking, and I felt self-conscious to the point of horror. I couldn't let him drag me around like a rag doll without him even explaining where we were going.

"Let go of me," I hissed, trying to wriggle free.

Connor stared ahead and continued walking. As if I was a piece of furniture he had to move from one point to the other. "Yes, boss," he barked into his cell, pacing faster, "she'll be there before takeoff."

"Get your hands off of me. I mean it," I demanded.

Wait, *takeoff?*

What the hell did Troy have in store for me now? I was really in no mood to find out. I was done playing nice with Troy's crew.

I jerked my arm hard enough to catch Connor off guard and ran in the opposite direction of both him and my friends. Since running was my passion and Connor was about as wide as he was tall, outrunning him in the crowd was easier than I hoped. I was half way to the street I wanted before I twisted my head to see if he was behind me.

I saw his pink, furious face as he tried to catch up. I picked up my pace, worried about what Lucy and Daisy might be thinking after that little scene. They probably thought I was going to get killed or something. And maybe they weren't so wrong.

I cut into a side street, where the pavement narrowed and bumped into a wide shoulder full force. The impact propelled me backward, but a warm hand steadied me, righting me before I hit the ground.

Brock.

I shook my arm free of him. "He sent you, too?" I seethed, feeling my body temperature rising. *Goddammit, Troy Brennan.*

"What?" Brock looked puzzled. "Sparrow, I'm here to do some shopping with my son. Kindergarten is only half-day and I decided to take the afternoon off. No one sent me. Is something wrong?"

I glanced over my shoulder. Connor was getting close, waving his fist in the air like he was about to break me to pieces. And Sam was right there as well, clutching his father's palm and looking at me like I'd gone completely mad.

"Oh, hi." I looked down at him and forced a reassuring smile.

"Hi." He nuzzled into his dad's pants leg shyly.

"Okay, gotta run." I was anxious to resume my escape. My heart slammed against my chest when Brock grasped my shoulder.

"Don't run," he said. "Connor is an idiot, but he's not going to hurt you, even if he certainly looks like he'd like to. I know why he's after you, and I can promise you, it's not something bad. Do you trust me?"

His hand was still on my shoulder. I blinked. Did I trust him? Why would I? I don't know anything about this man, other than the fact that he looked like the closest thing to Adonis.

"Umm, no," I answered honestly.

He laughed, the kind of laughter that you felt dancing in the pit of your stomach, even though you weren't the one who laughed. I eased, my muscles relaxing.

"That's right," he said, looking at his son. "Never trust strangers, Sam." He patted Sam's brown hair, and then he pulled me into a sudden hug.

I froze, but this wasn't an intimate embrace.

"Listen," he whispered, his mouth close to my ear. "You're starting a new chapter in your life. I promise you, I'll do everything I can to make you feel at home at Rouge Bis. Go back with Connor. Go to Troy, but make sure not to get too involved with him. Lay low, play your part, and I'll make it worth your while. Deal?"

I felt the tears I'd held inside for so long threaten to spill, but raised my chin. "You're doing it again. Being nice to me. You're *his* friend."

"No, Sparrow, I'm not." His voice was even lower now, almost inaudible. "I'm on *his* payroll. That's all."

When he released me, Connor was already too close for me to run again.

Brock's expression changed to unruffled, and he gave me a light shove in Connor's direction. "I think you've lost something. Here, she is."

I stumbled straight into Connor's arms.

Flushed, confused, and most of all, angry as hell, my bodyguard scanned Brock up and down. "She ran," he spat.

"That tends to happen when people have legs." Brock's tone was clipped. Tough. *Different.* Like Troy. "Don't let it happen again."

He turned around and walked away, holding Sam's little hand without sparing me a second glance. I knew right there that Brock was playing a game in front of his boss and his crew.

I needed to start doing the same, if I was going to survive Troy Brennan.

"You stupid little banshee," Connor growled. He was panting like he had just completed a Tour de France.

This time he grabbed me harder by the arm, He'd been caught losing me, and it looked like his fury had boiled to a point he couldn't control. He shook me aggressively just for kicks, then shook me more as he led me God knows where.

I was almost relieved when I spotted the car he'd driven me here in. *Almost.* I ducked my head and dodged a bruise as he threw me into the passenger seat like I was his duffel bag.

By the time, I righted myself, he was already behind the wheel and starting the engine. "What the hell is wrong with you?" I demanded.

He just pumped the gas in response, to spite me.

"Where are you taking me?" I tried again.

"Back home," he answered. "You need to pack. You're leaving for Miami."

My throat tightened. "Miami? Why? When? For how long?"

Connor kept on staring at the road. He looked fed up, gripping the steering wheel like he wished it was my neck. "Ask your husband," he said through clenched teeth.

I decided to do just that. I sent a quick text to Daisy and Lucy, claiming there'd been an emergency at Rouge Bis and that I was needed in the kitchen. Hopefully that would reassure them for now. Then I turned my attention to dialing Troy.

I realized that I didn't even have my husband's phone number. Up until now, I hadn't really thought about it. The idea of trying to reach him was so absurd, it never occurred to me that I might need to ask him something at some point. I looked outside the window, then at Connor, then out again. Was I really going to ask my husband's employee for his phone number?

Then again, I had too many questions: Why Miami? Why now? Was he sending me alone or coming with? *Plane!* I was going to fly on a plane! How long was the flight? How long were we going to stay? Was this our honeymoon?

That one stopped me cold.

So what if Brock told me it was safe. Tons of things, bad things, could happen to me.

I was *not* going to Miami, I decided. The car stopped at a red light, and I opened my side of the car, determined, ready to run, but Connor grabbed my arm, his fingers digging deep into my skin. I felt the air leaving my lungs as I tried to contain the white-hot pain.

He was hurting me. On purpose.

"Let go!" I yelled.

"You're coming with me," he said, leaning across me to yank my door shut and then leaning back, only to hit the gas.

I didn't think. I just hurled my cell phone at him. It hit him in the side of the face and dropped into his lap. Blood trickled from his nose down to his chin. He swiped it away silently, glancing sideways at me, glaring like he wanted to kill me. I knew he probably would have, if it weren't for his boss.

My heart began to pound as my cell bleeped with a new message.

"Give it to me." I motioned for the phone between his legs. "I swear to God, Connor, you better do it now."

He continued to weave through the traffic. It was an idle threat, and he knew it. I had nothing to fight him with, no way to escape. He'd locked the doors and engaged the child safety locks.

"Here," he said, surprising me and offering me my phone.

When I read Lucy's text, my heart beat so fast I almost felt it leaping out of my throat.

Lucy: *Tell me I don't need to call the police about this.*

With shaky fingers, I wrote back: *I can handle it myself. The joy of being a mobster's wife, y'know. Speak later. x*

I wasn't sure whether it was bold or stupid, but that was the moment when I realized that it was true. I was going to handle Troy and Connor myself.

And I was going to find my freedom, my happiness, inside this golden cage.

TEN

TROY

I NEEDED TO GET MY ASS TO Miami ASAP, and I'd decided to take Sparrow with me. Paddy had been dying of cancer for a few months now, and rumor on the street was he wasn't going to make it through the summer. Debt had to be collected and paid, and revenge was about to be served, cold and punitive.

It felt only fitting that Sparrow was there, even if she had no idea what I had planned. Plus, I didn't trust her alone in Boston.

I was packing my suitcase when Cat showed up at my bedroom door, leaning her shoulder against its frame, wearing nothing but a suggestive smile and her fuck-me black dress that was tight like an undersized condom. Her eyes on me felt like a lap dance not worthy of the fat tip. I fought an eye roll.

"Hey, baby," she rasped, licking her bright red lips. I kept my eyes on the suitcase I was filling, wide open on the bed. "Mom told me your wife's out and Brock picked up Sam from school to take him shopping, so I thought I'd drop by to say hi."

What the fuck was up with Brock. *Shopping?* I'd given him a job to do.

"What do you want?" My voice was clipped.

"You, mainly." She took a step into the bedroom, the echo of her heels click-clacking on the marble floor sending shivers of annoyance down my back.

The bitch had no right to be here. She clasped me from behind, her hands roaming over my chest as she rested her forehead between my shoulder blades. Her flowery perfume attacked my nostrils, hanging in the air like a tasteless joke.

"Where are you going, Troy? For how long?"

I didn't answer, reaching down and zipping the suitcase. Red was supposed to get back home any minute. I'd called Connor and told him to bring her in immediately. I fucking hated it when Maria let her daughter into my apartment just because she could, especially as Maria couldn't tell her daughter no about anything. I made a mental note to take my housekeeper's head off for this.

"You need to come see me on Friday. We have an arrangement," she pressed.

I turned around to face her, buttoning my white dress shirt. "Brock seems pretty pissed off with you. You acting up again?"

She pouted like a kid, but didn't answer.

"This…" I pointed between us. "Is just fucking around. Don't you forget that. Invest more time with your family."

Her chin started quivering, but instead of crying, her face broke into a coy grin. "But you *are* my family, baby."

Her hand reached down to cup my balls and I raised an eyebrow, grabbing her wrist and twisting it behind her back. Even though I didn't physically hurt her, I wanted to make a point.

I brushed my lips against hers and growled into her face. "Tell your mother that next time she lets you into my apartment without my permission, you're both walking out of here with one of my shoes shoved into each of your sorry asses. Understood?"

Cat's cleavage bumped into my lower chest, and I felt her rocking against me blatantly. Such a fucking trainwreck. Not an ounce of self-control.

"Since when do you give a flying fuck about Brock? About my family?" She grazed her teeth over my chin seductively, her tongue trailing down my neck. "C'mon, baby. There's no way in hell Pippi Longstocking keeps you busy between those sheets. Look how neat they are. I doubt she even shares that bed with you."

I grabbed her by the hair and spun her, throwing her against the wall face-first and grinding against her curvy ass from behind. "You better shut your pipe," I snarled into her ear. "It's never been too good for anything other than sucking cock, and even that is growing old."

Catalina threw her head back against my chest and laughed hysterically. "You didn't even fuck her yet, did you? Oh, how I wish I could have seen the look on her sweet little face when she unwrapped the gift that I bought for her." Her ass slammed into my erection. "I'll wear it for you, baby. All the leather and garters in the world."

"You're crazy." My impatience and anger felt sour on my tongue. "Have you relapsed?"

"I'm as sober as a nun. I just came to remind you that you're still mine." Cat snaked her hand behind the small of her back to grab my cock through my pants.

She couldn't have been more wrong. I wasn't hers. Never had been. Never will be.

Not again.

But she was right about one thing. I didn't sleep with my own wife. The woman who I took into my house, who slept in my bed, who I have given a job and bought tickets to Miami for.

And it pissed the shit out of me.

"Forget about her," she purred. "She'll never be yours."

"Bitch."

I flipped the hem of her dress up and ripped her panties in one sharp movement, leaving a red trail of on her skin. Her ass was round and golden brown, perfect, unlike Sparrow's small and white one. But I still closed my eyes, and for whatever fucked-up reason, pretended that this was my wife as I unzipped.

I rode Cat from behind, my balls slapping against her ass, like I was spanking the venom out of this vile woman. Soon enough, devil woman started moaning as loud as she possibly could, no doubt to make sure Sparrow would hear if she walked in downstairs. I balled her ripped panties in my fist and shoved them in her mouth to muffle the sound of her whimpering my name.

"*Tr-ror-roy…*" Her voice was garbled, and she spat the underwear from her mouth, which only made me more furious. "*Troy…*"

Thrust.

"Shut up," I ordered. Her voice made me remember it wasn't my wife I was having sex with. Hell, with each sound she made, my dick softened a little. She wasn't who I wanted to fuck, and that was oddly disappointing.

"Oh my God, I love you baby, I love you."

Thrust.

"Shut. The hell. Up."

I felt her legs shaking against mine as I pumped harder into her. Catalina was molded between my body and the wall, banging her head against it in frustration and pleasure, and that was my cue to pull out, still half hard, still thinking of Red for some crazy reason.

I didn't come, and knew it would be pointless to try. She wasn't Sparrow. Didn't feel like her, didn't taste like her, didn't move like her.

Cat barely had time to turn around and face me before I zipped up. I threw the stained dress she gave Red earlier that week in her direction.

"Get the fuck out of my place and never come here again," I ordered. "We're done."

I always told her we were through. Every week. Yet somehow, we always ended up rolling on her bed. And carpet, floor, Jacuzzi and even on her lush, neatly cut lawn. But it was always at her house. She was never allowed, not physically and certainly not mentally, into my kingdom. This was a breach.

And yet another goddamned excuse to finish what I wanted nothing to do with anymore. *Her.*

She caught the dress mid-air and examined it, shocked. Tugging at the stained fabric, she let out a grunt. "The little witch ruined my dress."

Pulling the suitcase from the bed and resting it on the floor, I stifled a sarcastic laugh. I reached for my back pocket and yanked out my wallet, plucking a wad of cash and throwing it in her general direction. "It was your brilliant idea to send my wife your dress. Ever heard of the dry cleaners? Time to use 'em."

"Dry clean what? It's a mess! Can't you see?" She waved the dress in the air. "I can't believe the little skank!"

I walked right past her, and when I reached the open door, I nodded for her to get out. Catalina huffed and marched out of the room, a sulky expression on her face. She stomped down the curved staircase, deliberately stabbing her pointy heels into the wooden treads. At the bottom she spun back to face me, but I stopped before the bottom step, towering one stair and several more inches over her.

"You're an asshole." She shoved a long painted fingernail into my chest.

"And this asshole is done with you."

"Don't you realize that she doesn't want you? I know exactly why you had to marry little Sparrow, so don't pretend like it's a real relationship. She is a *girl*, and I am a *woman*. As a woman, I can see what you refuse to register into that cocky brain of yours. She ain't gonna fuck you like I do or shut up and just be there for you like I can. Stop betting on the wrong horse." Her voice was spiked with sadness, and with that, she turned around and marched out of the apartment.

I waited to hear the door shutting after her with a loud bang before slamming my fist into the nearest wall. *Good riddance.*

I walked straight to the liquor cabinet, pulled out a bottle of whiskey and a glass, and poured myself a drink. Maria stepped out of one of the guestroom and gave me the stink eye. She knew more than I felt comfortable with about my relationship with her daughter. Then again, no one forced her to work here for me.

Understandably, she wanted Cat to stick with Brock and make it work. Brock, the lovable fucking golden boy. But the truth of the matter was that Cat loved danger more than she loved cock. She always crawled back to me, no matter how hard I tried to push her away. In all fairness, I never tried too hard. But after this little stunt today, barging into my apartment unannounced, I knew I would have to put her in her place when I got back from Miami.

"You let your daughter in here without my permission one more time, and you're fired." I took a sip from my glass, my eyes trained on the city view through the wall of windows.

Maria muttered something in Spanish and headed for the kitchen. The sound of glass breaking filled the air. She always had "accidents" around the house every time she was mad at me for screwing Catalina. I paid no attention.

A few minutes later, the door swung open and Connor and Red stormed in. Connor had a fresh bruise on his left cheek, a bleeding nose and murder in his eyes. Red looked flustered too, a furious little thing, trying to shake Connor's arm off her elbow. My eyes jumped directly to her arm, clasped between his chunky fingers, and he immediately let her loose.

Oh, hell no.

"The fuck happened to you?" I emptied my glass in one swig and pointed at him with it. His eyes darted straight to my wife, as if the answer depended on her. My attention moved to Sparrow.

She looked confused and furious, scurrying to the corner of the living room. She was blushing again and didn't even do her usual routine of glaring at me disapprovingly for drinking at ungodly hours. Something had happened between these two, and an uneasy feeling settled in my stomach.

"Nothing," Connor said in a tight voice.

She pointed her cell in his direction. "I threw my phone in his face," she announced, not a hint of apology to her tone.

I squared my shoulders and shoved a tensed hand into my pocket, knowing I'd need to keep it there if I didn't want to add more color to Connor's already bruised face. "Care to elaborate?"

Maria walked back into the living room just then, looking all kinds of interested in the new drama. I think she got off on knowing that I had bullshit to deal with in my personal life. Especially as she held me responsible for her daughter's own mess. Throwing her out was tempting, but Sparrow seemed ridiculously attached to the help, and she was already too pissed off for me to deal with, so I let Maria stay, doing my best to ignore her.

"He grabbed me by the elbow in front of my friends and now I have a mark." Sparrow stretched out her arm, exhibiting a thick, purple-green ring around her snowy skin.

My jaw tightened.

She yanked her arm back and narrowed her eyes at me. "I know that you think that you rule me, own me, that you can destroy me. But I'm not scared. I'm not going to be pushed around by you or your staff. And I am not going to be touched by anyone without my permission." She spewed her words out like hot lava. Her eyes, aflame with rage, burnt my skin everywhere they landed.

I took one leisurely step in her direction, every inch of my body itching with the need to launch at Connor and smash his skull on the granite tiles. I brushed my knuckles against her bruised skin.

She jerked away and hissed like a snake. "That includes you, Troy."

So Red didn't mind riding my face like a cowgirl, but still had trouble letting me touch her in front of Connor and Maria. I was beginning to see a little bit of me in her.

"Go upstairs and pack a bag," I ordered, pretending that it didn't sting when she rejected me in front of my two employees.

Maria grinned, getting her money's worth, and turned on her heel, back to the kitchen sink.

"I'm not going anywhere. Not until you tell me why, when, where and how," Sparrow demanded. "Oh, and FYI, I don't even have your phone number. No driver's license either, so good luck with getting me on that plane. Guess it's not as easy as you think, bossing me around. You should've really thought about it before..."

She was rambling, and I wanted to press my index finger to her lips and shut her up. But I knew better than to try touching her again. Instead, I raised my hand to cut through her stream of babbling.

"This is the last time I'm going to ask nicely. Go upstairs and pack your shit, understood?"

She stopped talking, her eyebrows flying up in outrage, flipped me the finger, and turned around and climbed upstairs. It was only when I heard her slamming drawers in the bedroom, no doubt to make a point, that I realized how worried I was that she wouldn't do as I said. Red had fight in her. She was the kind of woman to lead a revolution, not to be kept in a luxury penthouse with a cheating husband.

I was clipping her wings, and I knew it.

Squinting at Connor and feeling the familiar eye-twitch I got every time I wanted to yank someone's heart out of their chest, I turned my whole body to face him. Up until Sparrow, he was my part-time muscle guy when I required one. He received clear instructions and was paid to act, not to think.

Shortly before we got married, I'd hired him full time to keep an eye on my new wife. Honestly, Connor wasn't there to keep her safe—no one would go after her. I wasn't in the mob and even if I were, the underworld didn't involve wives and children when retaliation was needed. I kept Connor on her tail because I didn't want her to run away and fuck up everything I'd worked hard to achieve. To make sure I always knew her whereabouts. She was safe without him, but I didn't want her to know that.

I wanted her small and scared.

What I hadn't taken into consideration was the fact that like most muscle guys, Connor had very little brain to accompany his impressive size. And so, by trying to protect our fake marriage, I'd paired her with an idiot who hurt her.

"Boss…" Connor lifted one sweaty, trembling palm. His face looked like a ball of wrinkled paper, his glistening eyes begging for forgiveness.

I had none to spare. Connor now raised both hands up in surrender, walking backward while I strode toward him until his back hit the wall. His head banged against the polished concrete with a thud.

He was too scared to notice. "You wanted her to get here as soon as possible, and she was stalling on purpose. Then she tried to run away. I had no other option."

"When you poke a bear, Connor..." My voice was low, smooth and threatening. "Prepare to be bitten."

Stepping into his face, I curled my fingers around his neck and pinned his head to the wall. I squeezed his throat experimentally, watching his eyes bug out, pain and horror dripping from them. I wanted to leave him marked like he left his dirty fingers all over Sparrow's arm.

"Come near my wife again," I said, "and I'll show the world just how much of an angry motherfucker I can really be when someone touches what's mine."

"Boss," he gurgled, blood flooding his face and mapping it with little red veins. Sweat dotted his forehead. "Please, I'll never touch her again, no matter what. I wasn't thinking—"

"That much is true." I squeezed harder, not easing the pressure until his cheeks doubled in size and became unmistakably blue. I let him drop to the floor.

He landed with a bang, collapsing like a Jenga tower. His arms shielded his head and body, like he didn't know where the next blow was going to land. I looked down at him disgusted, a worm I was tempted to squash.

He crawled away, across the room, afraid to look up at me. "I'll apologize," he whimpered into his chest, still crawling his way in the opposite direction.

"Don't," I spat. "Don't fucking go anywhere near her ever again."

I left him to collect what was left of his self-esteem from the floor and climbed upstairs, finding Sparrow sitting on the edge of the bed, staring out the vast window. She didn't look up when I came in, just continued studying whatever it is she was fixated on outside. The sky? The tall buildings? A bird? Who the hell knew?

Her face was wrinkled in concentration, and the thought of Catalina being right about her hit me hard. She *was* a fucking kid. She sure looked like one now. She was a kid, and I ate her pussy without even blinking. What's more, I surprisingly enjoyed her sleek little body, and I knew I'd do it all over again the next time I got the chance. Eat her, fuck her, lick her, toes to skull, and ride her in every fucking position until every bone in her body hurt.

She was a kid, and I still wanted to do very grown-up things to her.

"This is the weirdest summer ever," she pondered aloud. "The sunshine today is a lie. The sun's out, but it's still cold. Sunshine," she repeated, "but a lie."

"Lies are what keeps this world running, baby Red." I took a step closer. She was so sweet. So fucking weird, too.

"Why does it smell funny in here?" she asked dully, her forehead crumpling.

Of course, the room reeked of sex, but she couldn't put the finger on that. Good thing I'd planned ahead and kept her sheltered from other men. I didn't have time to chase all the dickheads who wanted to touch her and rip their heads off.

"He'll never touch you again." I dodged her question, taking a seat on the bed next to her. So many people had touched Sparrow without her permission. Connor. Paddy.

Even I fucked around with her on the night of our wedding. Sure, she wanted it, but I gave her an unnecessary push, because she wasn't really ready for me, hence her attempt to show me she was on her period.

The mattress sank under my weight, and I noticed my wife was so short, her feet were still dangling off the floor. She kept her hands tucked between her thighs and didn't look at me, still staring ahead.

"Listen, Red. It's not okay by me when people touch you against you will. Not Connor. Not me. Not anyone."

"Fire him," she ordered simply. Under any other circumstances, I would have laughed or scared the shit out of her, but at that moment, when the lingering smell of my infidelity still hung in the air, I couldn't. Even I had to draw a line somewhere.

"I need you protected," I argued.

"I'm a big girl, and last time I checked, he was the one with a bruised face and asthma attack after our encounter."

"Fine," I agreed, but not easily. My lips twisted. I wasn't sure if I wanted to scowl or smile. "Consider Connor gone." I fished my phone out of my pocket and punched it with my thumb, placing it over my ear. "Calling you so you'll have my number. Happy?"

"Never with you." Her face was neutral, void of feelings when her ring tone sounded in her purse.

I hated that look. It was the look she gave me before I hired her. Before I went down on her. Before I thought she'd cracked.

You're a tough nut, Red.

"So what's that smell?" she repeated. "And where's that dress Maria gave me?"

"I took care of it for you. Thank me later."

Her hooded eyes told me she was not expecting any favors from me.

"Have you packed, or are you in the mood for testing my patience again?" I tried claiming some of my bite back.

"Already told you, I don't have a driver's license. Not a passport. Not even a library card. Nothing. I can't get through airport security."

I stood up and swung aside the painting of a nude that hid my safe. I pressed my thumb against the biometric pad and retrieved her brand new passport. I tossed it to her, and she opened it, staring inside the pages wide-eyed. It had a picture of her, a recent one, and it was legit. If possible, she looked even sadder.

"I would have gotten you a license, too, but I don't trust you behind the wheel, what with your temper."

"Really?" she sniffed, peering past me at the open safe. "The Department of State is on your payroll, too?"

"Even God can be bought for the right price." I slammed and locked the safe, hoping she wouldn't freak out at all the cash I kept there. You never knew when you might have to make a run for it.

She began to pace, not unlike a caged animal. "This is wrong. You can't just get a passport for me without my permission. I'm not a child."

"Look, you don't have to be such a pain about it. It's a fucking honeymoon, okay? We'll spend a few days in Miami, do some shopping, wolf down some Cuban sandwiches and Key lime pie, suffer mild sunburn and get our asses back to Boston before you know it. Now pack."

She stopped her stalking, her feet rooted to the ground as she waved her clenched fist at me. "You plan to drag me on a plane without prior notice like I'm a Chihuahua you can fit into a handbag and you expect me to just pack? What if I have plans for the week?"

"Postpone them." I was losing my patience. The Paddy Rowan business was so much more important than girl-time with her friends.

"And what if I don't want to?" She crossed her arms over her chest, jutting one hip forward, challenging.

"Christ." I closed my eyes, trying to control the impending arrival of another twitch.

Was this what marriage felt like? I was starting to seriously consider giving up the assets and money my father had left me. Any other woman would probably jump up and down with joy to hear I was taking her on a honeymoon, housing her in a luxury suite and shoving a credit card in her hand. Sparrow? She acted like I was going to kidnap her and deliver her straight into the arms of ISIS. Frankly, I wouldn't be surprised if they, too, found themselves struggling to contain the wrath of this girl.

Red walked to the corner where Cat and I fucked, and my stomach knotted. She stared at the exact spot where Cat banged her head against the wall. There was a trail of makeup right underneath my Yoskay Yamamoto painting. My heart picked up speed. Why did I care? This marriage meant nothing to me. I shouldn't give a damn if she found out.

She blinked slowly, turning her gaze back to me, and serenely asked, "Was this really necessary?"

She knew.

I hitched one shoulder up.

Red chuckled bitterly, closing her eyes and taking a deep breath, like she was gathering strength for her next sentence. Despite everything, she didn't lose her shit. It made me eerily proud of her. When she'd stood before me and repeated her vows, I'd imagined the girl I married would break in no time. Little did I know that Sparrow possessed the same quality I had when it came to people: For the most part? She didn't. Fucking. Care.

I changed my mind. Cat was wrong. She was not a kid—she was a woman who refused to turn a blind eye when it came to her husband's infidelities. She was more of a woman than my mom and Cat, combined.

"If you can afford a Maserati and a penthouse the size of a medium-sized island, you can also afford a nice hotel room downtown. This…" She pointed at the wall - was she able to detect Cat's sweet, unbearable fragrance? - "Is the last time it happens under the roof where I live. God, I can't believe I messed around with you. I feel so filthy."

There wasn't anger in her voice. I was so used to crazy-ass women tailing me around, begging for what Sparrow had carelessly rejected, I was almost disappointed with her reaction.

But I just leaned toward her, my posture relaxed. "If I tried to take you right now on the floor, you would do it all over again. You can run. Run all the way across the country, but you can't run away from your mind. And Sparrow, my little birdie…" I flashed her a confident smile. "I'm deep in your head, and you know it. Now, pack."

She tipped her chin up, marching straight to the walk-in closet, and disappeared between the vast, dark-oak shelves.

"You need a suitcase?" I got up from the bed.

"I'll find one myself," she snapped from the depths. "Meet you downstairs."

Hesitating only for a moment, I turned around and headed for the living room. Fuck it, I wasn't a gentleman, and if she wanted to handle a heavy suitcase, I really wasn't going to argue with her.

It wasn't until I walked into the kitchen and saw Connor's head under the running tap as he gasped for air, crying like a goddamned baby, that I realized that I'd just had my ass handed to me on a plate by a twenty-two-year-old virgin.

She didn't even give me a side of ketchup.

Just sent me to the fucking naughty spot.

I narrowed my eyes on the sturdy man in front of me, furious that he was being more of a pussy than my underweight, five foot three wife.

"Connor, you're fired. Take your shit and leave. I'll send you your last check when I get back from Miami."

His mouth fell open, water dripping from his hair in fat drops straight to his mouth. His imploring eyes fell to the floor, and he pushed himself slowly, depressingly, to a stand-up position.

"But what about your wife? Who's gonna watch over her?"

"She doesn't need watching over." I snorted, opening my front door and prompting him to get the hell out of my place. "Just look at the state of her and look at the state of you."

ELEVEN

SPARROW

H E CHEATED ON ME in our room.

In my room.

This was crossing the line. Hell, it was sprinting right past it, crossing a dozen more lines I never knew even existed. Yeah, we weren't a real couple, but this had nothing to do with love. It was about respect.

Obviously, Troy had none for me.

After a silent cab ride, in which I stared out the window and moved my jaw from side to side while he made some cryptic business phone calls, we made it to the airport. We checked in, light-jogged our way to the terminal, two strangers with a mutual destination but very different paths, and waited for the flight wordlessly, both of us engrossed in our cell phones.

When my ass hit the seat on the airplane, it dawned on me that I was scared of flying. Scared of everything, really. Scared of leaving Boston for the first time, scared of doing it with Troy, of all people, and scared of the prospect that Brock had lied to me. Flying to Miami wasn't going to do me any good, after all.

I'd told my husband that I wasn't scared of him, but that was a lie. I was frightened. Not that he'd hurt me physically. I knew that'd never happen. But that he'd break me mentally. That, I had no doubt, was something he was more than capable of doing.

Naturally, turning to Troy for comfort was like turning to a hooker for abstinence tips. I quietly sank into my blue, first-class seat, chewing on my fingernails and hoping that the plane wouldn't crash. Or maybe that wasn't such a bad idea, after all. A whole life with Troy felt like a burden only convicted war criminals should serve.

"Before I fired him, Connor mentioned that you tried to run away. You think you can run away from me?"

I didn't give him the satisfaction of turning to look at him in his seat. I watched him from my peripheral vision as I choked the armrest with my grip. His gaze was on his iPad, but his stone-cold-killer mask was on full display, his jaw hard. I half shrugged, pretending to stare out the window. I wanted to let him second-guess my next move. Be the one to keep him in the dark for once.

"It wouldn't be a good idea to cross me, Sparrow." He lifted his face, his menacing voice caressing my cheek. Every word echoed between my thighs.

I grimaced. This was not a good time to be turned on.

I licked my dry lips as the plane taxied down the runway, the wheels eating up the ground with incredible speed. Shit, it was fast.

His hand moved between us, hovering over my inner thigh but not touching.

I angled my hips away from him. "I'm a good runner."

"And I'm an excellent chaser," he whispered.

MIAMI TURNED ME INTO a sweaty mess of auburn curls, but it still stole my breath away. Like a first date with your high school crush, your first kiss underneath the bleachers and that very first cupcake from the overpriced bakery down the road.

Boston was a concrete jungle full of grungy-gray and staid-red brick buildings, whereas Miami was colorful, sunny and vivid. Boston was rainy, Miami, sunny. Boston was suited, Miami, bikini-clad.

It's like I'd stepped into a parallel universe, where everything and everyone were more alive and vital. Well, other than the man who brought me here. He was much the same. All cold efficiency and barely contained fury. Troy was munching on a toothpick, as he always did. Toothpicks were his pacifiers, and he left them everywhere he went, like a fingerprint.

Our cab stopped in front of a resort-style hotel, two rows of tall palm trees leading to its entrance. I looked up and saw the vast, glassed-in balconies of each room, every patio boasting its own small, real-grass garden and swimming pool. The driver hopped out and ran to the trunk, yanking out our two suitcases. I got out, sucking in the humid air and fanning myself with my hand as I scanned the very foreign surroundings.

Brennan stayed in the car, rolling the toothpick between his teeth and tongue, his dark aviator shades hiding those eyes that pinned me every time they glanced my way. The suitcases sat between us on the walkway like bouncers trying to make sure we weren't going to pounce instinctively and kill each other.

"Are your legs too precious to walk anymore? Do you need to be wheeled into the premises?" I mocked, venom dripping from each word. "Oh, I know, maybe I can give you a piggyback ride."

"Funny." He spat the toothpick to the sidewalk and leaned back into the seat of the cab. "I'll be back in a few hours."

"You're leaving me here?" My voice prickled with edge.

He looked around us, like he wasn't sure I was talking to him. "You don't want me to touch you. You certainly don't fucking want my conversation and you have my credit card. It's your honeymoon. Check-in. Go have fun. I, myself, am planning to do the same."

What? After everything he'd done, practically shoving me onto the plane against my will for this so-called honeymoon, he was going to just dump me in a hotel and abandon me like I was a stray cat?

I offered him a sly smile. "Aw, I'm hurt. Are you saying I'm no fun?"

"I'm saying that if I can't eat it, fuck it or kill it I have no interest in it," he answered dryly.

He was messing with me again, capitalizing on the fact everyone feared him. And let's face it, he knew what I was ashamed to admit—his dangerous aura did appeal to me. People were like onions, made of lots of layers. The deeper you went, the rawer the layer. With Troy, I'd found a layer in myself that wanted to be scared. That got off on the adrenaline and rush of being with a savage.

I bit on my inner cheeks, tasting the metallic tang of blood. A cheater, a criminal and perhaps even a murderer, my husband wasn't exactly a catch in my book.

And sadly, I still wanted him around.

"Fine," I said. "Have a good meal. Find a hooker. Fuck her. Kill her. Do your little homerun of fun. Just don't expect me to sit here and wait."

He laughed when he shut the cab's door with an unpleasant thud. It wasn't a spiteful laugh. He laughed like he was genuinely enjoying our mutual exchange. Then he rolled down the window. "Dinner is at nine. Be ready and dress nice," he had the audacity to say.

I folded my arms over my chest. "Is that a request or an order?"

"That depends on your answer." He tipped his shades down, the storm behind those frosty blues threatening to sweep me off my feet.

I took a step back and watched my husband tapping his palm over the headrest of the driver. Anger boiled beneath my skin, and I held my lip between my teeth.

Don't lose it, Sparrow. That's exactly what he wants.

"Semantics." He shook his head in amusement. "You women just love it. We're outta here."

The cab rolled back into the traffic jam ahead, leaving me with our suitcases and a sour mood. But this time, I wasn't going to just take it. I was going to up my game.

In true Brennan fashion, I turned around, took out my purse and shoved a few bills into the hand of the nearest bellboy. I didn't have much money, but whatever I had, I gave him.

"Keep the suitcase somewhere safe until I'm back and get me a taxi. Now, please."

A minute later I was sitting at the back of a bright yellow sedan, an elderly Cuban driver asking me where I was going.

"Wherever they're going." I pointed at Troy's cab. The other yellow car was still buried deep inside a traffic jam. We'd have no trouble tailing them—they wouldn't even notice.

Oh, yes. If Troy was going to treat me like a prop, I wanted to find out why. Why we were here, what was he up to and especially, why the hell I was his.

TWELVE

TROY

I WAS GOING TO MAKE THE most out what was left of Paddy Rowan.

I hated the man with a passion, and if there's one thing I knew, it was that passion never fails. Passion always fucking delivers.

Back in the days when the Irish ruled Southie, Paddy shaved some serious commission money off of my dad. Protection money, mostly. He was in charge of the bookkeeping, just like Brock, and just like Brock, he was not to be trusted.

I didn't discover the truth until after my father was dead. Rowan had skipped town months before. Of course, by then the Armenians were after him, too. That's why I'd let Paddy alone when I set out to avenge my father's death and chased down everyone who had wronged him over the years. Rowan's theft was ancient history and he had reason to lay low after he fled. He was, therefore, pretty far down on my list.

Then Red told me about what Rowan did to her, and it reawakened all kinds of dark thoughts I had about this man and put him straight up on that list again. He may not have been responsible for the death of my father, but he still stole our money.

He touched a girl.

He touched *my* girl.

Of course, killing Rowan was pointless. The man was already half dead and I wasn't dumb enough to be that impatient. All the same, I couldn't wait to get to Miami, especially after the news Jensen – a private investigator who was on my payroll - had sent while we were waiting to take off. Red was in for a hell of a wedding gift.

I also wanted her around just to make sure my cock wasn't doing anything overly stupid, like getting itself buried in other women. Even though I had no illusions about my icicle of a wife, taking her with me guaranteed I wouldn't find myself getting up to any old bad habits. The emptiness of the aftermath was intolerable. Case in point, tapping Cat today was about as fun as doing my own taxes.

I was getting too old for this shit, and frankly, the only woman I was vaguely interested in screwing right now hated my guts and happened to be my wife.

Paddy Rowan lived in Little Havana. A Cuban neighborhood where nobody knew him or gave a shit about who he was, so I figured that's exactly why he chose it in the first place. Laying low was easy in a place where no one had the slightest interest in you. In Little Havana, he was just another old dying senior with no history or future to speak of.

He lived in the nicer part of the neighborhood, though definitely a downgrade from his upscale house back home. It was a yellow, Spanish-style house with arches and all that jazz. The stucco was clean, the yard looked remarkably well tended, and there was a young Latino woman sweeping the floor of the walled front courtyard, humming to herself. She wore a cleaning company's uniform and looked up at me when she heard my footfalls. Her smile faltered, and her humming and sweeping stopped. A gust of hot wind blew on her face and a strand of dark hair teased her forehead.

The innocence of her expression reminded me of Red. Then again, pretty much every fucking other thing in the world reminded me of my wife nowadays. *Focus, asshole.* Revenge first, pussy later.

"Can I help you?" she asked, cautious and scared. She flinched when I sauntered toward the door without acknowledging her. I didn't have time for a chit-chat.

"Sir!" she objected behind me, leaning her broom against the yellow archway and stalking my footsteps.

The front door was locked, so I kicked it open. Most people don't realize that kicking-in a door is a fucking walk in the park to anyone over 150 pounds. I didn't even break a sweat. I marched into the house, the door behind me swinging on its hinges, not stopping to admire the Spanish artwork on the walls or the nice interior design Paddy has decided to go for in his retirement. He'd always liked pretty things.

Shame one of those things belonged to me.

"Where's Paddy?" I growled in her direction. It was a two-story house, traditional, vast, with a shitload of doors. I wasn't going to play hide and seek with the motherfucker.

"Who are you? I'm calling the police," the maid announced, but she made no move to pull out a cell phone or lunge for the one on the table in the foyer.

I offered her an impatient smile. "Don't be stupid. Tell me where he is and get outta here." I reached into my pocket and jerked a stack of money from my wallet.

She jumped back, watching the hundred-dollar bills feather-float all the way to the Spanish tiles. She then looked back up to face me and silently stared up to the second floor, tilting her head toward its right wing. Her gaze was steady, but her body shook.

"That's where he is?" I tipped my chin down, inspecting her.

Her full lips were pursed and her thick eyelashes fluttered. She was having a hard time giving him away, but knowing Rowan, he couldn't have been nice to a maid. He was notorious for putting women through shit, especially powerless ones. The Irish mob was always into the pussy business (mainly strip clubs that offered some extra attention to their clients—it was too profitable to turn down), but most men weren't particularly anxious to leave their mark on the girls. Paddy, however, liked them young and suffering. Preferably the latter, if he had a choice.

The girl nodded wordlessly.

"Are you giving him away because of the money or because he messed around with you?" I tucked my wallet back into my breast pocket, waiting with interest for the answer.

She gulped hard and studied the floor, knotting her fingers together. "Both."

A brief, heavy silence fell between us.

"Get out of here and if anyone asks, he gave you half the day off because you caught a stomach bug. I was never here. Understood?"

She nodded again.

"Who am I?" I asked.

"No one," she parroted. "I never saw you."

"Good girl. Now off you go."

When I walked into the darkened master bedroom, the stench almost knocked me over. So far the house looked nice and taken care of, but the thick and suffocating scent of illness crashed into me the minute I stepped into his room.

There was a tall king-size bed, and right in the middle of it, tucked inside dozens of fucking duvets and fluffy pillows lay the man I hated. Or, at least what was left of him.

He looked frail, skinny, the opposite from his old burly self. He used to be stocky, bald, short, ugly and healthy. Now blue veins traveled up and down his hands like vicious snakes and his skin was dotted yellow and brown. He was withering. An autumn leaf sticking out like a sore thumb in green Miami.

Paddy was wearing some kind of an oxygen mask, hooked into a silver and green tank that was sitting right next to him by the bed. The curtains were all drawn.

It smelled like death. Rotting, in-process death. I'd seen death before, but it was always quick and unripe. There was the rusty scent of blood, sour scent of fear and sweet scent of hot metal and gunpowder. It wasn't an unpleasant combo, albeit one that would stick in your nose and throat for days. But that was the photogenic side of death. Rowan was on the other side.

He was a living, breathing corpse, decaying like the bad apple that he was—and it fucking reeked. We both knew men like him were better off dying somewhere on the job, hard and quick and in a blaze of glory, rather than the mess of being on death row, hooked to a fucking oxygen tank, looking like a shadow of your former self.

I walked inside the room and yanked a handkerchief out of my jacket. I usually kept one for when I needed to touch shit without leaving fingerprints. I used it to cover my nose and breath through the stench of a body eating itself alive.

"Ah," I heard him say or, rather, cough. I wasn't sure if he was awake or asleep. In fact, the only thing that gave away the fact the bastard was still alive was his labored breathing. "I see the devil wants his pound of flesh. So the little bitch told you."

I continued strolling in his direction wordlessly until my legs hit the edge of his bed. I kept the handkerchief over my nose and stared at him. He shifted uneasily but kept his eyes on mine.

"I believe congratulations are in order." He attempted a chuckle. "I'm guessing you ain't here for some fatherly advice. Rumor has it you know all about the birds and the bees."

I stared down at my hands, fighting the urge to pick at the scabs on my knuckles. I wanted to touch something, to *break* something.

Of course Paddy knew about Sparrow and me. At this point, every single person in South Boston did.

"You should know by now, your sins always catch up with you at the end," I said, my tone flat.

He tapped his oxygen mask, rolling his sunken eyes. "Remind yourself of that when little wifey realizes who you really are and what you did to her mother, will ya, boyo?"

His words hit me hard. How the fuck did *he* know? There were only two people other than me who knew about Robyn Raynes and about my promise to my father...and now there were three. Fucking Cat and her big mouth. She probably told him too, in one of her visits to his notorious coke parties in Boston.

I couldn't let him see the surprise in my eyes, so I glared, trying to hide the hurricane swirling in the pit of my stomach.

"So, am I going to finally meet my maker today?" He tried to laugh, but it somehow rolled into a full-on cough. It sounded like he was going to throw up his lungs. The coughing got shallow and throatier, then died down.

"You don't deserve to go like a mobster," I answered. "No bullet to the head for you. I'd much rather know you're decaying here like roadkill no one bothered to scrape off the pavement."

"I like your touch, T-boyo. You remind me of your father." Paddy turned his head to spit out some phlegm. Grayish-black fluid, a souvenir from his long years of smoking, landed in a bucket next to him on the duvet. "He always was a sick, violent bastard. Runs in your blood I guess."

"How many young girls have you touched?" I asked, concealing the fury I felt with a condescending smirk. I wasn't a prime example of how to treat women. I didn't do love, fucked rough, never called the day after, but I always had their consent. And I never touched someone underage.

"If what you're looking for is guilt, boyo, you better turn around and walk back the way you came. You ain't no saint yourself. News travels, and from what I hear, you shame your family name on a regular basis. Being the errand boy for the rich and corrupt of Boston. At least we had pride. We put our lives in danger for our families, for our children, to bring food to the table. We weren't the upper class's hired help. Breaks my heart." He chuckled. "Cillian's son, a lap dog to the rich."

I rolled my shoulders back, looking amused. Underneath the tailored suit and easy grin, though, my blood boiled, my veins bubbling with fury. Killing Rowan was an itch I was desperate to scratch.

"How many girls, asshole? Tell me now, how many children have you molested?"

Paddy threw his head back with whatever energy he had left in him and hooted loudly. When his head bounced back from the pillow, a flicker of insanity danced in his eyes. He almost looked well again. At the very least, it appeared he was he was vital enough to taunt me.

He ran his nearly white tongue over his upper teeth, then sucked in air. "Oh, how I loved your wife's tight little pussy. Is it still as taut as it used to be?"

Don't kill him, I reminded myself.

"You know I did it for a while. Almost a year, maybe, before her father got a little sober and got himself a girlfriend to babysit her when he was at work." He laughed like a hyena.

I felt my fist tightening around the Glock inside my holster.

Clench, release. Clench, release.

Fuck, I wanted to end him so badly. But at the same time, I knew that's exactly what he wanted me to do. He'd pushed all the buttons. Pressed the soft spots. Tried to get me to react.

He had nothing to lose.

Other than *her.*

I looked down, taking a deep breath. Calm washed over me. I was going to do right by Sparrow, by my dad, by all the little girls Patrick probably molested over the years. I pulled my brows together, raising my eyes to meet his gaze slowly and steadily.

"You've got a lot of assets and shit to leave behind once you drop dead, now don't you, Captain McPervert? Got a few bucks saved in your offshore accounts. I know of at least three of'em in the Caymans and there are a couple in Belize, too, right?"

This melted his smile off faster than acid. A rookie's mistake his former self never would have made.

Bingo, motherfucker.

I shook my head and took a step forward, so he could see just how much I was enjoying it. Paddy yanked off his oxygen mask and reached toward the nightstand, patting it while keeping his eyes fixed on me. His fingers landed on a soft cigarette pack. He tugged one out and lit it, taking a breath so labored I could actually hear his lungs squeak under the pressure.

"Ah, crap," he said.

I nodded. Crap, indeed.

"So I was thinking, who's gonna get all of this assfuck's money and assets when he dies? You cheated on all your wives, collecting divorces at an impressive rate. Not one of 'em gives two shits you're dying. No one to take care of you. Send letters. No one to inherit all the hard-earned money you stole from my old man. So I started snooping around, asking people, taking an interest." I paused as I turned my back to him. "Nobody cared about Paddy, so I wondered if maybe there was someone *he* cared about."

Pacing, I folded the handkerchief and tucked it back in my jacket. The scent of cigarette smoke was enough to dilute the reek of death. Besides, I'd gone nose-blind to the stench. I tipped my chin lower so that he could see the amusement flickering in my eyes. "And as you mentioned before, news travels fast. Wife number two had a few details to share about your cheating."

Paddy's face collapsed into a heap of wrinkles, like he was one of those shar-pei dogs, and he winced, a sure sign of his inner torture. I was glad I hadn't pulled out my Glock after all. This was far more entertaining.

"How dare you! I was your father's best friend. When your girl needed rehab, I hooked you up with the best place in the States."

I almost laughed out loud. That had ended up being just another disaster.

"Paddy," I warned.

"Don't touch her." His voice shook, after a stretched silence that spoke volumes of his love for her.

"Touch her?" I let the words roll off my tongue lazily, like I was weighing on this option. "I'm not going to stop at touching. This *errand boy* knows the fucking drill." I walked over to a painting hanging on his wall, my arms folded behind my back, and scanned it with a playful smile. A cheap print of *The Nightmare* by Henry Fuseli. How ironic. A vision of a woman's deepest fears.

The painting was covered in glass and reflected Paddy's face. He bit his lower lip, releasing it slowly as he blinked away what was beginning to look like actual tears. Taking another drag and coughing it out, his eyes narrowed on my back.

"Leave her out of it."

"You mean, just like you left Sparrow alone?" I rubbed my chin with my finger thoughtfully as I turned to face him.

"Get to the point, asshole. What is it that you want?"

"I want everything, Paddy. Every. Single. Fucking. Thing. You stole money from my father for years, fuck knows how much, and you molested the girl who is now my wife. I hate you way too much to just kill you. So here's how it's gonna play out. You sign over every damn penny you have in those accounts to Sparrow, and I spare your illegitimate daughter's life. What's her name? Oh, yes. Tara. Sweet fucking Tara. Only nineteen, isn't she?"

"Eighteen." He pursed his lips, stubbing the cigarette with force into a nearby ashtray.

"Even better." I shrugged, spinning on my heel to face him and smiling good-naturedly.

"You can't do this," he mumbled to himself.

"I just did."

"And what if I won't?" He hesitated, pressing his hand to his neck, like he was choking.

"Then I swear to God, I will kill the little bitch. But before I do, I'll make sure every single junkie in South Boston rides her ass six ways from Sunday. And trust me, I will hunt down the kinkiest motherfuckers the city has to offer. I do my research, as you can tell."

Paddy's jaw ticked, and I knew he was terrified. I'd definitely hit a nerve.

When I booked the flight to Miami, I was under the impression that it was going to be another joyless kill. But then Jensen followed the money trail to Paddy's daughter. She was living outside of Boston with her ex-stripper mom. Paddy was sending them money every month, and according to Paddy's wife #2, it didn't stop there. He was in contact with Tara. Phone calls, Christmas cards and all the rest. Apparently Tara didn't know her father was a world-class douche. She was just a college freshman looking to bond with her dying no-show of a dad. Looked like a sweet enough girl, if you ignored her problematic gene pool. I never would have touched her. But Paddy thought like a psychopath, so I knew he wouldn't put it past me to do what he would have done if he still had a chance.

"How will I know you won't hurt her anyway?" Paddy pressed his head to the headboard, closing his eyes in frustration. He was coming to terms with this arrangement.

I wanted Sparrow to have everything this fucker had to his name, like he took everything from her when she was just a little girl. An eye for an eye.

"Why, I'll give you my word." I opened my arms in a friendly manner.

He stared me down and spat again into his bucket, reaching back for the oxygen mask. "Your word ain't worth shit."

"Then it's a crying shame that's all you're going to get. Either you hand over the money to Sparrow, knowing I intend to keep my promise not to touch your girl, or you let me walk away from this place, knowing my generous deal is off the table and that I'm going to do horrible things to your kid. Your call, old man."

The look on his face told me everything I needed to know. He loved his daughter, even though he was a monster. I'd broken him. He had lost everything he'd worked for. He was going to die a poor man, leave nothing to his only family. He was going to pay his debt.

"You are worse than your father, Brennan."

I smiled in agreement and fished out my phone. "I'll call a lawyer and have him draw up the papers right away. And you can start by signing this Power of Attorney. Don't worry, *boyo*, I brought a pen."

THIRTEEN

SPARROW

From my cab at the end of the block, I watched Troy walking up to the Spanish-style house. Once he was out of sight, I instructed my driver to wait and slowly strolled up the sidewalk, noting his idling cab. His driver was busy with his cell phone and didn't seem to notice me.

I eyed the stucco mailbox at the end of the driveway. Who was Troy visiting? What was so important at this house? Maybe Daisy was right. Maybe he *did* take his dick on a tour and was now visiting another mistress.

There was a house number on the mailbox but no name. I doubted I'd recognize the name anyway, but what the hell. I'd come this far. Trying to look casual, like I belonged, like this wasn't illegal, I pulled open the mailbox, hoping to find a letter with a name. I got far more than I bargained for. I read the address on the first envelope, and my breath caught in my throat, and I froze.

It said "Patrick Rowan."

Patrick Rowan. *Paddy.* The man who molested me.

Troy Brennan was at my molester's house. My husband and the only person I'd ever told about my dark, awful secret.

Stupid girl.

I stumbled back from the mailbox, like a nest of snakes was inside. My heart pumped wildly against my ribcage. Maybe he'd come here to kill him. After all, everyone said he'd killed before. Maybe he would punish this vile man the way I never could.

I forced my gaze back to the house, just as a girl in a maid's uniform hurried down the drive toward me, looking flushed and concerned. For a moment, I was afraid she was going to confront me, but instead she glanced right and left, like she was the one who was afraid. The girl made her way to a bus stop further up the street, hugging herself defensively and looking around every now and again.

When she was out of sight, I got my shit together and jogged to a spot behind a square bush. I watched the courtyard at the front of the house intently.

Twenty minutes after he arrived, Troy left the premises.

He had a stack of documents under his armpit and an easy expression. A few seconds later, a thin, frail man appeared beside him in the entry to the courtyard. He looked sick and old, nothing like the Paddy Rowan I knew and remembered, but then I saw his eyes and choked. It was him.

They shook hands and nodded at each other. I couldn't see Troy's face, but I heard him laugh before he walked back to his cab. He climbed right into its backseat, leaving Rowan very much alive.

I'd seen all I needed to see, and I wished I could unsee it.

The asshole was here for business. He didn't give a damn about what this man did to me.

I threw up between the bushes, feeling the bile bubbling in my throat like poison.

I hated them. Hated them both. But I knew one thing for sure. I wasn't going to give Troy the pleasure of knowing that I knew he was still in business with the man who molested me. Especially not after he disrespected me by having sex with someone else in our bedroom.

There was nothing I could do to get back at him, so I might as well not let him know that I was privy to his atrocious deeds.

No. I would hate my husband quietly, pretend like it never happened—and would never, ever let him touch me or get to me again.

Troy Brennan was dead to me. This time for good.

FOURTEEN

TROY

A s my cab pulled away from Paddy's house, I let out a groan and eased my head back, rubbing my palms against my eye sockets. It was difficult to come to terms with not being able to kill the person who assaulted Red, and probably other girls, too. I wasn't a saint, but like all criminals, I, too, had my individual, custom-made moral codes. And those codes were strict about molestation and sexual harassment.

Those people deserved to die.

Fuck, I even felt a little guilty about playing with her like that the night of our wedding. Sure, I knew she wanted it, saw it in her eyes, felt it in the way her body arched into mine, begging, writhing, but she'd been broken before. I didn't want to break her again.

Well, at least not this part of her soul.

My phone buzzed in my pocket and made me open my eyes. I had an incoming call from George Van Horn.

"Crap," I muttered as I placed it near my ear. Van Horn was business.

A real estate mogul turned politician who really fucking wanted to become mayor, and was about to run over his whole family to get to his goal. His campaign was absurdly aggressive and, since he had more skeletons in his closet than in a fucking graveyard, he'd hired me to keep his name clean.

Shit had to be handled, and I was the one handling it. I waited wordlessly for him to speak first. It was a good habit if you wanted people to cut to the chase.

"Brennan," he barked, "I need you to take care of a package for me."

"This'll have to wait until Friday," I said calmly. "I'll be back in Boston then."

"It can't wait until Friday."

"I'm on my honeymoon, George."

He gave a humorless laugh. "And let me take a wild guess, it's not exactly a Motel 6 in the middle of fuck-knows-where, and your wife ain't bargain shopping at T.J. Maxx, right? Yeah. That's because people like me pay people like you a good buck to work for us. It's not a nine-to-five job, Brennan. Get your ass back here. Now."

I answered with silence, knowing it would drive him mad. He should thank me. If I told him what I was really thinking, the words would cut so deep he'd be the first person in the world to be seriously injured by a telephone call.

"Brennan? Brennan! God-fucking-dammit…" He took a deep breath. "Look, okay, I get it. It's your honeymoon. But it's also an emergency. My package needs to be delivered somewhere discreet ASAP. I can't have it sitting around in the house any more. This could sway my voters and stain my image."

Another beat of silence on my end. If you wanted to win a negotiation, rule number one was to talk less. Show minimal interest. Let the other person sweat it.

I heard Van Horn hit something hard and curse in pain. *Yup, definitely sweating it.*

"Dammit. How much?"

"Double the amount you're paying me now."

"You gotta be fucking kidding me."

"I wish I were." I fumbled for a toothpick and stuck one in my mouth. "But I'm afraid I have a terrible sense of humor."

"Whatever. Fine. And you'll cut your honeymoon short?"

It wasn't like Sparrow and I were enjoying the sun, alcohol and the deluxe king-size bed the hotel had to offer. And I fucking hated Miami anyway. Too lively for my taste.

"I'll be on my way as soon as I can. I have to take care of one minor matter first."

I heard him lighting up one of his rancid cigars. "Some lucky wife, you got yourself."

"Leave my wife out of this. I don't want you mentioning her or even thinking about her. As far as you're concerned, she doesn't exist."

"Ah, so he has a soft spot after all." Van Horn said.

I almost gave a mocking laugh, but I tightened my jaw, clamping hard on the toothpick between my teeth. "I'll have my business associate Brock Greystone send you the new payment terms by tomorrow morning."

Click, and the line went dead, and so did any good thought I had about George Van Horn.

RED WASN'T THERE WHEN I got back to the hotel suite. Not that it surprised me. She was more independent than I pegged her to be. She was also a pain in the ass, and from what I'd noticed, hadn't touched my credit card even once. Consequently, Red was broke as hell. I had no idea how she managed to walk around without spending a penny, but she did it and hadn't complained about it even once.

She was stirring some very fucking strange shit in me—shit I wasn't prepared to deal with. Not when I still had to find the missing person on my list, my impending revenge hovering over our lives like a black cloud of suffocating smoke. I took the crumpled note out of my pocket again just to remind myself I had a goal in life, something bigger. Something that didn't involve money or ass.

1 = Billy Crupti
2 = Father McGregor
3 – The asshole who hired Billy?

I kicked off my shoes and walked into the bathroom, turning on the faucet and taking off my clothes. The heat and humidity killed me. Summer was my idea of hell. I was dark, cold person who enjoyed dark, cold weather. That's why Boston was my kingdom, my home. The unseasonable cold in the city this June suited me perfectly.

But the weather was the least of my worries after meeting with Paddy.

The important thing was that tomorrow morning Paddy's lawyer showed up with a check for Sparrow. Then I was going to get the fuck away from this place and back home to deal with the George Van Horn problem. Sparrow would enjoy a fat payment for her suffering all those years ago, and maybe she'd feel a little less reluctant to spend the bastard's money than she did mine. Though this money wasn't only for Sparrow, I kept reminding myself.

It was also for my dad.

I took a quick shower and by the time I got out, my wife was back. I was always hypersensitive to the presence of other people. Especially when I couldn't see them. A survival instinct I'd inherited from my father, I guessed, though it had failed him in the end. She didn't make much noise—she never did—but I heard her shuffling about, and the sound of her soft footfalls on the carpeted hallway filled the quiet presidential suite.

I walked out with the towel wrapped around my waist, not thinking much of it. She already seen me in my underwear dozens of times and didn't seem to mind. Most of the time, she even sent hungry looks my way. Leaning my hip against the doorframe of the double doors leading from the bedroom to the suite's foyer, I watched her intently.

Of course, she was still wearing the same pair of baggy jeans and tight blue-and-white striped tee she'd worn on the plane. I knew her play. She wasn't going to wear anything special tonight just to spite me. Red was standing on the balcony, her back to me, staring out at the turquoise ocean and tall palm trees. It was late, the sun was setting, and pink, orange and yellow hues smeared the sky like a perfect painting.

"Your resistance is growing old, you know that?" I spoke softly, pushing off the doorframe and walking toward the balcony's sliding door. There was a beat of silence before she answered.

"Then do us both a favor and let me go."

Stopping a few inches from her back, I placed my hands on the railing she was leaning against, caging her with my arms, my chin on top of her head. "That's not what you said when I was eating you like a seven course meal at an Italian wedding."

She twisted out of my touch and spun around, facing me, anger written all over her face. For the first time since I married her, she looked genuinely disgusted by my touch. This wasn't pretense or shyness. She really didn't want me anywhere near her. I took a step back.

"That was before," she spat, every muscle in her face quivering.

Right, that unfortunate Catalina fuck in our house. It seemed like a decent idea at the time, to try and kill the little obsession I'd started nurturing toward my wife. But in retrospect? Worst fuck I'd ever had, and entirely not worth it.

I pivoted back into the room, not wanting to show any kind of emotions. Hell, what was I talking about? I didn't *have* emotions toward this weird kid. I stopped at the mini bar and grabbed a bottle of hard liquor, not even sure which, twisting the top and taking a sip straight from the bottle. She followed me into the room, pouring angry heat from every pore of her body.

"Don't pretend to give a damn about who I fuck, Sparrow. Not when you keep on saying everything we do is a fucking mistake. Stop acting like the betrayed wife."

"You think I care about you screwing around?" She threw her hands in the air, frustrated. "Sorry you didn't get the memo, Brennan. For all I care, you can dick your way to every STD known to mankind and even create new ones in the process."

I turned around and got in her face, still holding the bottle by its neck. "Then what the hell are you talking about? What made you so pissed off now?"

"Forget it!" She shoved me back, her eyes glinting with impending tears.

Fuck, she wanted to cry. Red never cried, even when she married me, when I took her in, when crying was the only thing she could do.

I felt my anger faltering. "What happened?" My voice came out so gentle it startled me. "Why are you so upset?"

"Like it matters. You wouldn't share anything with me, won't tell me anything." She wiped the tears from her face, and I hated that a part of me wanted to do it for her. "Just leave me alone."

"We have reservations for nine."

"I'm not hungry," she bit out.

"It's the best place in Miami. Two Michelin stars. You can hate me tomorrow, the day after and for the rest of your life, but who knows the next time you'll be able to visit a world-class restaurant other than the one your husband owns."

Why was I trying to convince her to go out with me? I could have picked a woman better dressed and more agreeable at the hotel bar and actually enjoyed my time tonight. But for some screwed up reason, I wanted her to go ape-shit when she saw the restaurant. Red was food-crazy.

"Still not interested," she said coldly, yanking the bottle from my hand and taking a long sip, fury in her eyes. I grabbed the bottle back and pointed its neck in her direction.

"Put your fucking shoes on, Sparrow. I won't ask twice."

Okay, this was not the best strategy, but damn, she frustrated the living shit out of me.

"Yeah? What are you going to do if I won't? Will you kill me, like you killed Billy Crupti?" She hit me with her tiny balled fists. She was too small to make an impact, but that didn't mean Sparrow didn't try. Shoving me deeper into the room, she continued, "Will you cut me into tiny pieces? Throw me into the ocean? Make sure there's no trace of me left, but not give a damn that the whole freaking city knows?"

I shook my head, scrubbing my face and raking a hand through my hair, so frustrated I wanted to punch something. If she was bringing the Crupti shit up, she had nothing more to lose. She wasn't scared anymore. Or at least not as much as she was pissed off.

Sparrow was not going to come to dinner, and for the first time in my life, I knew there was nothing I could do about it.

I had no leverage over her. I couldn't restrict her, because she refused to use my money. And I couldn't hurt her, because I didn't want to.

She didn't deserve to be ruined. She wasn't Catalina.

Quietly, I turned around and stalked into the bedroom. I got dressed, put on my Rolex and some cologne, tousled my hair and walked out of the room, leaving her to polish off the alcohol I had left.

When I marched out to the hotel bar, she was still lying on the carpet, drinking herself to oblivion.

I took a seat on one of the stools and ordered a whiskey. A tall blonde of the model variety who was sitting two seats away from me smiled in my direction. I didn't smile back.

I drank two, three…four drinks before she came over and offered me her hand.

"Kylie." She pouted her name, but I didn't reach for a handshake. "And you are…?"

"Not interested. Sorry."

Two hours after I'd left, I walked back into our suite, drunk as hell and way beyond fed up with the Red situation. Talk about a liability.

I found her laying in the darkness, curled on the sofa, the dim light spilling from the TV, highlighting the curves of her face. She had a pillow under her head and a duvet covering her body, all the way up to the chin. We weren't going to share a bed tonight.

"I'm only going to ask one last time. Tell me what crawled up your ass, Sparrow."

"And what good would it do me? You'll never give me any answers. You never have."

She was right, and there was no point in denying it. I was keeping her in the dark.

"Pack your stuff. We're leaving first thing in the morning." I didn't even bother to watch her reaction as I strode straight to the bedroom.

The Paddy business was going to be over in a few hours. His lawyer probably had him signing the papers to make the transfer as we spoke. And I had to get back to Boston to take care of the Van Horn issue. Clearly, my wife was in no mood to play, and let's admit it, Miami was a nightmare to someone like me.

"I never unpacked," she replied with boredom.

"The fuck not?"

"I knew we'd be back in Boston in twenty-four hours. This isn't a honeymoon." I heard the bitterness. "Like everything else in your life, Troy, this was nothing but business."

FIFTEEN

SPARROW

WE SLICED THROUGH THE GRAY Boston streets, the brownstone buildings, jaywalkers and dead-end streets flying by. I pressed my forehead to the glass, trying to ignore my husband as best as I could. His hard eyes were fixated on the road ahead and I knew he wouldn't talk to me. Knew he'd given up.

I moved my stuff out of the bedroom and into the guest room downstairs, and he let me. A part of me struggled to remember why I didn't try this approach in the first place, and another part reminded me that for some unexplained reason, I liked sharing a bed with Troy.

Pathetic, I know.

I decided to start at Rouge Bis the next day. No reason to wait until next week. Surprisingly he agreed to let Brock know my first shift would be tomorrow. I tried to fuel my excitement by talking about it with my Lucy and Daisy that night. They still thought I was in danger and demanded I call the police, but both of them knew better than to take matters into their own hands. Rumor was that Troy had a tight relationship with some of the cops around, and besides, they wouldn't go against my wishes. And my wishes, apparently, was not to do anything about it.

Not because I didn't want to, but because I wanted to make it to my next birthday.

The next afternoon, Troy double-parked in front of the alley that led to the side door to Rouge Bis, again blocking traffic, this time a delivery truck. I twisted my body, grabbing my backpack from the backseat, when I heard a thump on my side of the window. Brennan rolled it down, and Brock's face appeared. He shoved his head straight into my side of the car, his lips bare inches from mine. Knocking twice on the car's roof and the air out of my lungs, he attempted an easy smile.

"I see a tan wasn't on the menu for the Brennan couple."

That was an understatement. I was still as pasty as a freshly painted wall.

Troy's face broke into a devious grin. "We were busy doing things far more interesting."

Yeah, like getting drunk in separate wings of the hotel and hating on each other. I had no idea why he made it sound like we were a couple in front of Brock, but with all the shit he kept from me, I didn't even stand a chance to figure out the reason for this behavior.

"Thanks for the ride," I ground out, pushing my door open and not giving a damn that Brock was still on the other side. He took a step back, but his gaze fell to my thighs when he saw Troy resting a hand over one of them. First time he touched me since I'd refused to have dinner with him.

"Have a good day at work, Red," he said.

Why was he acting weird all of a sudden? More specifically, like we were civil with one another.

I looked from his hand to his face. "Yeah, whatever." And before he'd decided to accompany this little gesture with a goodbye kiss, I dashed out.

"Brock," Troy barked, making him stick his head back into the car. A traffic jam formed behind Troy's Maserati, and embarrassment heated my neck again. "You're needed at the cabin."

Brock groaned. "I have work here. I'll be there in the evening."

Troy glanced at me as he clutched the steering wheel angrily, and then he seemed to relax. "One hour and you're on your way. I need you. Bring the kit."

With that, Brock straightened and walked over to join me. Troy still didn't budge.

Brock opened the side door for me and I entered Rouge Bis. I still had paperwork to sign before I started, and he led me down a back hallway, past the kitchen.

"Aren't you going to ask where the cabin is? What's that kit Troy was talking about?" he asked

"How do you know I don't already know?"

A small smile tugged at his flawless face. "Because I know your husband, and he is very good at keeping secrets. Especially from you."

True, Troy hid stuff from me. Mainly, he hid the reason why we got married in the first place. I knew that. And then there was Rowan...the thought of him made my spine stiffen.

I rolled my eyes, feigning boredom. "No thanks. I'm perfectly fine staying in the dark with this one. You guys can break the law as much as you like. No need to keep me in the loop."

"That's not what I do." He stopped in front of a glass door. Behind it, I noticed a gray brick wall, trendy office desk, several paintings and leather chairs. "I never break the law."

"But you break your promises," I challenged, not sure where all this strength came from. Maybe I was sick of being pushed around by his boss. "You said it'd be worth my while to go to Miami. It sucked."

"What I meant is I'd cheer you up when you got back. Sorry it didn't work out for you, sweetheart."

"Don't sweetheart me." I spun, marching into his office. I took a seat on the chair opposite from where he was supposed to sit. "Let's just get it over with."

Since I arrived a trillion years earlier than I should have for the dinner service, I was also the first to greet Pierre in the kitchen. The short, fat man walked in with a sneer on his face, smoothing his thick, black moustache with his finger. I jumped up on my feet from a milk crate I was sitting on and flashed him an enthusiastic smile.

"Hi!" I chirped.

"Well, if it isn't Miss Nepotism. I thought you weren't supposed to start until next week." He made his way to the large stove, leaning against it and folding his arms as he somehow defied physics and, despite being even shorter than my humble 5'3" still looked down at me.

Cringing inwardly, I wiped off my smile. "I'm ready to work hard and to prove I'm not only here because of my husband."

"No," he agreed, pushing off from the stove and walking over to me. "You're also here because of Greystone. He instructed me to let you pick a station. So you think you can rule my kitchen, do you?"

I wrinkled my forehead and took a step back. If Brock told him to give me my pick, it was all on him. I knew Troy would never offer me the easy way out. It was not his style. He was more the let-her-work-for-it type of guy. Brock, however, was the sweet let-me-help-you-out gentleman. The perfect man to bring home to mom. If I had one, that is.

"Station me wherever you want." I raised my chin. "I'm not scared of hard work, chef."

Pierre took a step toward me and smiled into my face, his breath reeking of cigarettes. "We'll see about that."

I gutted, scaled and cleaned dozens of fish, cutting myself several time with the thin-bladed boning knife just to keep up with all the work Pierre gave me. By the time my shift was done, I looked like I had just played rock-paper-scissors with Edward Scissorhands. Thoroughly bruised and cut, I helped cleaning up the kitchen, even scrubbed up the stove.

I got out of the place at eleven, and started walking the distance from Rouge Bis back to the penthouse. It wasn't close, but the trip back home was on crowded, main streets and I needed the time to think. I wrapped myself into my navy fleece hoodie—this was the coldest June to be recorded in Boston for the last fifty years, perfectly orchestrated with the breakdown of my personal life—swung my backpack over my shoulder and started for Brennan's building. My legs shook from exhaustion as I passed by the expensive stores and galleries, and I dug my hands into my pockets to brave the weird summer chill. Picking up the pace, I rounded the corner and immediately halted when I saw him.

He smiled at me and offered me his hand. I took it, despite knowing that I smelled like fish. Despite knowing that it was monumentally wrong. Despite knowing that by taking his hand, I was cooking up a disaster.

"How was your first day at work?"

"Brock." I swallowed. What was he doing here? Wasn't he supposed to be at home with his family, or at the cabin with my husband? Or anywhere else for that matter. We weren't friends. I was mean to him. He wasn't supposed to care.

Though, damn, he was still pretty darn beautiful. A pool of yellow light streaming from a streetlamp enhanced every handsome feature in his face, and he looked ridiculously Brooks Brothers in his blazer.

"Coffee?"

I shook my head. "No, thanks. I better get home."

"Hot chocolate, then." He reached over and placed his hand on my back, and it was only because of the shock that I didn't pull it back straight away. "I know it's your favorite."

It was creepy, but I went along with it. Frankly, going back to the penthouse wasn't that appealing. I was either going to be greeted with an empty house or with a house full of Troy, my arch enemy nowadays.

Besides, I couldn't say no to hot chocolate on a cold Boston night after a hectic first day at work.

Brock and I walked to a nearby diner and sat in a red vinyl booth. I drank my hot chocolate silently and messed around with the jukebox. He was beautiful, and nice to me. It was a lethal combination, and I knew it was wrong to ache for a married man, so I didn't.

I stubbornly flipped songs, frowning as I stuffed coins into the jukebox at the side of the table. "Bizarre Love Triangle" by New Order blurted from the jukebox. By mistake, of course.

"So, tell me about yourself." He leaned over the table and tried to catch my eye.

I couldn't look at those grays without wondering how it'd feel having them scanning my bare body. Would it have as much effect as Troy's icy-blues?

I huffed, focusing on the jukebox. "What for? You seem to know everything about me as it is. Why Troy married me, my favorite drink..."

This should have alarmed me, but truthfully, so much had happened the past few weeks, Brock was the least of my worries. He seemed harmless enough.

A middle-aged waitress with fake boobs and enough makeup to sculpt a small-sized vase brushed past us and eye-licked Brock, confirming he really was stupidly gorgeous. She leaned over to the table in front of ours, where a trio of teenage girls sat. Hunching over their tabletop, they kept stealing glances toward the man across from me and whispering. Couldn't blame them.

"I'm just trying to be attentive. I want you to know you're not alone when it comes to Troy. I'm here for you."

I shook my head and snorted, yanking a few sugar packets from their holder and ripping them open on the table. "Why do you pretend to care, Brock? We don't know each other, and it's not like you're hitting on me. You've got a wife and kid at home," I reminded him.

His interest in me was starting to piss me off. It had no basis. Or future, for that matter.

Brock reached over and dragged his pointer finger through the sugar I'd spilled on the table. Leaning across the table, he put his sugar-dusted finger on my lower lip, pulling it slowly and letting the sugar sprinkle all over it. My eyes met his and he used the same hand that touched my mouth to yank me by the collar over the table to meet his face, taking my lips with his.

He kissed me hard, diving into my mouth and darting his tongue inside with no hesitation. My stomach dipped as he took my face in his palm and the sweet of the sugar exploded between our tongues. I heard the girls from the other booths gasping their amazement and jealousy. Time seemed to have stopped before I managed to twist away from his touch.

Springing to my feet, my head swimming, I pressed a palm to my cheek to make sure I wasn't hallucinating. "What the hell?" I breathed.

He just sat there, a serene smile on his face. "You said I don't care. Well, I do. You also said that I'm not hitting on you. And well...I am."

"Is this a good time to remind you that you're married?" I stamped my foot, heat rolling off my body in waves. I wasn't sure if I was angrier or hornier.

Angrier. Definitely angrier.

"Just for my son's sake." He arched one eyebrow. "Only for Sam. Cat and I are not a couple."

"Yeah, well, I still have a ring on my finger." I grabbed my backpack and shoved my cell and other crap into it in a hurry.

"Again, not a real couple," he said, dragging his finger once more through the sugar and sucked on it, releasing it slowly. "We owe them nothing." He enunciated every word. "We owe ourselves everything."

I let out a low growl. My head was already a mess, what with Troy and his secrets. This was another disaster waiting to backfire in my face.

I didn't want Brock. Even if he did have a great heart and a flawless face. He was Cat's, and even more importantly, he was Sam's.

"Touch me again and I'm telling your boss," I said, turning around and storming toward the exit. I felt his gaze on my back as I pushed the diner's door open, almost slamming it in a random jogger's face.

Brock stayed put in his seat, knowing he'd done enough. He'd planted a seed. Knew I drooled over him like all the other women with functioning organs, and that now I knew I could have him.

Passing by the diner's window as I bolted down the street, I saw him easing back into his seat with a stupid smile on his face, tapping his lips with his sugar-coated finger.

I ran all the way back home, not stopping to catch my breath, and had an ice-cold shower the minute I stepped in.

Brock was the last thing I wanted.

And the first thing I needed to get over Troy's betrayal.

SIXTEEN

TROY

T HE IDIOT ARRIVED IN THE MIDDLE of the night, just when Flynn Van Horn threw up all over my Derby shoes, crawling on the floor toward the wooden table at the end of the hideout cabin and trying to get to the phone on top of it.

"Damn junkie," I muttered, stepping over his puke to open the door for my employee. Brock stood on the other side, looking stupidly smug. His car lights were still on, illuminating the hills around us.

Originally, my dad bought this place, in the middle of The Berkshires and faraway from civilization and Boston, to spend time with Robyn. When I inherited it, I used it mostly to take care of business. And right now I had a junkie to detox, only I didn't know shit about shit when it came to rehabbing a drug addict.

But that's what I had Brock for.

Flynn's father, George Van Horn, had insisted that his son could not attend a regular rehab facility, where someone could find out about his loser spawn. I took him to the cabin because its walls swallowed the secrets of my clients. They were soaked with them, big and small, dirty and crazy. Secrets everywhere. The blackmailing mistresses I had to deal with. The coercing gang members I had to throw out of town. The rich people who needed to disappear for a while. I swear, if these walls could talk, Boston Metro Police would have enough work for the next three centuries.

"I said one hour, not nine." I flashed my teeth angrily, and Brock pushed past me, walking into the cabin with his kit. He was looking all kinds of chirpy. *What the fuck have you done now?*

"Where's our little patient?" he asked.

Just then, Flynn began to gag, reaching up for the table and trying to struggle to his feet. He fell flat, facedown and the sound of a bone cracking filled the air. I shook my head and sank into the squeaky yellow sofa my dad's mistress picked. She had a horrible taste. Cozy braided rugs all throughout, a small, wooden kitchen and a bunch of deer heads mounted on the log walls. The cabin looked like a perfect place for a Stephen King character to murder his victims.

"I'm going to die!" Flynn yelled, just as Brock squatted down to take a look at him. He hovered over the frail kid and spoke to him calmly, explaining what he was going to do in order to determine his physical situation.

In truth, I believed Flynn. From the moment I stepped into his rundown apartment and yanked him off of his junkie girlfriend while he was trying—and failing—to nail her in their dirty sheets, he'd been shaking, purging and crying uncontrollably, muttering throughout the whole car drive to the cabin that he was sick and needed his next fix. I wasn't a doctor, but the fact that he was blue didn't leave me optimistic about his physical wellbeing.

"He needs to get to the hospital," Brock announced, getting up on his feet from Flynn and yanking off a pair of disposable black gloves. "Immediately."

Snarling, I kicked a nearby footstool.

I couldn't take Flynn to the ER, and Brock knew that damn well. I was paid to handle him quietly and discreetly. Failing wasn't an option. Never was in my line of work.

As if on cue, Flynn passed out on the rug, a trail of puke running from the side of his mouth and pooling beneath his cheek. Nothing but watery fluids. His eyes were shut and a coat of cold sweat began to settle on his damp skin.

"Oh, fuck me." I kneeled down, pressing two fingers to his neck. He was still alive. The pulse was there. It was faint, but it was there. "No hospital." I jerked my head to the heroin addict. "Do it here."

"It's dangerous."

"His dad would rather he be dead than getting well in a public hospital. We don't make the rules," I fired back.

"He could have a heart attack," Brock argued, quiet and stern, staring down at me from where he was standing, leaning his shoulder against a wall. "We can't just give him Imodium, a hot bath and a peanut butter sandwich. It's risky. I don't want it on my conscience."

Frustrated, I rubbed my knuckles against my cheekbone. Taking two steps toward him, I wrapped my hand behind his neck and jerked him closer to my face. We were nose to nose now. "Your conscience is already tainted, pretty boy. Just do as you're told."

Eyes narrowed, we stared at each other before he shifted, moving sideways and walking back to Flynn. He unzipped his duffel bag—AKA his detox kit—and took out a syringe and a small bottle. I looked away, out the window, closing my eyes as I inhaled deeply. I heard Flynn gasping and Brock fiddling with plastic and pill bottles.

Yeah, rich kids had the tendency to screw around with the hard stuff, and Brock knew how to detox. At least he was good for one thing.

"How was Red's first day?" I asked, not because I cared, but to remind him who she belonged to. My eyes remained fixed on his car outside the cabin, the headlights still on, illuminating the cold rain. I liked it when it was cold in the summer. It was like the universe was on my side.

"Why don't you ask her?" Brock sounded amused. "Thought you were on good terms."

I turned around to face him, and he motioned with his head for me to help him move Flynn onto the sofa. I took him under his armpits and Brock took his feet, and we laid his limp body on the yellow couch. Brock strode to the bedroom and came back with a blanket, swaddling Flynn like he was a baby.

When it was all done and dealt with, Brock took a seat on a stool near the couch and dropped his head to his hands. Lighting a cigarette, he threw the still-burning match toward Flynn. The match jumped on the young man's skin, putting out slowly against his bare wrist. Flynn was too out of it to feel the burn. Yup, Brock's good-boy façade always cracked around me.

I wasn't Catalina, Maria or Red. I was an asshole, just like him, and he didn't need to impress me. I already knew who he was. He was like the first scene in David Lynch's *Blue Velvet*, the insect underneath the well-kept lawn. That was Brock. A cheesy, Hollywood smile disguised the outside, while he was rotting beyond repair inside.

"She came back pissed off. From Miami, that is," he said, his eyes on the floor. "Tell me you're not abusing her in any way, because I told her I would keep her safe."

He told her *what?* What business did he have butting into my shit?

"And if I am?" I taunted, leaning against the countertop of the galley kitchen. "What if I made it my mission in life to make her miserable? Don't pretend like you have any power over this, Brock."

"Oh, but I do." He lifted his head, blowing a plume of white smoke directly in my face. "Don't forget I have the key to your can of worms. I know exactly why you married her. What you did to her mother. In fact, I know enough about you to want someone as innocent as her to stay the hell away from you, but since what's done is done, let me explain myself slowly." He blew another cloud, grinning behind it. "Harm this girl and I'm giving away every single secret you have to the highest bidder. And you and I both know the competition would be tight. Got it?"

Was he fucking threatening me? Did he forget who I was, what I could do to him? Did he forget he was on my payroll, that I paid for his wife's fancy shit, for his son's school and for all those goddamn, David-Beckhamwannabe preppy clothes?

Not thinking clearly, and perhaps not thinking at all, I charged at him, slamming my fist straight into his face. He didn't see it coming. The sound of my fist against his bone filled the air. Brock dropped his cigarette on the floor and stood up, swaying. He balled his fist and tried to throw a jab my way. I dodged it, and he fell on the floor, still dizzy from my punch. His nose bled all over the floor as he lay there, grunting. He rolled into a fetal position when I stood over him, took my handkerchief out and wiped his blood off my hands. Squatting down to my colleague so he could hear me clearly, I tipped his face up with my finger, looking him in the eye.

"I wouldn't threaten someone like me when it comes to my secrets. Remember, the reason my secrets are so extreme is because I do extreme things. You don't want to mess with someone who does what I do. If you think you have some kind of leverage on me…" I snorted a laugh, my hand snaking to the front of his neck, wrapping it around his throat firmly. "Well, it's a mistake that could cost you a lot. More than you're willing to pay."

"Fuck you." Brock spat blood toward my face, missing it by mere inches. His eyes were watering and his pretty face completely fucked.

I let go of his neck and offered him a casual smile, lifting the burning cigarette he dropped on the floor and tucking it back between his lips. I patted his shoulder like we were old friends. "Good talk, buddy. Now, turn off your fucking car lights. You're gonna be here awhile."

Slamming the bedroom door behind me, I sighed into my chest. We were going to spend some time in this shithole trying to help Flynn, but that didn't mean I had to tolerate the idiot. A sudden urge to smash someone's head into a wall washed over me, and I took the list from my pocket, observing it again.

1 – ~~Billy Crupti~~
2 – ~~Father McGregor~~
3 – The asshole who hired Billy?

The shit storm Paddy stirred in my life recently had made me dig up my original goal. It was easy to get lost in *life* when your quest was to avenge *death*, but make no mistake. Getting my hands on the person who had my father killed was still my first priority, still what made me tick.

Balling the yellow paper in my fist, I tucked it back into my pocket. I was close. Knew I was close. Felt it in my bones.

And I was going to show no mercy.

SEVENTEEN

SPARROW

YOU DIDN'T CHEAT.

My feet thumped against the concrete and I drew in the chilly air of the dawn, Nonpoint's "Alive and Kicking" roaring through my earbuds. I rounded a corner toward Marlborough Street, my muscles straining as I sped.

If anything, your fake husband is the one who takes his dick out on tour every time he leaves the house. You didn't ask for that kiss from Brock. Didn't initiate. Sure as hell didn't think it'd ever happen. Brock's cheating is none of your goddamn business.

My feet were burning and I felt my pulse in my neck, fast and furious. I crossed the road, heading back to the penthouse.

You don't have to tell Troy. It'll only bring more trouble, and it's not like you're suffering from a domestic bliss overdose.

I stopped in front of the revolving door leading to our building complex as I tried to regulate my breathing. I was not going to tell Troy about what happened with Brock, even though it made me feel really crappy about myself.

Troy was in the penthouse when I opened the door, must've arrived after I went out for my pre-dawn run. Still in his clothes from the day before, he lay on the sofa, a glass of whiskey in his hand.

I didn't acknowledge him. I took a shower and made my bed in the guest bedroom, and when I came back to the kitchen to fix myself some coffee, he was still there, in the same position. He looked exhausted, but any sympathy my heart could muster toward this man had vanished after the Paddy Rowan incident. I leaned my hip against the kitchen counter as I waited for the water to boil.

"Hello to you, too," he grunted into his drink.

I didn't answer. Christ. It was eight a.m. Too early to be drinking.

"You know..." He looked into the glass, swirling the amber liquid. "For someone who's been upgraded to living in a penthouse and got the job of her dreams, you seem a little ungrateful."

I threw my head back and gave a bitter laugh, my hands on the counter behind me for support. "Oh, you're good, Troy. I see the mistress you spent the night with managed to put all kinds of crazy ideas in your head. See, in order for me to be grateful, I needed to *want* this in the first place. No one asked me before you kidnapped me. We both know I'm not here out of choice. So why don't you tell me why you're keeping me here? I'm sure it's good." I turned around, pouring myself some coffee and clucking my tongue. "Yeah, I'm sure it's real good."

He got up from the L-shaped sofa. I heard him padding barefoot over the gold granite tiles even before he appeared by my side. He poured a cup of coffee, a smirk tugging at his lips. I knew he got high on this exchange, too. Our fighting recharged him. He already looked a little better, like he'd caught a quick nap.

"You seem to give all kinds of fuck about who I'm screwing nowadays. Are you jealous, Red? Because I already told you, you can always use me for your personal needs. The offer still stands." He deliberately brushed his arm against mine.

"Don't worry, I'm used to the idea of you cheating. I couldn't care less who you were with last night." I took my cup of coffee, intending to march to the guest room. His rough hand landed on my arm, stopping me.

His touch was gentle, almost like he was extra careful not to hurt me, but it was also firm. "I never cheated on you, because we were never really together. You know that and I know that. If we ever were together, I wouldn't even look at another woman."

"But we're not," I hissed into his face, just like he loved doing to me. "So I'm sure you had fun."

"I wasn't with anyone else last night. It was work."

I looked down at the hand that touched me. His knuckles were red, traces of dried blood in the creases. It seemed I wasn't the only one giving him a hard time this week. I scanned his body through my lashes. Yes, he wasn't with anyone else last night, and as much as I hated to admit it, that made me feel slightly better.

"I hope whoever you bloodied your knuckles on managed a few decent punches, too."

An unsettling grin spread on his face. "Who, Brock? In order to hurt me, he'd need to be a man first. And since I can't trust him to be one, I'll have to warn you myself. Stay away from him."

I felt like the blood was draining from my face. My mouth dried. How did he find out about the kiss? Did Brock tell him? No, Brock had no reason to. And even though I had no illusions about my husband's feelings toward me, I was pretty sure Troy wouldn't stop at punching if he knew Brock kissed me.

No, Troy was still in the dark.

He scanned my face, his hand still resting on my arm. I jerked free and hitched up one shoulder, shrugging off his order. Who was being jealous now? It felt good knowing that he cared. *If* he cared.

I hated him, yes, but my panties were on fire every time he was in the room. Troy stimulated something wild and aching in me in a way Brock was unable to. It didn't matter that Brock was kinder, easier on the eyes and overall, a better candidate as a lover. No, it was Troy who made lust and fear buzz under my skin. My blood ran hot and wild for him, and only for him. Even, and especially, because I had so many mixed feelings toward him.

Worst of all, Troy knew it. How much I wanted him, how I was his.

"Or what?" I stuck out my lower lip. "I work with Brock."

"Or..." He took a step closer, grazing his bloody knuckles against my cheek and down my neck, raising a trail of desire and excitement on my skin. "I'll have to make sure you and he spend less time together."

"You're going to fire me?" I swallowed the lump of anger down my throat but stood my ground, still staring straight into his frosty arctic blues.

"I wouldn't do that to you, wifey." His lips floated over mine, his blues never leaving my greens. He leaned back, taking a sip from his coffee, his free hand still traveling over my body, down my ribcage.

I didn't pull away, despite wanting to. Despite needing to.

"No. I'll fire Brock," Troy said. "Don't worry, I'm sure he'll be able to find a job that pays enough to support cute little Sammy in no time. I mean, it's not like Catalina works, but damn, she could use getting out of the house and doing something productive with her time."

Jesus, he played dirty. My dad had been on the Brennan payroll for years. If it weren't for his family, we wouldn't have had a roof over our heads. Food on our table. Presents under our Christmas tree. I couldn't have Brock fired. He was Sam's dad, and Sam deserved, at the very least, everything I was given as a kid.

"You're an asshole." My voice was hoarse. I was staring at his lips. Why the hell was I staring at his lips? Why was I still attracted to him? What kind of fuckery was that?

"I'm an asshole, and you can't stay away from me." He was so close his warm breath blew against my temple. "I'm the asshole who is on your mind twenty-four-fucking-seven. And I'm telling you now, if Brock has it in his head that he can take you too, he has another thing coming. You're mine, got it?"

My defiance collapsed into a frown. What did he mean by *you, too?* Who else did Brock take away from him? Then it hit me, stealing the air out of my lungs and making my stomach tighten with revulsion. I backpedaled, my face crumpling in disgust. My ass hit the wall behind me and I felt my chin quivering. My anger was uncontainable. It filled my chest and stomach, washing every inch of my body with hot, red rage.

Yes, I was jealous. I was screwed up and weird and jealous of the woman who dated my fake-husband. The guy who freaking kidnapped me.

"You dated Catalina?" I felt the pinch of tears behind my nose.

He laughed, a laugh that made his chest heave and his whole body shake with amusement.

Nausea washed through me and I felt lightheaded. Damn Catalina. Who broke up with who? Why did they break up? When did Brock get into the picture?

"Can you please answer one miserable question for once in your life?" I breathed. "It's not even about our marriage or your job."

"Stay away from Brock," he said again, suddenly serious. He slammed his coffee cup onto the island and started up the stairs leading to the master bedroom.

The faint scent of his expensive aftershave wafted through the air, dissolving my knees into jelly. But I stood rooted in my place, "What makes you think that I will?" I shouted behind him.

He continued climbing upward. "Because you'd only mess around with him to piss me off, and if you think I'm not nice now..." He turned his head to flash me one of his wolfish grins. "Then you should see my pissed-off version. That's some scary shit."

"Stop seeing your skanky mistress, and I'll keep my distance from Brock," I challenged. "Continue screwing around, and you bet your ass I'll do the same."

That made him stop mid-step. He spun around, his lower lip jutting out, impressed. "This sounds a lot like a threat, baby Red." He bobbed his head, zeroing in on my last words. "Is it one?"

"Semantics." I clucked my tongue, feigning amusement, just like he did when we were in Miami. "You men just love it."

The way his eyes lit with glee, you'd think I told him he won the lottery. That was Troy. He liked it when I pushed back. Loved it when I shoved enough to leave an impact.

I continued. "I won't sit here with my legs tangled together and take orders like a good little soldier." My voice was surprisingly calm. "I'm not my father, and I sure don't intend to comfortably fit into the tidy, screwed-up box you created for me. You want me to stay away from Brock? You do the same with other women. You mess around with me, and me only."

Where did that come from? I wasn't entirely sure, but I liked extra-feisty Sparrow. Knew she might be the death of me, but still rooted for her. She was the crazy underdog who wasn't afraid of biting the ass of its owner.

"Are you offering me what I think you're offering?" He tipped his chin down. "Because I won't be gentle."

"I don't want you to be gentle." I walked across the kitchen to fix myself some breakfast, my tone bored. "I want you to be badass, and cut the jealous tantrums. You act like a chick."

As I opened the fridge and shoved my head in, in search of something interesting to eat, I smiled to myself. I'd learned Troy, knew that he would take the bait. The harder I fought back every time he messed with me, the more he liked me. I bet if I set his penthouse on fire, he would laugh like it was all a big, fat joke.

"Hell, wifey, I'm game. Let's play."

And with that, I knew there would be no more mistresses in the immediate future. For the first time since we got together, I'd won. And victory never felt so sweet.

EIGHTEEN

SPARROW

I SPENT MY SHIFT AT ROUGE BIS dicing vegetables that Pierre tossed in the trash in front of his *sous*, saying they were too inconsistent to be used. Pierre made it a point to make sure I knew my ties with Brock and Troy didn't intimidate him. Guess he had every reason to hate me after the stunt Troy pulled, but I still couldn't keep my mouth shut.

I answered back and no one answered the head chef back. I was giving him trouble, and like most men in my life, he saw me as a walking, talking headache. An environmental hazard to steer clear of.

After my long day, all I wanted to do was take a hot shower and crawl in bed. I walked into the darkened guest bedroom. I'd already changed out of my kitchen whites at work, so I kicked off my shoes and threw my street clothes in a messy pile by the bathroom door. The immense shadow on the bed didn't register at first, but then his voice boomed, filling the room with a presence that was much more than physical.

"Get your shit and move back upstairs." It was an order.

Troy.

I stilled, clad only in a purple undershirt and matching underwear, the boyfriend-shorts style.

"I want to mess around." I smiled into the darkness, staring at a spot above his head. I could faintly make out the shape of his body. He had one foot propped on the bed, his knee bent, his dress shirt rolled up to his elbows.

"Nobody said anything about getting back to playing house," I said.

This was a blunt provocation, a way to lick the Paddy Rowan wound that he split open so brutally when he visited him in Miami. It almost made me feel better, hearing his breaths picking up speed, both of us engulfed in the pitch black. He was getting restless. Annoyed. And more than likely, hot for me.

He rose from the mattress, striding in my direction. A warm shiver ran down each of my nerves like a bomb fuse. It exploded somewhere between my thighs, sending sparks of adrenaline to the rest of my body.

I was going to pick a fight tonight.

"You know, Red? It's hard to hate you all the way when you stand toe to toe with me." He chuckled, circling me, his arms clasped behind his back.

The room was dark, too dark, and I was disorientated by the long workday and the fact that he came here for something.

For something I wanted and waited for.

For something I feared and dreaded.

For him to take my innocence.

"Is that your version of sweet nothings?" I snorted, shaking my head. "Because you suck."

"I'm rooting for you," he continued, ignoring my jab. "I'm fucking your life up, and you're still trying to claw your way out of the quicksand. It's hard not to admire that."

His body hovered over mine like a cloud of sweet mist, almost touching. I sucked my cheeks in, feeling my cool façade faltering. I didn't want him to be nice to me. It made our war so much more dangerous.

"Get to the point," I hissed.

"You refuse to be a victim. You always fight back, boots on the ground."

"Troy…" My voice nearly broke. It was the first time I called him by his first name without having a hidden agenda. "I said get to the point."

"When we were in Miami, I was doing you a solid." His lips found my skull.

More hot shivers. More want. More lust. *More Troy.*

Idiot, I thought. *You ruined me in Miami.* "Oh?" I asked, fighting the need to let my arms loose, to allow my hands to touch his strong, male body. I wanted him despite everything, and worryingly, maybe even *because* of what he did to me.

"Paddy…" His name was like a smack in my face leaving Troy's mouth. "I paid him a visit in Florida. Went there and got your payback for you."

I choked on my saliva, and felt my eyes flaring, but I didn't say a word. His lips fluttered between my shoulder blades, and he planted a kiss between my neck and shoulder, his tongue darting out briefly to remind me of what was to come.

"He's dying from cancer, y'know. Will be dead soon. He will die a poor man. He will die a broken man. Every dime he had to his name…" He caught a loose strand of my hair, rubbing it between his fingers like he was examining fine silk. "Is now yours."

"Mine?" I repeated.

"Yours." He nodded into the crook of my neck, his hot lips landing on spots I didn't even know were sensitive.

Calm washed over me. Realization, too.

This was retaliation.

Not business…but the sweetest form of comfort. *Revenge.*

"Six hundred thousand dollars." His voice sounded like it was coming from far away.

I like him. I like him and I hate it.

"In the form of a check," he continued. "Yours to cash, whenever you're ready."

I let it sink in, processing the meaning of it. He'd forced Rowan into signing over everything he had to me. More than half a million dollar. The kind of money I'd never even dreamed about. And it was for me to take.

"It's dirty money," I said on auto-pilot.

"This whole world is filthy," Troy shot back. "You deserve it after what he's done. Hell, the only reason I let him live is because it's so much more fun to know every day is a Russian roulette of live or die for him."

Deep down, I already knew I wasn't going to turn the money down. Not out of greed, but because the check had my name on it. Literally *and* figuratively. I didn't want Rowan's money to find its way back to something or someone he cared about. He sure as hell hadn't cared about nine-year-old me.

Six hundred thousand dollars. *Fuck.* Was I supposed to thank my husband?

Before I had a chance to decide, Troy's palm found the small of my back and he pulled me into his body. Hard. "Nobody fucks with what's mine. Even my late dad's friend. Upstairs," he demanded sharply. "Now."

I couldn't believe he flew us all the way to Miami to avenge my pain.

My legs found their way out of the guest room. I stared at my feet as I climbed up the stairs, him ascending behind me in perfect rhythm.

I felt his eyes on my ass. "When I was a kid," he said, "my mother had lovebirds. She used to clip their wings so when she let them out of their cage, they wouldn't fly away. The lovebirds always tried, but they never got far with their short, fucked-up wings."

I inched the bedroom door open and stepped into the pool of warm light spilling from the street outside.

He moved behind me, tucking my hair behind my right ear aside, pressing his face to it. "Until one day, one managed to escape. My mother forgot to clip her wings. A moment of distraction cost her her favorite lovebird."

I knew why he was telling me this, and the happiness in my gut swirled with a shot of sudden pain.

"Failure is inevitable," he continued in a flat tone that didn't hold much emotion or hope, "and heartache is unstoppable. One day, I'll forget to clip your wings. When that day arrives, when you run away, I guess I'd be happy to know you'll still have some money and the means to make it in this wild, tough world."

Was it wrong that I adored the way the word *lovebird* rolled off his tongue? I knew he hadn't told me that he loved me, but I still enjoyed the warm buzz in my chest when he said it. The truth about Miami had changed a lot. His visiting Paddy was not only forgivable but redeeming.

"It was more than a solid," I whispered, averting my gaze from the window to the bed. Still not daring to turn back and look at his face. "What you did for me."

"Sparrow," he warned. "Don't get any ideas into that pretty head of yours. I told you how things will play out. This…" He took a step back and walked deeper into the room, spinning around so that we faced each other. "This doesn't have a happy ending."

"Maybe I won't run away." I swallowed hard. "If you came clean about everything, about why you married me, maybe I'd stay. Break the lock to my cage, Troy." I took a deep breath. "What are you hiding? Who are 'they'? What did they do to 'us'?"

"Can't. It's illegal. I won't chance you running to the police with it, and I certainly won't chance the police finding about it through other sources and questioning you about it. You'd be considered my partner in crime for not notifying them. And risking your ass…" He shook his head. "Not gonna happen. Sit."

He patted the expensive mattress I kind of missed. Or maybe it wasn't the mattress. Maybe it was the smell that clung to it. Of the person it belonged to. My shoulders fell and I lowered my head, but I sat.

Still standing, he kissed the nape of my neck. "Obedient. That's new."

"Not really." My tone was flat. "But I'm in my underwear. In your bed. We had a deal. I intend to keep it."

He tilted up my chin up. I stared up at his blue eyes, getting lost in his gaze. My breath quickened. He wanted to play. I wanted to play, too, even though we both knew he was going to break the toy. *Me.*

He was behind me. I loved the thrill of never knowing what was going to happen next. He favored this position, when my back was to him. We both knew I didn't trust him. Which only made it more arousing.

"I believe you have something that belongs to me," he whispered into my shoulder. It felt like warm feathers traveling down my body. Addictive, awakening my senses again.

My eyes fluttered shut as I breathed him in.

"Your virginity, Red."

"Take it." I leaned into his touch, pressing my head against his hard abs. "'Cause that's all I'm going to give to you."

I was a liar. I was reckless. I was an idiot. But I was his.

He yanked me up and spun me to face him. Pulling my hair and extending my neck, he ran the tip of his tongue between my breasts. I stilled, holding my breath when his free hand fisted the hem of my shirt.

"I've been waiting for this moment for a while now," he said.

He likes me, my heart chanted. *He likes me and he is going to show me just how much.*

Yanking the neck of my undershirt down, he ripped it apart slowly, painfully over my skin. He studied the ball of fabric with cold eyes and tossed it behind him.

"You won't be needing that," he said, ducking down to meet my hungry lips.

Goose bumps rose on my skin, a shiver breaking along my scalp. I didn't moan, didn't give him the satisfaction, but when his hand cupped one of my bare breasts and kneaded it, his thumb circling the ridge of my nipple, I clenched inside without even meaning to.

The way Troy touched me was worth every horrible, self-loathing feeling that I would have tomorrow.

His lower lip caressed my ear. "Guess your magical period is over, huh?"

His fingers moved from my breast down my stomach, making their way between my quivering legs. He spread my thighs, using his fingers alone, and nudged my panties to the left. His strength made me dizzy with want, and I knew once he'd touch me there, I would collapse and lose control again.

"Are you here to talk, or to show me what you've got?" My voice cut through the air.

He paused his leisured strokes along my sensitive skin. In one swift movement, he cupped my pussy hard, like it was a baseball he was about to throw, jerked me into his body, my stomach pressing into his cock, and shoved one finger into me while his thumb rubbed my clit.

It hurt. It freaking hurt a lot.

"Watch it!" I shrieked, flustered, my muscles tensing. I pressed against him nonetheless. "It's painful."

"Pain *is* pleasure," he elucidated. His finger still inside me, he pumped in and out as he threw me onto the bed and spun me around again. He climbed on top, his muscular legs straddling my body.

I was face down on the pillow, panting like a cat in heat and loving every second of it. He was rough, not romantic or considerate in any way. And hell, that's exactly how I wanted him.

I felt his teeth sinking into the soft flesh of my ass—more a tease than an actual bite. He ground his erection against me, and I almost begged for him to yank my panties down and enter me. But he didn't. He just shoved his finger deeper, faster. Even though I winced, I became needier. Rubbing my opening and crooking his finger into me, he found a sensitive spot and pumped it again and again.

I buried my face in the pillow to muffle my moans. "This is..." I could barely speak. "This is..."

"This is your G-spot." He bit my earlobe from behind. "Nice to meet ya."

I wanted to scream with both pain and pleasure, and I clenched against his fingers. He picked up the pace even more, screwing me with his fingers while grinding his cock against my ass. I loved it. Loved every filthy moment of it. The pain of his weight and fingers inside me was so much...

I gasped each time he slammed into me. I felt his lips traveling along my upper back, my neck, my hair, leaving bites and kisses.

"Tell me what I'm doing to you, or I'll stop."

"You're driving me mad," I groaned. This much was true. His hand was between my legs while he jerked off on my body, and I admitted it was hot. So hot I was beginning to feel dizzy. Lightheaded. Drunk. The Catholic guilt I had felt after he performed oral sex on me the other day evaporated. It was technically not a sin. We were married.

"What. Am. I. Doing. To you? Simple English, Red."

"You're fingering me," I said, blushing hard. Damn, why was it so hard to say it out loud?

"That's *not* fingering."

"Okay, okay," I panted when he momentarily stopped, his fingers still inside me. "You're fucking me with your fingers."

He resumed thrusting, increasing the numbing ache and the crazy desire thrumming in my crotch. My body felt electrified, the bed beneath us pooled with my want for him, and after a few minutes of buildup, of so much pain and pleasure and everything in-between, I came apart for the first time in my life. There was no mistaking the feeling. It was hard. It crashed through me in waves of heat.

The tingling calmed, and my body went limp. His fingers stopped, and after I droopily crashed on the mattress, he pulled his hand from under me, sucked on his two fingers, and flipped me to my back.

I was his rag doll, for him to flip, spin, toss, finger, use, repeat. And that's exactly what I craved. *In bed, anyway.*

"I wanted you since that night at Rouge Bis, you know." His lips dove to my neck and he bit me hard, making my back arch with desire. He licked the spot, moving his finger down my spine and grinding against me. "Such a breath of fresh air. Messing around with me like I can't break you in two."

I moaned, returning a favor by pushing my hips in his direction.

He unbuckled his belt, unzipping his dress pants as he spread kisses all over my face and chest. God, I wanted more of him. Not just his body, just more. More feelings. More sex. More everything. I wanted him to be my real husband, and I was lying to him, myself and the world when I said that all I wanted was sex. This was just the tip of the iceberg. I was addicted.

"It's going to hurt like a motherfucker," he warned.

"Of course it will." I smiled into our kiss, my lips still glued to his. "Everything with you does."

He yanked my underwear down and guided his cock to my entrance. We both watched through hooded eyes as he moved it up and down my slit. I was so ready for him after falling apart between his strong arms, coming so hard, so wet and in need, I barely had any second thoughts about it.

"I love this," he whispered wildly, his mouth traveling down my body, his tongue swirling around my nipple. Everything about him was scorching hot, and I threw my head back, my eyes closed. "Love that I'm going to rock yourworld and ruin you for every other man in the world."

When he entered me, I held my breath. It wasn't just painful—it was torture. So bad, in fact, that tears stung my eyes. Troy was equipped with something resembling a semi-automatic weapon, and even though his cock was the first I had ever seen, I had a feeling it wasn't a modest, fun-sized one. He moved inside me slowly, his eyes holding mine. Interest flickered in his gaze, and I tucked my head into his chest.

"Why are you looking at me like that?" I felt my face heating. He didn't look turned on anymore. Just...alert. He was searching me, looking for something, making me feel even more naked than I already was.

"Breathe, baby," he said seriously. "The pain will go away, but the pleasure will stay. I got you, Red."

He thrust in and out, and I winced every time he did, digging my nails deeper into his back, knowing I'd leave marks. Because I wanted him to stop. Because I wanted him to continue. Because I never wanted to leave.

He kissed away a tear that slid down my cheek, and I wish he hadn't, because my heart broke a little more when he showed me tenderness. I wanted the ruthless version of him, the one that didn't offer me hope, that didn't promise a happily-ever-after ending. Troy was the guy who not only broke your headboard, but also broke your heart. And I didn't want false hope to occupy any more space in my mind than it already did.

He was pumping in and out of me, faster, stronger, deeper. Soon, I learned his rhythm, and our hips moved together like a sensual dance.

The pain will go away.

No, it wouldn't.

The pleasure will stay.

"I want you to come in my arms again," he said, but I knew it wouldn't happen. Not when all I could feel was him ripping through me. He snaked one of his hands down between us and started rubbing my clit, applying pressure. I gasped a little when he flicked it up and down with his thumb.

"Oh, God," I panted. "That hurts in the best possible way."

He kissed me, darting his tongue between my lips. Even his tongue fucked my mouth. The massive bed creaked a little with every push, the headboard banging against the wall with every thrust.

Wild. Possessed. Abandoned.

And it turned out that was all I needed, to twist and writhe again under him. I felt the familiar sensation of losing control over my muscles and tried pushing him away, because this time, the orgasm threatened to tear through me.

He held me in place, nailing me to the bed with the firm hand that played with me. "Fuck, you're beautiful when you come."

And I came again, this time harder, screaming his name to the sky and back. I don't think anyone ever felt more intoxicated from another person as I was intoxicated from Troy Brennan. The scary stranger turned cruel husband.

It was only after my second orgasm that my husband started pumping harder into me, losing control himself. It was wild to see him letting go for once as he thrust deeper and deeper. He swelled inside me, filling me completely, and strangely, not only physically.

He was coming. His forehead rested on mine, his black strands of hair sticking to his temple. Our sweat mixed together.

Damn, it was sexy.

Hell, I was done for.

It wasn't him taking my virginity that made me feel vulnerable. Not the fact that I was lying in a pool of our lust and my own blood. It was what I felt for him that horrified me. I wanted to step away from whatever I was feeling, put some space between me and Troy, gain some control over my heart. I was spiraling down, fast. Drowning, sinking, free-falling. I was defenseless, helpless, completely exposed. A sitting duck waiting for him to fill me with a buckshot and strip my feathers clean.

He flopped down next to me, pulling me into his arms, my ass against his body. The sheets beneath us were so wet, the thought of Maria finding them made my face heat with embarrassment. I would change those sheets tonight and do the laundry myself. Tomorrow, it'd look like nothing happened.

We lay there in silence while he drew letters and patterns on my skin with his finger. He wrote "God" and then "Troy" and then "Red." Drew a house, raindrops and a pair of wings.

We weren't kidding anyone.

This was not just sex. It was more and it was scary. A good thirty minutes passed before one of us spoke. Surprisingly, it wasn't me.

"Tell me about your mom," he asked out of nowhere, me still in his arms. His tone was lazy, like we were familiar with one another more than just physically. And that was a lie I was tempted to believe.

My body must've stiffened, because suddenly, his fingers stopped stroking my back and his lips no longer pressed against my hair.

"I don't have a mom," I clarified. "The woman who gave birth to me ran off long before I was able to remember anything about her."

"Have you tried looking for her over the years?" The softness in his tone was rubbing me the wrong way. He was not supposed to care. He was a sorry douchebag who cheated on me, forced me into marrying him and broke the law for a living.

"Are you auditioning for *Dateline?* What the hell is your problem, Troy?" I wiggled out of his touch, pulling myself up from the bed and standing up in a hurry. I lifted items of clothes that weren't even mine from the floor and dressed in his shirt and my underwear without making eye contact. Tonight was not supposed to end this way.

He was still lying on the bed, his head supported on one of his arms. Naked, he watched me. "Just trying to be a good husband," he said.

"You're good for only one thing, Brennan." I pulled my panties up my legs in swift movements. "And that's for what happened between your sheets not too long ago."

"They're your sheets, too, Red."

"Thought I was supposed to be lovebird from now on?" I turned my back to him, already making my way out of the room.

I heard his laugh, and my heart twisted in anticipation and sadness.

"I changed my mind." His voice had a hard edge. "I'm not letting you fly away. Ever."

NINETEEN

SPARROW

"Consider this..." Lucy's hands were quick as she peeled potatoes at the speed of light at my kitchen sink. "You told him to fire Connor and he did. You told him to quit fucking around and it looks like he did that too. I think it might come as shocking news to you, but honey, your husband has feelings for you."

Standing next to her, I stirred the Alfredo sauce for the rotini, dunking my finger and having a taste. I added a dash of salt, stalling. She was no longer concerned for my safety. Now, she was more interested in my love life.

"Mmm," I said, not really eager to tell her about the part where the so-called loving husband dragged me on a plane with a fake passport against my will and screwed another girl in our bedroom.

On the same day.

Yeah, Disney wouldn't be calling him for tips on how to play a credible Prince Charming.

"Yeah, well, we've been married for three months, and he's still bottling up all these secrets, not letting me in on anything. Why did he marry me? Who did he refer to when he said 'they' that night before we went to Rouge Bis? He won't even tell me what happened with Catalina."

We were making tons of food for a charity event for the homeless shelter down the road. Over the past few months, I'd gone to the shelter often, bearing tasty donations. The volunteers who worked there were all too happy to ask me if I could help cooking for their little gathering.

Lucy was about to pour the drippings from the bacon for the Alfredo into an empty jar when I redirected her with a wooden spoon to the garbage disposal down our sink.

"Seriously? It'll clog up your pipes."

"Don't run the water either," I shot back.

She grinned, but did as I told her and poured the grease down the disposal.

I was still rebelling in small, mundane ways. Keeping him on his toes. Showing him that just because we shared a bed—and enough sex to make me walk all wobbly the day after—didn't mean that I was an agreeable little wife. So far I have managed a few "accidents," including breaking his iPad, staining his favorite suit with white sauce and keying his Maserati. The headboard we broke together, so that wasn't exactly just on me.

"Look at you, all grown up and having detached sex." Lucy gave voice to my thoughts, talking over the grinding of the disposal. "How can you hate him, doing everything you can to show him just how much, and still sleep with him at night?"

I didn't hate my husband, but somehow, I was horrified by the concept of admitting it aloud.

I downplayed the whole situation by offering a half-assed shrug, wiping my oily hands on a paper towel. "It's just sex. If I didn't do it with him, I would have ended up having to stay a virgin until he dropped dead. Even I'm not stupid enough to cheat on a Brennan."

Now that Connor was out of the picture, I spent more time in our neighborhood, cleaning and cooking for Pops, and also more time with Lucy and Daisy. Lucy was in the loop again. Knew that I was sleeping in the master bedroom. Knew that my nights were warm this stormy, cold Boston summer. A summer that somehow was bleeding into an even worse New England fall.

My best friend was also privy to the fact that we shared civil conversations when my husband came home from work. He got back at reasonable hours, sans lipstick stains and the cloying cloud of flowery perfume of a woman who desperately wanted to be acknowledged.

One time he even took a bite of my famous blueberry pancakes. Yup, *that sugary crap.*

"Humor me here, sister." Lucy started wrapping up some of the dishes in foil. "If he *does* happen to have feelings for you, would that change anything? I mean, would you ever consider treating this like…I don't know, a normal relationship?"

I snorted into my chest, eyes firmly on the dishes in front of us. "No. Not unless he came clean about everything."

Deep down, I knew that we would never be equals until he'd let me in on why he'd married me in the first place. I also knew that no amount of sex and small talk was going to prod the truth out of him. If I was detached, his heart was practically on another planet, nowhere near my own.

"Do you think he'll ever come clean?"

My gut twisted in pain. "Honestly? Fat chance. I think people like Troy spread so many lies to hide their secrets, they drown in them and forget their own truths."

But that wasn't completely accurate. Troy was as comfortable in his sea of lies as a synchronized swimmer in an Olympic swimming pool. I was the one who was drowning in them.

Worst of all? I was feeding myself even more lies. Because I told myself I didn't care. While slowly, he crept under my skin.

Piercing through layers.

Clawing his way deeper into me.

And I knew it was only a matter of time before he reached the most dangerous place in my body.

My heart.

TWENTY

SPARROW

THERE WAS A LOT I DIDN'T LIKE about my job at Rouge Bis. I didn't like how Brock tried to worm his way into my good graces like we were friends, despite my best efforts to show him how uncomfortable I was around him after that kiss. I didn't like Pierre's attitude toward me, and the way he tried to come up with little, creative ways to make my life hell, just like I tried coming up with ways to piss off Troy.

But there was one thing I definitely looked forward to every shift—my break. When Brock wasn't there to try and strike up a conversation, it was my favorite part of the day. I was granted thirty minutes and a choice of entrée to eat in a quiet corner of the restaurant, shielded from the rest of the tables and booths. It was my *me* time at work, before the hectic dinner service.

I was twirling a forkful of pasta, relishing the quiet when I heard a pair of heels approaching, clack-clacking on the floor like bullet fire in the dark. The woman's hip swayed seductively as she strode in my direction on her stilettos. I smiled when I noticed she was wearing a pair of exactly the same shoes I'd worn on my first date with Troy, the ones Maria's daughter had lent me.

But when I lifted my gaze from her feet to her face, my smile froze. Her glossy lips were pouted in disapproval as we drank each other in. I hadn't seen Catalina Greystone since my wedding day.

She slid into the opposite bench of my booth and tossed a folded napkin over my plate to signal to me that dinner was over.

Stunned, I put the silverware down, tilting my chin up.

Her shoes.

My feet burned with anger. Catalina was Maria's daughter.

Her eyes.

She was furious. Something had pissed her off, and it had everything to do with me.

"Looking for Brock?" My smile was raw. She was another secret Troy hadn't shared with me.

"Actually, I was looking for you."

The idea that Brock had told her we kissed crossed my mind briefly, but disappeared just as fast. *He kissed you, silly. Not the other way around.* Anyway, that was months ago. Why would Catalina suddenly confront me now?

I leaned back in my seat, acutely aware of my foot that kept bouncing underneath the table, making the utensils clatter against my plate. I toyed with my cell phone. "Well?" I asked.

"You know, Sparrow, we never really got to know one another properly." She propped forward on her elbows, like she was about to share a secret, but her voice was anything but friendly. "I'm kind of sorry we haven't had time to talk."

Every muscle in my body tensed. I felt the persistent hum of a catastrophe in the making.

"Catalina," I said evenly, "I have ten more minutes before I need to get back to gutting fish. Whatever you came here to say, just spit it out. I don't have all day."

That seemed to shake her a little. She reached for the cell I held in my hand and stopped me from scrolling my thumb over the screen.

"Troy's in love with me," she said.

It never ceased to amaze me how a few simple words could shake you to your soul.

"He is," she continued. "You know, we were engaged before I had Sam. Dated for three full years." She was trying to catch my eyes. Desperately.

I refused to give her the satisfaction of seeing my shock, but inside, the pieces of the puzzle were falling together, quickly, clumsily, with a screechy sound. They'd once been engaged. They were in love. They were a *real* couple.

"Funny, I don't see a ring on your finger. Oh, wait, there it is." I motioned at her left hand. "And whaddaya know? It belongs to Brock Greystone."

"What, this thing?" She sniffed, waving her hand dismissively. Her engagement ring was considerably smaller than mine, but still gigantic to anyone who wasn't a real-life princess. She wore a thin wedding band on the same finger. "Brock and I are just an arrangement," she explained, smiling coyly.

And I believed her. After all, Brock had said so himself.

"Troy and I are a real item. That's why he crawls back to me every Friday. You always work Fridays don't you? I'm the only thing that keeps his charade with you bearable. Don't get me wrong. He thinks you're a nice girl. But, you know, just not a woman."

My body vibrated with fury. My lungs squeezed, and every nerve and cell in me urged me to lunge across the table and strangle her.

Troy had a mistress.

And there she sat, in front of me, telling me that they were in love, no less.

Worst of all, I recognized her sweet, flowery, in-your-face perfume. The one that hung in the air in my bedroom the day we flew to Miami. The day Troy had sex with someone else.

"Bullshit." My voice was low, even though I knew she spoke the truth.

My lips kept moving, and what they said next surprised me. "If Troy loved you, he would have never shared you. It's not in his DNA. He wouldn't even share someone he doesn't love." *Like me.* "So if he had feelings for you? It would be you in his bed. Not me. Not anyone else."

I made sense.

I made sense and it gave me a little strength. I pushed to my feet, pointing my cell at her face. "He's stopped seeing you, hasn't he? Months ago, I'm betting. That's why you're here. You're desperate."

By the color rising from her chest to her neck and up to her cheeks, I knew I was right.

She got up herself, glaring at me through a pinched smile. "The only reason it's you in his bed and not me is because he made a deal with the devil. I know all about your marriage, Sparrow. It ain't real."

Somewhere in my mind, there was a tiny, cartoon version of me getting punched square in the face by a cartoon version of Cat. The cartoon-me stumbled backward and dropped to her knees.

But the real me strode toward the door that said Staff Only, knowing that if I stayed, I'd do something I'd regret.

Catalina followed, still taunting me from behind. "And the only reason you aren't six feet under and Troy hasn't gotten rid of you to make room for me is because I cheated on him with Brock. The little fling I had with my husband ended up with me getting pregnant with Sam."

Her words were rushed, leaving her no room to inhale. Cartoon-Me took a shot in the shoulder, blood smeared on the wall behind her.

"Last but not least," she said, making me hesitate in the doorway, "even after I crushed him, had someone else's baby in my belly, Troy still took care of me. Did everything for me. What he and I have…honey, you don't want to try and top that. It'd only mean more heartache for you, and I'd hate to see you getting your hopes up."

Cartoon-Me jumped back to her feet, summoning false-strength for what she had to do next. "You know nothing about my relationship with my husband. Know nothing about what's going on. All you know is this that Troy stopped showing up, and it's killing you. You're worried. And you should be." I smiled. "Things change. People, too. Move on, I know he has. Bye, Catalina."

With that, I slammed the door in her face so hard, the walls around me quaked.

Cartoon-Me kicked cartoon Catalina in the butt, sending her out of the blackening, shrinking cartoon frame. But the second Cat was out of the frame, it expanded again and Cartoon-Me went back to lying in a pool of her own blood.

Because Catalina was right. He might not love her.

But he didn't love me either.

And the truth was, she knew the one thing he wouldn't tell me—what made him marry me.

And what made him tick.

TWENTY ONE

TROY

I PARKED IN FRONT OF THE foggy graveyard.

My father was buried in one of the oldest cemeteries in Boston. Untamed grass, mud, moss and spider webs adorned the tombstones like Halloween decorations. The place was a rusty gate short of looking like a bad horror flick set, and I had to admit, I kind of liked the extra-touch of morbidity it had. Despite the cemetery looking like hell, I knew Dad wouldn't have wanted it any other way. The graveyard was at the back of the South Boston church we used to go to every Sunday. Practically his second home.

Here were buried not only my relatives, but also many memories. Some I remembered fondly, some I wished I could forget, like McGregor.

I came here every Friday afternoon, before the weekend rolled around and with it, new, fresh sins to commit. Came here to talk to the man I so desperately missed. He was my priest, his gravestone my confession booth.

He never judged.

Never gave me shit for being who I was.

And coming here also reminded me that I had an unfinished business to take care of. To find out who was responsible for my father's death.

I whistled as I wove through the graveyard, my own personal touch of irony. Visiting his grave wasn't a sad affair nowadays. It was like going out for a beer with an old friend.

Ignoring the drizzle—it really had been the weirdest summer I could remember in Boston, and to my delight, the fall was starting out just as grim—I squatted down in front of my father's grave, my elbows over my knees. Like all fathers and sons, we had our tough talks, even after his eternal slumber.

The past few weeks, I'd been pre-occupied again with trying to figure out who'd murdered him. Who sent Crupti. Whoever it was, they used a middle-man (a sorry ass local kid who died in an accident a few months after dad's death) and bitcoin. The person behind dad's death was smart. Calculated...*and as good as dead.*

I had people digging more, trying to figure out who sent Crupti to kill him. I intended to leave no stone in greater Boston unturned. But it was hard. All of my father's enemies were either dead or in the clear. Something didn't add up.

I was beginning to wonder if the person who sent Crupti was an enemy of *mine*, not of my father's.

At least I'd settled the score with Paddy Rowan, the old shit. Though this wasn't only for him, it was also for her.

I'd spoken about Sparrow with my father often recently.

"Was Robyn such a huge fucking pain in the ass, too? Sparrow must've gotten her sass from somewhere, and it's not from Abe."

Dad didn't answer. Of course he didn't. He never did. But I had a feeling that if he were here next to me, he would have snorted out a laugh and said something crude about the Raynes girls. I had a feeling that even if he'd loved Robyn, he'd never outwardly shown his feelings.

Couldn't blame him. I wasn't exactly in touch with my emotions either. Most of the time, I wasn't even sure if they existed.

And now I was fucking Red exclusively. I plucked a few blades of grass and threw them on his grave. It'd been a while since I'd limited myself to one woman. Catalina was my last attempt at monogamy, and that had ended up being a magnificent failure.

"Baby? Baby, is that you?"

Speak of the devil. Cat was struggling toward me in her high heels, her blow-dried hair flattened against her head, raindrops spattered on her forehead. Her teeth chattered in the cold drizzle.

It shouldn't have surprised me that she was there. She'd always had stalkerish tendencies. Even before I first broke it off. When she still wore the sweet, shy-girl mask that made me want her in the first place. She'd accompany Maria when she came to clean for us at my parents' house, always eyeing me through her long, curly eyelashes, smiling like I hung the moon in the sky and lit up the sun myself.

But she was also possessive as hell.

Always sniffing around to make sure I was only hers.

I stood straight, only then realizing how soaking wet I was from the rain, and stood in front of her, my face hard and unwelcoming. She stopped a good few feet away from me. The rain picked up making it difficult to make out her expression.

"She is a child," she announced. "Your marriage was supposed to be an arrangement, you said so yourself. You said she was a burden you had to deal with for your dad." Her body shook, and it wasn't from the cold. "I need you back, Troy."

She was crying, talking about Sparrow, and as much as it surprised me, I wasn't so hot about seeing her shattered.

"Let it go." I huddled in my soaked pea coat. "We had our farewell fuck, said our goodbyes in my apartment months ago. We're done."

"Troy, baby, no." She fell on her knees in front of me, mud splashing everywhere around us. She clasped my legs like they were an anchor as tears streamed down her face, mixing with the raindrops. "Please. She is nothing, no one. She doesn't want you. Doesn't need you. Doesn't deserve you. We've got history. Chemistry. We've got something fucked up and twisted, but it's ours. It's us. It's always been us."

"You really should've thought about that before you let Brock get you pregnant." My tone was harsh, but the edge was gone. I wasn't high on fucking Brock's wife anymore. Everything about the situation felt tasteless. Worthless. Guess I'd moved on.

"You told me to marry him." She sniffed, her nose dripping, her fingernails still clawing into my pants. "You said it'd be the best thing for everybody because of that goddamned pregnancy. Oh, Troy."

"Cat," I growled, "the *goddamned* pregnancy is now a kid. Maybe you should consider taking care of him." But I knew what Cat never said out loud. She resented Sam, because Sam was the final straw between us. I couldn't take her back after that betrayal.

"This could have been us. Married. Happy," she pleaded. "I belong in your bed, in your house, in your mind. I'll do anything. Tell me what to do to bring you back to me."

"You're a wreck." I turned around and started walking to my car. I hated that she barged into my time with my dad.

She stalked after me, crying hysterically, stumbling to the ground and then lurching back to her feet. Stiletto heels weren't exactly the best footwear for a muddy graveyard. But Cat had always liked putting on a show. Twenty-something-year-old Troy admired that. Thirty-something Troy knew this shit got old.

"Don't do this," she warned. "I'll ruin this for you."

I sighed. "Catalina, baby, you can't even ruin your own fucking life successfully, let alone someone else's. You've never been the overachiever type."

"Go to hell." She shoved me and then flailed at me with her fists.

I dodged her girly jabs and captured her wrists, walking her backward into the high stone fence that surrounded that graveyard and pinning her back to it. It felt so vacant to hold her between my arms. For a moment, I wondered if I ever really did love her.

"Enough," I said. "This stops here. Now listen to me carefully, and get it into your head, because I won't say it twice. You had your chance. I gave you everything. Worked my fucking ass off so you could afford your fancy shit. Took risks. Built a business, opened a French restaurant just 'cause it was your favorite food—*all* for you. But you betrayed me. You got coked up on my money, snorted through the majority of it, and I had to send you off to rehab, where you fucked up more. We had our fun, and now it's time to let go. Got it?"

Catalina threw more aimless punches at me and screamed, "Stop saying these things!"

I knew she had a hard time hearing this, but the funny thing was, I no longer had a hard time saying it, admitting this to her and me. I'd sent Cat to a Malibu rehab shortly before we broke it off. The most expensive fucking rehab in the States. Sauna rooms and twenty-four-hour spas. Only the best for my girl. She came back pregnant with her counselor's baby. With *Brock's* baby.

I still remembered the day I found out my initially unpregnant girlfriend had come back after two months in rehab with a new addition in her belly. She tried to convince me the baby was mine. Hell, I fought hard to believe it myself. But then I went with her to her check-up and the OB-GYN had spilled the dates. Cat was six weeks pregnant, and not with my child.

"No, no, no, no." She shook her head violently, raking her long fingernails down her face, streaking her cheeks with bloody scratches.

"Don't mistake my sympathy then for feelings." I said, surprised that the rage was gone. "When you were pregnant, I didn't throw your ass out of my apartment because I didn't want this shit on my conscience, not because I still loved you."

"Troy!" she pleaded, throwing her bloody fists in my face and crying like a tortured animal. "Stop this now!"

But it was true.

I'd felt guilty. Guilty because I couldn't give her what she'd wanted. What we both wanted. Our engagement didn't mean shit, and we both knew that.

I was going to marry Sparrow Raynes, the poor little girl down my street. The money, the clothes, the restaurants, the fancy-ass vacations. Lies, lies and more lies. A pile of distractions to make us forget we were never going to get married. In a sense, a part of me—the puppy-love part—thought Cat screwing someone else was my punishment. I couldn't be hers exclusively. Why should it be any different for her?

I remembered after we broke up, going back to the apartment Cat and I used to share. I'd wanted to take some of my shit, mainly clothes. I wasn't surprised to see the guy who knocked her up had taken a trip to Boston just so he could have another dip.

She was beautiful, broken and willing to do anything the man at her side wanted. It was a lethal combination for most men, something that was too hard to turn down. I fucking knew that first-hand.

Brock ended up staying in Boston, and I let him work for me. Gave him a job a few months before my father's murder, thinking I'd help her—and him—build a family. I'd thought it was my way to compensate. We were done, but I still had a chance to redeem myself in the eyes of the only girl I'd ever fallen in love with. Even if I couldn't have her.

"We should have stopped this fucking years ago," I told Cat, who was struggling for breath, her face blotched with tears and older since I'd last seen her.

"I love you. He was always just a plaything. I love you, Troy." Trying another strategy, she arched her back away from the stone fence, her hips meeting my groin.

I pulled back immediately. Jesus, she thought I was going to take her right then and there. How could I have loved someone so weak?

I sucked in a breath. "You don't love anything other than danger and cock. There's an abyss between us, and it swallowed every positive feeling I've ever felt toward you. Because even after I tried to help you and your husband, you had the nerve to go and spill every secret I ever told you to him." I let go of her wrists in disgust. "And that was the ultimate betrayal."

Catalina told Brock everything.

About the promises my dad made me make.

About Sparrow.

About fucking everything.

She put me in a vulnerable position, and jeopardized everything I'd ever worked for.

I wished Cat had never told Brock about it. I wished he'd never told me that he knew. On a drunken night when the two of us got back from the cabin after detoxing one of my client's daughters, Brock had revealed that Cat had spilled every single secret I let her in on. Brock had promised to keep mum.

Because it wasn't a friendly promise—it was a threat.

"So here's the deal." I rested my arm above Cat's head as I locked eyes with her. "I'm going to walk away from here. Next time I see you, it'll be on Brock's arm, playing the dutiful wife. You will never speak to me, mention this, or try and reach out to me again, got it?"

I admit I'd taken my revenge too far. Fucking Catalina under her husband's roof just to feel better about myself? About everything I had lost? Making her one of the endless women on my speed dial? Reducing her to nothing but a warm pussy to bury myself in occasionally? Below the belt, but I'd needed to rebuild my ego. I'd needed to make sure I was leaving her just as broken as she'd left me when she cheated, married someone else and spilled my secrets in his ears.

"She knows," Cat said, smiling a crazy, hateful smile. "I told Sparrow about us. Your wife knows."

"Go near her again, and I will kill you with my bare hands." I took a step back, watching her slide down the wall and collapse on the grass as she wailed.

I'd played this scene over and over in my head for years. Me leaving Catalina for good. Stepping away from this mess while I had the upper hand.

I'd imagined feeling triumphant and elated as I dumped her, breaking her heart, but as I left the graveyard, all I felt was incredible emptiness and an unbearable fury about her talking to Red.

I hoped Cat wasn't coked up again. Poor Sam didn't need two fuck-ups for parents.

And as thunder cracked the sky open above me, another downpour on its way, I slipped into the Maserati and turned on the stereo all the way up. "Last Night I Dreamt That Somebody Loved Me" by The Smiths blasted through the speakers. I knew that this time the rain would wash away most of my memories with Cat.

We were done. Through.

I couldn't wait for my next chapter.

TWENTY TWO

TROY

FLYNN WAS DEAD.

He was still among the living when I left him at the cabin with Brock on Saturday. The detox after Miami hadn't stuck—not much surprise there. I'd received a call from George Van Horn, complaining that his son had relapsed big time. I'd hauled Flynn to the cabin again and put Brock in charge over the weekend.

As planned, first thing Monday morning, I drove up to check on them. Flynn was sure as fuck dead now.

Guilt ate away at my insides. It wasn't that I was particularly fazed by death. I was even responsible for the horrific ending of two men, finished them without even blinking. But Flynn was innocent, and he'd died because his dad was too proud to seek professional help for his son at the hospital.

He also died because I cared more about the paycheck than doing the right thing.

Flynn was Sparrow. Everyone failed him. His parents. His family. His friends. The only difference was that Sparrow had me now, and I wasn't letting anyone harm my little lovebird. If she was going to be ruined, it would be by me.

The smell around Flynn told me he had given up the ghost, but not so long ago that he stank. Which also made sense, because if Brock left him alone, it wouldn't have been too long ago.

I rolled him from his stomach to his back with a shove, placed two fingers on his neck and checked for his pulse again.

Yeah, the kid was gone.

Looking around the cabin, I sighed and raked a hand through my hair. Brock was supposed to save him. He may have been a shithead, but he was also a badass when it came to detoxing. Why the hell has he abandoned ship without telling me, and how the fuck was I going to explain it to George?

I brushed my thumb against Flynn's eyelids, shutting his eyes. His lost-puppy eyes were staring at me, and I needed a breather from feeling like shit.

I made the call to George Van Horn, breaking the news in code. The parcel got lost in the mail. Can't be retrieved. What does he want me to do next. I was hoping not to hear what he answered.

"I see the post office is still overpriced and unreliable." He took a dig at me. "Just make sure nobody else finds the parcel." Then he hung up.

Van Horn wanted me to get rid of Flynn's body discreetly. Didn't even have it in him to stage an accidental overdose and give his son a proper funeral, a service of some kind. Of course, the latter would kill his political campaign. But the thing about the George Van Horns of our world, the ones who compromised their morals—who did nasty shit they don't feel at peace with—was that they woke up one day to discover they'd became a monster.

I myself didn't feel like a monster. Wholeheartedly believed that the people who killed my father deserved to die. I was cruel, but I wasn't unjust. I wouldn't off someone from my family, or deny them a respectable burial, just to get ahead in the game.

Other than Sparrow's mom, I reminded myself. She was still very much on my conscience, and I knew that Sparrow would never forgive me if she knew.

I dragged Flynn's body outside and deeper into the woods. Far enough from the cabin so that in the unlikely event that he was found, no one would make the connection, but not too far, because dragging a body was fucking hard, even if he was a scrawny little junkie.

Driving him to another spot in the woods was pointless. I couldn't get him into the Maserati and would never be able to get rid of all the evidence if I did.

After I placed him near a tree trunk, I walked back to the cabin for a shovel, then walked back into the woods and dug his grave for him. I dumped his body into the hole and buried him as best as I could, knowing I'd be better off burning the body, but somehow not being able to bring myself to do it. It was stupid. He was already dead. But my fucked-up, twisted morals kicked in.

I buried him next to *her*, so I would remember where he was in case I ever needed to dig him up. Everything was calculated, as usual, but it no longer felt right.

Especially not the fact that she was there, buried just a few feet away from him. Her daughter needed to know. Her daughter had to know.

When I got back to the cabin, I took a shower and threw my clothes into a small pit at the back. Looking down, I flicked a lit match between my fingers and into the pit, watching the fire race from the twigs to the fabric, the flames licking at the edge of the pit, swallowing the evidence of my sin.

Sweating away my guilt, I dragged the sofa out to the patio, doused it with gasoline and lit that too. Stinking fire rose from the old sofa, a long cloud of black smoke climbing up to the gray, cloud-covered sky. I scrubbed the cabin clean, everything Flynn touched, until my skin peeled and my knuckles bled. It took me a good few hours, but I couldn't take any chances.

On the drive back to Boston, I tried not to think about the Van Horns. It was that part of the job that I didn't care for. Normally, I was a bad guy messing around with bad guys. But every now and again, a Flynn would slip onto my radar, an innocent person who was just at the wrong place, or more often than not, born into the wrong family, and that's when things got messy. Fucking people over who didn't deserve my wrath wasn't my style. I had my own version for justice, and I applied it whenever I saw fit. I tried to tell myself that this was life. That sometimes you were Batman...and sometimes, the Joker.

Flynn didn't deserve to die, and I could have prevented it, but it would have cost me a client and caused trouble for me. Simply put, covering my ass was more important to me than Flynn's life.

Trying to push this thought and the looming confrontation I'd have to have with Brock about it away, I dialed Sparrow's number. I knew she had a shift, but an overwhelming urge to hear her smartass voice took over. She answered after the fourth ring.

"Why are you answering your phone? You should be working," I barked. She took her job seriously, and I knew she wasn't happy at Rouge Bis. Sparrow was born to be free. She wasn't built to function under the realm of the likes of Pierre. Or me. She also didn't care for fancy food. She was the opposite of Catalina. Her style was oily, homey, comfort street food. She was a pancake kind of girl.

"If you know that I'm working, why're you calling?"

"To piss you off, of course."

"Mission accomplished." I heard the amusement in her voice, and then a sigh and the rattle of pots. "Pierre's giving me shit."

"Sausage fingers?" I rolled a fresh toothpick in my mouth. I hated that she had a shit time at my restaurant, but loved that she hadn't given up. "You're doing a good job."

"I know," she said evenly. "That's why it kills me."

"Deal," I prompted her.

"Oh, I fully intend to. I'm going to raid your liquor cabinet the minute I get home."

Home. This wasn't the first time she'd called it that. In the beginning it was always *your* apartment, *your* sheets, *your* kitchen. I liked that it had become ours, even if I had a feeling it was a temporary thing.

"Wait up for me. I could use a drink or six."

"Another bad day at the office?" she asked.

"The worst."

"Maybe you should change your profession."

"Sure," I snorted. "To what, exactly? Social worker? Maybe an environmental specialist?"

"Perfect. I was thinking along the lines of saving polar bears or wild birds. Somewhere far from civilization would suit you."

"I've already saved one wild bird," I reminded her. "And she keeps me damn busy."

"Saved, huh?" She laughed, the sound an unintended accusation. "Pick this wild bird up some Chinese takeout before you come home. I'll open up a bottle. See you there."

I was almost tempted to come clean to her, on the phone, out of nowhere. Luckily, I came to my senses quickly. I knew it wouldn't do me any good—that she'd never forgive me. Or my father. Her mother. Any of us.

I turned up the volume on the radio. "In My Head" by Queens of the Stone Age blasted through the speakers. Was I pussy-whipped? Yeah. *Literally.* Spending time inside my wife had become my favorite hobby. I had finally found my weakness, and sure enough, it was between Red's legs.

That's where I wanted to live, and that's where I wouldn't mind dying.

But it wasn't just that. The thought of spending time with that little smart mouth tonight made me feel weird. Not exactly happy, but oddly excited. I hated liking her. In a sense, it was like handing her the keys to the pit of my soul while she was tanked as hell and telling her to drive carefully. No one fucking promised me that she would.

Our "arrangement" of fucking around without having any sort of relationship had me confused as fuck. There was nothing romantic in what we were. We didn't go out, share gifts or watched fucking Netflix together. We didn't make love, we made war. When she was pulling, I was biting. When she was scratching, digging her nails into my flesh, I slammed harder, faster. Our sex was furious, it was raw, untamed, wild...but it wasn't selfish.

It wasn't about who Red was that I liked—it was about who she wasn't.

She wasn't a woman who wanted me because of my power, status, job or bank account.

Buying her shit only pissed her off, and trust me, I'd had my people filling her wardrobe with designer shoes and dresses. She gave them all away to the homeless shelter down the street like they weren't worth a dime. In fact, there's a crazy homeless woman in downtown Boston walking around in a Stella McCartney suit and a pair of Jimmy Choo's, yelling at traffic lights that she was the real Messiah.

Yeah. Red either ignored my flashy gifts like they were contaminated, filthy, unworthy, or worse, tucked them under her slim arm and gave them all to charity. I wanted to kill and kiss the shit out of her in the same breath.

It pissed me off and delighted me all at the same time.

She wasn't a woman who cared for superficial shit, someone who was motivated by the wrong things. She was a blank, clean, white sheet for me to scribble on.

And I scribbled.

On her lips, on her jaw, her neck and collarbone. I jotted my hunger for her in vivid colors as I sucked on her pink nipples, grazing my teeth over them, at first slowly and very carefully, and then with more force, when I realized that inside little Sparrow, lay a wild bird waiting to be untethered. I rubbed her until she almost bled, until her moans became growls. I scrawled my initials all over her as I licked her up and down and made her cry my name. Again.

And again.

And again.

And the fucked-up thing was that I didn't want her to be done. I wasn't anxious to get it over with, to get my turn to climax. I let her have her fun. What's more, I enjoyed watching her through heavy-lidded eyes. For the first time in my life, sex was not about me, it was about her.

Hell, sex, I'd been doing it wrong all these years.

This was not me. I was not the caring kind. Last time I cared, I let Brock, Catalina and a bunch of other shit into my life, and it didn't end well.

Feeling a wave of angry heat wash over my skin, I punched Jensen's number. Jensen was my guy for everything hacking-related. He had access to Sparrow's bank account, among other things.

He answered the call but didn't utter a word. Yeah, he was that kind of guy. Cheap with his words and generous with his actions.

"She cashed the check yet?" I asked. *Paddy's money.*

"No," he answered, "Still as broke as her hell, same as when you married her."

"Beautiful. Let me know if that changes."

I hung up, feeling smug. Sparrow would cash the check, I had no doubt, but she'd do it when she ran away and needed the cash. After all, she still didn't know she'd be rich no matter what, seeing as my father made sure of it in his will.

I pressed back into the leather seat behind the wheel of my car and took a deep breath for the first time since I'd left the cabin. For now, she was here. With me.

I intended to keep it that way.

TWENTY THREE

SPARROW

I HAD TO DODGE BROCK's advances for another diner date. He hadn't been at work since my confrontation with Catalina, but he waited for me on the corner of the street again after my shift on Monday night.

"Forget it," I said, walking past him without sparing him a glance.

He caught up with my pace, his hands tucked inside his jeans pockets. "Give me a minute? It'll be worth your while."

"You keep saying that," I ground out, the memory of his wife's afternoon visit a couple of days ago still fresh in my mind. "But I don't think you know what it means. Look, I'm sorry if you and Catalina aren't working out, but I'm not diving headfirst into your mess. You're married, so am I."

It was disappointing to find out that sweet, beautiful Brock, whom I was initially attracted to, couldn't take a hint, even when it was the size of a mountain.

It was even more disappointing to know that his wife was screwing my husband until a few short months ago, including after he married me.

Naturally, it wasn't my business to tell Brock that. I was trying to put out fires, not ignite a blaze that'd scorch us all to hell, Sam included. That's why I hadn't talked about it with Troy since she came to see me. I didn't need unnecessary drama. They were done. He'd fulfilled his side of our deal. There was nothing else to talk about.

"Sweetheart, I don't want Troy to harm you. He's dangerous."

Was he kidding me? Did I give him a damsel in distress vibe? I was pretty sure I handled myself gracefully, even when help *was* needed. As it happened, I didn't need saving. I was standing up to Troy on my own.

"Come with me. Let me show you something." He stopped in front of a car, not as glitzy as Troy's toy but eye-catching nonetheless, and opened the passenger door for me. "I promise, if you still think it's not worth it, I will leave you alone."

"The answer is no." I picked up speed, almost breaking into a run. "Goodbye."

I ran all the way back to the penthouse, trying to tell myself that I wasn't scared, and merely pissed off. That Brock had good intentions, and I was just too drunk on Troy to realize that he was trying to help.

Back at home, I cracked open a bottle of something vintage and placed two glasses of wine near the white wool carpet by the fireplace downstairs. I polished off two drinks just to take the edge off the Brock encounter—the guy was radiating seriously stalker vibes. Then I went into the bathroom upstairs, the one I shared with Troy, to comb my hair and wash off the last of my day at Rouge Bis.

It saddened me that I put up with my husband's secrets. Saddened me because I was no longer able to deny the truth. I was desperately in love with my husband.

Every day he took up more space in my heart. With every moment, it became a bit more difficult to breathe when he wasn't around. My love for Troy Brennan wasn't romantic or sweet—it was violent and needy. It was a cancer, spreading inside my body, multiplying into hundreds and thousands of new cells with every beat of my heart. No chemotherapy, no miracle cure.

Every heartbeat, I slipped a little more. Drowned a little deeper. Fell a little further into the bottomless ocean of feelings for him.

I heard the bedroom door slamming shut and dropped my head back, closing my eyes just so I wouldn't have to see myself in the mirror. Facing yourself was hard when you'd given up yourself for someone else.

"Is it possible to feel your heart breaking, even when you're falling in love?"

I brushed my long hair. *Yes.* It was. Here I was, falling in love, and getting my heart broken at the very same time. A knock on the bathroom door reminded me of the first time we talked, on our wedding day. How much had changed since then. Yet, some things remained the same.

"You better not be decent. I'm coming in."

He opened the door, filling its frame with his impossible size. His azure blues scanned me intently. I dropped my gaze to his hands. They looked busted, his skin peeling. He smelled of bleach and gasoline. I shook my head.

"I can't believe you," I said quietly.

"It's not what you think." He threw a crooked grin my way. "I didn't forget the Chinese. It's downstairs."

I pointed at his hand. "What the hell have you done now?"

His gaze became hooded, guarded, and his shoulders tensed. Still, I didn't regret bringing this up. If he was going around killing people like life was a Quentin Tarantino movie, I needed to know.

He looked down to his knuckles, frowning. This was not him. He was always good at covering his tracks. It was almost like he wanted me to find out, consciously or not.

"Troy..." I narrowed my eyes at him. "I'm done looking past what you do. Tell me."

"Sparrow, really." He tried to stroke my arm.

I took a step back. "Now, Troy."

His smile vanished. "I'm going to go ahead and be really honest about one thing, but beware. It's not pretty, and I take betrayal very seriously, so I'm trusting you to keep your mouth shut."

I looked up at him as his chest bumped into my body. He was so close, I was able to smell his delicious sweat and everything else he carried with him that day in the mix of bleach and gasoline.

I nodded. "I won't betray you."

"I know." His tone was harsh all of a sudden. "Remember, you've been pushing for some kind of truth. So here's the thing I want you to know. I'm not a hitman. I don't kill people for a living. Never been paid to finish someone off, but…" He raised his hand, twirling a lock of my hair around his finger. "Where there's smoke, there's fire. I did kill Billy. And I killed Father McGregor, too. Both deaths were ugly, but so was what they did."

My knees buckled, and my stomach lurched, but it wasn't from fear. I was elated. He had confided in me. He was cracking. My monster, my capturer, my corrupter. *My lover.*

"What did they do to deserve this?" I croaked, watching his finger playing with my strand of red hair.

"Billy killed my dad, a cold-hearted murder for money. McGregor told him where and when to find him, knowing his intentions. They took away the only thing I cared about." His eyes dilated as he watched his index finger playing with my hair, his voice lost in thought. "They had to pay for their sins."

"And you're Boston's God," I finished softly.

I wanted to cry but was too stunned to do something so natural and instinctive. I shouldn't have been surprised—the gossip warned about my husband all along—but I was. How did he live with the fact that he'd taken not one, but two lives? Then again, no one ever murdered my parent.

"Does it scare you, little lovebird?" he breathed into my ear, his huge body engulfing my small one, "To know that I'm capable of these things? I'm still on the lookout for the person who sent them to kill my dad, you know. I'm not done with my list."

Troy let go of my hair, taking a small, yellow slip of paper out of his pocket, pressing it to my chest. I plucked it out of his hand and read it. Crupti and McGregor's names were struck through. He didn't know who the third person was. There was a question mark.

I dragged my eyes up to meet his. "Am I scared? No," I said serenely. "Because I know you would never hurt me. Am I happy about what you've done? I'm disappointed. Playing God is immoral. Not to mention dangerous."

His expression relaxed when he scanned my face, looking for a hint of fear or disgust. There was none. He was a monster, but he was *my* monster.

"A little bird told me my ex-fiancée paid you a visit a couple of days ago." His lips were still parted. "Sparrow—"

He was going to say something more, but I didn't want him to think that I was angry. Especially when I knew in my heart he wasn't seeing her anymore.

"I don't care." I gave him a wicked smile. "As I said, this is just an arrangement, remember? Are you keeping your side of the deal? Is your dick inside your pants when you're out of the house?"

The softness in his eyes turned dark and cold. "It is. Is your pussy still mine?"

"You bet," I whispered.

"You're a little fucked up, Sparrow. I like that." He moved his hand up my arm and thrust me lightly toward the walk-in shower.

I stumbled back until my back hit the glass door, pushing it ajar. I stilled, staring at my husband, waiting to see what he'd do. He ducked his head down to meet my throat, biting and then sucking the pain away. His hot lips dove lower to my cleavage, but I dodged another bite by moving deeper into the shower until my back was flattened against the black ceramic tile.

"Nice try, pal, but I'm still disgusted with your confession." My heart hammered against my chest like a woodpecker on speed.

"I'm not your pal." He flashed his teeth, leaning forward and turning on the water behind me in one go. The showerhead sprayed cold water over my clothes, soaking me, and I gasped. "I'm your husband, and I'm going to do very marital things to you right now."

There was no point resisting, and who the hell was dumb enough to say no to this anyway? He attacked my mouth again with his warm tongue, his suit-clad body pressing into mine. I got lost in his passionate kisses, found myself again in his little teasing bites and, at some point, despite the chill of the water, got hot on every stroke of his big hands. Troy groaned into my mouth, taking both of my wrists in one of his hands and placing them against the towel warmer above my head. He jerked loose his tie, and tied me to one of its bars, tight enough to stop me from breaking free but not so tight that it hurt.

"Jesus." I dropped my head, watching the soft lighting from the ceiling blur out of focus and the cold water drops raining all over my body. My clothes were getting heavy and soggy, but I didn't care. We were both fully clothed and dripping. "Daisy was right."

"I bet she was." He yanked my jeans down violently, but didn't take the bait.

My underwear followed just as fast, leaving me bare and ready for him. Intoxicated with want. "She said the rumor is you like it kinky."

His warm breath traveled between my breasts, and I trembled as his tongue brushed the valley between them.

"I like it interesting…" He dropped to his knees, his face disappearing between my thighs. He grabbed one of my knees and draped my leg over his broad shoulder. "I like it delicious…" he murmured into my pussy, his tongue, so incredibly warm in contrast to the freezing water, swirling in circles, hard and hungry.

Shockwaves ran through my veins like hot honey.

"I like it rough…" He grazed his teeth against my clit, up and down, up and down.

I moaned, trying to wriggle free when his tongue danced around my sensitive nerves, but the tie was tight against my wrists. My long hair stuck to my eyes and forehead, and I was barely able to see. I whipped my head sideways, but my hair still streamed in my face. He liked the fact that I couldn't see shit. He liked me little, small, *hopeless*.

"But most of all, I like it with you…" His mouth continued its relentless motion.

"I'm close," I panted. I was. And there was nothing I could do to ruin it. I felt the orgasm washing through me. Rocking back and forth, aroused to a point of insanity.

The faucet behind me turned slightly to the right, and the cold water suddenly ran warmer until it got hot. When he moved up to kiss me, I smiled. "I'd like to reciprocate."

"Oh, you will." He grabbed one of my thighs, holding my knee in the crook of his elbow.

He slammed into me hard and fast before I knew what was happening, and I gulped air. Shit, it was good. I was so full of Troy I thought I already was going to explode again.

"When did you have time to take off your pants?" I asked, laughing while he fucked me.

It was crazy, but with a few short, powerful thrusts, another orgasm was building inside of me, chasing the first one and threatening to tear me even harder apart. He grabbed one of my breasts through my wet shirt and pinched my nipple hard.

"Baby, oh…" I was moaning in a volume more suited to a heavy-metal concert, so he started swallowing my loud, happy sounds with dirty kisses, muffling my voice, his tongue fucking my mouth, his lips locked on mine. Toothy kisses, filthy kisses, hungry and desperate and wanting kisses. Kisses that were much, much more than kisses.

There was nothing gentle and romantic about it. He was banging the living hell out of me, screwing me so hard I could feel his cock pounding deep inside me. I felt my second orgasm rippling from the inside, rushing through me like a tsunami of warmth, when something sharp sliced the tie in two and my arms fell free without a warning. I almost dropped to the tiled floor, but Troy grabbed me by the elbow at the last minute, my knees just inches from the tile.

"Reciprocate," I heard his sharp voice ordering, and immediately knew what he wanted me to do.

Bending down, I lowered my head to meet his cock, taking as much of it as I could in my mouth. My gag reflex was impossible to tame, but I held my breath and covered some of his shaft with my lips. I was still self-conscious about my blow-job technique, or lack of, but I didn't need to be.

Before I had a chance to figure out what to do, he slammed into me, fucking my mouth. "Can I?" he asked.

I nodded, closing my eyes. I'd always thought it would feel degrading to go down on a man, but how could I with him, especially now when my wrists were still hurting after he ate me out and made me feel like I was the most delicious thing in the whole freaking world.

I felt him tense, spasm, and then the thick, warm liquid filled my mouth. I swallowed hard, a small shiver running through my body. Looking up, I saw the smile on his face when his head dropped back, his black hair dripping water on my face.

He stroked my hair twice with the hand that wasn't holding his cock and sighed with pleasure. "Fuck," he said.

Fuck, indeed.

DESPITE EVERYTHING, Troy Brennan was human. And he was the worst kind, too—enchanting enough to get away with anything. *Even murder.*

We ate cold Chinese food and drank buckets of alcohol in front of the TV while I forced him to watch *10 Things I Hate About You* with me. Well, he wasn't really watching. More like answering emails on his phone, twirling my hair around his finger and occasionally rolling his eyes whenever Heath Ledger and Julia Stiles shared a romantic moment, but it was more domestic bliss than I'd had in my whole life combined. We lay on the carpet, him taking another sip of his Guinness, when I rolled into his chest, seeking his warmth.

"You don't have to be so anti-love. You can learn a thing or two from rom-coms," I said.

"I'm not anti-love." He dove down to kiss my lips, his hot tongue flicking my lower lip sensually. "I'm anti-bullshit. I bet you good money that if a real life chick had a guy jumping on the bleachers, singing a love song for her in front of a bunch of pimply high school kids, she'd pretty much kill him."

I laughed. "Wrong. I would love to hear you sing for me in front of high school kids."

"I would love for you to come back from your shift tomorrow completely naked, with nothing to hide your lady parts but a rare steak."

"That would never happen."

"Neither would me singing you a song in front of snarky teenagers."

He was normal. And fun. Worst of all, he showed me another part to love. A new layer in his complex personality no one else had access to. A layer tucked so deep under layers and layers of apathy, brutality and abrasiveness, showing it to me was almost like learning how to walk again.

He hated that part of him. The softer, kinder part.

And the fact that he shared it with me made me feel special. Special to have Troy, the guy you watched chick flicks with, and not Troy, the kill-a-priest and fuck-your-brains-out guy. That old, tired version he gave to everyone else. With me, he was still rough around the edges, but he wasn't all bad either.

"You're impossible to deal with," I said, pouting, but hell, I was enjoying this ping-pong.

"And you love it." He planted another kiss, this time on my forehead, as he scooped me into his arms. "I'm myself. I make no apologies for who I am, and you like it, because you're so much like me. You're the girl who teased the son of a dead mobster, The Fixer, on your wedding day. You own your shit, consequences be damned. Have you ever wondered why your parents called you Sparrow?"

"Uhm, let's see. Maybe because my dad was a drunk and my mom was a hippie, and together, they came up with really stupid name ideas?" I tried disguising my embarrassment with laughter.

Inside, though, my stomach twisted in tight knots. Everyone around me called me Birdie, with Troy calling me Red. No one called me Sparrow for a reason. It was an awkward name and I hated it. I tossed my hair back, faking boredom. "Anyway, I wonder about the bigger stuff, like why the hell my mom left me, not why she saddled me with a name that's basically an invitation for bullying."

"You hate your name," he said.

I twisted out of his embrace, feeling my face heating. Peeling off layers was hard. Not only for Troy, but for me, too.

"Aren't you clever." I took a long sip of my drink.

He scooped me into a bear hug again, locking me in his arms. His lips grinned against my skin.

Did he find me adorable?

"You shouldn't hate it, it's perfect for you. It symbolizes freedom and independence. You're both."

"I'm not free," I reminded him.

He rolled on top of me, straddling me with his muscular thighs. I lay beneath him, admiring his strong body and knowing, deep down, that I'd gotten comfortable in my cage.

"No, not from me," he agreed. "But trust me, lovebird. Even if I let you out of this cage, you'd be flying back in no time."

It was true, but that was exactly what worried me.

We spent more time making out on the carpet like two teenagers, before he got to his feet and disappeared into his office. He came back with a small box. Simple, light green. The kind you can get at the dollar store. He kneeled down to where I sat on the carpet and placed it in my hand.

"I've been studying you for a while now," he said. "Every day is a class day, each conversation is homework, and I think I know by now what I would have picked if we had known each other before we got married."

My heart fluttered in my chest, my pulse picking up speed. It was a moment of true, raw happiness, and it scared me beyond repair. I knew a long time, maybe even forever, would pass before I'd have this kind of moment again.

I opened the box, a part of me still scared I'd find something offensive. Last time he gave me a gift, on our wedding day, I almost threw up yesterday's lunch on his lap. In the box sat a ring. It was very different from my engagement ring—monstrous, attention-seeking bling. No. This was a simple red ruby. It looked like a drop of fresh blood. Basic, beautiful, special and original. More than anything, it was very, very red.

It dawned on me that the ring was exactly how he saw me. This was Troy's version of trying, and he was doing it for me. This was him being thoughtful. I looked up, a mischievous grin on my face.

"My original engagement ring has a diamond the size of the moon. Some would call this a downgrade."

"Trust me, it's an upgrade." He took the ring and slid it on my finger, brushing his thumb over it. "Besides, the diamond in your first one ain't real."

My grin collapsed into a startled *oh*.

He laughed. "I'm kidding, kiddo."

When the evening rolled into night, we took things to bed, and I writhed beneath him, screamed his name, just like he told me I would on our wedding night. Arcade Fire's "Rebellion" played from the stereo, and the irony wasn't lost on me.

I was in love with a murderer who didn't love me back, who never explained why he took me for his wife. It wasn't fine, wasn't okay, but it was the ugly, embarrassing, uncomfortable truth.

Considering how fucked up my truth was, I began to understand why Troy gave me something far more convenient and beautiful.

He gave me lies, and I ate them from the palm of his hand.

He gave me lies, and for him, I closed my eyes.

TWENTY FOUR

SPARROW

I TOOK A LITTLE BREAK TO WATCH the birds overhead as they migrated out of my rainy city.

That was my first mistake.

I only paused for a second, and it was a second too long, because as I plucked out my earbuds, "Monster" by The Automatic playing, to watch the birds flee from the rain, my fate was sealed.

I smiled to myself when I thought about how, for the first time since I was probably born, I wanted to stay put and not take flight.

My happiness cracked, collapsing into a frown, when I spotted him. Brock stood in front of me, blocking my way on the narrow pavement between the tall red-brick buildings.

This time I was scared. It started to look less and less like a coincidence and more like the stuff Fatal Attraction was made of. Boston was not that small, and he'd shown up where I was four times.

It was almost like Brock *knew* where I'd be. I didn't want to admit it, but

I was all too eager to follow Troy's suggestion—*okay, order*—and keep my distance from the guy. He leaned against a lamppost, one foot bent, as he puffed on a cigarette. When he saw me, he pushed off the lamppost, his face cracking into a smile.

"Oh, hey," he said through an exhale. I twisted back to where I came from, trying to resume my run, but he grabbed my arm, his voice still easy. "I need to talk to you."

"No, you don't," I said, "unless it's work-related."

Things at Rouge Bis weren't going as planned. Pierre still hated my guts, no matter how hard I tried, and Brock still tried to get close to me. Still, I knew they wouldn't fire me, though a small part of me wanted out of the place just so I could look for something better.

Brock tucked his free hand into his heavy wool jacket. "It's about your husband."

"No," I stated, scowling. Why was it that every time Brock talked about Troy, I felt like my heartbeat slow and my breathing got more shallow?

Because I knew that he knew. Knew whatever it was that I didn't about why he'd married me.

I reached for my phone inside my hoodie pocket with every intention of calling Troy, but he yanked it from my hand and tossed it into an open dumpster. My eyes almost popped out of their sockets, and I felt the blood draining from my face.

"What the hell?" I roared.

He didn't answer, but his face changed. He looked seriously and royally pissed. He pulled me into his body, my chest bumping into his. No more easy and cutesy for Brock, I gathered. He was done playing nice with me.

"Come with me," he growled.

"I'm not going anywhere with you, asshole." And then I felt it. He shoved the barrel of a gun deep into my stomach, so hard I was sure it'd leave a mark. But my fear numbed my pain.

"My car's down the street. Be quiet, and don't make me hurt you more than necessary."

Shit. Even his accent changed. Suddenly, he sounded local. He sounded…
Boston?

I looked around me, frantically trying to spot someone on the street, but there wasn't a soul within earshot. My fault for running every morning right before dawn. I hadn't seen anyone else for at least ten minutes, and then it was a woman walking her dog in the opposite direction.

I was alone. No, worse—I was with Brock.

"Brock, please." I wasn't sure what I was asking. Was I asking for him to let me go? Fat chance, considering the fact he'd just thrust a gun in my side.

He spun me in the opposite direction and led me to his car, prodding me along with the gun. I felt his breath on the nape of my back, and it sent a shudder down my spine. My mouth was dry, and I fought not to panic.

"Get in the passenger seat," he said from behind me. He swung the door to his Audi open.

I did as I was told.

He walked briskly to his side of the car and buckled up, his fingers still wrapped around his gun. "See? Now we're on the same page. It's a shame you needed that little push in the first place, Sparrow. Men don't normally dig difficult women."

I didn't answer, staring at the gun like Brock's voice came from its barrel.

"It's beautiful, isn't it?" He smirked, admiring his weapon as he held it up and turned it right and left for me to see. "I love how it feels in my hand. Like the world is in my palm. Powerful shit, huh?"

But not as powerful as my husband, I wanted to bark back.

"Hands all the way up, sweetheart." Brock pointed the pistol at me, nudging it in my direction. I wanted to protest but then he pressed the cold barrel to my temple, the steel digging into my flesh.

"Jesus, okay." I lifted my hands up slowly.

Brock leaned into my space, opened the glove compartment, took out a syringe with his free hand, bit off the cap with his teeth and slammed the needle hard into my thigh. I screamed, reaching for his hand, but he smacked my arm with the gun. Then he did it again with my other leg.

I stared in horror at the needles sticking out of both thighs. "What the hell did you do to me?"

He waved me off, tucking his gun between his thighs. The fact that he was less guarded now frightened me even more.

"A small dose of anesthesia." He kneaded the area around the needles. "You have to make sure it distributes well. It will keep your legs numb during the ride. Don't want you trying to hop out and run. When Connor picked up his last check, he mentioned your little stunt with him. I thought it best to be prepared. But don't worry, you'll be completely alert."

He started the car, one hand on the wheel and the other squeezing my leg. "Get comfortable, we'll be driving for a while."

We left the city, taking side streets, and soon enough the car rolled onto a deserted two-lane road, heading west. With every mile and minute away from Boston, I became more and more paralyzed, and not just from the dead weight of my legs.

Why did I get out of bed so early? Why did I insist on jogging at unreasonable hours? Why did I always take the small, empty pavements, searching for those hidden Boston gems, the places no one knew or walked in? Why had I insisted on getting rid of my bodyguard? Why do I never carry mace on something else that could scare away potential attackers?

Why? Why? Why?

I was in trouble. Something that was much bigger than marrying the wrong person or being left by your stupid parent or a drunk dad. Brock might be crazy, perhaps even the psychopath I ironically believed my own husband to be, but he wasn't stupid. If Troy found out he'd kidnapped me, he was a dead man.

Which meant Brock couldn't let Troy find out. Whatever else Brock had planned for me, I wouldn't be making the drive back to Boston with him.

Still, it was worth reminding him of the consequences, in case Brock had second thoughts.

"You can still take me back, you know," I said, staring ahead at the front window. I couldn't feel my legs at all at this point. My mind, though, was as sharp as ever—and I wish it wasn't, because knowing what was about to happen was nothing short of devastating.

We were driving deep into the woods, dim morning light filtering through the tall pine trees. I was so far from crowded, hectic Boston, it almost felt like I was on another planet. "Don't do something you'll regret. Troy won't stop looking for me. Once he finds me, he'll kill you."

Brock just stared ahead too, smiling and rubbing his stubble with the gun.

"Not if I kill him first."

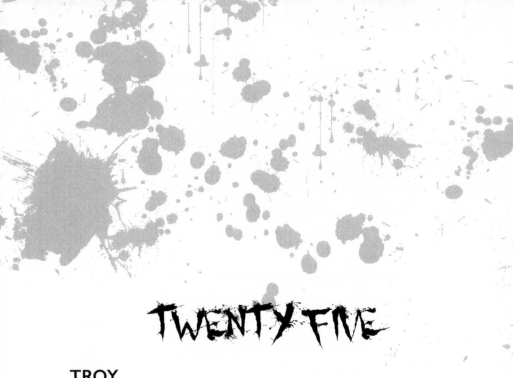

TWENTY FIVE

TROY

PATRICK ROWAN WAS DEAD.

It was my duty—and pleasure—to pay him a final visit and attend his mass. Paddy was being buried in Weymouth, where he was born and raised, just outside the city. His body had been flown in from Miami. Jensen had alerted me yesterday.

The funeral had attracted all kinds of old-schoolers. People my father and Rowan left behind, survivors of the chaotic mess they created with their own hands. Abe Raynes was there, looking high as a kite and just as incapable of forming a sentence as he usually was. He was deteriorating, despite the extra cash I'd streamed into his bank account since I married Sparrow.

I exchanged a brief hello with him, and only because I thought highly of his daughter.

Ignoring the other mourners, I walked straight to Rowan's open casket, peeking inside to make sure the fucker was really dead. A part of me wanted Red to see this, but I knew I needed to shield her from that sort of shit.

It wouldn't do her any good, anyway. She wasn't a monster like us, wasn't high on revenge and drunk on power like we were. She was strong, but also innocent. And she wasn't for me to corrupt.

I, however, planned to enjoy the event to its fullest.

I took a seat in the first row, next to two elderly men I didn't recognize. I glanced sideways, scanning them. From their attire, mannerisms and the faint scent of mothballs, I gathered the geezers were not ex-mob. They were ancient looking, with snow-white hair and gray flannel suits, and although probably Irish, they didn't mix with the rest. Outsiders.

Good. I wasn't in the mood to suffer the usual crowd.

The priest started talking and I tuned him out. Tara and her mother, the only relatives Paddy had left, sat on the other side of the church. Tara cried and sniffed, clutching torn, damp pieces of tissue in her fist, and although I felt a little sorry for her loss, knowing she'd inherit nothing from her deadbeat dad, I stood my ground. Sparrow deserved whatever Paddy had more than she did. It wasn't Tara he had hurt.

As soon as the service started, I found out exactly why the spot I chose in the front pew was empty in the first place. The men beside me were gossiping like fucking teenage girls. They were at it in full force, ignoring the priest and everyone else. Sounded like they were doing an inventory of who was there and who wasn't, and even though I didn't want to, I pretty much had to eavesdrop. Not that it was really eavesdropping when their voices could carry all the way to Cape Cod.

"Who else hasn't shown up?" One of the men clucked his tongue.

"Ah, the old wife, Shona. The one he married in the nineties. She ain't here either."

"I'm not surprised. Paddy gave her hell."

"That, he did."

"And the Kavanagh kid, surprised he's not here."

"I think his name is Greystone now. He changed it after his da died. I would, too, after what happened to him."

"David Kavanagh brought shame to his family. Killed by a drug dealer."

"Greystone," the old man continued, ignoring his friend. "Should be here. Paddy was his godfather, after all. He should show some respect."

"The Kavanagh kid's living in Boston now, you know. Moved back five, six years ago, I think. I saw him hanging around his da's favorite bar a couple of times. Makes you wonder why Kavanagh didn't show up when he lives just down the road."

"I told you his name's Greystone."

The old geezers were rambling, the thread of the conversation tough to follow, but I'd caught one thing. How many Greystones were there in the world, and even more importantly, Greystones who had moved to Boston five or six years ago?

Kavanagh. Greystone.

Kavanagh.

Greystone.

Brought shame to his family…living in Boston now…Paddy was the kid's godfather…Kavanagh.

David Kavanagh.

Who was David Kavanagh? I tried to remember. The name sounded familiar, like a childhood lullaby I hadn't heard in years but could still hum.

David Kavanagh. Who the fuck are you, David Kavanagh?

Then it hit me.

David Kavanagh. A beating gone bad. It had happened nine years ago, when the mobsters of America realized how poorly regulated the recycling industry was and cashed in big while going green. Cillian had Kavanagh roughed up after he tried to steal a shit-ton of recycled pipe and copper wire. Kavanagh got caught, pulled a knife instead of taking his medicine and ended up dead. There was blood. Everywhere.

Cleaning up the mess was one of my earliest jobs as The Fixer. I'd staged a drug deal, dumping the body in an alley with Kavanagh's knife, proud I'd handled things so neatly for my father.

David Kavanagh. Fuck, fuck. David fucking Kavanagh.

Trying not to let paranoia get the better of me, I eased back into the pew, but it was too late. I was all fucking ears, dying to hear what they'd say next.

One of the white-haired men nodded, spitting more info and a little saliva on the burgundy carpet.

"Brock," he said with conviction. "Brock was the kid's name. Nice boyo. I think he's married now."

My hand snaked to my breast pocket. I clutched the yellow slip of paper. All the pieces fell together. A moment of clarity washed over me, and I closed my eyes, taking a deep breath. Brock had a motive, and access.

Fuck.

Paddy was Brock's godfather. Of course he fucking was. That's why Paddy knew about Red's mom. Why he knew about the arrangement, about the marriage, about everything.

Jesus fuck.

And Brock? He'd reinvented himself as Greystone, even dropping a fucking clue by adopting a last name that was a little morbid and a lot angry. As a rehab counselor turned restaurant manager. *As the good guy.*

He knew I'd keep an eye on him if I realized who he was, that I would never have given him a job. My mercy, hospitability and love for Catalina had some hard limits, even back then. Shit, if I'd known Brock was Kavanagh's son, I'd have sent him back where he came from. His dad was no innocent victim. He sold us stuff, stole our stuff. Ratted on us. He did a lot of damage, was responsible for the loss of a couple of lives, too.

Brock Greystone was not a Greystone, and he wasn't a West Coast outsider either. He was David Kavanagh's son, one of us. An Irish kid from Boston who pretended to be someone else. He even had that smooth Cali accent to accompany his thick hair and Hollywood smile. No trace of Boston in his voice.

How could I not have known Brock was one of us?

I let him into my life without even checking who he was first. My mind was so messed up over losing Cat, over her betrayal, over her pregnancy, and how her baby-daddy needed a job on the East Coast, I got sloppy. Before I knew it, Brock had access to my business, to my secrets, to my father.

My fist on tightened on my list. I took out a pen and smoothed the paper on my knee. I crossed out the last question with a strikethrough and adding the missing name.

1 = ~~Billy Crupti~~
2 = ~~Father McGregor~~
3 = ~~The asshole who hired Billy?~~
3 – Brock Kavanagh

Excusing myself, I nodded politely to the two men as I stood up, buttoning my suit jacket and walking out of the church in the middle of the service. People frowned and followed me with their eyes as I strode to the wooden double doors and disappeared between them, heading to my car.

After I fired up the engine, I dialed Brock's number. He didn't pick up.

Somehow, that didn't surprise me.

I tried Red right after. The last thing I wanted was for her to somehow fall into his clutches. She didn't answer either.

I tried her again, and again, unsettling tension gripping me by the balls. My throat burned, and heat spread in my stomach. She was supposed to be home, or at the very least, available to take a call. She didn't have a shift that day, was supposed to come back from her morning run and if she wasn't home, she should have been with Lucy, Daisy or her dad.

Her dad was at the funeral. It left me with two more sensible, reasonable options.

Cursing Brock under my breath, I managed to get her friends' numbers and call them. Daisy said she hadn't heard from her in two days and Lucy claimed Sparrow had texted her before her morning run. They planned to hang out later. Sparrow never showed up at their usual spot.

Don't fucking panic.

I called Maria, and gathered from her broken English that Sparrow wasn't home. Feeling the blood freezing in my veins, I quickly used the GPS app I'd installed on my wife's phone when I snatched her, before we even got married. The location finder showed she was in central Boston.

Phew.

Fucking Red had me thinking irrationally. I was going to yell my lungs out when I got to her for pulling this kind of shit.

Once I got to the location, I called her number again and again, trying to reach her. I called maybe thirty times before I heard the faint sound of a ringtone and found her cell in a dumpster among cardboard, junk food leftovers and cigarette butts.

Desperation and distress coursed through my veins. I kicked the dumpster so hard, I left a dent.

"Fuck, fuck, fuck!" I yelled, not caring about people around me watching my very public meltdown.

She hadn't run away. Wouldn't run away. I knew my lovebird—she was the fighting kind. The only running she'd ever do was to get her cardio fix.

No, this was not her trying to break free. This was him trying to get even.

It was the moment I realized that, for the first time, Brock was one step ahead of me.

And it was also the moment I knew that I would burn down the city and stop at nothing to find my wife. Not because she was mine, I never believed that for a second, anyway.

Because I was so busy telling Sparrow how much she wanted me, I forgot a small little detail—I wanted her back. More.

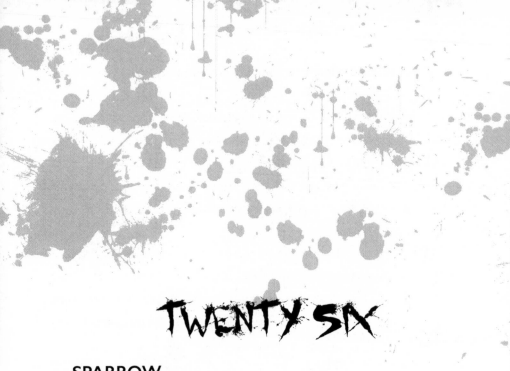

TWENTY SIX

SPARROW

<u>EXT. WILD FOREST – DAY</u>

THIS WAS IT. THE END. The final scene in my very short script.

Brock unbuckled his safety belt and tossed two pieces of gum in his mouth. "Have you ever wondered how come you had so little sexual experience before you met Troy?"

"Wh-what?" I stuttered. I had no idea what he was talking about. I couldn't feel my legs, and it was scaring the hell out of me.

He slammed his fist on the horn, and my heart jumped. *Jesus.*

When my head smacked the car roof, he let out a frantic laugh. "I asked if you ever wondered why guys stayed away from you before you married Troy."

The question made no sense, but then Brock kidnapping me made no sense either. At least the longer we were talking, the more time I bought. There was then more chance that Troy would find out I never made it home and come looking for me. Although, I knew that there wasn't much hope he'd find me. We were in the middle of nowhere and I didn't have my phone on me. Brock, on the other hand, had a loaded gun. The odds were not in my favor.

"Yes," I answered, finally. "Yes, I have wondered."

"Well…" Brock leaned into his seat with a smug expression, like we were gossiping. "That's because Troy threatened all of 'em. Every single guy who ever got slightly close to you or showed interest. He knew you were going to be his before you even hit puberty. Kept you a virgin all this time so he'd be the one to pop your cherry."

"I didn't know that." I swallowed loudly, trying to look upset. In another lifetime, I'd be eager to ask more, but even though the revelation was shocking (if it were even true), I didn't care about Troy's manipulative ways right now.

"That was the point." Brock laughed harder and pulled the empty syringes from my thighs.

At least I was able to feel my feet again.

He pushed his door open and walked around the car to open my door for me. Forever the gentleman. "He was a black shadow over your little head all this time. Guys wouldn't even breath in your direction, they were so scared of Troy. Get out."

I stumbled out of the car and fell headfirst. I watched as he pulled a shovel from the trunk, holding his pistol in the other hand. He carried the shovel and yanked me up from the mud by my arm, then spun me so that I had my back to him, just like before. Shoving the gun between my shoulder blades, he nudged me through a trail of long, half-naked trees. A thick carpet of red and orange leaves crunched under my dragging feet. The forest was beautiful, but the ugliest thing imaginable was about to happen to me.

I wanted to run. Knew I could run really fast, but not as fast as a bullet, and not with legs that felt like they had concrete blocks attached to them. I gained more control over my feet, but I doubted it would be soon enough to save me.

I wasn't giving up, though. If I was going to die, it wouldn't be without a fight.

It was freezing, and I was wearing nothing but my running gear. My teeth were chattering and my hair, a little damp from running earlier, was coated with a thin layer of ice.

We walked in silence. The crunching of the twigs and the occasional sleepy bird chirping a good morning were the only sounds reminding me that time didn't stand still.

I felt bile rising in my throat, my head swirling like I was going to faint. I'd rarely considered how I was going to die, and never imagined it'd be like this. But right now, with the shovel and the gun, with Brock looking like he did, wrath and cruelty dancing in his eyes, the odds of me leaving here in one piece, or leaving here at all, were growing slim.

We stopped near a tree stump marked with a slash of white paint. There was a fresh grave underneath it, carefully covered in mud. Brock pushed the shovel into my hand and cocked his head toward the leaf-covered ground.

"Start digging."

I looked down. The earth was soft from all the rain, but the shovel was damn heavy and my body and legs were still not working right, though getting better with each passing second. I knew exactly what he was asking. He was asking me to dig my own grave. Looking back up, I felt my tears pooling behind my eyes, but I had no time for self-pity

I needed to do something, quick.

"Why are you doing this? I'm not him. I'm not Troy."

"No, you're not," he agreed. "But you're important to him. If I can't steal you away, I will make sure he doesn't have you, too. It was your choice." He smacked his lips. "I tried my best to do it the easy way, but you didn't want me. Tough luck."

"Important to him?" I exclaimed, "You're wrong. I'm not important to him in any way."

"Yeah, you are." He thrust me forward, pointing at the ground with his gun. "Now dig."

Why was Brock so hell-bent on hurting Troy? He was the one who ended up marrying Troy's girl and got a job from the guy afterwards. Troy may have been a jerk to him and his family, but Troy was also a jerk to everyone else, too. It was a universal thing. He didn't discriminate.

Unless he knew about Troy and Catalina...then again, Brock himself said they were only two people living under the same roof for Sam's sake.

Nothing made sense.

There was no logic behind this scenario.

My vision blurred with unshed tears. The green of the forest and brown of the mud smeared like a bad painting. I didn't budge. Couldn't dig my own grave.

Brock shoved me again, but this time, I tripped. I fell into the mud, my knees buried deep. It was freezing, my damp pants sticking to my thighs.

"Please don't make me torture you more than necessary." His voice was disturbingly composed for someone who had just insinuated that he was going to kill me. "It's nothing personal. At least not against you. Come on now, sweetheart."

I felt his warm hand jerking me up on my feet. I couldn't look at his face, and sure as hell didn't want him to look at mine as he broke me like no one else ever had before.

"I promise to make it quick and as pain free as possible if you cooperate. You won't even realize what's happening."

I choked on my own saliva, gasping for air.

He took a step closer, his heat against my cold body. "I'll do it when you won't even notice, out of nowhere. You'll have your back to me. Deal?"

TWENTY SEVEN

TROY

I STORMED INTO ROUGE BIS in search of Brock.

No one had seen him that day, and nobody had spoken to him in recent hours.

Stalking into his office, I froze when I noticed the little clue he had left for me.

A toothpick. My toothpick. Sitting pretty in the middle of his newly empty glass office desk. A toothpick still tangled in the green fiber of Brock and Catalina's bedroom carpet.

His laptop was gone, so were the stacks of papers, pictures of his family and everything else he personalized the place with. Just my toothpick. And I knew why he put it there.

He realized I was fucking Catalina. Realized what I was half begging him to find out for fucking years. And now it was backfiring big time, blowing up in my face.

There were too many coincidences that day, and I knew the two disappearances had to be connected. He took her.

He took my wife.

A part of me wanted to smash the whole place down, walls included, but I didn't have time to fall to pieces. It was now my job to glue them together, to make sure Red was going to be okay.

I called my little pawn at the Metro police. John was one of the greediest bastards on my payroll. For the right price, he would have volunteered his own daughter to be diced up into steaks and served at Rouge Bis.

"How can I help you?" he asked

I gave him Brock's full name—both names, just in case—asking him to issue an APB.

"This could take a while," he said immediately. "Lotta paperwork involved."

"I'll pay whatever to make it happen fast." It wasn't like me not to negotiate, but time was not on my side.

Next in line were Sparrow's friends.

A half hour later, Lucy stormed through the backdoor of Rouge Bis, her face flushed. "It's all your fault. You, her stupid dad... For God's sake, I've never seen someone with as little luck as Birdie when it comes to the men in her life."

I couldn't agree with her more, so I gave her a nod, throwing my set of keys into her hands from where I stood. She caught them in the air, cocking one eyebrow in question.

Daisy, Red's other friend, followed her into the restaurant and looked around like it was the first time she'd walked into a fucking room. All wide-eyed and smiling, you wouldn't suspect her friend was missing.

"Go look for her in your culinary school, at her dad's, where-fucking-ever. Where does she usually hang out?"

"Yeah, why would you know?" Lucy growled. "You're only her husband, right?"

I saw Sparrow had taught her friend how to be snarky, too. I didn't answer her, and I ignored Daisy when she asked me how much it costs to rent Rouge Bis. I just shook my head and paced, trying to calculate my next move.

Instinct told me Red was with Brock, but I tried to convince myself I was being paranoid, thinking he'd harm her. Maybe they were just having an affair. Maybe Brock's goody-two-shoes façade got to her, too. But I knew that wasn't it. Red was pretty much bullshit-proof. She had more Boston in her fingernail than Brock had in his whole body. She was not to be messed with. And she couldn't be having an affair with him.

Because I knew it was only my name she screamed in bed.

"Lucy, just fucking cooperate, okay? You don't know what we're dealing with here." And neither do I, I refrained from adding.

Lucy's pulled out her cell. "That's it, I'm calling the police. This is my best friend we're talking about."

Daisy swung from staring at one of the paintings in the restaurant to staring at Lucy, her expression confused. "I thought I was your best friend?"

Idiot.

"No one calls the police," I said calmly, though inside, it felt like my heart was going to explode. I knew what I needed to do and didn't want to do it. "Now get your asses into the car and go look for her everywhere you can. In our old neighborhood. At her culinary school. Where she usually runs. Do whatever you can do and keep me updated."

That was also my order to everyone else around me. Employees. Colleagues. Ex-mob soldiers. Every single person on my payroll was already looking for Brock and Red. If they really were together, they'd be found— hopefully before I completely lost my shit.

I'd called Sparrow's friends because I was worried that I might be missing something, a place I might have overlooked, some place she could stay. Though deep down, I knew she hadn't run away.

A chill ran down my spine as I dialed Jensen's number for the fourth time that day. "Any news?"

"Didn't cash the check. Rowan's money is still there. I still can't track Greystone's license plate. Maybe he wasn't so stupid to use his own car, if he did kidnap her."

The word *kidnap* alone made me want to do to Brock things that would make Billy Crupti's death look like a pleasant stroll in the park.

"Brock is no criminal. He knows zero about shit like this. He only knows how to detox druggies." And it's not like he was doing that all that well either. Flynn was the perfect example. "Keep looking. Try the toll records. I bet you anything he drove his own fucking car."

There was a way to find out for sure, though.

I didn't want to do it, but I had no choice. I rushed into a taxi and gave the driver Cat's address. Lucy and Daisy had my car, because anyone seeing the Maserati would think of me and know they had my authority behind them. I needed as many eyes in Boston as I could get.

I shoved a fistful of money into the driver's hand. "Make it quick."

The cab flew so fast past the tall buildings, I actually thought it was going to take off.

And it still might not be fast enough, I thought as the streets flashed through my window.

That's what I was afraid of.

TWENTY EIGHT

SPARROW

I DIDN'T BUDGE.

"No," I said for the millionth time. "I'm not digging."

If Brock wanted to kill me, he'd have to do it the hard, messy way. I wasn't going to cooperate, and why would I? Even if every person I ever knew was looking for me, their chances of finding me were slim to none. We were so deep in the middle of nowhere I wasn't sure how Brock was going to find his way back from here when he was done.

"No?" He finally lost his patience. He hit me with the back of the gun, a smack straight to my face.

I fell to the ground. Blood trickled from my forehead, dripping into my eye, but I didn't feel a thing. I was so cold I was past feeling my skin. Blissfully numb. Maybe I wouldn't feel it when his bullet tore through my skin.

"Another one's coming your way if you don't start digging." He pointed at me with the gun, sounding cheerful.

Goddammit, how did I not realize the man was so sick? He'd hidden it really well, that's how. I used the shovel to push myself to my feet and stuck it into the soil, biting back a moan. I refused to give him the satisfaction.

"That's it. Now keep digging. Every time you stop, I'll smack you with this little baby." He kissed his gun, then took a seat on a stump with a white mark, crossing his legs

Yeah, Brock had tried extra hard to get me to like him. It had almost worked. But then it didn't. Even with Troy's awful reputation and obnoxious behavior, I was still more interested in him.

I started digging my hole, wincing every time the shovel hit the ground. I barely had any strength in me. I was weak, scared, hungry and furious. My body temperature was so low, I was afraid that I'd faint and Brock would finish me off while I'm unconscious. Maybe it was a good thing. Maybe I wouldn't feel a thing after all.

"Good job," he said.

"Screw you," I muttered under my breath. He heard. Even though it was weak and faint, Brock heard.

"What did you just say?"

My back was to him but I could still see him from my peripheral vision, and it was a good thing I could, because my rage boiled my blood back to a warm enough temperature for me to keep functioning. The digging helped, too.

"I said…" I answered slowly, trying to control my chattering teeth and shoving the tool deeper into the mud. "Screw. You."

He bolted up and strode to my direction. For the first time in months, I actually welcomed his proximity. I thrust the shovel blade into his stomach as hard as I could.

I stumbled backward from the impact as he rolled to the ground, his ass hitting the mud with a thud that almost made me smile. By the way he held his middle, I knew I'd managed to hurt him. I groped for his gun, eyes zeroing on the deadly weapon as it slid from his hand. I felt my fingers curling around the cold metal, so close to saving myself, so close to freedom…

A kick to the stomach sent me backward into the shallow hole. By the time I managed to blink the dirt away and regain my sight, he was already standing above me.

Brock stared me down like he wanted to smash his boot into my face. His gun was tucked into the waist of his jeans, the shovel in his hand. "Left or right?" he asked through clenched teeth.

Crap.

I swallowed. "Don't bother, I won't try to run again."

"Thanks a fucking bunch, like I'd take your word for it." He tried to laugh, but held his lower ribs. I'd hurt him. "You did a good job on Connor, and I should have done it before I even gave you the shovel. Left. Or. Right?"

I sighed, closing my eyes. Whatever he wanted to do, he'd do it with or without my permission. I didn't want to beg.

"Right," I answered.

"Good choice," he said, grunting as he swung the shovel and slammed it straight down into my right foot.

I was still lying in the hole.

I didn't cry out.

I didn't even wince.

I felt sharp poke in my skin, inside my running shoe, like something had shattered or snapped. A bone, probably. I knew it was bad, but the pain felt distant, removed. I stared at him, my eyes cold, my expression aloof, and awaited further instructions. The fact I barely felt any pain hurt me more than anything.

"What now?" I asked.

"Now you get up, and you continue digging."

TWENTY NINE

TROY

W HERE COULD THEY BE?
Anywhere. An apartment I don't know about that Brock had rented? A hotel, a motel, a barn somewhere, the woods, a lake, a basement? The options were limitless.

Where could they fucking be? Were they still in Boston? Were they on a plane going somewhere? No, they weren't on a plane. I would know. That's what I paid Jensen for. To let me know shit like that. Anyway, Sparrow didn't have her passport. I did. And her new driver's license would be in her wallet. She wouldn't go jogging at five a.m. with a wallet.

What was I worrying about planes for? If Brock had her, she for damned sure wasn't with him willingly. They wouldn't be strolling through security. I felt sure they were somewhere close enough to drive, and wherever they were, I needed to find her fast.

The cab pulled up to the curb at Cat's house, and I jumped out, instructing the driver to wait for me. I pounded on the front door so violently the windows rattled. Cat opened up, wide-eyed and obviously startled. She knew I meant business, because she looked more concerned than pleased to see me.

"What's going on?" Her forehead wrinkled, her short, skanky skirt swaying from rushing to the door.

"Where's your husband?" I strode right in. I wouldn't put it past Cat to let Brock keep Sparrow here. Didn't trust either of them. I might have been paranoid, but fuck it, they gave me every reason to suspect them.

"I have no clue. What the hell? Why are you looking for him?" She rushed behind me.

I climbed the stairs two at a time and started throwing doors open upstairs, Sam's room included. When his door flew inward and banged hard against the wall, he looked confused. He sat at a plastic children's table, with little trucks lined up neatly in front of him.

"Umm, hi, Mr. Troy?"

"Hey, Sam." I hesitated for a moment to take one last look at him before I did something I knew he might hate me for the rest of his life. "Have you seen your dad around?"

"Not today," he murmured, wheeling a truck to the edge of the table. He let it drop to the floor and made an explosive sound with his little mouth.

"Okay, bud. Be good." Don't do any stupid shit, I wanted to add. None of the stuff Brock and I did. None of the crap Cillian and David Kavanagh did, either.

"I will." He smiled at me as he picked up the truck from the floor and placed it back on the table.

Crap. So innocent. And Brock wasn't here. Fuck.

I turned to Cat, who was watching us from the hallway, and joined her pulling the door to Sam's room closed us so he wouldn't hear us. "You tracking your husband through GPS?"

"No," she said. "Why?"

"Let me ask again." I put my hand on her neck, not applying any real pressure, but hating the fact that I was losing control over the situation, and fast. "Can you tell me where his phone is through GPS or not? You don't want to lie to me, Cat. This is the one time I won't be so forgiving."

She looked down, chewing on her lip. "Is it about her?"

God-fucking-dammit. I didn't have time for this

"Catalina!" I slammed my fist against the wall behind her. I was lucky it was the opposite side of the hall from Sam's room, because it sounded like a bomb had exploded. "Answer me before I tear your fucking house apart."

"Fine! Yes! Of course I can freaking track him through his phone."

I knew it. If there was one miserable thing Cat and I had in common, it was that we craved control over our lovers. She wanted to track Brock for the same reason I wanted to know where Red was all the time. We both knew we weren't good enough.

"Get your phone for me. Now."

She was stupid enough to motion me toward her bedroom, but I stayed put in the hall. Pacing, I texted Lucy, Daisy and Jensen. None of them had any news, and I hated every single one of them for not being more helpful. It wasn't their fault, but I didn't have a single lead on where to look for Sparrow. She wasn't at Abe's. She wasn't in our old neighborhood, she wasn't at Rouge Bis, or the penthouse, or anywhere else around.

When Cat gave me her phone and showed me the app, I had a moment of hope. I quickly pinned the whereabouts of Brock's phone, but it was the address for Rouge Bis. The bastard hadn't taken any chances. He left his phone behind.

"Okay, Cat, listen to me, this is redemption time, okay? Every bit of bad shit you've ever done to me is about to be erased and forgiven, your place in heaven secured, if you can just answer one question." I held her shoulders, pinning her against the wall, my gaze hard. "Who might know where Brock is right now? Give me anything you think would help. Does he have any friends? Family I don't know about?"

Tick tock. Tick tock. Time was slipping away like sand between my fingers. I felt the walls of the hallway closing in, suffocating the shit out of me. I couldn't lose her. Wouldn't lose her. Red was the one thing I wouldn't let anyone take away from me.

Cat thought about it, raking her fingers through her hair and sighing loudly. It was all an act. She didn't want me to succeed. Didn't want me to find them. She knew whatever it was I was looking for had nothing to do with her and everything to do with my wife. I guess it killed her to know I'd moved on to better things. That she was no longer the center of my personal life.

"Cat, please…" I couldn't help it—my voice shook.

"My mom," she said finally, her voice brittle. "Mom might know where he is. They're close. She loves him, probably more than she loves me. That's why she hates you so much." She smiled bitterly, blinking away her tears.

I closed my eyes, taking a deep breath. "Thank you," I whispered, placing a soft kiss on her forehead. "Take care of Sam. He's the best thing that happened to you." *To us.*

"What? Wait, where are you going? Why did you say that?"

But I was already out the door, hopping back into the cab and throwing more money at my driver.

Maria was at my penthouse.

And she had some explaining to do.

THIRTY

SPARROW

I FELT LIKE I'D BEEN DIGGING FOREVER when Brock motioned for me to drop the shovel. "I'm going to the car to get some pain killers," he announced, rubbing his side. "For me, not you."

He hauled me over to a tree and tied my hands to the trunk.

That bought me time. I wriggled and pulled at the rope, and desperately prayed that somewhere in Boston, Troy was using that time to try and find me.

When I heard Brock returning, I slumped to the ground, pretending I'd been passed out all along. He untied me and put me back to work, but now he decided to be chatty. He sat on the stump, clutching his side every now and again, but generally as cheerful as a freaking girl scout.

"Oh, I just can't wait for you to get to her."

Cold and exhausted, I felt so physically sick, I wasn't sure I'd heard him right. I didn't answer.

"I just love it when families reunite," he continued, his face glowing with a smile.

"What the hell are you talking about?" I spat out. The blood on my forehead was beginning to dry and itch. I wanted to scratch it off but was afraid the psycho would think I'm was making some kind of move and shoot me. After all, I tried it before.

"Shit, I forgot he didn't tell you." He put a hand over his mouth like he had just let a secret slip and was now beyond embarrassed. "You're digging up the same grave where your husband buried your mom."

I shook my head trying to make sense of Brock's words. Troy didn't even know my mom.

"You lie," I seethed, turning around to face him. I couldn't stand on my injured foot, but I no longer cared. Not about anything, really, other than what I have just heard.

"I really wish I was, sweetheart." He cupped his bent knee, leaning forward and giving me one of his glorious smiles. So calm. So, obnoxiously calm. "He wrapped her in a white sheet, so even if you don't find her rotting body and she's all bones, maybe you'll still be able to spot her. Maybe you'll find a little souvenir of mommy dearest. Of course..." He scratched his forehead with the barrel of the gun, deep in thought, "That wouldn't do you any good, considering the fact that you're not going to stay alive for much longer."

"I know he didn't kill her," I told him. *And me.* "He was just thirteen when she took off."

"That's true. He didn't kill her. He just buried her out in the woods, oh, fifteen or so years later, so that no one would find out Cillian died in his mistress's bed. Right, I forgot you still have some catching up to do. Your mother? She dumped you and your miserable excuse for a dad for Cillian Brennan. Robyn used to meet up with him in a cabin in the middle of fucking nowhere, in these very same woods. Worked the lunch crowd at a diner in Amherst, but came here every Tuesday to start her second shift as Cillian's bitch. Yeah, this was her kingdom."

He opened his arms and gestured around him. "Must've been really crazy about him, and what good did it do to her? After Troy found them shot, he buried her right here in a deep grave. Come to think of it, you are awfully similar to Robyn, aren't you, Sparrow?" He strolled toward me. "You like to cook, and you're about to be buried here because of Troy Brennan, Cillian's son. Of course, you, at least, were his legal wife."

"Still am. Don't talk about me in past tense."

Brock dragged the gun gently along my cheekbone, his eyes drinking in my face. "I like that you're optimistic. It's a quality not a lot of city mice possess."

I didn't have to believe Brock. I just had to keep him talking. And even if he was telling the truth, it didn't matter now. Was I appalled at the thought of what Troy might have done? Yes. But even if my husband hadn't put me out of my misery and told me why my mother had left, where she was and what he'd done, it didn't matter because soon I probably wouldn't be able to feel a thing.

"So why did Troy marry me?" I heard myself asking Brock. That really didn't make any difference either, which is why I asked. No matter the pain, I could take it, because it wouldn't last very long. Not more than an hour, anyway. And Brock seemed keen on making conversation. It was more time among the living, something I wasn't exactly opposed to.

Brock twitched his nose and wiggled his index finger back to the hole I dug, which wasn't very big yet. "Keep digging and I'll tell you."

I picked up the shovel but only pretended to make any progress with my grave, mostly just moving the soil around. In the back of my head I remembered him telling me that he would kill me when I least expected it.

I knew the cabin Brock was talking about was here somewhere. That's why he brought me here. He wanted Troy to find my dead body, right here.

"Even though your mom was just Cillian's mistress, he apparently loved her. But she struggled with leaving her family, with leaving you especially. Guess it wasn't that difficult to walk out on Abe. Not that much of a catch, what with all his drinking and low-life friends. But you…she missed you. Talked about you a lot. At least that's what Troy told Cat and what Cat told me."

"Cat?" I choked. Of course. Troy's only true love. Not me, her. He told her everything, I reminded myself, hurting myself a little more.

Can Sparrows die of heartache?

"Oh, yeah..." He grinned, his face dipping closer to mine when he whispered, "Troy was so in love with my wife, he gave her his balls on a silver platter, and Cat, like the disloyal stray cat she is, spilled everything when we were in bed, while she was coked up to the max on drugs I personally smuggled into the rehab facility Troy checked her into in Malibu." He threw his head back and laughed, glee written on his face. "I was her counselor there. God, it was so easy to ruin him. He was Samson and she was his Delilah."

The fact Cat had been an addict was news to me, but one thing was clear. Brock planned this revenge a long time ago.

"Go on."

"So Cillian did the noble thing and made Troy swear that he'd take care of the little girl his mistress deserted for him. Marry you, to be exact. Fucked up, isn't it? But that's mobsters for you. And Cillian was one hell of a fucked-up man. The worst of 'em."

"You hate him," I said, turning to look at him.

"Of course I fucking hate him. He killed my dad, so I hired someone to kill him."

The missing name on Troy's list. The answer to Troy's question was Brock.

"Aren't you even a little bit sad?" I asked. "You were orphaned. Your dad was killed. Then you sent someone to kill Troy's dad, and now..." I trailed off, exhaling. "Now you're going to make Sam an orphan, too, because we both know Troy will hunt you down and make sure you're deader than dead after this. What about Sam? What about Cat?"

"Don't waste any sympathy on Cat. She's been fucking your husband under your nose. And don't worry about my son." He moved closer, stopping inches from me, and yanked the shovel from my hand. "After Troy finds your grave and sees how fucking symbolic it is that I buried you right next to your mother, I plan to kill your husband too."

Now it was my turn to smile. It was a grim, humorless smile, but I had a point to make. "Oh, Brock..." I pretended to laugh. "Such a rookie, even by my standards. You are so fucking dead."

"You first." He buried the shovel in the ground and started digging. "Ladies first."

THIRTY ONE

TROY

MARIA PRETENDED NOT TO speak English, but I knew her game. She did it so that no one would speak to her. Not at my mother's house in Sparrow's neighborhood where she originally started cleaning for us, and not at my place in Back Bay. It worked for the most part, but then I caught her at the mall, speaking fluent English to a cashier. She almost swallowed her tongue when she saw me waiting in line behind her, but I just smiled and let it slide.

She didn't want to converse, and it's not like I fucking needed her intellectual input in my life.

When I walked into my penthouse and saw that she wasn't alone, I almost lost my shit completely. It was only by a miracle that I pulled myself together. I bit my toothpick so hard, the wood crushed like tissue paper.

"Mr. Brennan…" A short man with no-nonsense clothes and small eyes got up from my sofa—my fucking sofa—and reached to shake my hand. "I'm detective Phil Stratham. My partner is on his way here, as well. I'm here to ask you a few questions about the disappearance of Flynn Van Horn."

This time it didn't even take me a second to do the math.

Brock. The fucker tipped the police about Flynn's death. This was orchestrated carefully. Wasn't a coincidence. Red was with him and not only did he not want me to find them, he deliberately put an obstacle in front of me. He wanted to serve me my ass on a plate.

Well played, Kavanagh. Too bad I invented the game.

"We have a very strong reason to believe Van Horn was with you the last few hours before his, er, disappearance."

The detective knew he was dead…and I had a feeling his death was a deliberate "accident" on Brock's part. You didn't leave a detoxing junkie alone in a cabin in the middle of the woods. His body was still fresh when I found him. Brock never answered my calls.

The walls were inching in. *Closer…closer…*

"Got a warrant?" My lips thinned as I walked straight to Maria. Her eyes widened. That was a good thing. She was scared. Maybe she knew something.

"Look, we got a tip and—"

"Got. A. Fucking. Warrant?" I repeated slowly, watching as the hair on his arms stood on end. "If not, get the hell out of my place right now. I won't ask twice."

"Brennan…" His voice pitched high. "Don't talk to me like that. I'm just here for—"

"Someone's fed you a pack of lies," I cut him off. "I don't know if Brock Greystone called you, or if he sent someone else to do his dirty work for him, but I didn't do shit to Flynn Van Horn other than to deliver him to Greystone. He was the one detoxing him, not me."

Pretty accurate. I got rid of the body, but for obvious reasons, that wasn't something I wanted to mention. "Look, I really have shit to do. Our little friendly talk will have to wait."

With that, I dragged Maria by the arm into the guest room, not caring about raising eyebrows. Pinning her against the closet, I got in her face, opening my eyes wide and giving her my crazy motherfucker look.

"Where's your son in law?"

"*Que?*"

"Cut the crap. I know you understand me. I know you speak English when you fucking feel like it, and you better feel like it right now, if you want to get out of this place with your tongue not ripped out of your mouth. Tell me where he is, now."

Maria started stuttering, a mish-mash of English and Spanish, throwing glances behind my head, hoping Detective Shithead would walk in and save the day. I was losing my patience, diving deeper into despair. Where the fuck could he be? Where could he take her?

"I don't know!" she shouted. "I don't know! He never to tell me anything!"

"You lie," I screamed into her face, losing every ounce of control I had left in me. Time was not on my side. Hell, no one else was, either. "You lie and Sparrow's life's in danger because of the fucker. Answer me now, bitch!" I slammed my open palms into the wall. "Answer!"

I wasn't proud of it, of course I wasn't. Maria was twice my age, and regardless, the word "bitch" wasn't really my style. I was more into the "fuck" business. But I'd lost it. Officially and genuinely lost my shit.

"You no see my Catalina anymore?" She blinked fast, checking me out from underneath her lashes.

Was this blackmail? Was my housekeeper extorting me so I would dump her daughter?

"I haven't seen her in months. It's over. Maria. Look, please…" I tried another tactic, pressing my palms together. Hell, I would have gotten down on my knees if I thought it would help. "Tell me anything. Tell me. I need to know where he is. Please. Just…please."

She looked left and right, ashamed and anxious. *Finally*, a fucking breakthrough. She was going to give me something. Something was better than nothing. At this point, I would take *anything*.

"He came on Saturday to home…" She cleared her throat, coughing a little. "My home. He taking the thing." She started making digging movements with her hands. "Then leave."

"The what? The what? The shovel? Did he take a shovel?"

She stared at me helplessly, unblinking. I fished my phone out of my pocket, the battery almost dead, and punched the word shovel into the search engine. I thrust the picture in her face.

"Is this what he took? That's what he left with?"

She nodded slowly, gulping. "This," she confirmed.

Fuck.

He took her to the woods. More than likely, to the place where I buried any chance of us ever making it as a couple. He took her to the woods, and I knew exactly where, because it was the last place I wanted her to be. Because it was the place that'd hurt her the most.

I stalked out of the guest room, praying that detective Fuck Face hadn't left the building yet. He hadn't. He was still in my living room, his arms crossed over his chest, planted on my sofa like a punished kid. Goddamn. This was a guy in charge of finding potential criminals and murderers? No wonder I was still on the loose.

"Can you spare me five minutes?" he asked, darting up and moving in my direction.

I nodded, passing by him as I headed straight for the door. "I can give you even more, but I need your car, and I need it now."

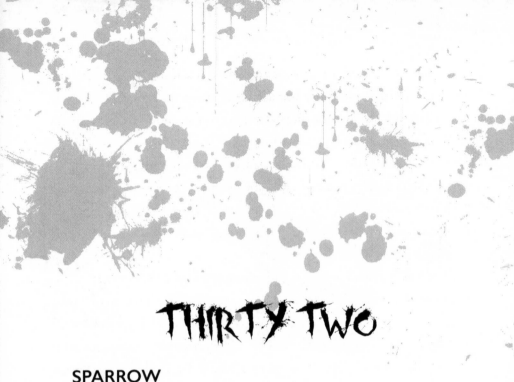

THIRTY TWO

SPARROW

"ALL DONE." BROCK STOOD UP and wiped off the coat of sweat on his forehead.

He'd taken over digging the grave two hours or so ago. Finally, he'd realized I was in no shape to do it myself, especially if he wanted that hole deep enough for my body before Thanksgiving.

He'd also found the damn white sheet, throwing it my way, victory printed all over his disgusting face. It wasn't so white anymore, but it was there.

I tried to smell the sheet, browned by dirt and mud, desperate to feel her, to connect to something that might have still been there. But I couldn't. All I felt was disappointment. Disappointment in my mom, in my husband.

"Why are you doing this?" I howled.

Brock was leaning against a tall tree, pulling at his brown hair, on edge. Well, he was about to take a life. *My* life. He was looking down at me while I was sitting on the ground. My forehead had stopped bleeding, the blood gluing my hair to my skin, and my foot throbbed like it was being slowly cut off with a chainsaw. It wasn't my best moment to say the least.

"I get that you hate Troy. I get that you loath the Brennans. But why do you feel the urge to hurt me?"

"I'm not sure." He pinched his eyebrows, actually giving it thought. "Maybe it's just my fragile ego, you know? I'm better looking, certainly nicer than Troy Brennan. Yet he always gets the chicks, doesn't he?" He snorted. "Yeah, that's it. Maybe I'm just bitter about you being so obviously blind to what he is and what I am."

"You're both as bad as each other," I shot. "Both monsters from hell."

But even as I said it, I didn't believe it. Because after all the secrets were out, after knowing what Troy did to my mother and what went down, I still couldn't hate him as much as I hated Brock. Troy wasn't malicious. Or maybe he was, but not toward me. Brock, on the other hand…he had every chance to stop the blood bath and everything that had happened, at least most of it, but he kept the freak show running.

"Aw…" He put his hand over his heart. "Now that's just straight out insulting. Any other last words, Mrs. Brennan?"

"Yeah," I said, letting go of the white sheet and watching it drop back to the ground. "There's someone behind you."

Brock pivoted to see who was coming, He gasped when Troy's panting figure sliced through the tall bushes like a storm.

He pointed his gun to Brock's head and shouted, "Don't shoot her!"

Brock dropped his gun, his mouth hanging open and realization washing over his face. It was over for him.

"Don't do this," Troy shouted again.

I was confused. *What?* Brock wasn't holding the gun anymore.

"You devil," Brock whispered, the accusation directed at my husband. "I'll save you a place in hell."

"Don't wait up." Troy's voice dropped considerably. "I'll be late."

Then, with a smile, Troy produced a panicked scream. "I said drop the gun now!"

A shot rang through the air. Brock fell to the ground, his body hitting with a thud that echoed between the towering trees. My head shot up. Still shaking, everything shaking, I gaped at his prone body next to me. Horror etched his face. I saw the surprise in his eyes as the dark red stain of blood bloomed on his mouse-gray jacket, spreading like an oil spill with every second that passed.

Too stunned and weak to try and get up, I lay there near the hole he dug for me.

Next thing, I saw Troy's shoes as he stopped inches from my face. Relief washed over me. I sobbed, releasing every single tear I'd been holding all day. He was here. Troy was here, and all of a sudden, everything was okay. Despite what I knew, what I didn't want to know, despite my life with him being over, it was okay. I knew I'd be okay.

I was so tired of being strong. Being taken care of, even by him, was a concession I was glad to make.

"Sorry, Red." He picked up Brock's gun with a handkerchief and walked to where Brock had been standing before the bullet hit him. "I promise I won't even graze your ear."

Then he shot me.

Troy Brennan, my husband, shot me.

He missed my ear by an inch, but I still felt the heat radiating from the bullet as it flew next to me. The scent of gunpowder burned my nostrils, and my eyes rolled back in their sockets.

I lost it for a moment, barely noticing Troy's arms closing around me. The next thing I knew he was picking me up. He carried me like an altar boy, and I was his cross. Swinging my arms over his neck, hugging me tight like I could evaporate at any moment.

I clung to my mother's white sheet and sobbed. I don't think he noticed the sheet. I'm not even sure that I noticed what I was doing at this point. So much had happened so fast, it was almost like I was an outsider peeking into a reality that wasn't really mine.

A second person ran through the trees in our direction. A small man with utilitarian clothes and sharp nose. *A cop*. He hurried toward Brock's body and felt for a pulse.

I was still woozy and incoherent, but I noticed Brock's gun was back in his hand.

My husband, ever the fixer.

"You shot him?" he roared at Troy.

Troy's arms tightened around my body protectively. It started to hurt. So did my forehead and foot. Everything hurt. Everything felt broken. Especially my heart.

"Self defense," Troy said, and I felt him through my shoulder pointing his chin at Brock. "He shot my wife, missed only by a few inches, and he was going to try again."

Not true. Brock never did any such thing. Troy was the one who shot him, and Troy was the one who used Brock's gun. Of course, I didn't utter a word to the cop. I let Troy carry me to a black SUV I didn't recognize, my arms flailing like they were no longer part of my body. I released my hold on the sheet, but he bent down, picked it up and flung it over his shoulder. He knew I knew, and somehow, that made me even sadder.

"Fuck, I'm so sorry, Red." He kept on repeating it, more to himself than to me.

"I know everything," I whispered into his chest. "How could you have done that to my mom? How could they have done this to *us?*"

His muscles tensed around my body. Chest, biceps and even his fingers stiffened.

"Sparrow—"

I fainted the second he placed me on the seat, and for the first time since everything happened, I truly didn't give a damn if I woke up or not. Nothing seemed to matter anymore. Nothing.

I didn't come to until I was at the hospital, and even then, everything was a blur. The first few minutes, I thought I was still in the woods, still with Brock, or even worse, dead. Then I felt the needle in my wrist and the scent of antiseptic and anesthetics attacked my nose. Blinking slowly, trying to gain some control over my vision, I saw a hazy figure sitting by my bed. I realized it was Pops, his head between his hands. His body shook, and I figured he was crying.

Lucy perched on the window sill, looking out, but mostly looking worried.

Daisy was digging dirt from under her fingernail absently, leaning against the wall, popping pink bubblegum.

I found comfort in the simplicity of everything around me. The walls were naked and everything was white or pale. The linoleum on the floor, basic furniture, blind-covered windows. It was boring, it was bare, and I loved it. My current self couldn't handle detail, or stomach anything more complex than what was in front of me.

And most importantly, I was surrounded by the three, only important people in my life.

My husband was no longer a part of this short list. Not after what he did.

Pops and Lucy must've heard me gasping when I tried to move my foot—unsuccessfully, by the way—because Lucy jumped from where she was sitting and appeared by my bed.

"I'm sorry, honey. You broke your foot."

"Actually, Brock broke it for me." I winced, but stopped trying to move my leg. It was so sore, no amount of morphine in the world would be able to subdue the pain.

By the looks on their faces, they were confused and still in the dark. I wondered how much they knew.

"Where's Troy?" I licked inside my mouth, trying to fight the dryness.

Lucy and Daisy exchanged glances, and I didn't like what was written on their faces. It pained me to admit that even though Troy did unthinkable things to a lot of people, the woman who gave birth to me included, I still cared about him. Still didn't want him to get into trouble. Even if I couldn't be with him, that didn't make him any less important.

If anything, it made me worry for him even more. The cancer has successfully taken over my whole body. I was infected head to toe. Resistant to any medicine, immune to anything he might do. In fact, I knew that even if the bullet he shot at me pierced my skin, I would still love him. Very much. It sucked, because I knew that I couldn't forgive him.

It also sucked to know he might be a free man, but he wasn't in the room, because he didn't want me anymore.

Pops was the one to break the news, since Lucy and Daisy were too empathetic to do such thing.

"He's at the police station," he said, unblinking. "Giving his statement about what happened."

I looked out the window. It was pitch black outside, a street lamp illuminating the fog and rain.

"What time is it?"

"One a.m."

Damn, it'd been almost twenty-four hours since I ran into Brock, but it felt like it was years ago.

"And Brock?"

This time Lucy had no trouble delivering the news. "He's dead. Don't worry. You poor thing. You were in quite a state when Troy found you. I can't believe Brock kidnapped you because he fell in love with you and couldn't stomach the fact you were married. What a psycho."

Ah. He now had a cover story, too.

"How did Troy find me?"

"The housekeeper," they answered in unison. *Maria.*

I let my head sink back into the pillow, closing my eyes and fighting the tears stinging the back of my eyeballs. Why was I crying now? Because I had my life back. Because I had my family around me. Because everything was supposed to be okay now, yet it wasn't. Never would be. Troy was right—I was bound to run away from him. I *needed* to run away from him. There was no repairing our relationship after what he'd done.

Even The Fixer couldn't fix this.

"Can we get you anything at all?" Daisy pulled at her gum, twirling it around her finger. I almost smiled. Almost.

"Hot chocolate," I said, and before I knew it, she dashed out of the room.

"Your forehead looks nasty," Lucy commented, brushing her hand along my temple in a motherly gesture.

"I bet my foot doesn't look too good either."

"No," she agreed.

I frowned. "You mean, my foot modeling days are over?"

"Afraid so."

The three of us laughed—me, Lucy and Pops—and the smile felt good on my lips again. Not natural, but good.

It would take a long time until I laughed again, really laughed, or felt genuinely happy, but this was a start.

I was taking baby steps, but with a broken foot and a shattered heart, this was something, too.

THIRTY THREE

TROY

I FIXED EVERYTHING.

That was me. I was The Fixer.

Sparrow was safe again. I managed to both kill Brock and stop the stupid Flynn investigation from happening—two birds, one stone. Fulfilled my promise to my dad. Crossed the final name on my list. Flynn's grave was found by the police, but so did Brock's sloppy fingerprints all over the cabin where he took care of him.

It wasn't so hard to convince them he was also the one to dig the grave. Especially as his mother in law confessed he had taken a fucking shovel to the woods.

The decaying remains of Robyn Raynes were found – and Detective Idiot and his crew were only too happy to dump the blame on Brock along with everything else.

And I made Brock's death look like self-defense. There was still a ton of paperwork to be done, and I knew it will cost me a pretty penny, but I fixed it. Everything was exactly as it was supposed to be. I had a reliable witness—Detective Stratham— who saw the gun Brock was holding in the woods, and the grave he dug for Red. There was no denying the man intended to harm her and me, and my intentions were well within the eyes of the law. I was bulletproof. Sparrow, though shaken, would be on her feet soon.

Everything was fixed.

Well, other than what was important.

I walked down the hallway of the hospital like I was on death row. Every door I passed brought me closer to the door I didn't want to knock on. I wasn't scared, I was petrified.

For the first time in my life, I was going to do the right thing, and I wished it felt better, because the truth was, it felt like fucking shit. It felt like hell, like torture, like a sharp butcher's knife digging into my chest, piercing into my heart and pulling it out slowly, breaking each and every one of my ribs on its way out.

I knocked on the door softly. If she was asleep, I didn't want to wake her up. She'd looked so frail when I found her. With blood running from her temple all the way down her face like a veil, her leg completely fucked and twisted, her foot the size of a basketball. She was freezing, too, in nothing but thin yoga pants and a Dri-Fit shirt.

An injured Sparrow.

The first thing I wanted was to tend to her, and then and only then to kill Brock slowly and painfully.

But I couldn't do it the way I had wanted it to happen. Because Brock needed to be finished before he could give away the fact that I buried Robyn and Flynn right there, in the woods. I had no doubt he'd spill the beans to Stratham the minute the cop took him into custody. Every moment he was alive and at a close proximity to the detective, my life as a free man was in danger.

That was fine. By the time I stopped Detective Impotent's vehicle in the middle of the woods and bolted out, all my urges and need for vengeance were irrelevant.

My quest was useless and irrelevant.

There was no time for revenge.

Everything darkened, and the only thing illuminated was *her*.

So I killed him quickly, coldly, efficiently, but not merrily. Still, I wouldn't change it for the world, because I managed to save Red, and that's all that mattered.

"Come in," she said from the other side of the door, and by the edge of her voice, I knew she figured it was me who came to visit.

I let her keep the rotting rag I wrapped her mom in before I buried her. In a way, digging holes for her mom and for Flynn were the darkest moments of my life. They both didn't deserve it. Even if I wasn't the one to kill them, I denied them a proper burial, and that was a lot.

In fact, it was so much, that in a way, not paying Robyn Raynes respect had cost me everything.

More specifically, her daughter.

I pushed the door open and walked to her bed. She had shit load of tubes in her wrists, and her leg was in a cast. And she was still nothing short of divine. My girl, my lovebird. The prettiest. Not because she had the pinkest lips or the greenest eyes, but because she was made for me. Tailor-made to make me laugh, to piss me off, to make me lose my shit. Hell, to make me *feel*.

I placed the Godiva chocolate box on her stand, right next to the orange gladiolas. The florist girl said they represent strength of character when I bought them.

I told her she had no idea.

Chocolate and flowers. That corny shit. But only for tonight, and only for Red. I hoped she'd find it funny, with her sarcastic sense of humor. I wanted to jump on bleachers and sing her a song. She deserved the whole nine yards.

But I also knew it was too late.

She looked at the flowers and chocolate and closed her eyes, taking a deep breath.

"Thank you," she croaked. But it was me saving her life she referred to. Not this stupid shit.

I took a seat next to her bed, looking down at my hands, or maybe my shoes. I wasn't even aware of what I was looking at, but it sure as hell wasn't into her eyes, because I couldn't deal with what was behind them.

"Don't mention it."

I was going to do it. I was really going to do something selfless for once in my life since Cat and Brock happened. The last time I did something altruistic, it became my ruin. I was about to do it again, knowing it would hurt ten fucking thousand times more than it hurt when I broke off my engagement with Cat. Because, looking back, the pain of Catalina's infidelity was nothing compared to the pain I felt knowing I inflicted misery on my wife.

And I was still going to do it, precisely because of that.

I really was a masochistic motherfucker.

"Are you all clear with the police and everything?" She sounded worried, but I didn't fool myself.

"Yeah." I inhaled, closing my eyes and falling backward on the chair with a soft thud. "I'll be fine." *Sort of.*

I opened my eyes and watched her for the first time since I walked into the room. She licked her dry lips, staring at the box of chocolate. This was us now. After doing the impossible and becoming something, this was us. Two strangers in a clinical room, looking for words that wouldn't do justice to what we really had to say. Again.

"My mom..." She sighed. "I can't believe you did that to her."

"Me neither, Red."

"Your father made you marry me. Why did you? Was there money involved?"

I nodded, peeling off a dead layer of skin from my palm. "The will said I'd get nothing until I married you. If we divorce, you get more than half."

She let out a sarcastic chuckle. "I don't need your family's money. Everything you Brennans touch gets tarnished."

"Nonsense. It's yours. Always will be."

"Let me go," she said quietly, her voice cracking. "I need to leave."

I nodded, knowing she was right but wishing she was wrong. Sparrow was my lovebird, and I couldn't clip her wings anymore. I have bent her with the weight of my actions and lies for the past few months, and she took it all and took it well, but this was the last straw. If I bent her even more, she'd snap. Forcing her to stay was too dangerous for me and too destructive for her.

Some said that lovebirds could die of heartbreak. That was the myth, anyway. I didn't look much into that, but I knew my lovebird, my Sparrow. She needed freedom, because even though she was incredibly good at accepting my shit, this was pushing it too far, even for her. I couldn't hold onto her anymore, even if I wanted to. Now more than ever.

She was my beauty, and I was her beast. But this was not a Disney flick. In real life, the beast goes back to his solitary life, a freak who lurks in the shadows and watches as his girl runs away back to the arms of her family.

She was my only shot at a semblance of normalcy and happiness, and I had to let her go.

Slouching down, my head so low my nose almost touched my knee, I croaked. "You're free."

The most painful words ever spoken by me. Sparrow was free to go, to spread her wings and fly. I'd give her everything, as my father's will ordered. And it still wouldn't be as painful as seeing her go. "I'm just so fucking sorry. I know it sounds absurd, considering everything we've been through, but I never meant to hurt you that way."

"I know." Her voice grew cold. She was already slipping away from me. From us.

"My door's always open," I added, as if it mattered.

She tilted her head slightly with a nod. "I know that, too. Now, please leave."

I got up from my seat. Walking in here, I thought I would never want to turn around and walk out. Thought I'd milk this conversation until the very last drop, get more time with her one last time before we said goodbye. But it turned out that when you really care, things don't work that way. Her pain occupied the whole fucking room, invading my space and knocking me off my fucking ass, and I couldn't tolerate it without feeling my pulse weaken and my body growing cold.

I reached for the door, about to walk away from her for the very last time.

"Just out of curiosity…would you have done things differently, all things considered?" she asked in her beautiful voice.

"All things considered," I said, not turning around because I know I'd break and do my usual thing, coerce her, threaten her, force her to stay, knowing that she shouldn't, "if I had known, I wouldn't have waited until now, or until our parents were dead. I would have asked you to marry me when you were nine, on that dance floor at Paddy's wedding, when you had your first slow dance, and damn the consequences."

She laughed.

She thought it was a joke.

It wasn't. This is what should have happened. We shouldn't have spent a minute away from each other while we had a chance. Nothing bad would have happened if I told nine-year-old Sparrow that she was mine.

No Paddy.

No Catalina.

No Brock.

I would never lay a finger on her mother's body, let alone hide it in the woods.

And now we were going to spend the rest of our lives apart. Damn that "Saving All My Love For You."

THIRTY-FOUR

TROY

Two weeks later

LAST TIME I SAW HIM, Paddy Rowan reminded me that I couldn't run away from my past. He was right. The truth was one hell of a runner, and it would eventually catch up with you. It caught up with him. It caught up with me. It was delivered coldly, like revenge, on a plate of misery, to my beautiful, wide-eyed, innocent, spitfire wife.

I wished I could cram all my lies into a ball of venom and shove it down my throat, swallowing the pain she felt, making it all better for her. But I couldn't.

When I first married her, I didn't tell her my father was responsible for our marriage because I didn't want this to shame my family, my mother, myself. I didn't want her to run off to the police with it. Didn't even feel like I owed her shit. The truth was mine, and for me to stew in. *Alone.*

I couldn't even stomach the fact that Brock and Catalina knew.

But as we got closer, things changed. I no longer cared about the stupid

Brennan pride, but I still didn't tell her. She didn't need to know that her mom ditched her for a married man. Didn't deserve to be saddled by more injustice and pain. For all she knew, her mom could have been kidnapped or murdered or just flat-out crazy, living with a herd of cats in the woods. I didn't want to reopen that old wound for Sparrow. The parent-child relationship was the most complex thing in the human race, I knew that first-hand, and that scab was too deep and tender to dig open.

A lot of puss and blood hid behind that old scab. It was going to hurt like hell for her.

I wasn't sure which part was the worst for Sparrow—how I hid her mother, got rid of the evidence, or that I didn't tell her about all this in the first place. One thing was for sure, yet understandable—my apology was not accepted.

Two weeks after I left that hospital room, it happened.

I expected the phone call, but that didn't mean it hurt any less. I answered the call with one hand, using the other to shove someone's head into a public toilet full of shit.

Not the best part of my job, but still better than rotting below fluorescent lights in an office all day.

I yanked his head back up and growled into his ear. "Last chance, buddy. Tell me where to find the scum who raped Don's daughter and I'll let you keep your balls."

Jensen, who called me, spoke from the other line. "I don't know any rapists."

The hustler I was dealing with didn't answer, so I shoved his head deeper into the toilet, this time keeping it for longer. Let him miss the privilege of breathing oxygen. Maybe that would refresh his memory as to the whereabouts of the guy who raped my client's kid. After all, I got a hot tip that he was the one who helped him hide for cash.

"I wasn't talking to you," I told Jensen. "What's good?"

"Your soon-to-be ex-wife's bank account," he said through tight lips. "That's what's good. It just got six hundred thousand dollars healthier."

She'd cashed Paddy's check.

"Thanks." I hung up and threw my phone against the dirty, heavily graffitied wall. I let out a few juicy curses before pulling the man's head back up. He was a little purple, but not enough for my taste.

"I just received some very bad fucking news, and I'm really in the mood for some torturing. One last time—where's the fucker?"

"Alright, alright. I'll tell you," he whimpered.

Disappointment slammed into me. He was going to cooperate, after all. Shame. I was hoping to have some fun beating the living hell out of him.

Then I remembered nothing was fun anymore.

Nothing was worth doing when Red wasn't around.

The only thing I wanted to do, and couldn't, sadly was her.

THIRTY-FIVE

SPARROW

Six weeks later

"**T**HIS ONE'S PERFECT! Can we have it? Please tell me we can have it. It's so, so, pretty. I really want it. It'd be perfect for us. So can we? Please say that we can. Lucy, tell her it's the best. Sparrow, we gotta buy it."

I leaned against Lucy's rental car, arms crossed. Laughing into a foam cup full of goodness, I watched Daisy practically hugging the white and pink food truck. It really was beautiful, and honestly, it was also perfect for a pancake business. All sugary and sweet. I wouldn't be surprised if Daisy started licking it, it looked so tasty.

"You don't have to decide now." Lucy bumped her shoulder into mine, laughing when she saw Daisy dancing around the truck like a drunk hippie.

We were standing in the middle of a trailer lot, looking for potential trucks for our new business. I was a few hundred thousand dollars richer than I was when I walked down the aisle with Troy, but also a few hundred thousand times less happy than I was right before our marriage fell apart.

True to his promise, he'd never contacted me after that hospital visit. Not directly, anyway. Didn't make any move on the divorce papers either. But I knew better than to think it was about the money.

We didn't care about the money. It was about betrayal.

After I quit my job at Rouge Bis, he sent me my paycheck to my dad's house. I bet he knew I no longer lived there, that I moved in with Lucy, since now I could afford the rent. I appreciated him not giving away he was still watching me.

Or *was* he?

It was bad to want him to follow me around. It was even worse to hope to bump into his employees or associates just so I could feel that he was still in my life. But in all honesty, that's exactly what I wanted. I wanted him, but was all too aware of the divide between us. Of its depth. Of the gravity of the lies our relationship had been built on.

He buried my dead mom in a forest and didn't even tell me.

Knew where she was all those years and never said a word.

He forced me into marriage so he could inherit his father's fortune.

He. Was. A. Monster.

And yet, I'd give anything to have this monster's claws back on my body, his cold eyes roaming my face. I missed the talks, the banter and everything this monster made me feel. Troy was the devil, but he breathed life into me.

"Earth to Birdie." Daisy snapped her fingers, her hot-red nails dancing close to my face, reminding me of the ruby ring I took off not too long ago. Its weight on my finger was unbearable without Troy in my life.

"Yeah, yeah, we'll take it." I waved my hand, and both Lucy and Daisy jumped up in the air, hi-fiving each other.

"Group hug!" Daisy announced, and before I knew it, I was buried in my friends' arms. I inhaled their scents, feminine and hopeful, closing my eyes, praying their happiness would seep into me. Sure, I was excited about chasing my dream. This was the original goal before *he* barged into my life. But now, even with this opportunity, these friends, that money—enough not only to build the career I wanted, but also to donate some to that homeless shelter down the road—life had an unpleasant aftertaste. Like nothing was going to be delicious again. Nothing would be blueberry pancakes and hot chocolate in the rain.

Nothing.

"I'm running into the office to tell them this one's off the market." Daisy bolted to the white trailer where the salespersons were watching us through the slits of their blinds.

They'd never come out to offer any help. I think they were under the impression that we were crazy. The truck was obviously hideous to anyone who wasn't starting out a *sugary crap* business. I bet it had collected dust for centuries before we walked in and decided we were going to take it.

Lucy turned back to me when Daisy disappeared through the office door. "How's your leg? Is your foot okay?"

I looked down to my cast. Every time I glanced at it, took a step or kept it dry when I was taking a shower, I thought about Brock. I supposed I should be more shaken by his death—the man died right in front of me. But the truth was he got what he deserved. The only things I couldn't wrap my head around yet were the reason why my mom had left us, and Troy's hideous secrets.

"Yeah, it's a lot better."

Lucy made a face like she knew exactly what wasn't a lot better. That thing beating for no one inside my chest.

"It's okay to miss him. It's that Stockholm syndrome. It'll go away."

It won't. I know it won't.

"Sure." I managed to flash her a smile.

Lucy offered me her hand, and I took it, as she helped me limp to the office to sign all the paperwork.

We were going to have our own business.

We were going to fulfill a childhood dream.

We were going to make freaking pancakes.

Then why did it all feel so pointless and sad?

"What if it's not Stockholm syndrome, Lucy? What if it's the real deal?"

"Then, my darling," she said, speaking patiently, "destiny will find a way to get you two back together. Real love doesn't disappear. It can turn into hate, and hate can turn into love, but those feelings won't ever turn into indifference."

She was right. Real love was cancer. All it took was one blink, and it would spread inside you like wildfire and consume you.

But that was okay, because I had a feeling that unlike cancer, real love didn't die. Ever.

THIRTY SIX

SPARROW

Six months later

"THREE...FOUR...FIVE BLUEBERRY pancakes," Lucy shoved the paper plates in my direction, and I bent forward, handing them to the two women who stood at the front of the long line to our food truck. Jenna and Barbara. They were legal secretaries, and they came here twice a week. Would visit more, if it weren't for their waistlines, they said. They always bought a few extras for other people in their office. *Or at least that was their version of things.*

"Thank you, Birdie. You know something is good if you think it's worth the calories *after* you eat it." Barbara laughed through a snort. "Now I just have to muster the courage to get on the scale. I've been avoiding it like plague ever since I found out about your truck."

"Oh, don't even go there." Jenna giggled, swatting Barbara's behind. "These girls need to come with a warning. I'll end up with type two diabetes if things continue this way."

Barbara and Jenna scurried along, leaving me to serve the next people in line. A woman and a man. They looked in love and I tried hard not to hate them for it.

"Go help Lucy." Daisy shoved me to the side all of a sudden.

I wrinkled my brow. We worked in a particular way, and never changed positions. I made our special batter before we opened up and took the orders, Lucy made the actual pancakes, and Daisy helped both of us where help was needed. But I didn't need her help.

"I got this," I said, but it only made Daisy pull me by the sleeve toward Lucy and the small kitchen.

"You can't stand here."

I pushed her away with my butt, "Why can't I…" But there was no need to finish the sentence. I already knew. My heart dove so low, I could feel my pulse thump in my toes. If winter were a feeling, this would be it. Everything froze, and I felt ridiculously unprepared. Shivers ran down my back and arms, raising the hair on my arms.

Something foreign washed over me, not unpleasant, but not exactly good either. It's like he grabbed me by my throat and pressed hard, depriving me of oxygen, yet made me feel so incredibly alive. I didn't breathe, blink or move. Just stood there and watched him, mouth slightly open. Eyes slightly wide. Heart completely broken. *My monster.*

"Are you still serving?" A woman in line scowled, and Daisy immediately took her order.

I continued standing there, unable to budge even though I wanted to, bad. I wanted to walk over, say something.

I wanted to talk to him.

I didn't want to talk to him.

He didn't even notice the truck yet.

Over the past few months, I had taken every precaution to avoid the local papers and Internet sites. I did everything, other than migrating out of the country. My darkest nightmare was to stumble across a picture of Troy with one of his Catalinas on his arm. I knew it would crush my soul into dust. Physically, I was fine. My temple was healed, and so was my foot. The cast was off, and I had even started running again. But inside, emptiness ate away at every corner of my being. No amount of blueberry pancakes was going to fill that void. Trust me, I'd tried.

Lucy paced over to me, pointing the spatula at my face. "Go. Talk to him. Stop being such a wuss."

But I couldn't. He stood next to a man twice his age. They both wore sharp suits and were engrossed in deep conversation, probably work, and I didn't want to interrupt. Yes, I was still his wife. I never had filed those divorce papers, didn't give a damn about the money I so-called deserved. Troy hadn't made a move to end our marriage either. But it seemed like we were together centuries ago. In a way, I almost feared he was a completely different person.

The man and Troy shook hands, and then the man spun on his heel, slowly fading into the crowd. Troy walked in the opposite direction, toward our truck. My breath caught in my throat. I looked around. There was no way he was going to notice me. The line was two blocks long and there was a good distance between us.

But Troy strode directly and purposely to the end of the line, fishing his cell phone out of his pocket and messing around with it, a smile on his strong face.

"Jesus," I muttered.

"He knows." Daisy grinned, still serving the people I obviously couldn't communicate with anymore.

I was standing in her way. The window was too narrow for the both of us, but she knew how much I wanted to see him again. *Needed* to see him again.

Troy didn't lift his head from his phone even once. He just kept on punching the screen incredibly fast, both thumbs on the touch screen.

Maybe he didn't know? But of course he knew. He would never have a blueberry pancake from a food truck willingly. It wasn't his style. No. He knew.

Closer…

Nearer…

The more Troy moved up the line, the more I felt like I was losing my grip on reality. Everything fogged around his silhouette, my eyes focused solely on him.

Maybe you're not ready to face him yet, a nagging inner voice teased. *Maybe you should just turn around and help Lucy, like Daisy asked you to.*

"Breathe," Lucy whispered, not lifting her eyes from the griddle as she flipped pancakes.

But I couldn't. He was quicksand, and I was drowning. Didn't even fight it. Just gave in.

"Would you like to take his order?" Daisy asked when there was only one person before him in line.

I felt my head bobbing in a nod. No matter what, I couldn't hide from him. That wasn't us. When he challenged, I stepped up. And by showing up here, he wanted me to react. I had every intention of doing so.

"If he wants to eat Boston's finest pancake, that's exactly what he'll get." I stepped to the center of the window. The person before him took her paper plate and walked away, and he moved forward. I'd forgotten how tall he was. He didn't even have to look up to capture my gaze.

"Hello." He stared at me hard, his face devoid of expression.

Daisy disappeared deeper in the truck, leaving us alone. Well, other than the dozens of people standing behind him in line.

"Hi," I said through a gulp.

He leaned his elbows on the order window and looked straight into my eyes with an intimacy you couldn't fake. I felt so exposed, it was almost like he ripped off my top and bra and left me naked in front of the throng.

"One blueberry pancake, please." His tone was neutral. Even.

What game was he playing now? I had no idea.

Averting my gaze, I punched the order in the cash register. I was disappointed. Confused, too. "Whipped cream?"

He slowly shook his head no. His gaze clung to my face, searching yet wary, like I was a rare mystical griffin, winged and ready to strike.

"One *sugary crap* coming up," I said.

His lips twitched, like he was fighting a smile, but he didn't let it loose. He just kept following my every move. Why didn't he laugh? He loved it when I taunted him, thrived on my comebacks. It was what made him notice me in the first place. Up until I'd answered back, I was nothing than a piece of furniture.

Lucy handed me a plate. She looked just as puzzled as I was. Why was he acting like we were total strangers? I wanted to strangle and kiss the hell out of him and jump into his arms and kill him all at the same time. His influence on me was dangerous still. My feelings toward him still crisp and fresh as a spring morning.

"Here you go." I lifted my gaze to meet his.

He dug his hand into his pocket and slammed the exact amount of the price on the counter. Did he know how much it would cost? Did he plan this? And he came all the way here...why? To show me that he didn't give a damn anymore? That was a low blow, even for him.

"Keep the money. Buy yourself something pretty," I told him, my face as stoic as it could be under the circumstances.

He didn't laugh at my joke, or budge. The line snaking behind him was growing thicker, more impatient, people craning their necks to see what was taking so long. I didn't say anything, not wanting to send him away, not brave enough to tell him to stay.

He was still staring. Why was he staring?

"Hey, man, are you done? My lunch break's almost over." A guy standing in line nudged him lightly from behind.

We paid no attention. "Do you know how Sam's doing?" I asked quietly. My chin was glued to my chest, my eyes trained on the floor of the truck. I'd thought about Sam many times over the past few months. Knew his mom wasn't exactly the most devoted in the world. I'd be lying if I said I wasn't worried.

"He's great. Living with Maria and Cat. Cat's in therapy. She is getting better at the whole parenting thing." He delivered the news flatly, no trace of emotion in his voice.

"Hey! You! Ask for her number and get it over with!" someone yelled from the end of the line.

"So you kept in touch with her." I inhaled. That stung.

But he just smiled at me easily, taking his paper plate. "Good to see you, Red." He winked before stepping out of the line.

My eyes drank him in as he strode to a nearby trash barrel, tossed his pancake inside and kept going. I spotted his Maserati—as always double-parked—and watched him disappear behind the wheel.

That was the second time my fake husband, who forced me to marry him, walked out on me. It was also the second time he took my heart with him.

But it was the first time I realized that I would never have it back.

He owned it, clutched it in his iron fist.

And sometimes, I knew, he squeezed too hard.

One hour later, we packed our stuff and closed for the day. Despite Lucy and Daisy doing their best to keep my mind off him, trying to persuade me to grab a few beers down at our local bar, I rushed home. I wasn't in the mood for anything other than running. Funnily enough, the Brock encounter didn't deter me from my favorite sport. I still jogged, but now, I only took the main streets, and went out in the evenings, when the city was buzzing with people. With *life*.

When I walked into our apartment that evening, I leaned my back against the door and squeezed my eyes shut. I never thought I'd fall in love with someone like Troy Brennan. As it turned out, love didn't give a damn about personal preferences.

Yanking my cell phone from my back pocket and throwing it across the sofa, I noticed a green text message flashing on the screen. It was sent at around noon. I had to rub my eyes to make sure I wasn't hallucinating when I saw the contact name the text was under. A lump of excitement forming in my stomach, I opened the text with shaky hands.

Troy: *I wanted to do the right thing. I really fucking did. But then it dawned on me that in order to do a good thing, you have to be a good person. I'm not good, and we both know that. I watched you over the past few months. Trying to tell myself that I was only looking out for you, making sure you're okay. Bullshit. I knew you'd be okay the moment Brock was out of the picture. I watched you because I wanted you for myself, because you belong with me.*

My heart beat faster, harder, wilder and I slouched on a chair, trying to remember how to breathe. There was a second message from him. I opened it right away.

Troy: *I changed my mind. You're not free. Not if you're flying away with nowhere to go, and for all the wrong reasons. What do you really want? Don't answer that. I'm about to find out. I'm waiting in line to see how you react when you see me again. Because Red, if you were so hot on getting rid of my ass, you wouldn't be postponing the divorce, knowing how much money's waiting for you. You wouldn't have kept my secrets to yourself. So what's it going to be? Am I going to see fear and loathing behind those greens, or want and need? Are you going to level with me? Fight back? Throw me away? It's about to go down in 3…2…1…*

That was it. Only those two messages. What the hell? Did he not see how much I longed for him? How much I wanted him? How I couldn't, for the life of me, form a coherent sentence when he was around? I darted up from my seat, eager to do something, anything, to distract myself. I got into my running gear, tucked my phone into my yoga pants and bolted out the door.

Running with my earbuds plugged in, "Sympathy for The Devil" by the Rolling Stones playing in my ears, I tried to burn all the extra energy I generated from reading his texts. My mind was too occupied to tell my legs where to take me. I ran without direction, without purpose. I ran because running was better than staying put and dealing with all those feelings.

With him.

Why was I so disappointed that he didn't text me after our encounter? I still hadn't forgiven him. Not for what he did to my mom and certainly, and more importantly, not for hiding all those secrets from me after we had already established a genuine relationship.

Forgiveness.

I never forgave anyone. Not necessarily because I held grudges, but because no one who had let me down ever asked for it.

Was I willing to forgive Troy? I stopped at the corner of the street, leaning against an industrial building and catching my breath. Yanking my phone out, I texted quickly, firing the message before I got the chance to let self-doubt, my ego and logic step into this mess.

Me: *You could have told me about why you married me. About what you did to my mother. You never even tried to confess and apologize.*

I tucked the phone back into my waistband and continued running. There was no point waiting for his response. I didn't even know if he'd answer. I got further away from my apartment, the streets blurring into nothing more than a faded background. My thoughts were louder than my vision. My phone vibrated against my damp skin and I looked down, swiping the screen with my finger to read his text.

Troy: *I didn't want you to know it was my family who was responsible for the falling apart of yours. By the time we became something, I didn't want the baggage to outweigh what we had. The last thing I wanted was to hurt you, Red. The first thing I needed was to keep you. And you know what I saw today behind those greens? Want. You still want me.*

I grimaced, shooting him back a text: *We can't be together.*

I picked up my pace, but was no longer able to hear the music in my ears.

Where was I running to? I had no clue. Maybe if I ran faster, quicker, harder, my pulse will drown all the noise in my head. This was crazy. We broke up six months ago. So what if I never pursued divorce? All I needed was a bit more time to get my head straight. I experienced a life-or-death situation when I was with Brock in the woods. Then I watched my husband kill him. Then I was *shot* by my husband.

Sure, he was a good shot, but that didn't make it okay. I just needed more time to get over it.

Troy: *We can. And we should. Do you think your mom really gave a rat's ass about where she'd be buried? She just loved being my father's, and wanted you to have the same thing. They knew. It's their legacy.*

Me: *This is crazy. My mother was a heartless woman who left me, and your dad was a cheating husband who forced us to get married.*

Running fast and reckless meant that my injured foot was beginning to make me limp again. I was way past feeling the pain, though. My body tried to keep up with my mind.

Troy: *Your mother was in love, and so was my dad. So are you.*

I stopped, realizing where I was. In front of his building. In front of the black revolving door. I stared at it, wide-eyed, knowing somehow that Troy would walk out of them within the next few seconds.

And he did.

It was crazy, but he did. I didn't even have time to catch my breath when I saw him walking out, his phone in his hand. Why did I run here? How did he know I'd be here?

He raised his head from his cell phone, the corners of his lips pulling up to a smile, and lowered his head back to his cell phone as he typed.

Troy: *And so am I.*

I stilled, watching him move closer. He wore a black pea coat, tailored jeans and matching Derby shoes. His coal black hair, impossibly thick and ridiculously touchable, slicked back casually. He always managed to make my heart float. Whether it was out of fear, out of fury or out of love. My heart always beat faster for him. My knees buckled, just for him. He was right. He did atrocious things, but it was him I wanted. Always, only him.

Troy stopped when we were nose to nose. Toe to toe. I loved watching those eyes from up-close. They were so ocean blue, no wonder they made my head swim.

"I love you, Red. I love you determined, tough, innocent, resilient…" His brows furrowed as he drank me in, stroking the curve of my face with his calloused fingertips. "I love you broken, insecure, scared, furious and pissed off…" He let a small smile loose.

I actually felt it, even though it was on his lips.

"I love every part of you, the good and the bad, the hopeless and the assertive. We don't just love. We heal each other with every touch and complete each other with ever kiss. And fuck, I know it's corny as hell, but that's what I need. You're what I need."

My eyes fluttered shut, a lone tear hanging from the tip of my eyelash.

"We don't have ordinary words between us. You always set my fucking brain on fire when you talk to me. We don't even have ordinary moments of silence. I always feel like I'm playing with you or being played by you when you're around. And I refuse to let you walk out on this, on us."

He cupped my cheeks and I locked his palms in place, tightening my grip. I never wanted him to let go. He dipped his head down, tilting his forehead against mine. I knew he was right. Knew that I'd already forgiven him. Probably before I even knew what he did, when we were still living together. Hell, probably on that dance floor, when I was nine.

My capturer.

My monster.

My *savior*.

"I'm an asshole, was an asshole, and have every intention of staying an asshole. It's the makeup of my fucking DNA. But I want to be *your* asshole. To you, I can be good. Maybe even great. For you, I'll stop the rain from falling and the thunder from cracking and the wind from fucking blowing. And yes, I sure as hell knew you'd come back. You came straight back into my arms, flew back to your nest, lovebird. Now why would you do that if you didn't love the shit out of me?"

My eyes roamed his face. His hands felt delicious on my skin. It was like he was pumping life into me with his fingertips. Like he made me whole before I even knew parts of me were missing.

It was wrong. All of it. To know what he did. To keep it from the police, from my friends, from Pops. To carry his burden for him in my gut.

It was wrong...*but it was ours.*

Troy waited for me to say something. His eyes didn't plead—he would never beg—but hell, they were curious, and full of beautiful, ugly, raw feelings.

"You're still an asshole," I concluded.

He laughed. His laugh sounded like the best song I hadn't heard yet, something I wanted to loop in my earbuds.

I laughed, too. For the first time in months, it felt genuine on my lips. "A brutal asshole. Not a lot of women can handle something like that. But I think I just might."

"I fucking love you, Red."

"I fucking love you, Brennan."

His lips found mine hungrily, demanding to be back where they belonged. His tongue parted my mouth, hot and familiar and addictive. His arms moving down my body, he placed one hand over my heart. His kiss not only told me I was doing the right thing—that I was meant and built to forgive this man—but also that this was it. It wouldn't get any better than this. There was nothing I'd rather do, nowhere I'd rather be, than right here with him.

His kiss was possessive, the warmth of his breath both comforting and thrilling. I tilted my neck sideways, inhaling his scent, letting it seep back into my hungry body. His skin on mine was bliss, and a rare, raw moment of happiness washed over me. I was so happy I wanted to scream. So happy it hurt. So giddy I couldn't even contain it anymore.

In theory, this should have ended in disaster.

In theory, stepping out of this mess with the upper hand meant that I had to rat on Troy Brennan to the authorities. Let my dad know what his family did to him, to *us*.

In theory, things were very complicated. Everybody had to pay for their sins, I had to grieve for the woman who gave birth to me, Troy had to turn himself in, and more lives had to be ruined.

Reality, though, was really quite simple.

I was his, he was mine, and everything else we did and didn't do to each other was just that.

Our past.

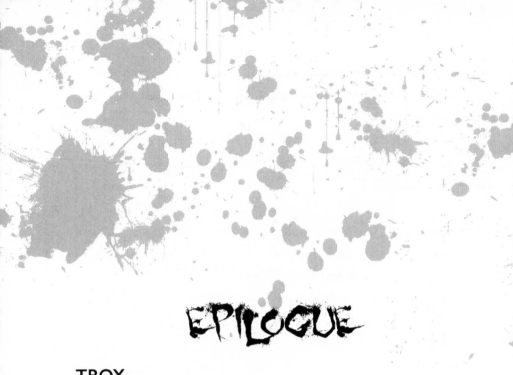

EPILOGUE

TROY

Sam grabs one of my toes, yanking it from the white sand it's buried in, victory written all over his face. *Brock's face.* I wiggle my toe like it's some kind of a small animal trying to break free. Sam's laughter drifts over me, drowning the noise of the waves crashing on the beach, the music from a nearby bar and the chit-chat of the beach-goers.

"I got it! I got it!"

"Good." Sparrow squares her shoulders, staring straight ahead to the ocean with hands on her waist and a small, navy blue bikini covering her little tight body. Her voice is smooth and serious. "Now let's feed it to the sharks."

"Aw…" Sam's eyebrows nosedive. He is frowning, worried and alarmed all of a sudden. "No, thanks. I'd rather…I dunno, build a castle or something. I don't want to hurt Uncle Troy. I will never hurt him."

It's amazing how forgiving kids can be. Nine months ago, I barely acknowledged his existence. Today, he is vacationing with us in Miami. Well, not just with me and Sparrow. Maria's here, too.

"Okay." Sparrow feigns disappointment. "But I will feed his toes to the sharks at some point."

Sam's still smiling, looking at her like she is life itself. "No, you won't," he declares as Maria approaches with sandwiches for them and a beer for me. "You looooove Uncle Troy."

I laugh, because I can't help not to. Maria grabs Sam by the hand and walks him over to a cart with an umbrella to get something cold to drink. I recently found out that he is pretty picky about what he likes to drink. No water for him. Just the fizzy stuff.

It was Red's idea to break the cycle. Sons killing fathers. Sons avenging fathers.

One night, when she was in my arms, just as I inhaled her cherry hair, she said, "You need to be in Sam's life. You owe it to him. You'll never be his dad, but he does deserve someone. Someone other than Maria and Catalina."

What she didn't add was that if I didn't want to end up like my dad, like David Kavanagh, and like Brock, I needed to mend the pieces I broke in Sam's life when I killed his father.

He doesn't know what happened, not yet, but it isn't a secret either. When the time comes, he'll know who pulled the trigger on Brock. And I don't want him to live with the hate that rattled in my gut, the hate that drove his father to lose everything. It eats you alive, consumes you from the inside, burns a hole in your chest, a void you fill with dark desires, with revenge that haunts you. The kid doesn't deserve it. One day, this kid will be a man. That version of him doesn't deserve it either.

I will tell this man that I didn't kill his father to avenge mine. I killed his father to protect the beautiful woman who makes him pancakes every now and then and has sunshine in her laugh, even when she faces the storm. Even when it was the coldest summer ever recorded in Boston.

So now I see Sam every other weekend. We go to fast food joints (all Sparrow's fault), Patriots games, and we even decided to take this trip to Miami while Cat stayed in Boston to look for a new apartment, just for her and Sam.

Red rolls on the sand until her shoulder bumps into mine. She is laughing hysterically, and even though I keep a stoic face, I'm anything but. God, I fucking love this girl.

"So…" She nuzzles into the crook of my neck, her arms flung over me. "Are you taking me to that fancy restaurant you booked for us last time we were in Miami?"

"Hell no," I snort. "That was before I realized you're a McMeal kind of girl. I can treat you to a hot, sexy dinner date at Wendy's if you're up for it."

"Make it IHOP and you're on. They have pancakes *and* hot chocolate."

"Classy girl. And I bet you'll still put out afterwards."

"Damn right I will. I'm only using you for your body, Mr. Brennan."

"And for the cash. Don't forget the cash."

"Nah, I make my own money, thank you very much." She plants a kiss on my jaw, and I beam like an idiot, because she's right. Red's rolling in it nowadays. Her business won't make us millionaires, but her pancake business is pretty solid.

I lean on one elbow, diving in for a deep kiss. I snake one hand to her taut stomach, still flat and gloriously pale despite the Miami sun.

"How is my little guy doing?"

"Could be a girl." She cocks one eyebrow.

"I kind of wish it is. Boys are such a headache. You should know." I'm just messing around with her, though. I have no preference either way. All I know is that I wasn't ready to be a dad until she told me I would be, and now? I can't fucking wait.

Even villains have a happy ending every now and again.

"Sparrow Raynes, anything you'll give me, I will happily take." I sound like a sappy dipshit, but sometimes you gotta pour some of the love in your heart out to make room for the next wave of joy. Ours is coming next fall. October 11th is the due date, by the way.

"I'm Sparrow Brennan now," she corrects. "I was only Sparrow Raynes when I used to be your nightmare."

"You were never a nightmare. At first, you were business..." I smirk, my fingers spreading wide on her stomach. "And then, at some point, you became my pleasure."

"And what am I now?" She covers my hand in hers over her stomach, squeezing it hard.

"Now, my lovebird, you're my home."

THE END

ACKNOWLEDGEMENTS

There are so many people who made Sparrow happen, and I just know I am going to screw up and forget a few of them, but I'll try and name every single person who helped me through this journey. Love, thanks and hugs to the following people:

My husband, who lived on In N' Out takeouts for five months straight. I'm so sorry, I bought you a gym membership to show my appreciation.

My son, who put up with a messy, all-over-the-place mother (I may have invented a new game called "Let's go over mommy's manuscript one more time". It wasn't a big hit, though).

My crazy-awesome street team, who actually did all the marketing for Sparrow for me, including Lin, Sabrina, Hen, Avivit, Donna, Dana and Mandy. Also, to my PA, Amanda Faulkner, for being patient and supportive, even through my meltdowns and anxiety attacks. You the real MVP, girl.

I'd like to thank my beta readers, who made this story so much better than it initially was. To the amazing Cat, Amy, Eliya, Bree and Ilanit. Special thanks to Lilian, who has read this book a gazillion times and was still patient enough to go over every single small detail. Thank you all for the great input and helpful suggestions. You put so much heart and soul into Sparrow and Troy's story, and it shows. I will never forget that.

The wonderful people who sprinkle magic all over my books – Karen the editor, Sofie the illustrator, Cassie the formatter and Cat the proofreader. I don't know what I would have done without you, and I sure don't want to find out.

Most of all though, I'd like to thank you, the readers, for making my dream come true. If it wasn't for you, I'd need no street team, no betas, no editor and no formatter. You make it happen by purchasing my book. Each and every one of you counts.

AUTHOR'S NOTE

I started writing Sparrow when I fell pregnant. I wrote every night and plotted every morning. I had time, plenty of it, and I used it to obsess and tweak every single word.

Then the baby came out, and time became a precious luxury I didn't have anymore.

But I still kept writing. And editing. And stealing moments – rewriting and obsessing.

Why am I telling you this? Because after giving up my life, sanity and sleeping hours, I need to know what you think. What you *really* think. Writing books is a lonely job, your only companion are four walls, a keyboard and lukewarm coffee. So now I'm dying to know what went through your mind when you read it.

Please leave an honest review if you have the time. Not just for this book, but for all books. The author appreciates it.

A lot.

Now, if you'll excuse me, I have approximately seven hundred hours of sleep to catch up on.

Love,

L.J. Shen

Contact me on my author page - https://goo.gl/e7m8n0

You can also join my reading group and discuss my books, Tyed and Sparrow, freely - https://goo.gl/IszvvG

Coming up:

August 2016 - California Love #2 – "Mr Left", The story of Izzy and Shane

Made in the USA
San Bernardino, CA
19 February 2020